"I rather fancy her," he said. "You don't mind if I borrow her for a while, do you, Vaughan?" It wasn't really a request, not the way he said it.

Clenching her hands into fists, Kadie sent a pleading glance to Vaughan. He looked at her, his eyes filled with pity.

"A

V

g

f

h

h

s

s

r

Other titles available by Amanda Ashley

A WHISPER OF ETERNITY

AFTER SUNDOWN

DEAD PERFECT

DEAD SEXY

DESIRE AFTER DARK

NIGHT'S KISS

NIGHT'S MASTER

NIGHT'S PLEASURE

NIGHT'S TOUCH

IMMORTAL SINS

EVERLASTING KISS

EVERLASTING DESIRE

BOUND BY NIGHT

BOUND BY BLOOD

HIS DARK EMBRACE

DESIRE THE NIGHT

BENEATH A MIDNIGHT MOON

Published by Kensington Publishing Corporation

AS
TWILIGHT
FALLS

AMANDA
ASHLEY

ZEBRA BOOKS
KENSINGTON PUBLISHING CORP.
http://www.kensingtonbooks.com

ZEBRA BOOKS are published by

Kensington Publishing Corp.
119 West 40th Street
New York, NY 10018

All Kensington titles, imprints and distributed lines are available at special quantity discounts for bulk purchases for sales promotion, premiums, fund-raising, educational or institutional use.

Special book excerpts or customized printings can also be created to fit specific needs. For details, write or phone the office of the Kensington Special Sales Manager. Attn.: Special Sales Department. Kensington Publishing Corp., 119 West 40th Street, New York, NY 10018. Phone: 1-800-221-2647.

Zebra and the Z logo Reg. U.S. Pat. & TM Off.

ISBN-13: 978-1-4201-3039-3
ISBN-10: 1-4201-3039-0

First Printing: May 2013

eISBN-13: 978-1-4201-3040-9
eISBN-10: 1-4201-3040-4

First Electronic Edition: May 2013

10 9 8 7 6 5 4 3 2 1

Printed in the United States of America

For Evie Norris

*Thanks for the love
and the loaves!*

Chapter 1

Kadie Andrews eased her car to a stop when she reached the narrow bridge. She wasn't afraid of heights, or bridges, but the wooden expanse didn't look as if it would hold a VW Bug, let alone her SUV. Still, she had taken a wrong turn somewhere along the way, and now it was dark, and she was lost and very nearly out of gas. Peering through the windshield, she saw what looked like a gas station in the distance.

She had just decided to park the Durango on the side of the road and walk across the bridge when the storm clouds that had been following her for the last few miles decided to release their burden. There was a jagged flash of lightning, a deafening roar of thunder, followed by a sudden deluge.

Walking was out of the question.

With a sigh of resignation, Kadie turned on the windshield wipers, put the SUV in gear, and drove across the bridge as quickly as she dared, praying all the way that the bridge wouldn't break and dump her in the shallow river below.

When she reached the other side, she headed straight toward the gas station, her sense of unease growing as she drove down what appeared to be the main street. Only there were no lights showing in any of the nearby buildings. No cars on the street. No people in evidence.

The place looked like a ghost town, and she knew all about ghost towns. As a freelance writer and photographer, she had visited ghost towns from Bumble Bee, Arizona, to Vader, Washington. Some were truly ghost towns, with little left but the spirits of those who had once lived there. Some, like Virginia City in Nevada and the city of the same name in Montana, were not really ghost towns. Saloons had been revived and buildings restored, giving people a glimpse of what life in the Old West had been like.

Her most recent adventure had been to Rambler, Wyoming. It had been a difficult trip and not worth the effort, since little remained. But Wyoming was a beautiful place.

Kadie glanced out the side windows of the Durango. If there were any ghosts lingering in this old Wyoming town, she was certain they weren't the friendly kind.

Pulling into the gas station, Kadie stared in disbelief at the pump. Instead of the modern, automated kind she was used to, this one had to be pumped by hand. She had seen pictures of old pumps like this. They dated from the 1920s. She wasn't surprised to see a CLOSED sign on the office window. The place looked as if it had been out of business for decades.

Now what?

Grabbing her cell phone, she flipped it open and punched in the number for the auto club, only to receive the message that there was no service available.

Chewing on the inside of her lower lip, she drove slowly down the main street, hoping she might be able to get a signal at another location.

She passed a quaint two-story hotel built of faded red brick. The lights were out.

The lights were out in every store she passed.

She tried to use her phone several times in different locations with no luck.

Tossing the phone onto the passenger seat, she made a right turn at the next stop sign and found herself in a residential section. The houses were mostly made of wood, set on large lots, well back from the street. Most of them had large front porches and old-fashioned picture windows. A few had cars in the driveway, cars that came from the same era as the gas pump. Every house was dark inside and out.

Pulling up at a stop sign, she glanced down the street, then smacked her hand against her forehead. Of course! The lights were probably out due to the storm.

She made a quick U-turn and drove back to the hotel. The Durango sputtered and died several yards short of her goal. Taking her foot off the gas, she coasted to the curb.

Kadie sat there a moment, reluctant to leave the shelter of the SUV. Rain pounded on the roof and poured down the windshield. No doubt she'd be soaked clear through before she reached the entrance.

She glanced at the hotel again. If the storm had caused the power failure, it was odd that the hotel didn't have a backup generator, or at least have some candles burning.

Leaning forward, she rested her forehead on the steering wheel and closed her eyes. Maybe she would just sleep in the Durango. She'd done it before.

She jumped a foot when someone tapped on the driver's side window.

When she looked up, she saw a man peering at her through the glass. For the first time, she wished she had taken her father's advice and bought a gun to keep in the car. "The way you go gallivantin' around the country, you might need it someday," he'd often said.

And now someday had arrived.

"Are you all right?" the stranger asked.

Kadie stared at him, surprised she could hear him so clearly in spite of the rain and the thunder.

"Fine, thank you," she said. "Except I'm out of gas. Is there a station nearby?"

"Just the one, and it's out of business."

Kadie frowned. She'd seen cars in the driveways. Where did they buy gas?

"You're gonna freeze to death in there," he said. "There's a tavern down the street that's open late. You can warm up inside."

Kadie shook her head. She wasn't crazy enough to follow a stranger down a dark street in the middle of the night.

"You'll be perfectly safe. Cross my heart," he said, his finger copying his words.

Kadie took a deep breath as she weighed her options. If he meant to do her harm, there was nothing to stop him from breaking into the SUV. And she was cold, and getting colder by the minute. Lightning lanced the clouds. A rumble of thunder shook the car.

"They have hot coffee," he added.

That did it. Grabbing her purse and the keys, she pulled the hood of her jacket up over her head and unlocked the door.

She was careful not to get too close to him as they walked down the street.

The bar was only half a block from the hotel. Kadie hesitated when the stranger opened the door; then, taking a deep breath, she stepped inside.

Warmth engulfed her. The light from a dozen flickering candles revealed a large room dominated by a bar that ran the length of the back wall. A number of booths lined one side of the room; a dozen small, round tables occupied the other side.

She felt suddenly self-conscious as five men and a woman turned to stare at her.

Ignoring them one and all, she followed her companion to an empty table.

"Here, let me take that," he said as she shrugged out of her wet jacket.

Kadie murmured her thanks as he draped it over the back of an empty chair, then took the seat across from hers.

A tall, skinny woman who looked almost anorexic approached the table on silent feet.

"Do you want anything besides coffee?" Kadie's companion asked.

When she shook her head, he ordered a glass of wine for himself and the skinny woman walked away as silently as she had appeared.

Kadie clasped her hands in her lap, looking everywhere but at the man across from her.

"I'm Darrick."

He had a faint English accent. Dark brown hair brushed the collar of his black shirt and his eyes were a shade lighter than his hair.

"Kadie," she said.

"What brings you to Morgan Creek?"

"I took a wrong turn," she admitted, and felt a faint flush of embarrassment warm her cheeks. She had always prided herself on being able to find her way around. "And ended up here."

"Far off the beaten path, to be sure."

The silent waitress returned with their drinks, and silently departed.

"Is there something wrong with her?" Kadie asked.

He lifted one brow. "With Frankie? She's a mute."

"Oh, how sad." Kadie watched the waitress move from table to table. The woman never smiled at anyone.

"You'll be needing a place to spend the night," Darrick said, drawing Kadie's attention once more.

"The hotel . . ."

"Out of business. The place is empty. Has been for years. But I'm sure we can find you a bed somewhere."

She didn't like the sound of that. "That's all right. I'll just sleep in my car. I've done it before."

He shook his head. "Not a good idea."

The look in his eyes, the underlying warning in his voice, sent a chill down her spine. "Do you have a better one?" She blew on her coffee, then took a sip. It was stronger than she liked and she added a packet of sugar.

"There's an empty house over on Fifth Street. The people took off in a hurry and left all their furniture behind. You can stay there."

"You mean, break in?"

"The people aren't coming back, so the house is just sitting there. You might as well use it."

Kadie fidgeted in her chair. What he was suggesting didn't seem right, but it was a lot more appealing than sleeping in her car, especially with the rain falling steadily and no end in sight.

She looked up to find Darrick regarding her over the rim of his wineglass. It was hard to think clearly when he was looking at her like that, as if she was the last cookie in the jar and he was starving for sweets.

He sipped his wine, his gaze never leaving hers.

His stare made her uncomfortable. He looked harmless enough. There was nothing threatening in his manner, and yet . . . She shook off her disquieting thoughts. She was probably just upset by the day's events.

She finished her coffee and set the cup aside.

"Do you want another cup?" he asked.

"No," she said, smothering a yawn. "I can hardly keep my eyes open."

Putting his wineglass aside, he pushed away from the table. "Let's go, then."

"What about the check?"

"Don't worry about it. I'll take care of it later."

That seemed odd, she thought, getting up from the table. But then, maybe he knew the owner or ran a tab.

He helped her into her jacket, then followed her toward the door.

Kadie pulled her hood up as she stepped outside. "Aren't you cold?" For the first time, she noticed he wasn't wearing a coat.

He shook his head.

"I need to get my things."

Nodding, he fell into step beside her, waited on the sidewalk while she pulled her suitcase from the backseat. He took it from her, then reached for her hand.

Pretending not to notice, Kadie shoved her hands into her pockets.

"This way," he said.

Filled with trepidation, she followed him down the street and around the corner. They didn't pass anyone else, but then, who would be out on a night like this if they didn't have to?

They went another block before they came to a neat, ranch-style house. Kadie hurried up the porch stairs, grateful to be out of the rain.

She hesitated when he opened the door, sent a quick prayer for protection to heaven, and stepped inside. She grunted with pain when she bumped her knee on a table.

"Stay here," Darrick said, closing the door. "I'll find a candle."

Kadie bit down on her lower lip. What on earth was she

doing in a strange town, in a strange house, with a strange man? She had always hated those silly heroines who were too stupid to live, but she had a feeling she was acting like one.

She was giving serious thought to running back to her car, but she wouldn't be any safer there than she was here.

He returned carrying a hurricane lamp. The lamp's light cast eerie shadows on the walls and ceiling.

"I think you'll be comfortable here," he said, handing her the lamp. "There's some wood in the hearth, if you want to start a fire."

Kadie nodded, her tension growing with every passing moment.

"The power should be back on in the morning," he said.

She nodded. "Thank you for your help."

He looked at her, his expression enigmatic. He took a step toward her. She took a hasty step backward when she saw his eyes.

"What's wrong?" he asked.

"Your eyes . . ." She blinked and looked again. "Nothing." For a moment, she could have sworn his eyes looked red. Probably just a trick of the light, she told herself. She placed the lamp on the mantel. Turning around, she said, "Thank you for your . . ."

Kadie stared at the place where Darrick had been standing only moments before. How had he disappeared so quickly? And how had he gotten out of the house without opening the door?

Chapter 2

The vampire sleeping deep within the earth stirred, aroused by the scent of fresh prey in town. Gathering his senses, he deduced that the newcomer was young, healthy, and female. But it was the rich, warm scent of her life's blood that called to him, drawing him to full awareness.

Just a single whiff, and he knew he would not rest until she was his.

Anger stirred within him when he realized that Darrick Vaughan had already claimed her. The man had been looking after the town's affairs for too long, but that was about to change. It was time to remind Vaughan and the others who was in charge here.

Burrowing up through yards of earth, he made his way home. He would need to clean up and feed before introducing himself to Miss Kadie Andrews.

He paused outside the gray stone house that held his lair, listening to the sounds of the night. Morgan Creek was a quiet place after dark. He didn't know or care what the humans did during the daylight hours. The only people seen on the streets after dark were those who had been fed upon recently. Not that holing up inside their houses did the residents a lot of good. Out of sight, out of mind didn't work on his kind. But he had little interest in the mortals who lived and died here.

After a quick shower, he donned a pair of jeans and a shirt. The hunger clawed at his vitals, yet he hesitated to leave the security of his lair. Though thirty years had passed since he had gone to ground, he remembered all too vividly his last foray outside Morgan Creek . . .

It had been a beautiful summer night and the city had been alive with people. Walking among them, their combined scents had aroused his thirst. A Fourth of July celebration was in full swing at the park. After the fireworks, there had been music and dancing.

Spying a beautiful young thing in shorts and a halter top heading away from the crowd, he had followed her. He had been closing in when he felt a sharp pain in his back. Too late, he realized he had walked into a trap. A dozen hunters swarmed over him, driving him to the ground. He fought back, breaking a neck here, a leg there, sinking his fangs into another, but they never let up. Fear had been like ice in his belly when they splashed him with gasoline. He fought with renewed energy when he caught the scent of sulphur, roared with pain as his clothes and his hair caught fire.

The flames had driven the hunters back. It had taken every ounce of preternatural power remaining to will himself back to Morgan Creek and bury himself deep in the earth so the healing could begin.

The pain had been constant, relentless. Even trapped in the dark sleep of his kind, there had been no escape from the agony of blistered preternatural flesh. It was definitely an experience he didn't want to repeat. Even now, it was hard to believe he had been so careless. It was a mistake he would not make again.

Shaking off his morbid thoughts, he willed himself to the nearest city. He needed blood to complete the healing before he approached the woman whose mere presence had called him from the arms of the earth.

Chapter 3

Kadie woke with the sun shining in her face. A glance out the window showed a beautiful clear day.

Fighting down a surge of guilt for spending the night in a house that wasn't hers, she went into the bathroom to take a shower.

With the water sluicing over her head and shoulders, her thoughts turned to the strange man she had met last night. Who was he, really? He had seemed ordinary enough, and yet there had been something strange about him. She recalled the odd red glow in his eyes, then shook her head. It had to have been a trick of the light. Nobody's eyes turned red.

After drying off, she pulled on a pair of skinny jeans, a long-sleeved T-shirt, and her favorite high-heeled, black boots. Glancing around to make sure she had everything, she shoved her dirty clothes inside her suitcase, grabbed it and her handbag, and left the house.

The houses she passed were all older homes, circa the thirties and forties, but they were all in good repair, the yards well tended. Now and then she saw people staring out their windows at her.

Mostly women. Mostly young and pretty.

They all seemed surprised to see her.

She passed a handsome young man mowing his yard.

An older woman rocking on her front porch.

A pretty young woman pulling weeds along the edge of the driveway.

They all watched her, their eyes filled with curiosity. No one smiled. No one spoke to her, not even when she offered a tentative hello.

Not a very friendly town, Kadie thought, wondering at their reticence.

When she reached the edge of town, she glanced left and right. The streets were deserted. No sign of people hurrying to work, no children walking to school. No cars on the road. Of course not, she thought glumly. There was no gas to be had. How was that even possible in this day and age?

Her SUV was where she had left it. Unlocking the car, she stowed her suitcase and her purse inside, locked the door, and shoved her keys into the pocket of her jeans.

The tavern Darrick had taken her to last night was closed. Was nothing in this town open? And where was everyone?

"Hi, honey, you look lost. Can I help you?"

Kadie turned to find a woman walking toward her. She had short, curly, gray hair, brown eyes, and a friendly smile.

"What are you doing here?" the woman asked, frowning.

"Excuse me?"

"I'm sorry, but we don't get many new people in town. I mean, we're not even on the map anymore. How did you get here?"

Kadie gestured at her car, parked a few yards away. "I ran out of gas."

"That's unfortunate," the woman said, sighing. "We haven't had any deliveries in ages. Where are my manners?" she exclaimed. "I'm Donna Stout."

"Kadie Andrews. What do you do for transportation if there's no gas?"

"We walk," Donna said with a shrug. "Where are you staying?"

"Well, I'm not sure. Last night I . . ." Kadie broke off, wondering if she should admit to where she'd spent the night. She had a feeling Donna Stout was the town gossip. But she was leaving, so what did it matter? "I stayed at a friend's house," she said, stretching the truth a bit.

"You look like you could use a good hot cup of coffee. The restaurant should be open now if you'd like some breakfast."

"Sounds great."

Inside the restaurant, Kadie followed Donna to a table near the front window.

After ordering coffee and a short stack of pancakes, Kadie folded her hands on the table. "Is the town always this quiet?" she asked, noting that the streets were still deserted. "I mean, where is everybody?"

Donna looked at her, cleared her throat, then glanced away. "We . . . that is . . . you see, it's like this. Morgan Creek isn't an ordinary town. We're kind of . . . um, unique."

"Unique?"

"People move in from time to time but . . ." She looked over her shoulder, her expression troubled. "As long as I've been here, no one has ever moved out."

Kadie stared at the woman. What was she trying to say? Or not say? "I don't understand."

"Of course you don't." She patted Kadie's hand. "I wish I could explain it, but I can't."

"Why not?"

"Because I can't."

Kadie pondered Donna Stout's words while she ate. What was the woman hiding? It was almost as if she was afraid to tell Kadie what was going on. Was Morgan Creek the home of some kind of cult? Like Jonestown?

The waitress returned a few minutes later. "Can I get you anything else?" she asked.

"No," Kadie said. "Just the check."

The waitress looked at Donna, one brow raised.

"Kadie is new here," Donna said as if that explained everything.

With a nod, the waitress moved away.

"What was that all about?" Kadie asked.

"Nothing," Donna said brightly. "Don't worry about the check. I'll take care of it later."

"I can't ask you to do that."

"You didn't ask."

"Well, thank you." Kadie pushed away from the table. "It was nice meeting you."

"Where are you going?" Donna asked, following her out of the restaurant.

"I don't know." Kadie chewed on the inside of her cheek. There were no other towns nearby. Unless she could find a ride or some gas, she wasn't going anywhere. "Do you know a man named Darrick?" she asked, thinking maybe he could help her.

"You met Darrick?"

"Only in passing. I met him last night," Kadie said, wondering at the woman's shocked expression. "Do you know where he is?"

Donna shook her head, her curls bouncing. "No. No. I mean . . . no. It was nice to meet you, Kadie," she said, and hurried down the street without looking back.

Kadie stared after her. What was that all about?

And what was she going to do now?

She would go for a walk, Kadie decided. Maybe it would help to clear her head. Returning to her car, she put on a pair of sturdy walking shoes, stashed her suitcase and handbag in the backseat of the Durango, locked the car, and tucked her keys into the pocket of her jeans. Standing on the curb, she played eeny-meeny-miney-mo, which way should I go, and struck off toward the west to keep the sun out of her eyes.

Maybe she was dreaming, she thought as she walked briskly down the sidewalk.

Maybe she had stumbled onto a movie set.

Maybe she had landed in an alternate universe when she'd crossed the bridge last night.

She walked for several blocks, passing a movie theater, a number of department stores, a drugstore, a barbershop, and a beauty salon. All were empty. A swimming pool was set in the middle of a large park edged with tall trees.

Kadie was about to turn back toward town when she saw the house. Located on a hill behind a tall, wrought-iron fence, it was three stories high. An old-fashioned veranda spanned the front of the house. There was a balcony on the third floor. The paint had faded to a weathered gray; there were iron bars on the windows, a wrought-iron security screen on the front entrance. There was no sign of life, yet the yard looked freshly mowed, the bushes recently trimmed.

She stared at it for a long time, wondering who lived there. A sudden chill had her wrapping her arms around her waist, and with the chill came the uneasy feeling that she was being watched.

Spooked, she turned on her heel and hurried back the way she'd come.

She hadn't been able to get any cell reception in the town. Maybe if she crossed to the other side of the bridge, she could get a signal near the road.

The thought quickened her steps until she was practically

running. The bridge. She had to get out of here. She had to get across the bridge.

Her steps slowed as she approached it. The uneasy feeling she had experienced earlier returned, sending a shiver down her spine.

Fighting a wave of panic, she ran across the wooden expanse, a startled cry erupting from her throat when she reached the other end and suddenly couldn't go any farther. It was like trying to penetrate an invisible shield. Try as she might, she couldn't get past the end of the bridge to the road beyond. Her feet moved, but it was as if she were on a treadmill, going nowhere.

She glanced around, only then noticing that the entire town was surrounded by mountains. There had to be another way out. A road, a deer trail, another bridge. There just had to be.

She spent the rest of the day looking for an exit, but if there was another way out, it remained elusive.

This had to be a dream, she thought. A nightmare. Soon, she would awaken in her own bed.

"Please," she whispered as she turned and walked wearily back to town. "Please let it be a dream."

Darrick woke with the setting of the sun. His first stop was the tavern, where he eased his thirst. From there, he headed to the house he'd given Kadie, curious to see how Morgan Creek's newest resident was getting along.

She answered the door at his knock, a wary expression on her face.

"Good evening, Kadie."

"What's good about it?" She stood in the doorway, blocking his entrance.

"Mind if I come in?"

A shadow of doubt passed behind her eyes before she stepped back to allow him entrance.

"Something wrong?" he asked as he crossed the threshold.

"Everything." Obviously distressed, she went into the living room and sat on the sofa.

"Want to tell me about it?" He sat in the rocker across from the couch. "Maybe I can help."

"I tried to leave here today."

"It's a long walk to the next town."

"I wouldn't know," she said, her voice tight. "I couldn't get past the end of the bridge."

Damn. He hadn't expected her to try to walk out.

"Why couldn't I leave?"

Unless he could come up with a plausible lie, he was going to have to tell her the truth, he thought. Although that really wasn't a good idea.

"Answer me!" she demanded, her agitation growing. "Why can't I leave? What's going on here?"

He blew out a sigh. "It's a little hard to explain."

"Yeah? Well, give it your best shot."

"I guess you could say Morgan Creek is like a gated community without the gates."

"That doesn't even make sense." She frowned at him. "That's why everyone looks so unhappy, isn't it? Because they can't leave."

"Unhappy? Hmm, I never really thought about it."

Kadie leaned forward, her hands gripping her knees. "Why can't I leave town?"

"I really can't tell you that."

She stared at him, shock and fear chasing themselves across her face. "Who are you?"

"I guess you could say I'm the sheriff of Morgan Creek. I uphold the law."

She swallowed hard, then cleared her throat. "That doesn't explain why I can't cross the bridge."

"In a way, it does."

"I didn't have any trouble coming into town."

"That's right. We welcome everyone."

"And everyone who comes here has to stay. Is that it?"

He nodded, his gaze lingering on the pulse throbbing in the hollow of her throat. "In one way or another."

And with that cryptic remark, he took his leave.

Chapter 4

Kadie followed Darrick to the door, stood on the porch watching him as he walked away. "Wait!"

He turned slowly to face her.

"I'm hungry."

A wry smile twisted his lips. "Sorry. I should have thought of that. Come on, I'll take you to dinner."

Kadie grabbed her jacket, then followed him down the street. There were more people out tonight—a middle-aged woman walking her dog, a young couple strolling hand in hand, a tall, blond man who stood out from the others. Kadie stared at him, trying to decide why he looked different from everyone else. She couldn't put her finger on it, but it occurred to her that Darrick had that same indefinable something.

She looked up at him, trying to decide what it was.

"Here we are," Darrick said.

Drawing her gaze from his face, she saw that they were in front of the restaurant.

He went inside and she followed him, sliding into the booth he chose, reading the menu he handed her.

"Order whatever you like," he said.

She glanced at the menu, then frowned. "There aren't any prices."

"I'll take care of it."

Feeling like she had fallen down the rabbit hole, Kadie stared at Darrick. Nothing in this place made sense. She was Alice and he was the Cheshire cat, speaking in riddles.

She ordered a Caesar salad, shrimp and rice, and a glass of lemonade. "Aren't you eating?"

"Not now."

"Did you mean it when you said I couldn't leave here?"

He nodded. "You'll get used to it."

"I don't want to get used to it. I don't want to stay here. I have a life, a job that I love, a family. . . ." She fought back tears of frustration as she thought of her little sister, anxiously waiting for her to return. "I have to go home."

"You are home, Kadie. The house is yours."

"What do you mean, it's mine?"

"Just that. It's yours for as long as you're here."

"How can you give it to me? You said it wasn't yours. That the people who lived there left in a hurry."

"So I did."

"Why would you give me a house?"

He shrugged. "You need a place to stay. Do with it whatever you wish. Buy whatever you need. Groceries, clothing, furniture for the house. Just charge it all to me."

"I have money of my own."

"Your checks and credit cards are no good here."

"I have some cash."

"It's no good here, either."

She had to be dreaming, Kadie thought. Whoever heard of a town where your money was no good? And if they didn't use checks, cash, or credit cards, what kind of currency did they use? And why was Darrick willing to buy her a house and pay her bills? She was certain it wasn't out of the kindness of his heart.

Did he expect her to be his mistress? She took a deep breath, hoping to calm the sudden flutter of anxiety in the pit of her stomach. "What do you want in return for . . . for keeping me?"

"Only what you're willing to give." It wasn't an out-and-out lie, but it was close.

Kadie glared at him, her eyes narrowed. "I'm not willing to give you anything."

He didn't reply, just sat there, watching her through hooded eyes. He didn't move, didn't blink. It was eerie, almost as if he wasn't human, but a statue.

She felt a rush of hysteria rise inside her. Maybe she wasn't dreaming. Maybe she was dead. Maybe he was the devil and this was hell.

When the waitress brought her dinner, Kadie pushed it away, her appetite gone.

"Kadie, you should eat something." His gaze held hers. "You're hungry and thirsty. You need to eat to keep your strength up."

Overcome by a strange lassitude, she picked up her fork. She didn't really feel like eating, but the food was suddenly irresistible, and she ate every bite.

The next thing she knew, she was outside, walking toward her house with no memory of leaving the restaurant.

Darrick walked her home. "Good night, Kadie," he said quietly. "Just one more thing. Now that the house is yours, be careful who you invite inside."

And with that enigmatic message, he left her standing on the porch.

Kadie stared after him a moment before going inside. She locked the door behind her, then stood there, wondering what to do with the rest of the night. It was too early to go to bed.

In the living room, she glanced at the clock over the mantel, surprised to find it was almost midnight.

That couldn't be right, she thought. They had gone to dinner around six. It certainly hadn't taken her six hours to eat, but a look at her watch confirmed the time. She didn't know how it was possible, but sometime between dinner and returning home, she had lost six hours. How could that be? She recalled feeling a little disoriented during dinner, eating when she wasn't hungry, but she didn't remember anything after that. Had she fainted?

Worrying about it had her tossing and turning all night long. It was near dawn when she fell into a troubled sleep populated by white rabbits and Cheshire cats and a frightened Alice who ran through the night, fleeing from an unseen terror with bloodstained fangs and hell-red eyes.

In the morning, Kadie stared at her reflection in the bathroom mirror. She looked pale, the bags under her eyes mute evidence of a mostly sleepless night. She didn't usually remember her dreams, but she remembered the nightmare she'd had. She had never dreamed about monsters before. But maybe it wasn't so unusual, considering her bizarre circumstances.

There was nothing to eat in the house. With her stomach growling, she dressed quickly, grabbed her handbag, and headed for the grocery store.

She bought the necessities—coffee, milk, bread, eggs, butter, sugar, flour, salt and pepper, as well as some fruit, mayonnaise, blueberry jam, and ice cream. Thinking ahead to dinner, she added a package of chicken legs and a box of stuffing.

The woman at the register smiled as she rang up Kadie's groceries. "You must be Kadie Andrews," she said. "I'm Maricela Romero, but my friends call me Marti."

Kadie nodded, surprised by the woman's friendly welcome. She guessed Marti to be in her late twenties, with glossy black hair, brown eyes, and a figure Kadie couldn't help envying.

"Welcome to town. I hope you'll learn to like it here. If you get lonesome, some of us meet at the library Wednesday mornings at ten thirty. We have coffee and doughnuts and talk about books and things. Sometimes we go out to lunch. You should come."

"Thank you," Kadie said politely. "Maybe I'll do that." She bit down on her lower lip, suddenly uncomfortable at the thought of telling Marti that Darrick was paying for her groceries. But it wasn't necessary.

"I'll just put this on your bill," Marti said, handing Kadie a receipt.

Kadie looked at the white slip of paper. There was nothing on it except her name. Curiouser and curiouser, she thought, fighting a rush of hysterical laughter.

"Can I put those in your car for you?" the bag boy—his name tag identified him as Jeremy—offered.

"I'm afraid I don't have a . . ." The words died in her throat when she saw her SUV pull up to the curb. Groceries forgotten, she hurried outside to confront the man behind the wheel. "What are you doing in my car?"

"Hey, back off," he said, holding up both hands as he exited the vehicle. "I was just bringing it to you per Mr. Vaughan's orders."

"Who's Mr. Vaughan? And where did you find gas in this town?"

"You're Kadie Andrews, right? His protégée?"

"Protégée!" she exclaimed. Well, that was a new word for it.

"You must be something special," he said, his voice tinged with envy.

"Why would you say that?"

He snorted. "You're the only one in town with a car that runs." He thrust the keys she'd left in the SUV into her hand, then turned and walked down the sidewalk.

Kadie stood staring after him. Protégée, indeed!

"Shall I put these in your car, Miss Andrews?"

Glancing over her shoulder, Kadie saw the bag boy—who wasn't a boy at all, but a young man who appeared to be in his early twenties—standing behind her with her shopping cart. "Yes, please." At least she wouldn't have to walk home weighed down with her groceries. "Who was that man?"

"Oh, that's Claude Cooper. Nobody knows much about him, except that he's a real grouch. Keeps to himself, mostly."

Thinking that she couldn't blame the man for being out of sorts, all things considered, she thanked Jeremy for his help, and climbed behind the wheel. After checking the gas tank—it was full—she put the car in drive, and drove straight toward the bridge. It was one thing for Vaughan's magic, or whatever it was, to stop her. Let him stop a four-thousand-pound SUV!

When she reached the other end of the bridge, she stomped on the gas pedal. And the engine died.

After restarting the car, she put it in drive and pressed gently on the gas. But the results were the same. The engine died.

She pulled her cell phone from her handbag, knowing even before she looked at the display that the battery would be dead.

Shoulders slumped in defeat, she stared at the road that

led to freedom. She really was trapped here, she thought dully. Like a rat in a cage.

She didn't know how long she sat there, staring into the distance, before she restarted the car and put it in reverse, but the ice cream was melted when she returned to the house.

A house that was, in reality, a prison. She was never going to get out of here, she thought bleakly. Never see her parents, or her sister, again.

By Wednesday morning, Kadie was heartily sick of her own company. She had spent the last four days rattling around the house, rearranging the furniture for want of anything better to do, reading the books she had brought with her until the words blurred on the page.

It might not have been so bad if the house had been equipped with a TV, a radio, or a computer, but there were no connections to the outside world.

Deciding to take Marti up on her offer, Kadie showered, ate a quick breakfast, and walked to the library.

The gray-haired lady at the front desk looked up. Taking off her glasses, she smiled at Kadie. "You're the new one, aren't you? Kadie?"

"Yes."

"Are you looking for a book? As you can see, we have a large selection."

"No, thank you. Marti invited me to visit her readers' group."

"Oh, of course, they meet in the back room. I'm Brittany Thomas," the librarian said. She gestured at a door to the left of the desk. "They meet in there."

"Thank you."

"Hold on a second, hon. Marti made up a list of addresses for you. so you'll know who lives where."

"Oh, that was thoughtful of her," Kadie said, taking the list the woman offered.

Squashing her nervousness, Kadie opened the door and stepped inside.

Marti and six other women were seated at a rectangular table. They all looked up when Kadie entered the room.

"Kadie!" Marti exclaimed, rising. "I'm so glad you came."

"Thanks."

Kadie took a seat at the end of the table amid a chorus of "Pleased to meet you's" and "Welcome to our group."

"Let me introduce you to the others." Starting with the woman on her left, Marti introduced the group.

Shirley Hague was middle-aged, with short, curly brown hair, brown eyes, and a faint scar near her hairline.

Leslie Miller looked to be in her early twenties, with long, straight black hair, dark brown eyes, and skin so pale it was almost white. She wore a bright red scarf around her neck. So did several of the others, Kadie noticed.

"We're discussing one of Stephen King's books," Marti said, when the introductions were complete. "*Salem's Lot.* Have you read it?"

"Actually, I have," Kadie said. Funny, she had finished reading it just a few weeks earlier. "Scared me half to death."

Murmurs of agreement ran around the table.

"What did you think of Mr. Barlow?" Rosemary Holmes asked. She appeared to be in her early fifties with short gray hair and gray eyes. She regarded Kadie through a pair of wire-rimmed glasses.

"Pure, unadulterated evil," Kadie answered without hesitation.

Chelsea Morris nodded. "I agree! I slept with the light on

for a week after I finished that book." Chelsea was rail thin, with shoulder-length blond hair and blue eyes.

"He made the vampires seem so real," Kadie said. "I almost started to believe they truly exist."

"And when Ben Mears destroyed Barlow. . . ." Nancy Dellenbach shivered. The plump woman with long, wavy, red hair touched the red silk scarf she wore around her neck. "I've often been tempted to try it when Nolan or one of the others come to my house," she said, her green eyes flashing. "But I just don't have the nerve."

Pauline Stefan nodded. She was a lovely woman, with clear blue eyes and long brown hair she wore tied in a ponytail. Like Nancy and Leslie, she also wore a bright red scarf loosely tied around her neck. "I know what you mean. They're so much stronger than we are."

"Wait a minute," Kadie said. "Are you saying . . . ?" She shook her head. What she was thinking was impossible. They were just messing with her.

"You don't know, do you?" Rosemary asked.

"Know what?" Kadie felt a sudden uneasiness as the women exchanged glances.

"Maybe we shouldn't tell her," Pauline said.

Chelsea leaned forward, her hands folded on the table. "She needs to know."

"Know what?" Kadie repeated, her unease ratcheting up a notch.

"Morgan Creek has a lot in common with King's book," Nancy said, fiddling with the ends of her scarf.

Kadie shook her head. "I don't understand. What are you trying to say?" She frowned. "Does it have anything to do with the reason why I can't leave?"

"Everything," Rosemary said succinctly.

Kadie's gaze moved quickly around the table. The women were all watching her, some with curiosity, some with pity.

"Just tell me!" Kadie said. "What's going on?"

"You've probably noticed the mansion up on the hill," Shirley said quietly. "Blair House?"

Kadie nodded.

Still watching Kadie, all the women leaned forward, waiting for Shirley to go on.

"Morgan Creek is home to a coven of vampires. They all live in the house on the hill. Well, all but one."

Kadie sat back. She would have laughed if all of the other women didn't look so serious.

"You don't believe me, do you?" Shirley asked.

"Of course not. There's no such thing as vampires. *Salem's Lot* is fiction, not fact."

Shirley looked at Leslie, Nancy, and Pauline. As if on cue, the three women removed their scarves.

Kadie frowned, wondering at their odd behavior. And then she saw the bites. They weren't mosquito bites. Or spider bites. The imprint of teeth—fangs?—looked eerily like the bite marks usually seen in vampire movies. She sat back, feeling faint.

"Are you all right?" Nancy asked.

"I haven't seen any vampires," Kadie said. "At least, no one's tried to bite me."

"Are you sure?"

"Well, of course I'm sure. I'd know if someone bit me, wouldn't I?"

"Maybe," Rosemary said. "If you were awake when it happened."

"And if they didn't seal the wound to make it disappear," Pauline added.

Kadie's mind flashed back to the six hours she had lost. Had Darrick Vaughan bitten her while she was unconscious and then sealed the wounds? "Why do your bite marks show?"

"The vampires don't bother to seal them," Chelsea remarked. "We all know what's going on."

"Then why hide the bites with scarves?" Kadie shook her head, unable to believe she was having this conversation.

"They aren't to hide the marks," Leslie explained. "They're to let the vampires know that we're not available."

"Available?"

"They aren't allowed to feed on any of us more than a couple of times a week," Marti added as if that made everything all right. "A red scarf means you're off-limits A black one means a vampire has claimed you."

Kadie's stomach churned. "*Feed* on you?"

"Of course. That's why we're here," Leslie said. "Why they won't let us go."

She was dreaming, Kadie thought. It had to be a dream. This couldn't possibly be real. There was no such thing as vampires. "I thought vampires couldn't be out during the day?"

"They can't." Pauline lifted a hand to her neck. "We don't always get home before dark."

"Oh."

"In a way, you're lucky," Shirley said, a note of envy in her voice. "Darrick has staked you out for himself."

"Darrick?" Kadie choked out the word. "He's a vampire?"

"Of course. Most of the men in town are vampires. Since Darrick has claimed you for himself, the others are forbidden to feed on you."

"Until he tires of you," Chelsea said.

"Just be glad Rylan Saintcrow didn't set his sights on you," Pauline said, a shiver in her voice.

"Who's that?"

"He's the head vampire. Very mysterious," Marti said. "None of us have ever seen him. All we have are rumors."

"What kind of rumors?" Kadie glanced around the table. Were they really having this discussion? She would have thought it was some kind of grisly joke, except they all looked so sincere.

"It's said that when he picks a woman, she's never seen or heard from again," Shirley said, her voice a whisper.

"You mean . . . ?"

"No one knows for sure if he kills them," Chelsea said. "But what other explanation is there?"

Kadie shrugged. "Do you know any of the women who disappeared?"

"Well, no," Rosemary said as if she hated to admit it. "Saintcrow hasn't been seen in town since I've been here."

"So, it's all just speculation," Kadie said.

"Well, the rumor must have come from somewhere," Pauline remarked. "But I wouldn't worry about Saintcrow, since you belong to Vaughan now. I wish he'd picked me. Vampire or not, I think he's hot."

Kadie shook her head, unable to believe her ears. Hot or not, she didn't want anything to do with him. Or this place. She pushed away from the table as panic washed through her. She had to get out of here. Now. Before it was too late.

Heedless of the calls of the other women, Kadie fled the library and raced for home.

Inside, she bolted the door, then stood there, her heart pounding in her ears. Darrick Vaughan was a vampire. All the women she had met were there for one reason—to feed the vampires.

How many vampires lived in Morgan Creek? No, that wasn't right. Vampires weren't really alive.

Had Vaughan fed on her without her knowing?

She gagged as revulsion swept through her.

She had to get out of this place!

Moving into the living room, she sank down on the sofa. If there was a way out of here, she would have found it by now. If there was a way, surely the other women would have left long ago.

She sat there, staring blankly out the window, as the clouds chased the sun from the sky.

The sound of the doorbell brought her to her feet. For a moment, she considered pretending she wasn't home, but what good would that do?

Gathering her courage, she went to answer the door. After all, there was always a chance it wasn't him.

Taking a deep breath, she called, "Who's there?"

"It's me. Marti."

Weak with relief, Kadie opened the door. "Come in."

"We were worried about you," Marti said. "I came to make sure you're all right."

"All right?" Kadie repeated, locking the door. "I'll never be all right again."

"I know how you must be feeling," Marti said, taking the seat Kadie indicated. "But once you get used to it, it's not so bad."

"Not so bad? I don't believe what I'm hearing! How can you say that?" Kadie sat down, then stood and began to pace the floor. "You tell me this town is filled with vampires, that you and the others are food, and it's not so bad?"

"Kadie, sit down and listen to me."

With a shake of her head, Kadie sat on the sofa, her hands clenched in her lap.

"I'm not saying it's wonderful or that I wouldn't leave at the drop of a hat, but it could be worse. We have the run of the town during the day."

"So, how does it work?" Kadie asked.

"Oh, it's all very civilized," Marti replied. "Like I said, they aren't allowed to feed on any of us more than two or three times a week. And as long as you belong to Vaughan, no one else can touch you."

"Lucky me," Kadie muttered. "So, the vampires just come knocking on your door and expect you to let them take what they want?"

Marti nodded.

"Darrick told me to be careful who I invite into the house," Kadie said. It hadn't made any sense at the time.

"The vampires can't enter a person's home without an invitation. By giving you this house, he gave you more than just a place to live. It's a haven. None of the other vampires will be able to come in unless you invite them."

"You mean your house isn't yours?"

"No, all the other houses belong to the vampires."

"How many vampires are there?"

"Nine. Eight men and one woman."

Considering she hadn't even known vampires existed, it seemed like a lot. "And they all live here?"

"Yes. I don't know for sure, but I don't think they can leave, either."

Marti drew in a deep breath and let it out in a long sigh. "Vaughan has given you a wonderful gift, Kadie. Something none of the rest of us have."

"The only thing I want from him is my freedom. That would be wonderful."

Marti nodded in agreement. "But it isn't likely to happen."

"How long have you been here?"

"I'm not sure. I tried to keep track of the days when I first got here, but . . ." She shrugged. "What year is it?"

"Two thousand and thirteen."

Marti stared at her. "Five years," she said, blinking back her tears. "My daughter will be in first grade by now. Brad's probably remarried."

Kadie laid her hand on Marti's arm. "I'm so sorry."

Blinking back her tears, Marti said a hasty good-bye and took her leave.

Kadie closed the door, then went to the window. She wondered how the vampires could be so cruel, separating a mother from her family? Silly question. They were vampires. Monsters. Bloodsucking fiends.

She thought about what Marti had told her about the vampires. There were nine of them in Morgan Creek. She frowned. How many people resided here besides those she had met?

She wondered why Vaughan let her have a car when none of the other women had one. And how she was supposed to keep him out of the house when he had already been inside?

The rest of the day passed with agonizing slowness. Kadie found herself constantly watching the clock, counting the minutes until the sun went down. Would Vaughan show up when the sun set and expect her to . . . to feed him?

The very thought made her stomach churn with revulsion. And then she heard a knock at the door.

Mind racing, she moved through the house, seeking a weapon of some kind, but there was nothing more menacing that the table knives in the kitchen. They didn't look sharp enough to cut butter, let alone kill a vampire.

If only she had listened to her father and bought a pistol. Vowing that a gun shop would be her first stop if she ever got out of this place, she went to answer the door.

Chapter 5

Kadie took a deep breath, then opened the door. As she'd feared, it was Darrick. "What do you want?"

"I just wanted to stop by and see if there was anything you needed."

"The only thing I need is to get out of this horrible place."

He shifted from one foot to the other. "Haven't we already had this conversation?"

"Well, we're having it again. I want to go home. Back to California," she added before he could tell her again that she was already home.

"Now that we've covered that, would you like to go to a movie?"

"A movie?"

He heard the disbelief in her voice. "What's the matter?"

"Whoever heard of vampires going to the movies?"

"Who said anything about vampires?"

"The ladies in town, of course."

Vaughan looked thoughtful. "So, what do you think vampires do?"

"Drink blood and kill people."

He chuckled softly. He couldn't argue with that.

Kadie stared at the door, wondering why he didn't come in, and then she frowned. What was it Marti had said? Something about vampires being unable to enter a home without an invitation. Surely that didn't apply to Vaughan, since he had been in the house before. Then again, it hadn't belonged to her at the time.

Curious, she opened the door a little bit wider. "You can't come in, can you?" she asked, a note of wonder in her voice.

"Told you that, did they?"

Kadie nodded. So, it was true then. He couldn't come in without her permission. She found that immensely reassuring.

"Have you nothing to say?"

Feeling safe within the walls of the house, she asked, "Do you feed on everyone in town?"

If he was startled by her bold question, it didn't show. "Not everyone."

"Why did you give me this house if I can keep you out?"

He considered a lie, then opted for the truth. "I didn't want any of the others preying on you." He flashed a wicked grin. "You might say you're my own private stock."

"That's disgusting!"

"Really? I thought you'd be pleased."

"Why on earth would you think that?"

"If you're opposed to the idea, I can revoke your ownership of the house and let you fend for yourself."

The threat should have scared her. Instead, it made her angry. "Do it then!" she snapped, and slammed the door in his face.

* * *

Eyes closed, Kadie stood with her back against the door. What had she done? If Vaughan took the house away from her, she would be at his mercy, and at the mercy of every other bloodsucking vampire in town.

Lifting a hand to her neck, she tried to imagine what it would be like to have them feeding on her, one after the other, until there was nothing left.

With a shake of her head, she went into the kitchen and poured herself a glass of cold water, then splashed some on her face. She was letting her imagination run away with her. None of the women she had met looked as though they had been abused. . . . Good grief, what was she thinking? Just because the women hadn't been drained of blood didn't mean they weren't being mistreated. They might have the run of the town. Food and shelter and entertainment might be provided for them. But, one and all, they were prisoners here, nothing but a food source for the vampires—a supply of fresh blood whenever the monsters got hungry. It was despicable!

Leaving the glass in the sink, Kadie went back into the living room and dropped down on the sofa. What was she going to do?

Kadie was still pondering her questionable future when she woke late the next morning. Later, sitting at the kitchen table over a cup of coffee, she considered her options and decided she really only had two—she could accept Vaughan's offer, or she could join the ranks of the other women.

Neither option was particularly appealing, but if she had to pick one, Darrick seemed like the best choice. Kadie didn't know how often he ate—or drank—or whatever, but better to nourish one than many.

Would he give her a black scarf to warn the other vampires away?

Feeling as though the walls were closing in on her, she ate a quick breakfast, dressed, and left the house.

Filled with a restless energy, she walked through the town, nodding to those she passed. Most waved back; a few people she hadn't met stared at her, their eyes narrowing suspiciously.

Without conscious thought, she found herself in front of the house on the hill.

Was Vaughan in there? Resting in his coffin? Waiting for the sun to go down so he could rise and terrorize the townspeople?

Why didn't the people in town break into the old house and destroy the vampires while they slept? If the vampires were dead, would it break whatever spell kept the human inhabitants of Morgan Creek from leaving? Had they ever tried to destroy the vampires?

She frowned. If killing the vampires didn't break whatever spell prevented the people from leaving, they would all eventually starve to death.

With that cheerful thought, she returned home, where she ate a leisurely lunch. After washing the dishes from breakfast and lunch, she rearranged the furniture in the living room.

A glance at her watch showed it was only two o'clock.

Sighing, she took another walk through the town and ended up at the library. Perhaps she could lose herself in a good book. It wouldn't solve her problem, but it might take her mind off her predicament for an hour or two.

After chatting with the librarian, Kadie picked up the latest mystery by her favorite author, then found a chair in a secluded corner where she spent a few minutes wondering how the vampires managed to have the latest movies, books, and DVDs before losing herself in the story.

Kadie woke with a start, fear piercing her heart when she realized she had fallen asleep and hours had passed.

She stood abruptly. The book in her lap fell to the floor with little notice.

It was dark outside.

Marti had told her that the human population had the run of the town during the day, which, by implication, meant it belonged to the vampires at night.

And it was night.

And she was human.

And terrified.

She stared at the front door of the library, wondering why no one had awakened her, and what her odds were of getting safely home. There were a lot more people in town than vampires. Maybe she was worrying for nothing. It wasn't that late. Only a little after seven. Maybe it was too early for the vampires to be out and about and there was nothing to worry about.

Nothing to worry about.

Startled, she shivered as the words whispered through the room. She glanced around, a nameless fear raising goose bumps along her arms. "Is someone there?"

Even as she called out, she knew there was no one else in the library, and yet she felt a presence in the room beside her. A frightening, almost tangible presence, as if a ghost had wandered inside and was now hovering nearby, watching her every move.

She flinched, certain someone—something—had just brushed against her arm.

"No such things as ghosts," she murmured, her gaze exploring the shadowy corners.

She didn't see anything, but there was something in the room with her. She knew it. And while there might not be ghosts, she knew there were vampires.

The thought had no sooner crossed her mind than a man was standing in front of her, a speculative gleam in his eye. A man who was, without doubt, one of the Undead.

"You must be the new one." He smiled. His teeth were very white.

Kadie stared at him, her panic growing when she realized his wasn't the presence she had felt earlier.

That same unembodied *thing* was still in the room.

The vampire took a step forward. "Just as pretty as I was told." He took another step toward her. "You smell delicious," he said, licking his lips. "Do you taste as good as you look, I wonder?" He took another step toward her, his nostrils flaring as he leaned over her.

He was sniffing her, she thought, the way he might appreciate the aroma of dinner cooking. And she was dinner.

He was reaching for her when he suddenly froze, his expression changing from lust to fear as he backed away from her, his gaze darting nervously around the room.

"I never touched her!" he shouted, and as quickly as he had appeared, he was gone.

Kadie slumped down in the chair, her heart pounding as she glanced around the room. What had the vampire seen—or sensed—that had frightened him so?

She jumped out of the chair at the sound of footsteps, her hand pressed to her heart in relief when she recognized Darrick walking toward her.

"What are you doing here after dark, Kadie?"

She waved her hand toward the chair. "I was reading

and I . . . I fell asleep and when I woke up, I was afraid to go outside, and then a vampire showed up. . . ."

"What? Who?"

"I don't know. But something scared him off and then you came in."

Darrick glanced around the room, then shook his head. "Saintcrow," he hissed.

"What?"

"Nothing. Come on, I'll take you home."

"How did he disappear so fast?"

Vaughan shrugged. "He didn't really disappear."

"Well, he certainly vanished from sight. What else would you call it?"

"Vampires can move faster than the human eye can follow."

"So, he just left the room at the speed of light?"

"Something like that." Vaughan opened the door for Kadie and followed her outside. "Vampires get stronger as they get older."

"Really? How long have you been a vampire?"

"A little over five hundred years."

Kadie blinked at him. Five *hundred* years. Try as she might, she couldn't believe it. Sure, people were living longer these days, with more and more men and women living to be over a hundred. But five hundred?

"It's true," Vaughan said. "I was turned in 1513. Henry the Eighth was king of England."

Kadie turned that over in her mind as she crossed the street toward her house. She had always been fascinated by Henry the Eighth and his second wife, Anne Boleyn. Kadie had always questioned Anne's wisdom in defying Henry. Had Kadie been the queen at the time, she would have taken young Elizabeth and fled the court. In Kadie's opinion, being queen wasn't all it was cracked up to be, especially if you were married to Henry, who had divorced two wives and beheaded two others.

They had reached the house. Kadie stopped at the door. "Thanks for walking me home."

"If you'd really like to thank me . . ." His voice trailed off as his gaze moved to the pulse throbbing erratically in the hollow of her throat. "I know a way."

Kadie shook her head. "No. I know you're stronger than I am. I know fighting is useless. But I'll never surrender to you willingly. I don't care what you do."

"Is that right?" He closed in on her, his hands flattening on the door on either side of her head. "Look at me, Kadie."

She tried to look away. She tried to close her eyes, but she had no will of her own. She stared into his eyes and all thought to resist fled her mind.

"I want to drink from you," he said. "And you want me to."

"I want you to." She hadn't meant to say the words aloud, but they passed her lips of their own accord. She stood there, helpless, as he brushed her hair aside, then lowered his head to her neck. She felt a faint sting as he bit her. It wasn't really painful, but the thought of what he was doing filled her with horror and disgust.

When he released her from his preternatural power, she slapped him as hard as she could, then escaped into the house and slammed the door.

She stood there, breathing heavily. Had he gone? Stepping closer to the door, she pressed her ear to the wood, but heard nothing. Was he still there?

Going to the window, she peered outside. At first, she saw nothing, but then, from the corner of her eye, she saw movement. She stared at the scarf fluttering in the breeze for several minutes. Vaughan had gone, but he had left a black silk scarf tied to the porch rail.

The scarf was still there the next morning. Black. The color of death. Removing it from the railing, Kadie let the silk slide through her fingers. If she wore it, she would be admitting to everyone, and to herself, that she belonged to Darrick Vaughn. A shiver of unease slithered down her spine as she wadded it up and shoved it into her back pocket.

Feeling a sudden need to get away from the house and everything it represented, she quickly changed out of her nightgown and into a pair of jeans and a sweater, grabbed her car keys, and left the house, deciding a drive was just what she needed.

At the end of town, she turned onto an unpaved road flanked by stands of timber that grew taller and closer together the farther she went.

She turned off the road onto a trail that wound through the forest, hit the brake when she saw a deer bounding away. Easing her foot off the brake, she continued down the trail, her troubles momentarily forgotten when she saw a pair of deer grazing on the sparse grass. Braking, she spent several minutes admiring the animals. They were such beautiful, graceful creatures with their large eyes, big ears, and delicate legs. She watched them until, for no apparent reason, they turned and bounded out of sight.

Kadie drove on, her gaze darting left and right. Could this be a way out of town that no one else had found?

After a number of twists and turns, the trail ended at the foot of a mountain that appeared to be made of solid rock and went up and up, seemingly with no end in sight.

Backing up, she turned left onto another trail. She'd gone about a mile when she saw the cemetery. Curious, she grabbed one of her cameras. Maybe she could get some good shots as long as she was out here.

She opened the rickety wooden gate and walked toward the nearest grave. It was marked by a wooden cross and nothing more. Glancing around, she saw row after row of weathered wooden crosses. No headstones. No flowers. No names or dates to identify the dead. Just crosses of various sizes. Maybe it wasn't a real graveyard. Whoever heard of burying people without identifying the deceased?

She shook her head. It was just one more piece of the increasingly strange puzzle that made up Morgan Creek.

Ignoring a growing sense of unease, she took several photographs. "Good thing I don't believe in ghosts," she mused. But it sure felt like she was being watched.

As she approached one of the graves, she was struck by a sudden coldness, as if she had stepped into a freezer. A TV show she'd watched claimed that cold spots indicated a ghostly presence.

Deciding she had enough pictures, she left the graveyard. She wasn't a Ghostbuster and if spirits of the dead lingered here, she didn't want to meet one. She had enough supernatural creatures to deal with, thank you very much.

She thought about the peculiar graveyard as she fastened her seat belt, then put the SUV in gear.

A short time later, she reached a fork in the road. Wondering if she would ever find her way back to town, she turned right. She hadn't gone more than a mile or so when she came to a large, square house made of gray stone. There were turrets at the corners of the building, which gave the place the look of an old English castle. Thick iron bars covered the front door and the windows.

Thinking maybe whoever looked after the graveyard lived here, Kadie opened the door of the SUV, hoping to find someone who could tell her how to get out of this accursed town. She gasped when an unseen force slammed into her.

Pulling the door closed, she put the Durango in reverse and got the hell out of there as fast as she could. An hour later, she was hopelessly lost and almost out of gas. Again.

Chapter 6

Whistling softly, his hands shoved into his pockets, Darrick left Blair House and strolled toward Main Street. Now that Saintcrow had returned, maybe he'd ask the head vampire for permission to leave, and to take the new woman with him. She was his now, to do with as he wished.

He was opening the door to the tavern when Kadie's image popped into his mind and with it a frightened plea for help.

Letting the door to the saloon slam shut, he lifted his head and sniffed the air. Though faint, her scent was borne to him on the breeze.

With preternatural speed, he left town, heading for the forest that grew along the foot of the western mountains.

He found her shivering under a blanket in the front seat of her car, which was parked in the middle of a stand of timber.

She shrieked when he rapped on the window.

"Kadie, it's me."

She stared at him, wide-eyed, then opened the door and practically fell into his arms.

"Easy, girl," he said. "You're safe now."

"I got lost," she said, hating the tremor in her voice. "And I ran out of gas."

"Come on, let's get you back to town before you freeze to death."

"My car . . ."

"I'll have someone come out and gas it up tomorrow."

"But . . ."

"We can argue about it later," he said, and wrapped her in his arms.

The next thing she knew, they were standing on the front porch of her house.

Being told that vampires could move at light speed was one thing, being part of it was another.

Seeing her startled expression, Darrick grinned and said, "Vampire mojo."

Before she could think of anything to say, her stomach growled loudly, reminding her that all she'd had to eat was a granola bar, and that had been hours ago.

She crossed the threshold, then paused to look over her shoulder.

Vaughan stood on the porch, his hands shoved into his pants pockets.

Kadie huffed a sigh; then, hoping she wouldn't regret it, she said, "You might as well come in."

With a nod, he entered the house.

A faint shimmer of energy played over her skin when he crossed the threshold.

Seeing her quizzical expression, he said, "Preternatural power. Not every mortal can sense it."

She pondered that while she made a sandwich.

Darrick watched her from the kitchen doorway, his arms folded over his chest.

"Do vampires ever eat . . . food?" she asked, pouring herself a glass of milk.

"No."

"Never?"

"Never."

She nibbled on her sandwich a moment before asking, "How did you find me?"

"I followed your scent."

Brow furrowed, she blinked at him. "But I was miles away."

He nodded.

"More vampire mojo?"

"Something like that," he replied with a wry smile.

"There was a house. A big house made of gray stone. With bars on the windows."

He nodded again. "It belongs to Saintcrow."

"Saintcrow?" She frowned. The name sounded familiar. And then she remembered where she had heard it. Pauline had remarked how lucky she was that Vaughan had found her first, and Shirley had said that none of the women taken by Saintcrow were ever seen again.

"He's the oldest one of our kind I've ever met," Darrick remarked. "Morgan Creek belongs to him."

"He's older than you?" she asked.

"Oh, yeah. Saintcrow rode with King Richard during the Crusades."

If she remembered her history correctly, the first crusade started in the year 1095 or 1096 and was fought to regain control of the Holy Lands. To the best of her recollection, there had been nine crusades. It was inconceivable that anyone living back then could still be alive.

She was about to say as much when there was a ripple in the air and a tall man with dusky skin appeared in the doorway beside Vaughan.

"Speak of the devil," Darrick remarked sourly, "and he appears."

"Kadie Andrews," the newcomer said. "I think it's time we met since you were prowling the grounds of my lair earlier today."

Kadie stared at Saintcrow. He was taller than Vaughan, broad-shouldered, and lean-hipped, with an air of confidence and authority that was almost tangible. He wore black jeans, black boots, and a black silk shirt open at the throat. His inky black hair brushed the collar of his jacket; his eyes were like deep pools of ebony. A thin white scar ran from the outer corner of his left eye, down his cheek, and disappeared under his shirt collar. Power radiated from him, making the short hairs rise along her arms. Even if no one had told her what he was, she would have known he wasn't human.

Saintcrow took Kadie's hands in his. "I regret that I was not able to welcome you when you arrived," he said.

Kadie nodded. His voice moved over her like a caress, deep and whiskey smooth.

Eyes narrowed, Saintcrow took hold of the black scarf hanging out of her back pocket and tossed it aside.

"I rather fancy her," he said. "You don't mind if I borrow her for a while, do you, Vaughan?" It wasn't really a request, not the way he said it.

Clenching her hands into fists, Kadie sent a pleading glance to Vaughan. He looked at her, his eyes filled with pity. "As you wish, my lord," he said, and vanished from sight.

Kadie stared at Saintcrow. She had been afraid of Vaughan, but that was nothing compared to the terror that gripped her when Saintcrow looked at her through those fathomless black eyes.

"Come along, Kadie Andrews." His gaze burned into hers, hotter than hellfire, yet strangely compelling. When he held out his hand, she dared not refuse.

With a predatory smile, his fingers—long and incredibly

strong—closed over her own. A rush of preternatural power surrounded her. It was like being caught in the center of a tornado. The world spun out of focus. Darkness swallowed her.

When she came to her senses, she was in a large, square room, trapped in Rylan Saintcrow's embrace.

Kadie didn't move, could scarcely breathe. He was close. So close. His power engulfed her, a mysterious pulsing energy unlike anything she had experienced before. His unique scent, alien and yet somehow enticing, filled her with an emotion she couldn't define. When she risked a look into his eyes, she felt herself falling, tumbling from this world into times past where knights on horseback vied for supremacy in the lists. She saw brightly colored banners fluttering in the breeze, the spires of an ancient castle, swords flashing in sunlight, weary men gathered around campfires. It took her a moment to realize she was seeing scenes from his past. How was that possible?

When he released her from his gaze, she wriggled out of his arms. Retreating several steps, she glanced at her surroundings. A fireplace large enough to hold a horse dominated the room. The tables were made of heavy wood, the sofas covered in a dark green fabric. Oriental rugs covered the floor. A tapestry, its colors faded by time, hung from one of the walls. An ornate bookcase took up space on another. She ran her hand over the suit of armor in the corner, wondering if he had worn it in the Crusades. A pair of crossed swords hung over the fireplace. She jumped back, startled, when flames sprang to life in the hearth.

Wrapping her arms around herself in an age-old feminine gesture, she dared a glance at Saintcrow. "What are you going to do with me?"

She had intended to speak boldly; instead, her voice came

out sounding as frightened as she felt. Belonging to Darrick Vaughan was suddenly very appealing.

"What does any man want with a woman?"

She didn't like the sound of that at all. Gathering her courage, she lifted her chin. "You're not a man."

"You think not?" He took a step toward her. "Shall I prove it to you here and now?"

"No!"

His deep black eyes lit up with amusement. "Would you rather be with Vaughan?"

"Yes."

He lifted one brow. "What is it about him, I wonder, that the women find so appealing?"

Kadie stared up at him, mute, her heart racing like that of an animal caught in a trap. He towered over her, as solid as a block wall. He might not be a man in the usual sense of the word, but he was undeniably, blatantly male. Something primal deep within her responded to him.

He took another step toward her. As though hypnotized, she watched him lift his hand. Her heartbeat increased tenfold when his knuckles caressed her cheek, slid down the side of her neck. She shivered when his fingertips traced her collarbone, then rested lightly on the pulse throbbing wildly in the hollow of her throat.

Every nerve and cell in her body came to sudden, vibrant life at his touch.

He smiled at her, an insufferably smug, knowing smile. "You're mine now." His voice was like the low rumble of distant thunder. "No other shall have you."

She nodded, unable to speak or object when he was looking at her like that. Unable to move as he lowered his head and claimed her lips with his in a long, searing kiss that threatened to turn her blood to fire and her bones to mush.

She felt bereft when he lifted his head.

He gazed down at her, noting her bruised lips, the two bright spots of color in her cheeks, the slightly dazed expression in her eyes. She was a remarkably pretty woman. Thick, dark brown hair fell in soft waves down her back, almost to her waist. Her eyes were a warm golden brown above a nose that tilted upward at the end. And her lips . . . ah, those lips. Pink and perfectly shaped; made for his kisses.

He could take her, here, now, but he didn't want to compel this woman as he had so many others. When he made love to Kadie Andrews, he wanted it to be her idea, and he wanted her to remember every glorious moment of it.

"How old are you, Kadie?"

"Twenty-four."

He nodded. She would serve him well for a good long time.

"Why me?" Marti had told her that none of the others had ever even seen Saintcrow. Shirley had said that those who were taken by him were never seen again.

"Why *not* you?"

She crossed her arms over her chest again. "Are you going to kill me?"

His brows rushed together in a frown. "What kind of question is that?"

"I just want to know. I was told . . ." She bit down on her lower lip, her courage failing her. Maybe she didn't want to know the answer.

"The women. They told you it wasn't safe here, with me?"

She nodded. "They said you kill the women you bring here."

"And you believe them?"

"What kind of question is that?" she exclaimed. "Of course I believe them. You're a vampire. Isn't killing humans what vampires do?"

"It is, indeed."

His hands, large and strong, folded over her shoulders, pulling her closer, holding her immobile. Every instinct urged her to flee, but she couldn't escape his hold. Fear coiled around her insides, colder than ice. Shirley was right, she thought frantically. He was going to kill her.

"Relax, Kadie," he said soothingly. "You're in no danger." He stroked her cheek with the knuckles of one hand, then drew in a deep breath. "Have you any idea how delectable you smell? So fresh and clean." He brushed a kiss across the top of her head, his lips moving in her hair. "So soft," he said quietly. "No wonder Vaughan wanted you." He drew back abruptly, his gaze suddenly fierce. "Did he have you?"

"I . . . I don't know what you mean."

"Did he take you to his bed?"

"No!"

"I always knew the man was a fool. But in this case, it likely saved his life."

Kadie stared at him, horrified. It was bad enough that he wanted to drink from her. That, at least, she could endure. But to share his bed . . . Revulsion speared through her. She would rather die! Still, a little part of her mind couldn't help wondering what making love to him would be like. Did vampires make love like other men? If his lovemaking was as mind-blowing as his kiss, how would she survive?

He smiled at her in a way that made her glad he couldn't read her mind.

Taking her by the hand, he led her to the high-backed sofa in front of the fireplace and drew her down beside him, his arm sliding around her shoulders to hold her close.

"Time for a taste," he said, and bent his head to her neck.

"No!" Panic surged through her. She tried to wriggle out of his hold, but his arm, as hard and unyielding as iron, held her fast.

She gasped when she felt the faint sting of his fangs at her throat. His mouth was incredibly hot against her skin. He was drinking from her. She expected to feel revulsion, disgust, horror. Instead, a delicious warmth spread through her whole body, pooling deep within her, culminating in a rush of unexpected sensual pleasure that stole the breath from her body. Hardly aware of what she was doing, she grabbed a handful of his hair to hold him in place, afraid he would take his mouth away.

She moaned softly, heard his soft chuckle as he ran his tongue along her neck, and then drank again. She was lost, she thought, lost in a world of sensation unlike anything she had ever imagined. It was almost beyond bearing.

If only he would stop.

If only he would never stop.

When he lifted his head, she stared up at him, suddenly ashamed of the way she had responded to him.

"That wasn't so bad, now, was it?" he asked, a gentle chiding evident in his tone.

"Of course it was." She would not give him the satisfaction of knowing how much she liked it.

"What a little liar you are." There was no censure in his voice, only mild amusement. "You will stay here from now on. You may have the run of the house, but you will not invite anyone else inside. You may come and go as you please, spend your days as you see fit, but your nights will be spent here, with me. Do you understand?"

She nodded.

"There are a number of bedrooms upstairs. Take whichever one pleases you. Redecorate if you wish. You'll find several catalogs in one of the drawers. In the kitchen, I think. Make a list of whatever you want and I'll see that you get it."

"Where do you sleep?"

"That's something you don't need to know."

"How did you get in my house? I was told none of the vampires could come in without an invitation."

"I don't need an invitation. The town—and everything in it—belongs to me."

And she was part of "everything."

"My car is out back. Go get your things. You won't be going back to Vaughan's house again."

"But . . ." She glanced out the window. It was dark as pitch outside.

"No one will bother you."

She lifted a hand to her neck. "My scarf . . ." Without it, she would be vulnerable.

"You no longer need it. My scent is on you now. No one will touch you on pain of death." He withdrew a key from his pocket and handed it to her. "You might want to stop at the store and purchase a few groceries and whatever else you need. Just tell the clerk you're with me now."

Too overwhelmed to speak, Kadie nodded, then hurried out of the house, anxious to be away from Rylan Saintcrow and the conflicting emotions he aroused in her.

Outside, she took a deep breath. She had a feeling that living with Saintcrow was going to be like living with the Prince of Darkness. She had his protection, but she was afraid it might come at the cost of her soul.

It didn't take long for Kadie to pack up her few belongings. Still, she was in no hurry to return to Saintcrow, so she lingered in the house, alternately sitting on the sofa staring into the fireplace, and pacing the floor.

After an hour and a half, she climbed behind the wheel of Saintcrow's silver ZR1 Corvette and drove to the store. She didn't know much about cars, but she recalled seeing an ad for a car like this one in a magazine. If she remembered correctly, it cost over $100,000.00. How would a vampire come to have so much money?

Of course, she thought, he probably took it from those who came here. The humans had little need for cash in this bizarre place. Or maybe, being a vampire, he just took what he wanted and killed anyone who objected. She shook her head. He was over nine hundred years old. Even a small savings account would acquire a lot of interest in that amount of time.

She was turning onto Main Street when she made a hard right and headed toward the bridge. She was driving the head bloodsucker's car. Maybe it could bypass whatever spell prevented her from leaving. It was certainly worth a try.

Hands gripping the wheel, she held her breath as she drove across the wooden expanse, but then uttered a very unladylike curse word when the car stopped a few feet short of her goal.

Expelling an aggravated sigh, she backed up and drove to the store, wondering what Mr. Rylan Saintcrow would do if she deliberately drove his luxury automobile into a brick wall.

Later, while pushing her cart up and down the aisles, she wondered why he even had a car, since vampires seemed to be able to whisk themselves wherever they wished to be.

She was standing in the bread aisle, trying to decide between white, whole wheat, or potato, when a sudden tension in the air warned her she was no longer alone. She didn't have to turn around to know that Saintcrow was standing behind her.

"Finding everything you need?" he asked.

"Not really."

"If there are things you want, all you need to do is make a list and I'll see that you get them."

"Is that so?" She turned to face him, and wished she hadn't. She had forgotten how tall and broad he was. How intimidating. But she refused to be cowed. "Who do you think you are—Santa Claus?"

He laughed—a deep, masculine chuckle that made her toes curl.

Annoyed by his amusement, she moved to the next aisle, all too aware that he was following her.

When they passed the liquor aisle, he added several bottles of red wine to the cart.

"I don't like wine," she said curtly.

"I do."

His nearness made her nervous. Deciding she would do her shopping during the day in the future, she headed for the checkout line.

Apparently Saintcrow made everyone nervous. The woman at the cash register refused to look at him or at Kadie. The bag boy kept dropping things. The checker handed her a receipt.

Saintcrow picked up the bags and followed her out to the car.

"You didn't pay for anything," Kadie said while he loaded her groceries into the trunk. "Why not?"

"No one here pays for anything."

"Then why bother with receipts, or checkers or bag boys and cash registers?"

"The computer keeps track of what's 'bought' so we know what to restock. As for the rest . . ." He shrugged. "It makes the humans feel more at home if we keep things the way they're used to." He shut the trunk and opened the passenger door for her.

After a moment's hesitation, Kadie got into the car. She was living in The Twilight Zone, she thought as Saintcrow slid behind the wheel. No doubt about it.

When they reached the stone house, he carried the grocery bags and her suitcase into the kitchen, then stood in the doorway while she put the groceries away. The appliances were all state of the art. There were dishes in the glass-fronted cupboard, a set of stainless-steel utensils in the drawer. Since he had no use for the stove or the refrigerator or anything else, she supposed he kept all of it for his human slaves.

"Slaves? That's a bit harsh, don't you think?" He'd never thought of it like that. True, most of the residents would rather not be here, but they had stopped asking for their freedom. After all, life here wasn't that bad. The people lived in nice houses. They had enough to eat, stores to shop in, a movie theater, a park, and a swimming pool. The ones who wanted to work had jobs. Hell, they were a lot better off than most of the people living in the outside world these days. They didn't have to worry about the high price of living or anything else.

Startled, Kadie whirled around. "How did you know what I was thinking?"

He crossed his arms over his chest. "Don't you know?"

Grimacing, she put away the last of her groceries. She would have no secrets from him, she thought irritably. No privacy at all.

Sweeping past Saintcrow, she ran up the stairs, entered the first bedroom at the top of the landing, and slammed the door.

The sound of Saintcrow's amused laughter followed her all the way.

Chapter 7

Needing some semblance of reality, Kadie went to visit Marti first thing in the morning. Marti hugged her as soon as she entered the house.

"Oh, you poor thing!" Marti exclaimed. "Is there anything I can do?"

"You heard?" Kadie asked.

"It was all over town this morning, how Vaughan let Saintcrow take you without a fight."

"But how did it get around so fast?"

"Vaughan told Pauline. Of course he didn't say it right out like that. And Pauline passed the word. Let's talk in the kitchen. Rosemary is here. I just made a pot of coffee. Judging from the circles under your eyes, you look like you could use a cup."

"You're right about that," Kadie said, trailing Marti into the kitchen.

"Kadie, we heard all about it," Rosemary said with a sympathetic smile.

Kadie nodded as she took the seat across from Rosemary. Morgan Creek might not have a morning paper but that didn't keep people from knowing the latest news.

Marti set another mug on the table, filled all three cups,

then sat down. "So, what's he like?" she asked, cutting right to the chase.

Stalling for time, Kadie added sugar and cream to her coffee. What was he like? "I really have no idea," she said at last. "He seems nice enough on the surface, I guess."

"Nice!" Rosemary rolled her eyes. "He's a killer. They're all killers."

"Maybe you've misjudged him," Kadie suggested. "I mean, I asked him outright if he was going to kill me. . . ."

"You what?" Marti shook her head in disbelief. "What did he say?"

"He said I wasn't in any danger."

"And you believed him?" Rosemary asked.

Kadie stared into her coffee cup. "I have to," she said quietly. She had to believe him. It was the only way she could get through the days ahead without going crazy with fear. "He let me drive his car to the store last night. Told me to buy whatever I needed, and then he showed up and followed me to the checkout line." She shook her head. "It was all so . . . so . . . I don't know. Bizarre."

Rosemary and Marti both sat back, their expressions thoughtful.

"He's probably just lulling you into a false sense of security," Rosemary remarked. "They're all monsters."

Kadie nodded, remembering that Saintcrow hadn't denied it when she accused vampires of killing humans. What had he said? *It is, indeed.*

"You're not wearing your scarf," Marti observed.

"I know. He said I didn't need it, that none of the other vampires would dare touch me now, on pain of death."

"I wonder why he keeps the other ones here?" Marti glanced at Rosemary. "Do you know? You've been here the longest."

Rosemary shrugged. "I have no idea. Maybe he just wants the company of his own kind."

Marti snorted. "I never thought of vampires as being social creatures."

"Me, either," Kadie said. "But then, until I came here, I never thought of them at all."

Marti and Rosemary both looked at her, and then, to Kadie's surprise, they burst out laughing.

"What's so funny?" Kadie asked.

"Nothing," Marti said, wiping tears from her eyes. "It's just that we've all said that very thing at one time or another."

Rosemary nodded. "Welcome to Morgan Creek, Kadie. You're truly one of us now."

One of them. It was a sobering thought and yet, to Kadie's amazement, it gave her a surprisingly unexpected sense of camaraderie.

"How long have you been here, Rosemary?" she asked.

"About twenty years, as near as I can figure."

"Twenty years," Kadie exclaimed softly. A lifetime of memories lost, she thought, thinking of all the birthdays, holidays, and graduations Rosemary had missed. Never knowing if her sons had married, if she had grandchildren, great-grandchildren. It was so unfair.

Kadie frowned thoughtfully. Rosemary was certain the vampires were killers, but if the vampires intended to kill the inhabitants of Morgan Creek, they certainly didn't seem to be in any hurry.

"It seems much longer," Rosemary said. "There's nothing to look forward to here, no reason to live."

Kadie murmured, "I'm sorry," because she couldn't think of anything else to say. The utter hopelessness in Rosemary's voice, the stark defeat in her eyes, tugged at Kadie's heart. "How did you get here?"

"Just stumbled into the place, the same as everyone else," Rosemary said. "We were on vacation. My husband and my four teenage sons had gone fishing. If only I'd gone with them! Instead, I decided to do a little sightseeing. I ended up here." She blinked rapidly, but not before Kadie saw her tears. "I don't want to talk about it."

"Of course you don't," Kadie said sympathetically. She sipped her coffee. It was hot and strong. She tried to think of a topic of conversation that was safe, but in the end, she asked the question that was uppermost in her mind. "Do either of you know anything about Saintcrow that you can tell me?"

Marti shook her head. "He's a mystery to all of us."

"In all the time I've been here, I've never seen him," Rosemary said. "The other vampires don't talk about him."

"The only thing I know is that he rode with King Richard in the Crusades," Kadie said.

"Did he tell you that?" Rosemary asked.

"No, Vaughan told me."

"That's so hard to believe." Marti looked bewildered. "Are you sure he didn't make that up?"

"I guess he could have," Kadie replied with a shrug. "But why would he?"

"Who knows why they do anything they do?" Rosemary's voice was tinged with bitterness. "They're vampires."

It explained everything.

And nothing.

"Tell us about yourself, Kadie," Marti said.

"There's not much to tell," she said wistfully. "I'm a free-lance photographer and writer. I live in California with my folks and my younger sister, Kathy. She's very ill, but none of the specialists she's seen can diagnose the disease." Kadie bit down on her lower lip, blinking rapidly to keep her tears at bay. "I've got to get home before it's too late."

* * *

It was midafternoon when Kadie took her leave. Reluctant to return to Saintcrow's house, she walked the few blocks to Main Street, her mind replaying the conversation she'd had with the women. She had a lot to learn about vampires and life in Morgan Creek. It seemed Marti and Rosemary had given up any hope of escape, Kadie mused, but she never would. There had to be a way out of here. There just had to be!

And what if there isn't? queried a little voice in the back of her mind. *What then?*

At loose ends, Kadie decided to check out the movie theater. She was surprised to discover there were four auditoriums, all playing different movies. She was a little disappointed that she had already seen them all, but she frequently saw movies she liked more than once.

There was no charge, of course, no one to take tickets, but Leslie and Chelsea were behind the concession counter, handing out popcorn, candy, and soft drinks.

"Hi, Kadie," Leslie said cheerfully. "What'll you have?"

"Popcorn and a root beer, please."

"Coming right up," Chelsea said.

Leslie leaned her elbows on the counter. "So, have you settled in yet?"

"I guess so."

"I hear you belong to Saintcrow now."

"I don't belong to anybody!" Kadie exclaimed indignantly, then quickly apologized for her outburst.

"It's all right," Leslie said. "We all get frustrated now and then."

"Do you two work here every day?" Kadie asked.

"We all take turns," Chelsea replied, handing Kadie a bag of popcorn and a large soda. "It helps to pass the time."

Nodding, Kadie thanked the women for their help, then went into the first auditorium. No one else was there.

The movie had been playing about twenty minutes when a man entered the auditorium. He glanced around, then took a seat in Kadie's row, leaving one seat between them.

"I'm Carl Freeman," he said, his voice gruff. "You must be Kadie Andrews." He didn't bother to whisper, since they were the only two in the place.

"Pleased to meet you," Kadie said.

He gestured at the screen. "This is a good one. Have you seen it?"

"Yes, back home."

"Where's home?"

"Morro Bay."

He nodded. "Pretty country down there. I'm from L.A." He grinned wryly. "Hard to believe anyone could miss the smog and the congested freeways, but I sure do."

"What did you do there?"

"I was a draftsman for a successful firm."

"How long have you been here?"

"I don't know, it's hard to keep track of time. Five years, maybe six. What difference does it make?"

Kadie nodded. His voice held the same note of despair as Rosemary's. "I've only met a few men who aren't vampires."

"We're few and far between."

"I was told there's a female vampire here. Have you met her?"

"Oh, yeah. Her name's Lilith. She's as ugly as sin and meaner than hell. She prefers to feed on men and, lucky me, I've become her private stock." He stared at the screen for a few minutes, his hands clenching around the scarf at his neck. "I tried to get one of the others to kill me, but they won't do it. I can't blame them. They're afraid of repercussions, I guess." He looked at Kadie intently. "I don't suppose you'd . . . ?"

"No," Kadie said quickly, horrified by the mere thought of taking a life. "Don't even ask."

He sank back in his seat, fidgeted a few minutes, then got up and left.

Kadie stared after him. Had his only reason for coming in here been to find out if she'd put him out of his misery?

It was dark when Kadie left the theater. Caught up in the misery of others, she paid little attention to her surroundings as she left Main Street. Earlier, with the sun shining brightly, she hadn't realized just how long a walk it was from Saint-crow's house to town. Now, strolling along the quiet, shadowy streets, she wished she had taken his car.

She had never been afraid of the dark, but then, she had never lived in a town full of vampires before. She jumped as a cat ran across her path. She told herself there was nothing to worry about. She was perfectly safe. Still, she was almost running when a man stepped out of the shadows to block her way.

She came to an abrupt halt, her heart pounding like that of a rabbit's caught in the jaws of a fox.

He didn't say anything, just stared at her. And then, before she even saw him move, he was on her, one arm holding her close while he sniffed her hair and skin. She opened her mouth to scream, but there was no need.

Muttering an oath, he pushed her away, then disappeared into the darkness.

My scent is on you now. No one will touch you on pain of death. She heard the words in her mind as clearly as if Saintcrow was standing beside her.

He was waiting for her in the living room when she entered the house. Dressed in black jeans and a gray T-shirt, he might have been an ordinary man but for the power that radiated from him like heat from a furnace. His hooded gaze swept over her, his nostrils flaring like a wolf scenting its prey.

She stood in the doorway, uncertain of what to do or say.

He crossed his arms over his chest. "Did you enjoy your day?"

Kadie shrugged. "Not really."

"Did you enjoy your visit with Rosemary and Marti?"

"How do you know about that?"

"I know everything that happens in my town. You've been to the movies. You ate popcorn and drank a soda. You talked to Carl. He's still looking for someone to end his life. Quinn accosted you on your way here."

Kadie fisted her hands on her hips. "Why do you bother to ask about my day if you already know everything that happened?"

"Conversation brings people closer together."

"Maybe, but you're not people," she said flippantly, then swept past him on her way to the kitchen.

She decided on breakfast for dinner. Two slices of French toast, a couple of sausages, a glass of orange juice, a cup of coffee. It was quick and easy.

She refused to acknowledge Saintcrow, who stood in the doorway, one shoulder braced against the jamb, his arms folded over his impressive chest.

She carried everything to the table, sat with her back to him, and picked up her fork. She could feel the weight of his gaze on her back, knew he was watching her every move.

She tensed when he pushed away from the doorway and dropped into the seat across from hers.

"Tell me about yourself," he said.

"No."

He lifted one brow. "No?"

"Is something wrong with your hearing?"

"Is this how you want it to be between us?" he asked darkly.

"There is no 'us,'" she retorted. "There's you and there's me. I can't fight you. I can't escape, but I don't have to like you, or talk to you."

"That's true." His eyes narrowed ominously. "I would remind you, though, that this is *my* town. *My* house. The vampires do as *I* say. The humans do as *I* say. You would be wise to remember that."

"You can threaten me all you like. It won't change the way I feel."

He laughed softly, but there was no humor in it. "You put on a brave front, but it's all bravado. I can smell the fear on your skin, hear it in the rapid beat of your heart, see it in your eyes. Try as you might, you can't hide your thoughts from me."

She glared at him, hating him because he knew there was nothing behind her bluster but sheer terror. Try as she might, she couldn't wrap her mind around the reality sitting across from her. If vampires were more than myth, what of the other storybook monsters? Maybe there really were trolls under bridges and monsters under the bed.

Saintcrow unfolded from his chair and rounded the table. He stood next to her, his expression enigmatic, and then he lifted her to her feet. "I'll show you what's real," he said, his voice whiskey smooth.

Before she had time to think what he might mean, he bent her back over his arm and kissed her, his lips punishing hers, his tongue invading her mouth.

There was nothing of tenderness in his kiss. It was meant to humiliate her, to prove he was the one in control.

She didn't fight him. What was the use? There was no

escape from the arms that imprisoned her, just as there was no escape from Morgan Creek.

He deepened the kiss, one hand sliding up and down her back. His lips were warm and firm. His kiss gentled, his arm loosened around her, and she found herself kissing him back, clasping her hands at his nape.

He whispered something that sounded like an endearment in a language she didn't understand, and then he kissed her again. Heat engulfed her, spreading to every part of her body, arousing a need deep within her unlike anything she had ever known. What was he doing to her?

She was gasping for breath when he let her go.

He stared down at her for stretched seconds, his dark eyes flashing ebony fire. "Go to bed, Kadie," he said gruffly.

She didn't argue.

Her first instinct was to run up the stairs as fast as she could, but some ancient sense of self-preservation reminded her that she was prey and he was a predator. With that in mind, she made her way slowly up the stairs and quietly closed the door.

Saintcrow stood in the kitchen, hands balled into tight fists, as Kadie climbed the stairs to her room. He had known hundreds of women in his time, perhaps thousands. Old and young; pretty and not so pretty; sassy and submissive. None had appealed to him the way this one spitfire of a girl did. She didn't beg for her freedom. She didn't pretend to like him in hopes that he would relent and let her go. She would never stop trying to escape. He had to admire that.

He drew a deep breath, his nostrils filling with her unique scent. He could taste her on his tongue—warm and sweet, vibrant and alive. He had taken women in the past, used them as long as it pleased him and then thrown them away without a second thought.

But this woman—Kadie—he had known the moment he'd woken to her scent that he had to have her. He had sought her out in the library and other places, making sure she didn't see him.

He grinned inwardly. One of the perks of being the oldest, biggest badass of his kind was that no one ever dared oppose him.

Which meant Kadie Andrews was now his for as long as he wished it.

And whether she liked it or not, it was going to be for a good long time.

Kadie stood with her back against the door, her thoughts spinning round and round like a hamster on a wheel. She couldn't escape Morgan Creek. Saintcrow knew everything she did. She wasn't sure how, but it didn't alter the fact that her comings and goings, her innermost thoughts, were his. He was like a Greek god and she a lowly mortal, a minor piece on the chessboard of his life.

She trailed her fingertips over her lips. She couldn't escape from Saintcrow. And now, with the memory of his kiss and her reaction to it fresh in her mind, she didn't know if she wanted to run from the man or beg him to kiss her again.

She had been kissed before, many times. Most had been pleasant, a few had been remarkable, but none had been as amazing as Saintcrow's. Of course, he'd had over nine hundred years to perfect it.

Nine hundred years. Feeling suddenly weak, she slid down to the floor. What would it be like to live that long? She shook her head. It wasn't normal. Or natural. People weren't meant to live forever, at least not on Earth. Even contemplating eternity in the hereafter was beyond her comprehension. What would people do when forever stretched ahead of them?

Leaning her head back against the door, she closed her eyes. Saintcrow's image immediately sprang to the forefront of her mind. Piercing dark eyes. Broad shoulders. A massive chest. Long, long legs. Large hands . . . She shivered, remembering the touch of those hands in her hair, on her skin. The hard length of his body pressed against hers. The way his tongue had ravaged her mouth . . .

"Vampire." She forced the word past her lips. "Vampire," she repeated, more forcefully this time.

But first a man. Saintcrow's voice slid through her mind like honey warmed by the sun. *A man who wants you. Who burns for your touch. Who hungers for your sweetness.*

And with his words came the image of the two of them locked in each other's arms.

Clapping her hands over her ears, she shouted, "Get out of my head!"

She felt his withdrawal like a physical ache.

Gaining her feet, she undressed down to her underwear. Crawling under the covers, she pulled the blankets over her head, curled into a ball, and burst into tears.

Chapter 8

Darrick Vaughan stared at the dark crimson liquid in his glass. Bottled blood. It was enough to make a vampire gag, yet all the females were off-limits for the next few days. It didn't happen often, but it was hell when it did.

As always, his thoughts turned to the new woman. The one who should have been his. Would have been his if Saintcrow hadn't asserted his right to have any woman he wanted at any time. One of the perks of being a master vampire, Vaughan thought glumly, and felt his jealousy and his frustration grow in equal measure.

Of course, he could have challenged Saintcrow, but he wasn't insane. There was no way he could hope to beat the older vampire, one-on-one.

He grimaced as he sipped his drink. If he could sway the other vampires to his way of thinking, they might be able to destroy Saintcrow and take over Morgan Creek, run it the way they saw fit. Instead of waiting for unwary mortals to stumble into town, they could go out and round up a dozen, a hundred, and gorge themselves to their hearts' content. But that would never happen as long as Saintcrow existed.

He drained his glass and set it aside. Right now, only Lilith agreed with him.

With enough persuasion and a little luck, he might be able to change that.

He thought again of asking Saintcrow for permission to leave Morgan Creek, but he was reluctant to do so. This place was a haven, a refuge from the hunters and slayers who were determined to wipe their kind from the face of the earth. Leaving Saintcrow's protection could be dangerous.

After signaling for a refill, Vaughan drummed his fingers on the bar top. Slow and steady wins the race, his father had always said. The best thing to do was try to sway the others to his way of thinking. It might take a year. It might take ten. But what the hell. If there was one thing he had, it was time.

Chapter 9

Kadie woke late after a surprisingly restful sleep. She had slept like the proverbial log, with no dreams that she could recall.

She stared up at the high ceiling. It was Sunday. Had she been at home, she would have eaten a late breakfast, read the paper, taken her little sister, Kathy, to church, if Kathy was feeling up to it. After lunch, she would have gone through her latest batch of photos, deciding which to keep, sorting them into groups, deciding if the pictures deserved a story and where she would send them. In the evening, after dinner, she would have read her e-mail, updated her Web site, maybe played cards with her mom and dad after Kathy went to bed. Her parents must be worried sick. She had promised to call as soon as she reached Wyoming.

Sitting up, she glanced around the room. She hadn't paid much attention to it before. It was a nice-enough room, large, with bare, off-white walls. The rug was deep green; matching drapes hung at the single window. The four-poster bed looked like an antique, as did the rocking chair in the corner. But maybe that was to be expected, since the owner of the house was somewhat of an antique himself! An old-fashioned mirror stood in one corner. What was that doing here, she wondered, since it was commonly believed that vampires had no reflection.

She swung her legs over the edge of the bed. She had a horrible taste in her mouth. After her grand exit from the kitchen last night, she had been too upset to wash up properly. Now, she was eager to shower and brush her teeth.

She did so quickly, thinking how much she hated Rylan Saintcrow for keeping her here.

Exiting the shower, she slipped into her bathrobe, then stepped into the hallway.

Were there bedrooms behind the other five doors? Did Saintcrow sleep in one of them?

Curious, she padded down the carpeted corridor, peering into each room. They were all furnished much the same as hers, and appeared to be unoccupied. Why did he need so many bedrooms when he lived alone? Had he once kept a harem?

In the kitchen, Kadie put on a pot of coffee. She scrambled a couple of eggs, made some toast, poured a glass of orange juice. While looking for the silverware the day before, she found the catalogs Saintcrow had mentioned. He had brochures and catalogs from dozens of stores and manufacturers from coast to coast. She couldn't help thinking that shopping online would have been a whole lot easier.

She browsed through several while she ate. He had told her she could have anything she wanted. She quickly made a list—a sofa from Jonathan Adler that cost a mere $3900.00, along with an equally expensive love seat and armchair, a pair of end tables, new lamps, a kitchen table and one chair (Mr. Saintcrow could stand, thank you very much—he didn't eat, anyway). She added a portable DVD player and fifty DVDs, a blender, a microwave, a new set of silverware, a set of Spode Blue Italian china, Egyptian cotton sheets for the bed, sage green towels for the bathroom, ten bars of

imported soap, a bottle of Clive Christian No. 1 perfume
(the world's most expensive fragrance—a steal at only
$2150.00 a bottle), the same scent worn by actress Katie
Holmes on her wedding day. Lastly, she added a diamond
tennis bracelet, something she had always wanted but could
never afford.

Kadie sat back, smiling. She couldn't wait to see Saintcrow's face when he read her list.

"Is this all?" Saintcrow asked as he perused the items she
had selected.

Kadie stared at him. If she had hoped to anger him or get
a rise out of him, she had failed miserably.

He folded her list and stuffed it into his pants pocket.
"What would you like to do this evening?"

"Do?"

"I thought you might like to get out of the house. Have
you eaten dinner?"

"No."

"There's a nice little Italian restaurant not far from here.
Would you like to go?"

"You mean, leave Morgan Creek?" she asked, her mind
racing.

"If you'd like."

"I would! Just let me change clothes." Not that she had
anything really nice to wear. When she'd left home, she
hadn't planned on eating out in nice restaurants, or being
gone long enough to need anything other than jeans, T-shirts,
and boots.

But she had packed one nice pair of black slacks and a
blue silk shirt, just in case, and she donned them now, along
with a pair of black sandals. She brushed her hair and her
teeth, applied fresh makeup, then scowled at herself in the

mirror. What was she doing? Was she actually dressing up for him?

"Of course not," she told her reflection. "I'm doing it for me." She grabbed her handbag. If things went as planned, she wouldn't be coming back here tonight. She hated to leave her cameras behind, but it was a small price to pay for her freedom.

Saintcrow stood when she entered the room. A flash of admiration gleamed in his eyes when he saw her. She ignored it, just as she ignored his hand when he offered it to her.

In the car, she stared out the window, refusing to be drawn into conversation with him. She didn't know what he was up to, or why he was being so nice, but she was sure he had some ulterior motive.

They crossed the bridge with no trouble at all.

Kadie felt a sense of anticipation as they approached a red light. With as much stealth as she could muster, she took hold of the door handle, held her breath as the car slowed to a stop.

Now! She jerked on the handle.

And nothing happened.

She tried again, with the same result.

Shoulders slumped in defeat, she slid a sideways glance at Saintcrow. He was looking straight ahead, but she didn't miss the wry grin on his face. He had known, she thought. He had known all along that she would try to escape and so he'd used some of that notorious vampire mojo to thwart her.

Anger and frustration rose up within her, threatening to explode like a cork from a bottle. She took several deep breaths. If only she had a dagger, she thought darkly, she would cheerfully drive it into his black heart.

"I had no idea you were such a bloodthirsty little baggage," he remarked mildly.

She glared at him. "Stop reading my mind!"

"It's hard not to when you broadcast so loudly."

Minutes later, he pulled off the freeway and into the restaurant parking lot.

Inside, Saintcrow asked for a table for two.

In spite of her anger, Kadie couldn't help noticing it was a lovely place as she followed the hostess. Murals of Italy covered the walls, the tables were spread with red-and-white checkered cloths. Music played in the background.

The hostess handed them menus and assured them that their waitress would be there shortly.

Kadie put her menu aside without looking at it.

"Have you already decided?" Saintcrow asked.

"I'm not hungry anymore."

"So, you only agreed to this in hopes of escaping." It wasn't a question.

She stared at him, mute, her hope of freedom shattered.

The waitress arrived just then. "*Buona sera,*" she said, smiling as she placed a basket of garlic bread in the center of the table. "Have you decided yet? Or do you need a few more minutes?"

"A bottle of your best chardonnay," Saintcrow said.

"Very good, sir." The waitress looked at Kadie askance.

"You may as well eat," Saintcrow said.

"Spaghetti and meatballs," Kadie said sullenly.

"Soup or salad?"

"Salad, please, with Italian dressing. And iced tea, no lemon."

"And for you, sir?"

"Just the wine."

With a nod, the waitress collected their menus and left the table.

Kadie spread her napkin in her lap. "You knew what I had in mind all the time, didn't you?"

He nodded. "It wasn't too hard to figure out."

"They told me no one has ever left Morgan Creek. Is that true?"

"You have."

"You know what I mean."

"No, no one's ever left."

"Do you think that's right, keeping us all prisoners for your amusement?"

"I'm no longer concerned with right and wrong the way you know it."

"Of course not. You're a . . ." She glanced around. "What you are. I guess the rules the rest of us live by don't apply to you."

"Exactly."

Kadie bit back her retort when the waitress arrived with the wine, Kadie's iced tea, and salad.

Saintcrow poured a glass of wine for himself, then looked at Kadie.

She shook her head.

"Are you sure? It's a very good year."

"I don't like wine. I don't like you, and I never will."

"You might not like me," he said quietly, "but you want me."

"I do not!" she said hotly.

"You can lie to yourself, Kadie, but you can't lie to me." He leaned forward, his gaze intent on her face. "I can taste the longing on you, smell it on your skin, hear it in the beat of your heart."

She stared at him, mesmerized by the blatant desire in his eyes. His words wrapped around her, his breath caressing her.

Swearing softly he drew back when the waitress reappeared with Kadie's dinner.

Kadie drew a deep, shuddering sigh. She could deny it until she turned blue in the face, but he was right.

She wanted him.

Kadie remained mute on the drive back to Saintcrow's house. She felt him watching her several times, but she refused to meet his gaze. He wasn't human. He was keeping her a prisoner in this accursed town. She might hate him, but there was no denying the attraction between them. But was it even real? If he could keep people from leaving here, if he could read her mind, how did she know that whatever she felt for him was genuine and not just more of his vampire tricks?

And even if what she felt was real, she wasn't going to do anything about it.

As soon as he pulled into the driveway, she jumped out of the car and hurried up the porch steps. When she tried the door, it was locked.

He took his time getting out of the car.

She was all too aware of him when he came up behind her. Every nerve and cell in her body came to attention. His breath fanned her hair, his arm brushed hers as he reached past her to unlock the door, which he did merely by touching it. A little push and it swung open on well-oiled hinges.

Lights came on when she crossed the threshold.

More vampire magic? Or merely some sort of sensor?

Without a word, she walked swiftly toward the staircase. Her hand was on the banister when his voice stopped her.

"Kadie."

Taking a deep breath, she turned to face him.

"I'm still hungry."

She frowned. What did he expect her to do about it? she wondered, then felt her blood run cold. He wasn't asking her to fix him dinner. *She* was dinner.

She turned away, her only thought to dash up the stairs to her room and lock the door, but her feet refused to obey. Was this how it was to be from now on? Would he feed on her every night? She told herself that wouldn't happen. The vampires weren't supposed to feed on any of them more than two or three times a week. But maybe the rules didn't apply to Saintcrow.

He closed the distance between them in three long strides and then he was standing on the stair beside her, towering over her. His hand slid around her nape, his fingers gently massaging her neck.

"What you feel for me is quite real, Kadie," he assured her, his breath warm against her cheek. "I could compel you to want me, but there's no fun in that. I could mesmerize you, make you do whatever I wished, whenever I wished. But again, there's little pleasure to be gained from bedding a robot."

"I can guarantee you'll find no pleasure in my bed if you take me against my will."

He lifted one brow. "That sounds like a challenge."

"It's not!" she said quickly.

"No?" He cupped her face in his hands and kissed her gently, his tongue sweeping over her lips.

Kadie refused to kiss him back. She kept her body stiff, her eyes open, even though she wanted nothing more than to surrender to the need burning deep within her.

He kissed her again, his hands stroking her hair as he pushed her back against the banister, his body pressing against hers, letting her feel the hard evidence of his desire.

She fisted her hands at her sides, determined to resist.

He gazed into her eyes, his own filled with amusement. "You are a stubborn wench," he remarked. "But I can wait. I have all the time in the world."

And so saying, he released her and vanished from sight.

Feeling suddenly weak in the knees, Kadie grabbed the banister, clinging to it as she climbed the stairs and hurried into her room. She locked the door, though there seemed little point to it. Nothing as flimsy as a lock would keep him out.

She climbed into bed, fully dressed except for her shoes, pulled the covers up to her chin, and closed her eyes. But sleep would not come. His scent was all around her. She licked her lips, and tasted him there. Her body throbbed with longing everywhere he had touched.

She wanted him.

Knowing what he was, how could she feel this way about him? He was a vampire, a monster.

A single tear slid down her cheek. How long would she be able to resist before she surrendered to him? How could she give in now, when she had so adamantly declared that she never would?

Kadie dreamed of him that night . . .

She was a peasant girl in a medieval village when Saint-crow came to town in the company of a dozen other English knights.

She had never seen anything like them, the stalwart men who rode into town, spurs jingling, banners flying. The village children ran to meet them, cheering and waving. There was little excitement to be had in their day-to-day lives. It was a struggle just to plant and grow enough food to survive from one year to the next. Church feasts proclaimed the time of sowing and reaping. From time to time, there were fairs, a chance to put aside all thought of work and enjoy music and acrobats. Knights came to challenge each other in the lists, merchants sold their wares, games of chance were held in the local tavern.

They were having such a fair when the knights came to town, but Kadie had eyes only for the one who rode in the front. Head high, shoulders back, he sat his charger like a king. She had never seen anything more beautiful.

When he deigned to look her way, her whole body tingled with excitement. As unobtrusively as possible, she followed him to the lists, stood in the shadows as he prepared to challenge the local champion.

With her hand pressed to her heart, she watched the knights ride toward each other, heard the harsh echo of lance against armor, gasped as their champion tumbled to the ground, rolling over and over.

Saintcrow reined his prancing charger to a stop beside the body. He dismounted in a fluid move, something that should have been impossible for a man encumbered by armor.

Tossing his helmet aside, he strode toward the fallen knight and knelt beside him.

He cried, "To the victor belong the spoils!" then buried his fangs in the defeated knight's throat.

She tried to look away, tried to run away, but she stood rooted to the spot, her mouth opening in a silent scream when he lifted his head and she saw his eyes . . . as red as the blood that stained his lips . . .

Screaming, "No!" Kadie bolted upright, her heart hammering, her body bathed in sweat. "Only a dream," she gasped. "Only a dream."

She was reaching for the light beside her bed when a dark shadow disengaged itself from the corner.

"Who's there?" She wanted to sound brave and bold; the quaver in her voice proved she was anything but.

"It's me."

Kadie's breath whooshed out of her at the sound of his voice. How was it possible to be relieved and frightened at the same time? "What are you doing in here?"

"It's my house."

"It's my room. Don't I have a right to privacy?"

"Not with me."

She switched on the light, shrank back when she saw him looming over her. "What do you want?"

"A midnight snack?"

Her hand flew to her neck in an unconscious gesture of protection. He was going to drink from her again. She wanted to protest, to rail against such a personal invasion, but how could she when she remembered all too clearly how much she had enjoyed it the last time?

Even as she tried to summon words of complaint, she couldn't deny that she was eager to be in his arms again, to experience that wondrous sensual pleasure she had known before.

And he knew it, damn him.

He was smiling when he sat beside her. One arm slid around her waist, drawing her up against him. Her cheek rested on his chest—his bare chest. Only then did she realize he was wearing nothing but a pair of jeans that rode low on his hips.

He stroked her hair and she marveled that his hands—so large and strong—could be so gentle, that the touch of a man who wasn't really a man could arouse her so quickly.

Placing his knuckles under her chin, he raised her head, his gaze meeting hers. "I want you."

His voice was low, but she had no trouble hearing him. Or knowing that he wanted more than just her blood.

He smiled at her again and she felt her heart slam against her ribs. It would be so much easier to resist him if he wasn't so outrageously handsome! If she had wanted to hire someone to pose for her ideal man, Rylan Saintcrow would have been the perfect model, from his long, black hair and deep ebony eyes to his strong jaw line. She had always been drawn to tall men with broad shoulders and well-developed arms, and Saintcrow fit that description to a T.

"Kadie?"

"Are you asking my permission to . . . to . . . ravish me?"

"Would you rather I forced you?"

She bit down on her lower lip.

"You would have a clear conscience then, wouldn't you?" he asked with a knowing grin.

"I hate you," she said between clenched teeth. "I really hate you."

He laughed softly. "Sure you do." He ran one finger down her cheek. "I'll take your blood when it pleases me. I am, after all, a vampire. I need it to survive." His gaze moved over her, his eyes smoky with desire. "But I won't bed you against your will. When I take you to my bed, the decision will be yours. I'm not a rapist. Not now, not during the Crusades."

Kadie couldn't help noticing he'd said *when,* not *if.*

He lowered his head ever so slowly, giving her ample time to avoid his kiss.

Undecided, she met his gaze. Surrender or not? His breath

was warm on her face when she turned her head to the side, denying him her lips but giving him access to her neck.

Moments later, she felt the brush of his fangs at her throat. And wished, fleetingly, that she had taken him to her bed.

Chapter 10

Vaughan's gaze moved over the other vampires seated at the table in the back of the tavern. The vampires didn't socialize very often. Even here, in Morgan Creek, they tended to be solitary creatures, suspicious of one another.

Nolan Browning had resided here for almost fifty years, longer than any of them except Saintcrow. Quinn and Felix were relative newcomers, having only lived here for the last thirty-five and forty years, respectively, while Wes Lonigan was their newest resident; he'd arrived less than thirty years ago. And then there was Lilith, the lone female in their group. She was a short, skinny creature, with straight brown hair, pale gray eyes, and the demeanor of a shrew. No one liked her. He'd often wondered why Saintcrow allowed her to stay. She'd been here almost as long as Browning. Only Kiel was missing.

"He'll give the new female to us sooner or later," Trent Lambert remarked with a shrug. "He always does."

Vaughan scowled at Trent. Lambert had long ago resigned himself to the way things were. He had a safe lair and a variety of prey and he was content.

"You can't blame Saintcrow for not sharing," Felix said. "After all, he hasn't had a woman in thirty years."

"What's the big deal, Vaughan?" Wes Lonigan asked. "This new female's no different from all the rest."

"She was mine," Vaughan said, slamming his fist on the table. "I saw her first. He had no right. . . ."

"He has every right," Browning said, his voice flat. "This is *his* town. We're here on *his* sufferance."

"Am I the only one who misses hunting?" Vaughan asked, his voice rising with his temper. "Sure, the women here are sweet, but where's the excitement? The challenge? It's been so long since I hunted, I think I've forgotten how."

Quinn nodded, his long blond hair falling over his forehead. "I hear ya."

"He took her out tonight," Vaughan said. "Did you know that? We can't leave here, but he took her out."

Vaughan's revelation gave rise to several disgruntled murmurs.

"If he can go out, why can't we?" Felix asked.

"You're forgetting that out there, *we're* the hunted," Browning reminded them. "We're here because we wanted to be here. Saintcrow didn't drag us here kicking and screaming. We all thought it was a good idea, remember? With hunters crawling out of the woodwork, there are damn few safe havens left. We're lucky to have this one. Saintcrow's one of the few master vampires this side of the Mississippi."

"Right," Gil said, nodding. "And if he wants that new female, so what? Without his protection, where would we be?"

"Anywhere but here," Felix mumbled.

"We're living like frightened sheep instead of wolves!" Vaughan exclaimed.

"You're right," Lilith said, speaking up for the first time. "We are living like sheep. And I'm damn sick of it."

Trent and Felix looked at each other, then nodded in agreement.

"So," Vaughan said, his eyes showing red, "what are we going to do about it?"

Chapter 11

The men were still making plans for their rebellion when Lilith left the tavern. Darrick always had such big plans, but he was all show and no go. All that talk about wolves and sheep had aroused her hunger.

A thought took her to Freeman's house. According to Saintcrow's rules, she wasn't supposed to feed on any of the sheep more than a couple of times a week, but she didn't like to feed on the women, and there were only a few men. And Carl was her favorite, simply because he hated her the most.

She didn't bother knocking on the door.

"Good evening, Carl," she purred. "Ready for a little fun?" She couldn't hold back a malicious grin when she saw the look on his face. "Surely you've been expecting me?"

He sat frozen on the sofa, his eyes reflecting the horror he knew was coming.

Holding out one hand, she beckoned him, felt her excitement rise when he tried to resist. She loved being a vampire, loved the power it gave her. Try as he might, the fool could not ignore her summons.

Falling to his knees, he crawled toward her.

"What a good boy you are!" she exclaimed, and dropping down beside him, she tore off his shirt, her long nails ripping the skin off his back. He shuddered with revulsion when she ran her tongue over the bloody furrows. She always loved a little taste before the main meal.

She bloodied his chest and his cheeks, licking the wounds dry, knowing her saliva would heal them by morning.

He shuddered again when she took him in her arms, a wail of pain and helplessness exploding from his lips as she buried her fangs in his throat.

One night, she might take it all. But not tonight.

Chapter 12

Kadie woke with a raging thirst. Flinging the covers aside, she hurried down to the kitchen and put on a pot of coffee, then drank two glasses of water.

Why was she so thirsty?

Of course, she thought with morbid humor, lifting a hand to her throat, she was a quart low. She was exaggerating, she hoped, but she was certain Saintcrow was the cause of her unusual thirst.

She knew now why the other women didn't complain about the vampires feeding on them. It was an amazing sensation. Sensual when it should have been sickening, amazing when it should have been abhorrent.

Would making love to Saintcrow be the same? Did vampires make love like human men? Or was it some totally different, bizarre experience entirely? And did she really want to know?

She poured herself a cup of coffee and carried it into the living room. At the window, she pulled back the curtain. There wasn't much to see other than rocks, trees, and the dark clouds rapidly gathering overhead.

She had always loved the rain. At home, she liked to wrap up in a blanket and sit on the front porch when it stormed.

Even though Kathy had been afraid of the thunder and the lightning, she had always crawled into Kadie's lap.

Kadie felt her throat grow thick as she thought about her little sister. Kathy had been a change-of-life baby. Kadie had been sixteen when her mother announced she was pregnant. Kadie remembered being horrified at the thought of her mother having another baby. Kathy had been spoiled and coddled by her parents from the day she'd been born. Kadie had never been jealous of the attention Kathy received. She had doted on her little sister, been heartbroken when Kathy took sick. Her father, a respected surgeon, had been unable to diagnose her illness. Specialists had been called in but to no avail. Her ailment remained a mystery. Recently, her father had discovered an infusion that enabled Kathy to enjoy several weeks at home before it wore off and she had to return to the hospital for another treatment.

With a sigh, Kadie turned away from the window, praying that a cure could be found.

The day stretched before her, as gloomy as her thoughts. Kadie began to understand why Brittany worked in the library, why Marti and Jeremy worked in the grocery store, and why Leslie and Chelsea handed out popcorn at the movie theater. They didn't get paid, but it gave them something to do, a sense, however false, of being useful.

Moving to the sofa, she wondered if there was something in town she could do.

She sat up with a start when the doorbell rang. Feeling a little apprehensive, she set her coffee cup aside, then went to the door and looked through the peephole.

It was Carl Freeman.

Curious, she opened the door. "Hi. What brings you here?"

"I was just taking a walk and thought I'd stop by."

"That's some long walk."

"Tell me about it." He shuffled from one foot to the other. "Can I come in?"

"No, I'm sorry. I'm not allowed to let anyone into the house."

"Maybe you could come out?" he suggested.

"I guess so." Leaving the door open, she stepped outside.

"How are you liking it here?" he asked.

"Is that a trick question?"

"Yeah, I guess it is. I mean, what's there to like?"

Kadie pondered that a moment. He was right. She could think of nothing in this town to recommend it. But there had to be something. "The trees are pretty," she remarked, glancing at the oak in the front yard. "The air is clean."

He looked at her in disbelief. "You're one of those 'the glass is half-full' kind of people, aren't you?"

She shrugged. "I don't know about that, but if you look hard enough, you can usually find something good in any situation," she said, and then frowned. Why had she said that? She hated it here, beautiful trees and clean air notwithstanding.

Kadie felt a sudden apprehension when he moved closer. She took a step to the side, then folded her arms over her breasts.

He cleared his throat. Not quite meeting her eyes, he said, "You're very pretty."

Murmuring, "Thank you," Kadie took a step backward, her apprehension turning to alarm when he took another step toward her. "What are you doing?"

"Scratching an itch."

Before she could retreat into the house, his arms closed around her and then he was kissing her, his body rubbing against hers, his hands stroking her arms, her face, her back.

At first, she was too startled by his behavior, too outraged by his brash assault, to react, until he plunged his tongue into her mouth. Gagging, she drove her knee into his crotch as hard as she could.

He released her immediately, his hands clutching his injured manhood.

Pivoting on her heel, Kadie escaped into the house and slammed the door behind her. She turned the lock with a flourish, then wiped her mouth with the back of her hand. What had just happened? She had never said or done a single thing to encourage him.

She pressed her hand to her heart. What would Saintcrow think when he found out?

What would he do?

He had told her that none of the vampires would dare touch her on pain of death. Did that apply to the humans in town, too?

She was suddenly certain that it did, and just as certain that she knew why Carl had rubbed his body against hers, why he had kissed her. It was no secret that he wanted to end his life. Had he finally found a way to make it happen?

Panic sent her into the bathroom. She showered for twenty minutes in hopes of erasing Carl's scent from her skin, washed her hair three times, brushed her teeth.

Pulling on clean clothes, she tried to relax, but it was hopeless. She fretted over Carl's actions the rest of the day, her tension growing with each passing hour. She didn't want to be the cause of anyone's death.

Her nerves were drawn tight as a bow string when Saintcrow appeared in the living room.

As usual, he asked about her day, only to pause, his brows rushing together, his eyes narrowing, as he looked her up and down, his nostrils flaring.

He didn't ask any questions, just looked at her as though awaiting an explanation.

Kadie glared at him. She saw no need to explain what he obviously already knew.

And still he stood there, waiting.

"Don't hurt him," she said.

"The man has been looking for death since he came here. He's found it."

Kadie placed her hand on Saintcrow's arm. It felt like iron beneath her palm. "You can't kill him just because he kissed me!"

"You think not?"

"I won't be the cause of a man's death!"

"He knew what he was doing. If I spare him, it will weaken my authority and put your life in danger."

"But . . ."

"The subject is closed," he said harshly. Then, more quietly, "I'll make it quick."

Before she could beg Saintcrow to reconsider, he was gone.

Unable to sit still, she paced the living room floor, her mind conjuring one gruesome image after another, all of them ending with Carl Freeman dead and drained of blood.

Kadie went to the window and stared out into the darkness. Where was Saintcrow? What was he doing? She sat on the sofa, her fingers drumming on the cushion beside her, then got up and went to the window again. She glanced at her watch, surprised to find that what had seemed like hours had been only a few minutes.

She was ready to scream when Saintcrow reappeared.

Kadie stared at him, mute, but when he said nothing, she had to ask, "Did you . . . is he . . . ?"

"No." He swore a pithy oath, then grabbed her arm and yanked her up close against him. "You owe me one, Kadie Andrews."

She stared up at him. "What . . . what do you want?"

Desire blazed in his eyes. "I think you know." One hand fisted in her hair. "That's my price. Is his life worth it?"

"You said you wouldn't force me."

"I'm not."

"Yes, you are! This is blackmail of the worst kind!"

"Yes, or no?"

"How do I know you didn't kill him?"

"Because I'm telling you that I didn't. Do you believe me?"

She met his probing gaze without blinking or flinching and she knew, somehow she knew, he was telling her the truth. She blew out a sigh. Giving him what he wanted— what she wanted, if she was honest with herself—seemed a small price to pay for a man's life.

"Very well, Saintcrow. The answer is yes. I'll sleep with you. As long as it isn't in a coffin."

His laughter startled her. "You win, Kadie. It's enough that you believe me. For now."

"You don't want me?"

"Always, but I want it to be your idea, not mine."

"Then what was this all about?"

The heat faded from his eyes. "I'm not sure."

Stunned, and unaccountably disappointed, she dropped down on the sofa. "Where's Carl now?"

Saintcrow leaned against the hearth, his arms folded over his chest. "I let him go. As far as anyone else knows, he's dead and buried."

"You let him go?"

"It was either that or kill him. I trust you won't tell anyone he's still alive."

"No, of course not. Can I ask you something?"

He nodded.

"I saw a graveyard. Are there people buried there? I mean, is it a real cemetery?"

"It's real, and yes, there are people buried there. People

who have died here," he added, anticipating her next question. "Most from natural causes."

"Most?"

"There have been casualties from time to time."

She didn't have to ask what kind of casualties. The town was filled with vampires, after all. "Have you ever seen any ghosts out there?"

"Don't tell me you saw one?"

"No, but . . ." She felt a flush of embarrassment heat her cheeks. "I felt something . . . something cold and kind of clammy. It was creepy."

He started to assure her that the dead couldn't hurt her, then changed his mind. Most of the Undead were more dangerous than the living.

"Anything else you want to know?" he asked, though he had no idea why he was answering her questions. He had never done so for any of the others.

"Just one. I was wondering why there are so few men here. Human men, I mean."

"Probably because men rarely get lost."

"Yeah, right," Kadie said. But she smiled in spite of herself. "Seriously, why?"

He shrugged. "Very few people find this place. Sometimes there are more men, sometimes more women. At the moment, the females outnumber the males. Women live longer. Men are more aggressive than women, less inclined to accept captivity, more likely to start fights they can't win."

She contemplated that for several minutes before asking, "Are you going to keep me here forever?"

"Perhaps." His gaze moved over her, as warm and tangible as a caress. And then he took her hand in his and drew her to her feet and into his arms. "But I think not."

Unbelievably, at that moment, with his arms holding her

close and his dark eyes making love to her, there was nowhere else she wanted to be.

She woke early the next morning, still thinking of Saintcrow, still wondering what it would be like to make love to a vampire.

Going downstairs, she came to an abrupt halt at the entrance to the living room. All the old furniture was gone, replaced by the Jonathan Adler furniture, the new end tables and lamps. Saintcrow had arranged it so the sofa faced the fireplace. The easy chair and one table were to the sofa's left, the love seat and the other table to the right.

How had he gotten everything so quickly? she wondered, and then grinned. More vampire mojo.

There was a note on one of the end tables.

Kadie—
    If you want to rearrange the furniture we can do it when I rise.

                                                                RS

The kitchen was also refurbished. She couldn't help smiling when she noticed there were two new chairs though she had only ordered one. The new blender and microwave were in place, new silverware gleamed in the drawer.

After making a pot of coffee, she pulled a new Spode china cup from the shelf. She hadn't seriously expected Saintcrow to buy all these things. She glanced at the cup in her hand. What if she broke it? It wouldn't be like breaking one of her cheap ceramic mugs back home.

With a shake of her head, she poured herself a cup of coffee. If he wanted to keep her, then he could keep her in the manner to which she was seriously unaccustomed!

Cup in hand, she returned to her bedroom. She hadn't paid much attention on waking, but now she noticed several packages on the dresser. No doubt she'd find her new sheets, towels, and bath soap inside. Not to mention a bottle of the world's most expensive perfume.

Unable to resist, she opened the smallest package and spritzed herself with Clive Christian No. 1. It smelled divine. Feeling like a movie star, she returned to the kitchen, wondering if Saintcrow would hire her a maid and a cook if she asked him to.

Kadie was sitting on the new sofa, watching a movie on her new DVD player, when Saintcrow appeared. As usual, her foolish heart skipped a beat—partly from the suddenness of his arrival, but mostly because he was such an amazing-looking man.

He glanced around the room. "So, how do you like it?"

"How do *you* like it? You paid for it."

He shrugged. "A sofa's a sofa. A chair's a chair. Do you need anything else?"

"Yes." Sitting up, she leaned forward, her elbows braced on her knees. "I want to know about you."

He lifted one brow. "What about me?"

"Gee, I wonder. Let's see. You're a nine-hundred-year-old vampire. Why don't you start there?"

He dropped into the chair and stretched his long legs out in front of him. "What do you want to know?"

"How did you become a vampire? I mean, who did it? Where did it happen?"

"It was during the Crusades. It was a messy business, that war. A lot of men died on the way to the Holy Land. Ships were lost at sea. They were the lucky ones. The rest of us marched across the desert in full armor. Some perished from lack of food, others from lack of water, some from heat exhaustion. But we kept going, marching to the battle cry of *Deus vult*. God wills it. That was our motto. Thousands of men, women, and children joined us."

He shook his head with the memory. "Getting to the Holy Land was only half the battle. Once we were there, we laid siege to the cities, sometimes for years. It was exciting at first, riding off to a holy war, but the excitement quickly died, replaced by the stink of fear and death. I was wounded in battle. I knew I was going to die, but I managed to drag myself away from the field where no one could find me. I guess I was delirious, but I was determined to die alone. A woman found me there. She gave me a drink of water, sang me a song."

His eyes took on a faraway look, and Kadie knew he was living it all again. He was quiet for several minutes before he continued.

"She talked to me for a long time. I don't remember much of what she said. I was fading fast. I remember she pinched me hard enough to get my attention, then she asked me if I wanted to die. I thought that, under the circumstances, it was a foolish question. I was weak. I could barely speak, my vision was gone. She shook me, then asked me the same question again, but I was past answering.

"What happened next remains a blur. I know she bit me. I remember feeling her teeth at my throat, but it didn't hurt. I felt myself drifting away and I knew I was dying, but I didn't care. I was floating in a sea of crimson when she slapped me. It jerked me back to reality. 'Drink this,' she said, and I opened my mouth. That's the last thing I recall until I woke the next night.

"At first, I had no idea what had happened to me. My memories of the night before were fragmented. All I knew was that I was filthy, my armor was gone, my garments were stained with blood, and I was ravenous, hungry for something, although I didn't know what it was at the time.

"I heard voices in the distance and I started walking toward them." He took a deep breath, held it for a long time before releasing it. "I found three men gathered around a fire. Deserters from the look of them. I called out and they invited me to join them." He dragged a hand over his jaw. "I guess my appearance was pretty awful. When they saw me up close in the fire's light, they drew their weapons."

His gaze met hers, dark and direct. "It was the last thing they ever did."

She bit down on her lower lip. He had killed them, she thought. All of them. "What happened to the vampire who made you?"

"I don't know. I never saw her again. I learned how to be a vampire the hard way, by trial and error. It didn't take long to learn that the sun was my enemy, or that I could no longer consume mortal food, or that everyone I met from that night on was my enemy.

"It took me quite a while to adjust to my new existence, to accept that I was no longer human, that I would never have a family of my own." He glanced at the fireplace. A moment later, flames sprang to life in the hearth. "For a time, I hated everyone, myself most of all." His gaze met hers again. "I became the monster of myth and legend, and I reveled in it."

"I'm sorry." It was a completely inane thing to say, but she couldn't think of anything else. It was so easy to visualize the story he had told her. She could feel his anger and his despair, and even though she couldn't condone what he had done, she could understand it.

He lifted one brow in what was quickly becoming a familiar gesture. "You think you understand?" He snorted his disgust. "You have no idea of the bodies or the carnage I left in my wake."

She wanted to go to him, to erase the torment from his eyes, ease the harsh lines that bracketed his mouth, but an innate sense of self-preservation warned her not to say or do anything that would ignite the anger simmering in his eyes. His preternatural power filled the room.

He was a big man, strong. Solid. He would have been a man to be reckoned with even as a human. Now, that strength, combined with his supernatural power, made him far more dangerous.

He glared at her for several tense moments, then vanished from her sight.

The flames in the hearth licked hungrily at the logs, their hissing the only sound in the room.

Weak with relief, Kadie sagged back against the sofa pillows, thinking she was lucky to still be alive.

Chapter 13

Saintcrow went to her as soon as the sun set the following night. He'd had many women over the course of his existence. Old, young, black, white, yellow, and red, but none had taken root in his heart so quickly, or so deeply, as Kadie Andrews. There was something about her that called to him, that made him want to keep her close, to tell her everything she wanted to know.

Had he said too much last night? He hadn't intended to reveal so much of his past, or confess to the lives he had so thoughtlessly taken. He didn't want her to be afraid of him and yet, for her own safety, she would be wise to remember what he was. It was rare these days that he succumbed to the kind of violent behavior that had consumed him in the beginning. He had learned to control his anger and his hunger. Most of the time.

Vaughan and the others thought he had been away from Morgan Creek these past thirty years when, in truth, he had gone to ground in the cemetery. Even after his body had healed, he'd had no desire to rise, until Kadie Andrews came to town. Her scent, the beat of her heart, had penetrated the thick layers of earth and darkness that had surrounded him, drawing him out of oblivion. One look at her face, one scent of her blood, and he had known he would not rest until he'd had a chance to meet her, touch her. Taste her.

And now she was his.

And he wanted her. All of her. He wanted to know her every thought, lose himself in her sweetness, take her in his arms and satisfy his every desire.

He smiled inwardly. He had no doubt that, sooner or later, she would fulfill his every desire, grant his every wish. She might deny it. She might not fully realize it. But she wanted him as desperately as he wanted her.

Looking up from the book she was reading, Kadie glanced around the room. She could feel Saintcrow's presence, detect the scent that was uniquely his, yet she was alone in the house. How was that possible?

She laid the book aside, frowning as her sense of his presence grew stronger. It was, she realized, the same presence she had felt on awakening in the library.

From the corner of her eye, she caught a faint shimmer, like sunlight dancing on a pool of water, and Saintcrow materialized in front of her, tall, dark, and handsome in a pair of faded jeans and a black sweater.

Kadie pressed a hand to her chest. "Are you trying to give me a heart attack?"

"Not at all. I was merely anxious to see you."

"Well, next time try coming in through the front door." She couldn't stop staring at him. So, she really had sensed him there. How long had he been in the room? Had he been spying on her? "Do you live in the house somewhere?"

"Live?" he asked with a wry grin. "I don't actually 'live' anywhere, you know. Vampires are technically dead." He swore under his breath, wishing he could recall his thoughtless words when he saw the look of horror on her face. "You must have known that?"

"Yes, of course, it's just that . . ." Feeling a sudden chill that had nothing to do with the weather, Kadie scrubbed her hands up and down her arms. "I've just never heard it put quite so bluntly, and by a vampire, no less."

She tilted her head to one side, her eyes narrowing as she studied him.

His body quickly responded to her perusal.

"Do you feel dead?" she asked candidly.

Saintcrow took a place in the chair across from her, long legs stretched out, his arms folded over his chest. "Quite the opposite. I feel more alive than I ever did when I was mortal."

"Really? Hmm. Why is that, do you think?"

"I don't know. Are you planning to write a thesis on the thoughts and feelings of the Undead?"

"No, just curious. You said dying was like drifting away, that it didn't hurt." She hoped that was true, for Kathy's sake.

He shook his head, thinking that, in nine hundred years, he had never had a conversation quite as bizarre as this one. "It was like falling asleep, until I woke up, cold and alone, with no real knowledge of what had happened to me. It was terrifying at first. Everything was brighter, sharper, louder. Any kind of light hurt my eyes. When I fed the first time, I was horrified by what I was doing and yet . . ." He shook his head. "I shouldn't be telling you this."

"Why not? It's fascinating."

"Fascinating?" He cocked one brow. "You're the strangest female I've ever met." And that was saying something, he thought, considering the length of his existence.

"Well, you know the old saying, know your enemy."

"I'm not your enemy, Kadie."

His voice poured over her like honey, warm and sweet.

She loved the way he said her name, drawing it out as if he liked the way it tasted on his tongue. She gazed into his eyes, those deep ebony eyes that seemed capable of looking past her defenses and uncovering the secrets buried in the nethermost parts of her heart and soul.

"If you weren't my enemy, you'd let me go." It was an effort to speak, and as she said the words, she knew that even if she was free to go, leaving him wouldn't be easy.

From the slow smile that spread over his face, he knew it, too, damn him.

"Kadie, shall I tell you something?"

"If you want to."

He leaned forward to take her hands in his. "I was asleep in the earth when you came here."

"Asleep?" Her brows lifted in astonishment. "In the ground?"

"I had planned to rest there for another decade or two. And then you came here. You woke me, Kadie. Your scent, your spirit . . ." He shook his head. "Whatever it was, I felt it through eight feet of earth."

"That's impossible."

"Is it?" His thumbs played back and forth over her hands. "You knew I was here earlier, didn't you?"

She nodded, unable to deny it. She had felt his presence in the house before he materialized in front of her. How was that even possible?

"And you sensed me in the library the night Kiel accosted you. There's something between us, Kadie, something I've never felt before with anyone else."

"I don't believe you. You're just making that up so that I'll . . ." She tugged her hands from his and sat back, her arms folded across her chest. "I don't believe you."

"You think I'm making it up to get you into bed? If that's

all I wanted, I could get you there with no trouble at all, and then make you forget it ever happened."

"How?"

His gaze trapped hers. "Come here to me, Kadie. Sit on my lap, put your arms around me, and kiss me."

His voice threaded through her mind, stealing her will, until all she wanted to do was please him. Rising, she crossed the short distance between them and did as he'd asked.

When he broke the kiss, she stared at him, startled to find herself in his lap, her arms around his neck.

She scrambled to her feet, then stared at him, her eyes wide. "What happened? What did you do?"

"A form of hypnotism," he said quietly. "If I wanted you in my bed, Kadie, you would be there. Now do you believe me?"

She nodded, frightened right down to the ground.

"I told you before I wouldn't take you by force. I haven't changed my mind." Rising, he drew her into his arms. "But I want you, Kadie, more than I've ever wanted another woman. And you want me. I can smell it on you, hear it in the beat of your heart. Do you deny it?"

"No."

"Then say yes, and I'll give you anything you want."

"You promise?"

"I do."

"If we make love, will you let me go?"

He shook his head. "I'll grant you anything but that."

"It's the only thing I want."

The arms holding her grew taut. A muscle throbbed in his jaw. "I can wait," he said, his voice harsh. "Like I told you before, I have all the time in the world."

His hands grasped her arms, his fingers digging into her flesh, though not painfully. Lowering his head, he kissed her, slowly at first, then with building intensity, his lips moving evocatively over hers, his tongue tasting her, branding her, until the rest of the world fell away and there was only his mouth on hers, his hand on her back, drawing her body up against the hard length of his. Everything that was female within her responded to his kiss, to his caress. He was man and she was woman and they were meant to be together.

When he released her, she sank to her knees. Head spinning, she closed her eyes and expelled a deep shuddering breath.

When she looked up, he was gone.

Saintcrow stalked the dark streets, his need at war with his promise not to take her by force. Why had he made such a ridiculous promise in the first place? This was his town. She was his woman, his slave, no more than chattel if he wished it.

He passed each house, knowing which woman was alone and which was entertaining one of his kind. If he wished, he could hear their thoughts, though that was something he rarely did. Mortal thoughts held little interest for him, especially those in Morgan Creek.

He paused outside Leslie's house. Quinn was inside, high on the woman's blood. He had taken far more than he should. The woman was unconscious, barely breathing. The beat of her heart was almost undetectable.

Cursing softly, Saintcrow entered the house.

"What the hell are you doing here?" Quinn demanded, gaining his feet. "She's mine for the night."

"You damn fool, she's almost dead!"

"So what? There's more where she came from. I'm tired of being careful. Tired of this place! I want to hunt. I want to kill something!"

"You want to kill something?" Saintcrow glanced at the woman on the sofa. "You just did. She's dead."

Quinn cleared his throat. "I didn't mean to kill her."

"Bury the body before you seek your rest."

Quinn nodded.

"If this happens again . . ."

"It won't," Quinn said, his voice sullen.

"See that it doesn't," Saintcrow said.

Quinn nodded. There was no mistaking the blatant warning in Saintcrow's voice, or the promise of destruction in his eyes.

Outside again, Saintcrow willed himself to the nearest town. He had long since stopped preying on those in Morgan Creek. He took the first woman he found. She was clean, her blood untainted by drugs or disease, but he found no satisfaction in it, no enjoyment, only an end to his hunger.

Kadie, damn her. She had spoiled his pleasure in anyone else.

Chapter 14

Kadie waited the rest of the night for Saintcrow to return. She yearned for him, craved his kiss, his touch, longed for him more than her next breath. But he didn't come back.

Not that night.

Not the next night.

Or the next. Where was he? Was it possible he was sick? Did vampires get sick? She grimaced at the idea. They lived forever, so it was likely that they were immune to human diseases. But what did she know? Maybe he had the vampire flu.

With a toss of her head, she plopped down on the sofa. He was probably just trying to make her miss him and, damn his hide, it was working.

By Saturday morning, she was tired of waiting and worrying. After taking a quick shower and downing a piece of toast and a cup of coffee, she jumped into his Corvette—noting that the gas tank was full—and drove to town. The car was insanely fast.

She pulled over to the curb when she saw Marti, Rosemary, Shirley, and Chelsea huddled together outside the grocery store.

She switched off the engine, then joined the others on the sidewalk. "Hi," she said brightly. "What's going on?"

"Mona passed away."

"Who's Mona?" Kadie asked.

"She's the elderly lady who lived across from Chelsea."

"Oh." The old lady on the porch. Kadie recalled seeing her a couple of times. "What happened to her?"

"She died in her sleep. Donna found her when she went to check on her this morning."

"And that's not all," Marti said. "Leslie is missing."

"Missing?" Kadie glanced from one woman to the next. "How could she be missing? There's no place to go."

"It's a polite way of saying she's . . ." Rosemary choked back a sob.

"She's what?" Kadie asked.

"Dead." The word whispered past Marti's lips.

Kadie heard the tears beneath her words. "What happened?"

"What do you think?" Shirley exclaimed. "One of those monsters killed her. Sooner or later, they'll kill us all."

"How do you know she's dead?"

"No one's seen her since Tuesday night," Marti said. "I went by her house yesterday afternoon. Her things were gone."

Tuesday night, Kadie thought. That was the last night she had seen Saintcrow. The night she had refused him. Had he taken his anger out on Leslie? Kadie shook the thought from her mind. He hadn't been angry. "But, if no one's seen her, how do you know she's dead?"

"Because her house has been cleaned out," Shirley explained. "It's happened before."

"Have you told the others?"

Shirley nodded.

"Why would the vampires kill her?"

"It might have been an accident," Chelsea said without conviction. "That's happened before, too."

"Do you know who did it?" Kadie asked, dreading the answer.

Chelsea shook her head. "We don't know, for sure."

Kadie glanced at the other women. "You don't think it was Saintcrow, do you?"

"I think it was Quinn," Marti said. "He saw her the most."

"What difference does it make who did it?" Rosemary wiped the tears from her eyes with the edge of her scarf. "Leslie's dead and one of those monsters killed her. Any one of us could be next."

Those words echoed in Kadie's mind as she drove back to Saintcrow's house. She pulled up in front, then put the car in reverse and continued down the road, hoping she was headed in the right direction.

As luck would have it, she found the cemetery without any trouble. Exiting the Corvette, she stared out over the grave sites. The two new ones were easy to find. The wooden crosses were untouched by wind or rain, the ground freshly turned.

How was she to know which was which? Did it really matter?

She would come back with a knife tomorrow and carve Leslie's name on one of the crosses and Mona's on the other so that they wouldn't be forgotten.

By the time Kadie reached Saintcrow's house, she was thoroughly depressed. She curled up in a corner of the sofa. She hadn't seen Saintcrow in days. She would probably never see her family again. And a woman she had known, however slightly, had been murdered. She remembered Rosemary saying any one of them could be next.

But they didn't need to be killed. In a way, they were already dead, sealed off from the rest of the world. How long before her parents stopped looking for her? So many people disappeared these days, never to be seen or heard from again. In time, they were declared dead and life went on.

Kadie had always felt sorry for the people left behind who never knew what had happened to their loved ones. Did they ever really get over the loss? Ever find any kind of closure? And now she was missing.

Tears stung her eyes as she imagined her father holding back his own tears while he comforted her mother and sister. No doubt they had all imagined the worst, she thought with a bitter smile. But they never would have imagined anything like this place.

She felt a growing sense of anticipation with the coming of nightfall, but again, there was no sign of Saintcrow. Had he left town? Buried himself in the earth again?

She told herself she was better off without him. He was a vampire, a monster. For all she knew, he was the one who had killed Leslie. In his time, he had probably killed hundreds—maybe thousands—of men and women. Perhaps even children.

Her grim thoughts weighed down on her, thick and oppressive, as did the silence, which always seemed worse at night. She dropped a DVD into the player, but couldn't seem to focus on the movie. Canned conversation did nothing to make her feel less alone.

The house felt empty without him.

The house. Sitting up, she glanced at the staircase. She had only given the house a cursory look.

Rising, she tiptoed up the stairs, then laughed at herself. Why was she being so quiet? There was no one else here.

She went into the first bedroom. She ran her hands over

the walls, looking for cleverly disguised levers that would reveal hidden stairways or secret doors, but to no avail.

She bypassed her room and explored the other three. Again, nothing out of the ordinary. Disappointed, she returned to the first floor. In the movies, old houses like this always had concealed passageways. And sometimes a bolt hole. Was he hiding in some hidden closet?

She frowned, then glanced around the living room. There could be a door behind the bookcase, only it was too heavy for her to move. Maybe the fireplace. It was big enough to hold a horse. She pressed one brick after another, hoping to find a hidden lever that would lead to a secret room.

"Looking for something?"

Kadie whirled around at the sound of his voice, a guilty flush climbing up her neck into her cheeks. "Yes, if you must know. I was looking for you."

"Looking for me?" One brow arched inquisitively. "In the fireplace?"

She folded her arms across her chest. "Where have you been?"

"Don't change the subject. What were you really looking for?"

"A way out."

"Are we back to that again? I was hoping you'd finally resigned yourself to staying here."

"That's never going to happen. I don't have the luxury of hundreds of years. I only have one short lifetime, and I want to go back home and live it."

"I'm sorry, Kadie, but you'll never see your home again, so you might as well accept that fact and move on."

"That's not fair! My family and my friends will never know what happened to me! How can you be so cruel? And what about Marti? And the others? They all had lives before they came here. You have no right to keep us against our will!"

She was crying now, her shoulders shaking, her tears coming faster and faster.

Saintcrow swore under his breath, moved by her tears in spite of himself. The others had cried, too, but he'd been immune to their pleas. He was a vampire. As such, he lived outside the rules of humanity. He scarcely remembered what it was like to be human, subject to pain, sickness, fear, and death. Family life was only a faint memory, but it surfaced now. He'd had a wife once. She had died two years after their marriage, and their daughter with her. He had never loved Eleanor, but he had grieved for the loss of his child.

"Dammit." He drew Kadie roughly into his arms.

Stiff as a board, she endured his embrace, her tears subsiding at the touch of his hand lightly stroking her back, the brush of his lips on the top of her head. His chest was rock hard beneath her cheek. He drew her closer, his thigh pressing against hers.

She looked up at him. His eyes were dark with an emotion that might have been guilt, but before she could be sure, his mouth covered hers, chasing away every thought, swamping her senses, until there was only Saintcrow, his strong arms holding her tight, his whiskey-soft voice murmuring her name as he kissed her again and again.

What was he doing to her? Standing on her tiptoes, she twined her arms around his neck, every part of her yearning toward him, wanting to be closer, closer.

She was drowning in a world of sensation. His lips caressed her neck and she turned her head to the side, granting him access, wanting to give him everything she had, everything she was.

"Kadie, forgive me, but I can't let you go."

Let her go? That was the last thing she wanted. She was repulsed by what he was and yet some part of her was attracted to the man he must have been before he became a vampire.

His fangs scraped lightly over her skin and then, with a low groan, he gave in to the need coursing through him.

She moaned softly, her body sagging against his as the world went red. There was no pain and, oddly, no fear, only a remarkably sensual euphoria. She closed her eyes, drifting, falling into velvet blackness that threatened to sweep her away into oblivion.

"Dammit!" Saintcrow knew a moment of genuine fear when she went limp. He scooped her into his arms and carried her to the sofa. Sitting down, he brushed a wisp of hair from her cheek, cursing himself for his weakness. Her face was pale, her breathing shallow, her heartbeat slow and labored. What the hell was he thinking, to drink from her like that? He could have killed her, but never, in nine hundred years, had anything tasted so good, pleased him so much, satisfied him so well.

Biting into his own wrist, he dipped his finger into the blood and slid it past her lips. He repeated it several times, until the color returned to her cheeks, her heartbeat grew stronger.

He stroked her cheek with his fingertips. Her skin was as soft as down, her hair like silk. It grieved him that she was unhappy here even as he fought down an irrational rush of jealousy for everyone she had known before she came to Morgan Creek. He begrudged her every minute she had spent with anyone else, every second of life she had lived before they met.

Bending, he brushed her lips with his, then jerked his head back, his eyes narrowing. Had she had a lover? The thought was beyond bearing. She was his. No other would have her. He would rip the heart out of any man who touched her.

She hadn't mentioned a husband or a lover. Was she a virgin then? In this day and age, that seemed highly unlikely.

She stirred in his arms, her eyelids fluttering open. "What happened?"

"You fainted."

She touched a hand to her head, then frowned. The last thing she remembered was Saintcrow's mouth on hers, his fangs brushing her throat.

She bolted upright. Another memory tugged at the corner of her mind, but it eluded her. She licked her lips, wondering why there was such a bad taste in her mouth, and then she stared up at him. "You gave me your blood!" She grimaced. "How could you do that?"

"You needed it."

"That's ridiculous! I'm not a vampire." Her eyes grew wide. "Am I?"

"No, Kadie. I got a little carried away and took more than I should have. That's all."

"That's all? That's all!" She pushed away from him and stood up, swaying as the room spun out of focus.

"Easy, now." He was beside her in an instant, his arm steadying her. "Rest a minute," he said, urging her back down on the sofa. "I'll get you something to drink."

She watched him leave the room, her mind filling with morbid thoughts. He'd taken too much. How could he be so casual about it? If he had taken it all, she would be dead now, just another body buried in an unmarked grave like all the others. The thought made her stomach roil and she leaned forward, her head down, afraid she was going to faint again.

"Kadie? Here, drink this."

He handed her a glass of orange juice. She hadn't realized how thirsty she was until she'd drained the glass and asked for more.

She drank the second glass more slowly. Not meeting his gaze, she said, "You could have killed me."

He didn't deny it.

"Was that what happened to Leslie? You took too much and killed her?"

"Is that what you think?"

"Did you?"

"It wasn't me."

"Do you know who it was?"

"Of course. I know everything that happens here. It was Quinn."

So, Kadie thought, Marti had been right about that.

"You should go to bed," Saintcrow said, taking the glass from her hand. "You'll feel better in the morning."

She lifted a hand to her neck, but there were no bite marks, at least none she could feel. "Will I?"

"What do you want me to say? I'm sorry?"

"Are you?"

"No. I can't make you understand. I don't understand it myself. But like it or not, Kadie, you're here to stay."

Her heart sank at his words. "Have you ever let anyone leave here?"

"Just once, under duress."

He was referring to Carl Freeman, she thought, smiling faintly. "One of the women said the other vampires can't leave either. Is that true?"

He nodded.

"So, they're prisoners, too?"

"In a way. They came to me for sanctuary. I agreed to give it to them, but only if they agreed to stay inside."

"Why?"

"I don't trust any of them not to betray this place."

"Why would they?"

"There is a rather large bounty on my head."

Kadie's eyes grew wide. "Really? Why?"

He shrugged. "Perhaps because I'm the most powerful vampire in the country."

"You are?"

"Impressed?"

"I don't know. Should I be?"

He laughed, amused by her bravado.

"How much are you worth?"

"Last I heard, they were offering a cool five million for my head."

Kadie's brows shot up. "Wow!"

"Thinking of trying to claim it for yourself?"

"Of course not!" She didn't think any amount of money would persuade her to do such a thing. "So, who wants you dead so badly?"

He looked at her askance. "You don't know?" Was it possible she really had no idea?

"Well, since you're a vampire, I suppose a lot of people want you dead," she replied candidly.

He laughed again. "True, enough, but there are others— hunters—who are more persistent, more knowledgeable about my kind, who have sworn to wipe us from the face of the earth."

Kadie's brows drew together. "But you leave town."

He shrugged. "I'm a master vampire. I can do whatever I wish."

In a voice dripping with sarcasm, she said, "Must be nice."

He nodded again. Then, reaching for her hand, he drew her to her feet and walked her up the stairs. "Shall I tuck you in?"

"That won't be necessary."

"Too bad." His gaze swept over her from head to foot. "Good night, Kadie," he said quietly. "Sweet dreams."

She closed the door, then stood there, his scent all around her, her thoughts muddled. How was it possible to hate him so much and still burn for his kisses?

Chapter 15

Sunday morning, Kadie returned to the cemetery. She studied the two newest graves, but there was no way to distinguish one from the other. She told herself again it didn't matter. Mona and Leslie were beyond caring. Tears stung her eyes as she carved Mona's name on one of the crosses, and Leslie's name on the other. She thought about Saintcrow. He had taken more of her blood than he should have the other night. Had he taken too much, she might be buried here, another casualty in an unmarked grave.

Blinking back her tears, Kadie bowed her head and prayed for the courage to endure what could not be changed, prayed that Saintcrow would relent and set her and all the others free, prayed that her parents would be comforted and not give up hope. Her father had become distant ever since Kathy took sick. More and more, he'd been away from home, and when he was there, he was always preoccupied. Men in dark suits came and went at odd hours of the day and night. They rarely stayed long, thank goodness. Her father never spoke of them. She knew little more than their names, but there was something about them that Kadie found disturbing.

Unable to hold back her tears, Kadie dropped to her

knees and prayed for Kathy, pleading for a cure to be found before it was too late, praying that Kathy would hang on until Kadie got home. She had never mentioned her sister to Saintcrow, but maybe she should. Surely, if there was the slightest bit of compassion in his soul, he would relent and let her go home.

Driving back to Saintcrow's house, she found herself thinking about vampire hunters. Until she came here, she had never believed vampires existed. Now it seemed that not only were they real, but there were people dedicated to destroying them. She could almost sympathize with Saintcrow and the others. It would be awful to be hunted, to have a price on your head. Still, the vampires could hardly blame people for hating them when they preyed upon humans. Maybe if the vampires could drink animal blood, people wouldn't hate them so much.

Even as the thought crossed her mind, she knew she was being naïve. After all, how could you expect someone to give up what they needed to survive? Still, she couldn't help wondering if they'd ever thought of it? Tried it? Vampires did it in the movies all the time.

It was still on her mind later that night when Saintcrow appeared. Without thinking, she blurted, "Can you live on animal blood?"

"Excuse me?"

"I was thinking about what you said, about being hunted. Maybe if your kind stopped preying on my kind, we could all live together without killing each other."

"All live together?" He laughed, his dark eyes filled with amusement.

Kadie stared at him a moment, her cheeks burning with embarrassment, before turning on her heel and running up the stairs to her room.

He was right behind her, his hand closing over her shoulder, stopping her flight before she reached the door.

"Let me go! No wonder people hate you! You're despicable!"

"Kadie." He turned her to face him. "I'm sorry. I shouldn't have laughed at you, but . . ." He shook his head. "You're so young, so innocent."

"I am not!"

"A leopard can't change its spots, and vampires can't stop being vampires. It's possible for us to survive on animal blood for a time, but sooner or later, we have to have human blood. There's no way around it."

"Do you like it? Human blood, I mean. Isn't it . . . gross?"

"No. Some is sweeter than others." He drew her slowly into his arms. "Yours, for instance, is remarkable. Warm, sweet, pure."

"Blood is blood. How can mine be any different from anyone else's?"

"Because you don't smoke. And you don't drink to excess. And you don't do drugs. And you never have."

"You can tell all that from my blood?"

Nodding, he drew her closer still, then lowered his head and brushed his lips across her throat.

And just like that, she wanted him. She knew it, and when his gaze met hers, she had no doubt that he knew it, too.

It was only a matter of time.

"Tonight, Kadie?" His voice, low and filled with the promise of sexual delights, made her stomach curl with anticipation.

Why not tonight? She wanted him. How much longer could she deny it? How much longer could she deny him?

"You want me." His hands stroked her back, ever so lightly. "You know you do. Why fight it when it's what we both want?" He pressed butterfly kisses to her cheeks, her eyelids. "You're so beautiful. Say you'll be mine tonight."

She closed her eyes, on the brink of surrendering, when she heard Shirley's voice in the back of her mind, predicting that, sooner or later, the monsters would kill them all. Quinn had killed Leslie. How could she have forgotten that?

With a low growl, Saintcrow released her. "I'm not Quinn," he said, his voice tight. And then he was gone.

Kadie wrapped her arms around her waist. She told herself she should be glad he was gone. It was for the best, after all. So why did she feel so bad?

He stayed away from home for a week this time. Teaching her a lesson, she thought. Proving to her how much she would miss him. And miss him she did.

One night, she gathered her courage and drove to the tavern in town, hoping to find Vaughan. As luck would have it, she found him sitting at the bar, alone.

"Well, well," he drawled. "Look who's here. What happened? You get tired of Saintcrow?"

"No," she said, taking the stool beside him, "I just felt like a night out on my own. Anything wrong with that?" She glanced around. Besides Vaughan, there were four other vampires in the tavern, all sitting at separate tables.

The silent woman, Frankie, was tending bar. She looked at Kadie, one brow raised.

"I'd like a glass of root beer," Kadie said in answer to her unspoken question.

"You didn't come here for a glass of soda," Vaughan remarked. "Why are you really here?"

Kadie nodded her thanks when Frankie brought her drink.

Picking up the glass, Kadie gestured at the other vampires. "Don't you guys like each other?"

"Not much."

"Are there really hunters on the outside?"

He nodded.

"Is it true that you can't leave here?"

"Yeah. Taking refuge here sounded like a good idea at the time. Safety in numbers. A secure location. A ready supply of . . . a ready supply. It was good for a while, but after forty-odd years, I'm ready to take my chances with the hunters."

Forty years in this place? Kadie shuddered. "Why won't Saintcrow let you go?" She knew what Saintcrow had told her, but she was curious to hear what Vaughan would say.

"He thinks he knows what's best for everyone, just because he's the oldest. Sure, we came here seeking a place to hide, but we didn't know he was going to keep us here forever. I don't know about the others, but I've had enough."

Kadie sipped her drink. "So, we're all in the same boat."

"Yeah," Vaughan agreed. "And it's time for a mutiny."

Chapter 16

A mutiny was exactly what was on Lilith's mind that night when she found a young couple who'd wandered across the bridge. They reeked of drugs and liquor, but she didn't care.

With the speed of a striking snake, Lilith broke the woman's neck, then carried the man up into the mountains.

He stared at her, his face white with shock. "You killed her." He shook his head, obviously trying to clear his mind. "Why?"

"She was in the way."

He blinked at her. "In the way?" He staggered back a step, tripped over a rock, and landed on his backside.

He let out a startled cry when Lilith flew across the distance between them and pinned him to the ground.

He shook his head again, fear penetrating the drug-induced haze that clouded his thoughts. "What are you?"

She grinned at him, displaying her fangs. "Just what you think I am."

"No. No, it's not possible."

She grabbed a handful of his hair and jerked his head to the side. "Oh, it's very possible," she hissed, and buried her fangs in his throat.

He struggled, but he was no match for her supernatural strength. She drank until there was nothing left but a dry, shriveled husk. Wiping her mouth on his shirt, she retrieved the woman's body, then returned to the mountain. It took only moments to dig a grave big enough for the two of them.

Throwing back her head, she gazed up at the sky. It had been years since she'd felt this good, this strong. This invincible.

And she liked it.

Chapter 17

Kadie thought about what Vaughan had said as she left the tavern. A mutiny? Was he serious? What a bloodbath that would be, vampire killing vampire. Would any of them, human or vampire, survive?

After getting into Saintcrow's car, she sat there a minute, her fingers drumming on the steering wheel. She didn't want to go back to Saintcrow's empty house and listen to the silence. It was too early for bed.

Putting the car in gear, she drove down Main Street, then turned right on Oak and drove through the residential area. Now that she was acquainted with where everyone lived, she knew that even though most of the houses were vacant, the people trapped here kept them in good repair. She hadn't gotten to know the few men in town very well, but she had seen Jeremy and Carl mowing the yards and trimming the bushes of the empty homes. It gave them something to do, like working in the market kept Marti occupied. She wondered briefly where Saintcrow had taken Carl Freeman, and what Carl was doing now.

When she reached the end of the residential area, Kadie turned right and drove until the paved road ended. She switched off the ignition, then sat there, staring at the

mountain. She had lost track of how long she'd been in
Morgan Creek. Three weeks? A month? With no contact
with the outside world, no newspapers, no calendars, how
did anyone even know what year it was, let alone the date?
She supposed you could count the years by the number of
summers passing. Maybe even make your own calendar to
keep track of the days and years. But what was the point?

Where was Saintcrow? Had he left Morgan Creek? What
if some hunter had found him and destroyed him? Would the
vampire mojo that kept them all trapped in the town be
broken if he died?

Would she care if he was dead?

The answer was a resounding yes. For some insane
reason, she had grown fond of him. More than fond. Maybe
she just had a case of Stockholm syndrome. She had read
newspaper accounts of hostages who had developed empa-
thy for their captors, seen it in movies, and thought it highly
unrealistic in spite of evidence to the contrary. Maybe it
wasn't as improbable as she had always imagined.

With a sigh, Kadie opened the door and stepped out of
the car. Hands shoved into the pockets of her jeans, she
walked toward the mountain. The night had turned cold. She
gazed up at the sky, thinking about the vampires.

Vaughan had been here over forty years, but he still
looked like a man in his prime. Saintcrow was over nine
hundred years old and didn't look a day over thirty. What was
it like for Donna and Rosemary to have been here for so long,
to watch themselves age while the supernatural creatures remained forever the same?

She couldn't help wondering if the other men and women
who had stumbled into this place had died of natural causes,
or if they had been killed when they were no longer young,
or when they got sick. Everyone she had met seemed healthy.
She thought of Donna Stout. The woman was probably in her

late sixties. It seemed obscene, somehow, for the vampires to feed on a woman old enough to be a grandmother. She thought again of Carl Freeman. He had been unable to endure living here any longer, had hoped to provoke Saint-crow into killing him. And it would have worked if Kadie hadn't pleaded for his life. How many other people, desperate to escape this place, had provoked one of the vampires into killing them, or had taken their own lives?

She was thinking about going back to Saintcrow's house when a subtle shift in the air warned her she was no longer alone. Hurrying toward the car, she reached for the door handle, only to have someone grab her from behind.

"So, what are you doing out here all alone?"

She cringed as she recognized Kiel's voice.

"You've been driving me crazy." His arm slid around her waist, holding her immobile while his free hand moved brazenly over her body, touching, squeezing, while his tongue licked the side of her neck.

Revulsion roiled in Kadie's stomach. Frantic, she jabbed him with her elbow, stomped on his instep, but he quickly captured both her hands in his, then backed her up against the car, trapping her between the Corvette and his body.

"Saintcrow will kill you for this." She was shaking so badly she was surprised she could speak.

"I'm willing to take my chances."

"Don't, please."

"I'm tired of this stinking place. Tired of the others."

She shrieked as his eyes went red, felt the bile rise in the back of her throat when his fangs scraped the skin of her neck, drawing blood.

"You taste even better than I thought you would."

"No!" She struggled in his grasp, but it was futile. Helpless, she closed her eyes and tried to pray, but she didn't know what to pray for. Rescue? Or death?

The decision was taken out of her hands when someone pulled Kiel away from her.

Afraid of what she might see, Kadie kept her eyes tightly closed.

She heard a terrible, high-pitched scream, a horrible sucking noise, and then silence.

"Kadie?"

"Saintcrow?" She opened her eyes, felt her knees go weak with relief when she saw him standing in front of her.

"Are you all right?"

"You lied!" She glared at him, her body trembling. "You told me no one would bother me. That they would smell you on me and I'd be safe."

"He'll never touch you again."

She glanced past Saintcrow, but there was no sign of the other vampire.

She didn't ask what had happened to her attacker.

She really didn't want to know.

She was still shaking when Saintcrow took her home.

A short time later, Saintcrow stood in the doorway of the living room, his arms folded over his chest. Regarding Kadie through hooded eyes, he asked, "What were you doing out there alone?"

"I was bored."

She was sitting on the sofa, wrapped in a warm blanket, a cup of hot tea clasped in her hands. She couldn't stop shaking.

With a wave of his hand, he dimmed the lamps, then ignited a fire in the hearth.

Kadie looked up at him. The light from the fire cast golden highlights in his thick black hair. It didn't seem right for a vampire to be so outrageously handsome. He was a killer. No doubt he had killed the vampire who had accosted her, and probably hundreds, maybe thousands, of others, human and vampire alike.

"Thousands?" Saintcrow asked, his voice thick with amusement. "Really?"

"Too few?" she asked sweetly.

Saintcrow shook his head. "You really have a low opinion of me, don't you?"

"In spite of your name, you're no saint."

"True, enough. But I'm hardly the monster you think I am, Kadie. If I was, you and all the others would be dead by now, drained of blood long ago."

"Only a monster keeps people enslaved. Whether it's for gold, glory, or blood, it really doesn't matter to the people you're keeping here. We're still slaves. Worse than slaves. We're like cattle to you, aren't we?"

"I'm guessing you see the world in black and white, don't you? Right and wrong. No middle ground. No shades of gray."

"Pretty much."

"Would you rather I had let Kiel feed on you against your will and then just let him go?"

"Of course not!"

"I warned him once. He knew what the penalty would be if he touched you again, and he paid it. I don't have many laws here, but the ones I have are inviolable. If I'd let him get away with it, the others would see it as a sign of weakness. I can't afford that."

"Weak? You?"

"I can take them all, one at a time, or all together, but I'd prefer not to."

"You let Carl go."

He nodded, but said nothing.

"Where have you been?" She put her cup aside, then clasped her hands in her lap.

"Not far. Why? Did you miss me?"

She thought of lying, but what was the point when he could read her mind? Her gaze slid away from his. "You know I did," she admitted, her voice little more than a whisper.

"I missed you, too."

She looked up at him, everything else forgotten when his gaze met hers.

"What do you want from me, Kadie?" he asked quietly. "Besides your freedom?"

"Nothing."

"Nothing?" He closed the distance between them. Kneeling in front of her, he ran his hands up and down her arms.

His touch was light, yet it burned through her like fire. His gaze trapped hers and images rose in her mind, images of the two of them lying on his bed, their bodies entwined, their skin slick with perspiration as they writhed together. Even though his hands were now resting on her shoulders, she could feel them moving over her, caressing her. She tasted his lips on her own, felt the sweep of his tongue.

She swayed toward him, gazing at him through heavy-lidded eyes. "Kiss me," she murmured.

He muttered something in the same foreign language he had spoken once before as he pulled her body to his. His kiss was bold, his tongue demanding as it dueled with hers in sweet, subtle seduction.

She leaned into him, her legs suddenly unsteady, her heart pounding a rapid tattoo in her chest.

Eyes blazing with desire, he said, "Tell me. Tell me what you want."

"You know what I want."

"Say it."

"I want you to make love to me. Here, now."

He growled low in his throat as he lowered her to the rug

in front of the hearth. His hands made short work of getting rid of her clothing and then his own.

Soft sounds of delight rose in her throat as she ran her hands over him. In spite of the scars that marred his chest, he was beautiful, each muscle sharply defined as though sculpted by an artist's hand. His skin was cool beneath her questing fingertips as she explored the width of his shoulders, his six-pack abs, the long, ridged scar that ran the length of his back.

Frissons of desire stirred deep within her every time she touched him. It was hard to believe he was a vampire when he lay quiescent beside her. His muscles quivered when she caressed him. It gave her a sense of power, knowing that her untutored hands could arouse such a magnificent creature. And he was definitely aroused.

He let her explore to her heart's content and then he turned the tables on her, his calloused hands quickly learning the contours of her body, stroking the hills and valleys, whispering words of endearment in her ear as he aroused her until she cried out, begging for him to take her, demanding that he put an end to the exquisite torture. Mindless with need, she held him close, her fingers digging deep into his shoulders as she urged him on, certain she would die if he didn't ease the yearning he had unleashed within her.

When she cried his name, he covered her mouth in a searing kiss as he rose over her, possessing her with one quick thrust.

She whimpered with mingled pain and pleasure as their bodies became one, heard him mutter something indistinguishable when he realized he was her first lover.

Chapter 18

"Why didn't you tell me you were a virgin?" he asked much later.

They were lying on their sides, face-to-face, arms and legs still entwined.

"The subject never came up, until now."

"How is it possible you were untouched? Most girls these days have sex in their teens."

"Well, I didn't. I grew up in a very religious home. My mother taught me early that sex outside of marriage was wrong, and I believed her. I was tempted several times to see what all the fuss was about, but then my best friend got pregnant at fifteen. The boy she loved, the one she was so sure loved her, refused to have anything to do with her when he found out. I decided then and there it would never happen to me. After high school, I went to college. I didn't hang around with the 'cool' crowd because I didn't drink or smoke and I wasn't a party girl." She shrugged. "I hardly dated at all. After I graduated, I was too busy working to have much time for anything else." She looked at him, her brow furrowed. "Who would have thought my first sexual encounter would be with a vampire?" She jackknifed into a sitting position. She had made love to a vampire. Unprotected love. Suddenly frantic, she stared at him. What if she got pregnant?

"Relax," he murmured. "It's impossible."

"You're sure?"

"I'm sure." He drew her down beside him so that her head was resting on his shoulder. "You should have told me you were a maiden."

Kadie smiled faintly, amused by the archaic term. "Why? Would it have made a difference?"

"I would not have touched you had I known," he said, a faraway look in his eyes. "I saw too many women ravaged during the Crusades, and later, in other wars in other places. I vowed then I would never take a woman against her will."

"You didn't take me against my will unless . . . Did you make me want you tonight, the way you made me kiss you?"

"No. Whatever you're feeling for me is real."

She nodded, wondering if she should believe him.

"The attraction between us is genuine, Kadie. I swear it on my honor as a knight."

She ran her hands over his chest. "So many scars," she marveled. "Were you in a lot of battles?"

"So many that I lost count."

She traced the thin white scar on his cheek. "How'd you get this one?"

"Knife."

She ran her fingertips over the shiny white scar that ran from his shoulder to his navel. "And this one?"

"Sword."

She grimaced, thinking such a wound must have been terribly painful. "I can't imagine what it must have been like, fighting with swords. Shooting someone seems much easier than skewering your enemy with a sword, feeling the blade penetrate his flesh," she said, shuddering.

Saintcrow chuckled. "Your idea of pillow talk is a bit

unusual. Most women want to hear promises of undying loyalty and affection."

"Women," she remarked, then bit down on her lower lip, refusing to ask the question now demanding an answer.

Raising himself up on one elbow, Saintcrow brushed a lock of hair behind her ear. He didn't have to read her mind to know what she was thinking. Lowering his head, he cupped her cheek, then kissed her gently. "There haven't been as many as you might think."

"One would be too many," she retorted, surprised by her jealousy. He was a man who had lived a very long time, not a monk.

"I've never truly loved any woman," he said. "Does that make you feel better?"

"It would, if I believed you."

"You don't?"

"You're over nine hundred years old, and you're gorgeous. I'm sure women throughout time have been throwing themselves at your feet."

"Well," he said, grinning, "I can't deny that."

"You've never been married?"

"Once. It was an arranged marriage, as most of them were in those days. Eleanor died in childbirth and our daughter with her. I joined the Crusades shortly after that."

"And then you became a vampire."

He nodded. "And marriage in the traditional sense was no longer an option."

"You could have married a vampire."

"Perhaps. But very few vampires marry. A mortal union that lasts seventy years is a rarity. A vampire marriage could last for centuries."

"But if you loved someone, wouldn't you want to be with her forever?"

"I've never met anyone I wanted to spend eternity with."

His gaze moved over her, leaving silky frissons of pleasure in its wake. "Until now."

Kadie blinked at him. She needed to say something, she thought. But what? He hadn't said he loved her, but maybe that was a given, if he wanted to spend forever with her. Of course, that was impossible. She didn't have forever. Did she want to spend the rest of her life with a vampire? Not that it made any difference. At the moment, she didn't have any other choice. She was his for as long as he wanted her.

"It's late," he said. "I need to feed, and you should get some rest."

"Is something wrong?"

"No."

She lifted a hand to her neck, a question in her eyes.

"I need more than I want to take from you," he explained.

"You're going to drink from one of the other women here?" The thought sent an unexpected bolt of jealousy clean through her.

"No. I stopped drinking from the women here years ago."

"But they said you take women home with you, and that those women are never seen again."

"It's only a rumor, Kadie. I don't know where it started, but you're the only woman I've ever brought here." The only woman he had ever wanted to share his home and his life.

"So, if you don't drink from the women here, where do you go?"

"Wherever I want," he said, his eyes twinkling.

"Right. You're the boss."

"Exactly." But these days he never went far from Morgan Creek.

Scooping Kadie into his arms, he carried her into the shower and turned on the water, then proceeded to wash her, ever so slowly, from head to foot.

"My turn," Kadie said, and taking the cloth from his

hand, she returned the favor. She should have known what the results would be, she thought, laughing softly when he took her, soaking wet, there, on the bathroom floor.

Sometime later, Saintcrow left Kadie sleeping in her bed. He needed to feed, but had business with Lilith first.

He found her in the tavern, alone.

She looked up when he entered. The guilt in her eyes was all the proof he needed.

"Where are the bodies?"

"I buried them, up on the mountain."

"I'm surprised you didn't keep the man."

"I thought about it, but it's been years since I've been able to satisfy my thirst, to take it all. So, what are you going to do about it?"

"Don't do it again. I don't want any killing in my town."

"Unless you do it."

"That's right. Don't make me tell you again." Turning on his heel, he left the tavern. The natives were getting restless, he mused as he drove to the nearest town. He could have gotten there faster using his own preternatural speed, but he enjoyed being behind the wheel, listening to the purr of the engine, being in control of a powerful machine.

He had left Kadie in bed, asleep. It had been hard to leave her, but he hadn't fed for a few days and he was afraid he might take too much. He was surprised by the depths of his feelings for her. In all his life, he had never truly loved a woman. He had not loved Eleanor, though he had grown fond of her. Since then, there had been no one in his life he loved or trusted, no one he wanted as he wanted Kadie Andrews. Making love to her was like nothing he had ever known. The fact that she cared for him was nothing short of a miracle. And miracles had been few and far between in his long existence.

There was a whole world to explore outside of Morgan Creek. If he took her away from there, would she stay with him? Or hasten back to her own home, her old life, without a backward glance?

It would be a risk in more ways than one.

He might lose Kadie.

He might even lose his head.

In the morning, Kadie woke aching in places where she had never ached before, but it was a wonderful kind of pain, a reminder of what they had shared. Remembering the night past had her smiling like a schoolgirl with her first crush.

"Rylan." She had never spoken his first name. It made him seem more human, somehow.

But he wasn't human. He was a vampire, hidden away in some secret place, sleeping the sleep of the Undead. Was he here, in the house? And if so, where? She supposed she couldn't fault him for keeping his resting place a secret. Was he completely vulnerable during the day? How scary would that be?

The other vampires hid out in Blair House when the sun was up. Kadie frowned, wondering again why the people in town hadn't tried to destroy them.

Kadie shook her head, surprised by her bloodthirsty thought. Even if the vampires could be destroyed, there was no guarantee that that would break the spell keeping Marti and the others in town.

Rising, she showered, dressed, and went downstairs for breakfast. Enjoying her first cup of coffee, she found herself thinking about making love to Rylan. If she had to belong to one of the vampires, she could have done a lot worse.

Needing something to do, she dusted the furniture, did a load of wash, mopped the kitchen floor.

Around noon, she drove into town for lunch. Of course, service in the restaurant depended on who felt like working that day.

She found Marti and Rosemary sitting at a table near the window.

Marti waved her over. "Come, sit with us. We just ordered."

"Thanks," Kadie said, taking the chair beside Marti's.

"We haven't seen you for a couple of days. Is everything okay?"

Kadie smiled, thinking of the night past. "Everything's fine."

Marti and Rosemary exchanged glances.

"If I didn't know better, I'd think you were in love with him," Rosemary said.

"Don't be silly," Kadie exclaimed, hoping no one would notice the flush climbing up her neck. She was attracted to him, there was no doubt of that. But love? Ridiculous. He was a vampire!

"Oh, Kadie," Marti said. "Say it isn't so."

"Of course it isn't," she replied hotly. Hoping to change the subject, she asked the question she had pondered earlier. "Speaking of vampires, why haven't you just destroyed them during the day?"

"Believe me, the men have tried," Rosemary said, "but there's no way into Blair House. The men tried breaking down the door, but that didn't work. And the windows are all barred."

Kadie nodded, pleased that her ploy to change the subject had worked.

"Besides," Chelsea said, coming to join the conversation,

"there's no guarantee that destroying the vampires will break whatever spell is keeping us here."

Kadie had recently come to the same conclusion herself. Not to mention the fact that, if the townspeople destroyed the vampires, they would have no one to bring them food and drink. Trapped in town with no way out, the inhabitants would all slowly starve to death.

"I'm on kitchen duty," Chelsea said, "so what would you like this afternoon?"

"A bacon and tomato sandwich and a cherry Coke," Kadie said. "Thanks."

"Coming right up," Chelsea said.

Rosemary waited until Chelsea went into the kitchen, then leaned forward as if she was afraid of being overheard, although they were the only three customers in the place. "You do know that all vampires have a certain sexual allure that's almost irresistible to mortals, don't you?"

"No, I didn't." Kadie groaned inwardly. So, they were back to that, were they? She bit down on the inside corner of her lip. Saintcrow had assured her that what she felt for him was real. Had he lied to her? Was she wrong to trust him?

"It's how they attract their prey," Rosemary said. "Vampires are incapable of love, of human emotions."

Kadie shook her head. "I don't believe that."

"It's true."

There was something about the way Rosemary said it that made Kadie look at her sharply. "Are you saying . . . ? I mean, have you . . . ?"

"We all have," Marti said.

"They took you, against your will?"

"That's what I'm trying to tell you," Rosemary said, her voice rising. "They can make you want them, make you think it's your idea."

Kadie didn't know why she was so shocked. Saintcrow

had told her that he could compel her to do anything he wanted. He had even proved it one night. But it had never occurred to her that the vampires used their preternatural power to seduce Rosemary and the others. Wasn't it bad enough they took their blood without stealing their will?

Rosemary sat back in her chair when Chelsea appeared with their orders. "Tell her, Chelsea," Rosemary said. "Tell her what those monsters are capable of."

Chelsea's cheeks flushed red.

"So, it's true," Kadie murmured.

Chelsea nodded.

Kadie felt sick to her stomach. She'd been a fool to trust Saintcrow. A fool to believe him when he told her that what she felt for him was real. And if her feelings weren't real, then neither was what they had shared last night.

After lunch, Kadie declined an invitation to go to the movies with Rosemary and Marti. She needed time alone.

Back at Saintcrow's house, all she could think about was what Rosemary had said. All vampires possessed a supernatural attraction. They couldn't fall in love. They were incapable of genuine human emotions.

She prowled through the house, too upset to sit still. It was bad enough that the vampires took the life's blood of the women, but to seduce them against their will . . . that just wasn't right!

And yet, argued a little voice in the back of her mind, if it was true, if all vampires could attract humans, then why hadn't she been attracted to Vaughan? Why had she been repulsed by Kiel? Maybe some humans were immune to their allure. For all she knew, Vaughan had tried to compel her and failed. As for Kiel, he hadn't wanted to seduce her. He had wanted her to be afraid of him, had taken pleasure in scaring her half to death. Why? The answer came quickly. He was a predator. He lived for the hunt, took pleasure in subduing his prey.

In the living room, Kadie sank down on the sofa, a book in her lap, but instead of reading, she found herself staring at the suit of armor standing in the corner. She couldn't imagine wearing anything like that. It must weigh a ton. She wondered again if Saintcrow had worn it during the Crusades, or if it was just a decoration.

Lost in thought, she was hardly aware of time passing until Saintcrow appeared on the sofa beside her.

"Oh!" Kadie exclaimed, one hand pressed to her heart. "You really have to stop that."

"You should be used to it by now."

"I guess." She ran her fingers over the spine of the book, wondering how best to bring up the subject that had been on her mind since lunch.

Saintcrow cocked his head to one side. "Something wrong?"

"Why do you ask?"

"I suppose, after last night, I was expecting a warmer welcome."

"Is that so?"

His eyes narrowed. "All right, what's bothering you?"

She took a deep breath, and said it all in a rush. "Is it true that vampires are incapable of feeling human emotions?"

"Who's been talking to you now?"

"Is it true?"

"Yes, and no."

"That's no answer."

"Most of us turn human emotions off because it makes it easier to prey on people if your feelings don't get in the way. After a while, it becomes second nature to hide what you're thinking, what you're feeling."

"Can vampires fall in love?"

"If they let themselves."

"How am I supposed to know what's real and what isn't? You already proved that you could make me want you against my will."

"I told you the attraction between us was real, and I meant it. There's no way for me to prove it to you. Either you believe me, or you don't. I guess you'll just have to trust me."

Trust a vampire. That was asking quite a lot.

Kadie stared into the distance. She wanted so badly to believe that what she felt for Saintcrow was real, but how was she to know if he was telling the truth? If only she could read his mind the way he read hers.

She could feel him watching her. Was he reading her mind even now? She had never felt like this about any other man. Did that mean Saintcrow was manipulating her? Or that she had finally found the man of her dreams? Just her luck that he was a vampire.

Kadie sighed. They were so different. Worlds apart, she thought, separated not only by hundreds of years but by the way they viewed life. And, most of all, by the fact that he was no longer human. He was, for all intents and purposes, dead during the day.

"Not dead."

The words were so faint, she wasn't sure if she'd imagined them, or if he'd said them aloud.

He needed blood to survive.

"Do you ever get tired of drinking blood?" As soon as the question was out, she wished she could call it back.

He lifted one brow. "Do you ever get tired of eating chocolate?"

"*Touché,* milord." She looked up at him. "What did you mean when you said, 'Not dead.'"

He shrugged. "I can move about during the day if it's necessary."

So, what was she to do? It was obvious that she wasn't going anywhere anytime soon. Saintcrow was handsome and charming and she enjoyed his company. Why not make the best of it?

"Is that armor yours? I mean, did you wear it during the Crusades?"

"No. That kind of armor came later. I wore chain mail. I got the tin suit at an antique store."

"Oh. Did you wear anything under the chain mail? I mean, all those metal links couldn't have been comfortable against bare skin."

"You're right about that. We wore bries. Think of it as medieval underwear. Over that we wore cloth chausses on our legs. Those were covered by another set of mail, also called chausses. A gambeson protected our body." Seeing the question in her eyes, he said, "A gambeson is a thick quilted coat. We wore our hauberk—the mail—over it. The thing weighed about forty pounds. A surcoat was worn over the armor to keep the desert sun off the metal, and to identify individual knights. Surcoats were usually embroidered with a knight's arms or family crest. During the Crusades, a lot of us wore a white surcoat emblazoned with a red cross to remind us what we were fighting for."

"Do you still have it?"

"No, why?"

"I'd loved to have seen you in it. In days of old, when knights were bold," she said, grinning. "Were you bold? Did you have a lady fair?"

"None so fair as you."

Five little words spoken in his whiskey-rough voice and she melted. Rosemary could insist from now until doomsday that vampires were incapable of human emotions, but she was wrong. Kadie heard the wanting in Saintcrow's voice, saw the desire in his eyes.

He slid his arm around her waist, drawing her up against him, holding her close. For a time, he simply held her, one hand lightly massaging her back.

Kiss me, she thought.

A moment later, he tilted her head up and claimed her lips with his. It was a kiss like none of the others they had shared, one filled with an aching tenderness that gradually grew deeper, more intense. It unleashed a wave of longing deep within her, a hunger for his touch, a yearning to touch him in return.

"Kadie?"

She gazed into his eyes, perhaps into his soul. He wanted her. He was a powerful creature, able to bend her will to his if he chose, capable of taking her by force. Yet he left the decision to her. How could she refuse him when she wanted him so desperately?

When she nodded, he stood, carrying her with him. His steps were long and swift as he carried her up the stairs to her room. He lowered her onto the bed, then stretched out beside her.

He cared for her.

She'd bet her life on it.

A poor choice of words, she mused.

Because that was exactly what she was doing.

He kissed her then, a searing kiss that made her toes curl with pleasure. If she was to die, she thought, there was no place she would rather do it than in Rylan Saintcrow's arms.

In the morning, Kadie woke smiling. She lay there staring up at the ceiling for a long time, reliving the hours she had spent in Saintcrow's arms. What an incredible lover he was, she thought, and then giggled because she had no one else to compare him to. But surely no other man was as tender. Or as inventive. A blush heated her cheeks as she recalled her wanton behavior, and the way he had urged her on, encouraging her to let go of her inhibitions.

Later, lying spent in his arms, she had asked him again where he took his rest, pouted when he refused to tell her. It wasn't fair. She trusted him with her life. Why wouldn't he trust her in return? Did he truly think she would betray him?

The thought made her frown. Had another woman betrayed him in the past?

She wondered about that as she showered, and again while she ate breakfast.

After doing the dishes, she felt the strangest urge to explore the turret rooms. To her disappointment, there was little to be seen. The two in front were empty. The third held a narrow cot and a wooden chair. A black iron cross adorned one wall. The fourth room had a bed, a chair, and a table. A tapestry that looked very old covered the far wall from the floor to the ceiling. The colors were faded, the edges frayed.

Head tilted to the side, she studied the tapestry. It depicted a knight in chain mail mounted on a rearing black charger. The knight wore a white surcoat emblazoned with a red cross. He held a sword in one hand and a shield in the other.

Frowning, Kadie took a step closer. Was that . . . ? It was. It was Saintcrow!

Just looking at his image made her feel warm all over. He hadn't changed at all in over nine hundred years. She ran her fingertips over the image, then pressed her hand to the cross painted on his surcoat. And heard a strange grinding sound, like stone moving against stone.

Curious, she moved to the edge of the tapestry, pulled it away from the wall, and peered behind it to see a narrow doorway. Filled with excitement and trepidation, she opened the door, revealing a long spiral staircase.

Was Saintcrow's lair down there?

Did she really want to know?

She worried her lower lip with her teeth, then turned and ran down the stairs to the living room. She wasn't going down into that dark tunnel without a light of some kind. Perhaps she could find a flashlight in town. If not, then she'd use a candle to light the way.

Kadie was sure she'd set some kind of record for driving to town and back when she returned to the house. Armed with the most powerful flashlight she could find, she ran up the stairs to the turret room, made her way cautiously down the spiral staircase behind the tapestry, then paused.

Was she making a mistake? Who knew what lay at the end of the tunnel? She suspected it might lead to Saintcrow's lair, but what if it didn't? What if that dark passageway led to a dungeon filled with skeletons, or worse, living prisoners who had displeased the master vampire? What if it was filled with bags of blood? Or bags of gold? That might not be as far-fetched as it sounded, she thought. He drove an expensive car. He paid for food and drink for all the people who lived in Morgan Creek, as well as the utility bills for his house, and the rest of the town.

Driven by a need to know what he was hiding, Kadie moved slowly, quietly, down the tunnel. It was eerie, moving through the darkness with only a flashlight to illuminate the way. Her footsteps sounded very loud in the silence that surrounded her.

The tunnel went on and on, straight as an arrow.

Overcome by an unexpected bout of claustrophobia, she came to an abrupt halt, suddenly certain that the tunnel extended far beyond the house.

Forward or back? Which way should she go? She took a step forward, then turned on her heel and started back, only to pause again. She had come this far; why not go on?

Tamping down her fear that the tunnel would collapse, trapping her beneath tons of earth, she hurried forward. To her surprise, the tunnel ended at another door after a few yards.

She ran the light over the door. It was made of oak, crisscrossed with iron straps. There was no lock. No handle. Placing her hand in the center of the wood, she gave it a push. Nothing happened.

Chewing on her thumbnail, she focused the light on the door again. There had to be some way to open it. Starting at the top right corner, she ran her hand over the entire door, then along the lintel and the sides. Nothing happened.

With a sigh of defeat, she made her way back to the staircase, only to find that the door she had come through was no longer open.

She pushed it. She kicked it. She beat on it with her fists until her hands ached and her knuckles were swollen and bloody. But the door refused to budge.

Alarm quickly turned to panic. What if this didn't lead to Saintcrow's lair? What if it led to some long-abandoned storeroom and no one ever came down here?

Her stomach churned with horror.

She was trapped in the tunnel with nothing but a flashlight.

And no one in Morgan Creek knew where she was.

Chapter 19

Saintcrow woke with the setting of the sun. For a time, he remained in bed, thinking about Kadie and the night they had shared. It still amazed him that, after over nine hundred years, he had found a woman who pleased him in every way, a woman who was rapidly becoming far too important to him.

Her scent lingered on his skin, reminding him of the intimacies they had shared. He felt a brief twinge of guilt for taking her virginity. He had done a great many things he regretted, but it had been a matter of pride with him that no matter what other atrocities he had committed, he had never defiled a woman nor killed a child. To ease his conscience, he reminded himself that he hadn't taken Kadie against her will. Far from it. She had been all too willing.

Jackknifing into a sitting position, he raked his fingers through his hair, then opened his senses, homing in on his blood link to her.

He felt her terror as if it was his own. She was trapped in the tunnel, had been trapped there, in the dark, for hours.

Not bothering to dress, he left his lair with all the speed at his command. Seconds later, he was at her side.

"Kadie, I'm here."

"Rylan!" She collapsed against him, her whole body trembling uncontrollably.

"It's all right now," he said, gathering her into his arms. "I've got you." A thought opened the door behind the tapestry, another carried the two of them into the living room, a third lit a fire in the hearth.

He sat on the sofa, holding her against his chest, cradling her head on his shoulder. The scent of her blood teased his nostrils. Taking her hands in his, he licked the blood from her knuckles, sealing the wounds, then whispered words of comfort in her ear until her trembling stopped.

"Thank you for coming after me."

"Did you find what you were looking for, Pandora?" he asked.

"You know I didn't."

"Are you so determined to see where I sleep?"

"I'm sorry. I should have respected your privacy," she said, "even if you don't respect mine."

"*Touché,* milady. But if you decide to explore down there again, you need to know that once you step through the door behind the tapestry, it closes automatically. You can't open it from my side."

"You did."

"I said *you* couldn't. Nor can anyone else."

She drew back a little so she could see his face. "Why is that?"

"It's my own form of revenge. Should anyone find my lair and take my life, theirs will also be forfeit."

She shuddered as she imagined being trapped down there in the dark for days or weeks with no food and no water. "Has that ever happened?"

"Not until today." He stroked her cheek. "You have all the tenacity of a pit bull."

"I don't like secrets. It's not fair for you to have them when I can't."

"Hasn't anyone ever told you that life is unfair?"

"What other secrets are you keeping from me?"

He sighed in resignation. "What do you want to know, Kadie?"

She shrugged. "I just want you to promise that you won't lie to me. You've taken away my freedom and everything that's familiar to me. You're all I have, and I want to know that I can trust you to be honest with me."

"All right, Kadie. I promise not to lie to you." Though he could not promise he would always tell her the whole truth.

Kadie rested her cheek on his shoulder and closed her eyes, content to be held, to feel his hand lightly kneading her back and shoulders. Vampire or not, she felt safe in his arms. He was impossibly strong and powerful. Nothing could hurt her as long as he was with her.

There was no sound in the house. Gradually, she became aware of his skin beneath her cheek. His cool, bare skin.

"Rylan?"

"Yes, Kadie?"

"Why are you naked?"

Laughter erupted from his throat, filling the room with pure, masculine amusement.

Stiffening, she frowned at him. "Did I say something funny?"

Still laughing, he shook his head. How had he lived so long without her? He had laughed more since Kadie arrived in Morgan Creek than he had in years. He was surprised by how good it felt.

When she started to slide off his lap, he wrapped his arm around her waist, holding her body to his. "I felt your fear in the tunnel," he explained with a grin. "I thought it might be more important to find you than pull on my pants. Next time you need rescuing, I'll take time to dress first."

She stuck her tongue out at him, then wrapped her arms around his neck and kissed his cheek.

His laughter turned to a groan as she wriggled in his lap.

"What's wrong?" she asked. "Am I hurting you?"

He inhaled sharply. "You have no idea."

"I'm sorry. Should I get up?"

"No." He buried his face in her hair as desire shot through him. He was an old vampire, practically indestructible, yet this fragile creature had the power to humble him, to bring him to his knees in ways no one else ever had. He had spent his life guarding his existence, hiding his true nature from the world, refusing to let himself care for those around him because he knew from experience that, in the end, they would wither and die.

And then Kadie had come along. Young, innocent, and ignorant of his kind, she had burrowed deep into his heart and taken root there.

He undressed her slowly, raining kisses on her cheeks, her neck, the hollow of her throat. He caressed her, delighting in her warmth, in the little sounds of pleasure that rose in her throat as his hands moved over her.

Stretching out on the sofa, he settled her on top of him and kissed her until she cried for him to take her.

Murmuring her name, he rose over her. He could never let her know the power she held over him, he thought as he buried himself deep within her. Never let her suspect she had the power to destroy him.

Kadie blew a strand of hair out of her eyes, her heart still pounding, her body bathed in sweat, Saintcrow's taste still on her lips. They were lying side by side on the sofa, their bodies still joined together. His eyes were closed and she studied his face. It was a strong face, a handsome face. She moved and his arm tightened around her. "Don't go."

"My foot's asleep."

Grunting softly, he lifted his leg from hers.

She loved being in his arms, feeling his body next to hers. He was so masculine, so tall and strong, with incredible powers at his command. What must he think of her when she was so weak, so human?

"I think you're beautiful," he said, his voice husky. And anything but weak. She had captured him, heart and soul. If she ever suspected the power she held over him, she could have anything she desired.

She tangled her fingers in his hair. "What's it like, to live so long? You must have done everything there is to do, seen everything there is to see. How do you stand it, when there's nothing new, nothing to look forward to? No surprises left."

He opened his eyes. "You were a surprise. Totally new and unexpected."

"Me?"

"I've never known anyone like you before."

"I've never known anyone like you before either," she retorted with an impish grin.

"Kadie, I'm being serious here."

She shook her head. "I'm just ordinary, no different from thousands of other women my age."

"Are you accusing me of lying when I've just promised to tell you the truth?"

"No, but . . . you must have known hundreds of women. What makes me so different?"

"There's no one else like you." He cupped her cheek in his hand, his thumb playing lightly over her lips. "I'm not sure how to explain it. You may think you're like everyone else, and to other people, maybe you are. But I perceive you differently. The beat of your heart, the scent of your skin, the sound of your voice . . . You're beautiful to me in ways others don't see." He stroked her cheek with the back of his hand. "Your skin is softer than the petals of a rose, your hair is like silk in my hands."

She blushed at his praise.

It was on the tip of his tongue to tell her he loved her, couldn't live without her, but he swallowed the words, afraid to appear vulnerable, afraid she would take advantage of his love and ask for her freedom. He would willingly give her anything. Anything but that.

Later that night, after Kadie was asleep, Saintcrow drove to town. He didn't often mingle with the other vampires, but lately, he had sensed some unrest among them, especially among Vaughan and Lilith. He wasn't surprised to find the whole vampire community gathered in the tavern when he arrived. Nor was he surprised when Lilith bolted out of her chair.

"Where is he?" she demanded, jabbing her finger into his chest. "Where's Carl?"

Saintcrow grabbed her hand and bent it back until she flinched. "If you point that finger at me again, you'll lose it." He bent her hand back a little more, until she dropped to her knees. "Remember who you're talking to."

She nodded, her lips compressed in pain.

"Carl and Kiel have both been dispatched," he said, his gaze moving over the other vampires. "They accosted my woman, and they paid the price. The rest of you might remember that." He released his hold on Lilith and she scrambled back to her seat. "So," he said, "what's going on?"

"We're tired of living like this," Vaughan said.

"Right," Wes agreed. "We're living like sheep instead of wolves."

Saintcrow glanced at the other vampires, his gaze resting momentarily on each of them. "You all feel this way?"

Trent stood, his arms crossed over his chest. "We do."

"I take it this is something you've been talking about for quite a while."

Vaughan nodded.

"You might want to rethink it," Saintcrow suggested. "The hunters have united. They aren't hunting individually now, but in packs. They're well armed and well informed. And relentless."

"You're just saying that," Felix said. "You like keeping us here."

Saintcrow snorted. "Why the hell would you think that?"

"Well . . ." Felix shrugged.

"It makes you feel like you're the king or something," Gil said. "Giving orders, keeping us here like we're serfs."

Saintcrow shook his head. "You want out? Fine. Get the hell out of here, all of you."

"You mean it?" Lilith asked. "We can go?"

"I said it, didn't I?"

"What about the humans?"

"What about them?"

"Are they free to go, too?"

"No. When you're ready to leave, let me know, and I'll escort you across the bridge."

Lilith looked at him, her eyes narrowing with suspicion. "How do we know you're not going to destroy us when we leave here?"

"I won't have to. The hunters will take care of that for me. Like I said, let me know when you're ready to go."

With a last look at the vampires, Saintcrow left the tavern. So, they wanted out, did they? Well, to hell with them. He'd taken them in, provided them with a comfortable lair and a variety of human prey. And now they wanted out. Well, good riddance.

"We're free!" Lilith exclaimed. "I don't know about the rest of you, but I can't wait to get out of here."

"Maybe we're being hasty," Vaughan said.

"Hasty?" Wes exclaimed. "This was your idea in the first place!"

"I know, but he's right. We don't know what's going on outside. We haven't had to seek a safe lair or hunt in years."

"I'm pretty sure we all remember how," Lilith said, her voice dripping with sarcasm.

"That's not the point," Vaughan said. "Saintcrow is the oldest vampire among us. If he's reluctant to leave here, maybe we should reconsider. Maybe we could convince him to let us know what's going on outside."

"Maybe," Gil said dubiously.

"What do you think he'll do with the humans?" Lilith asked. "He won't have any use for them when we're gone."

"Forget the humans. We need to know what's going on in the world outside," Nolan said. "When I came here, the people who believed we existed were few and far between. If that's changed, we need to know."

"So, we ask him to bring us up to date," Vaughan said.

"Fine," Lilith said. "You go ask him. And ask him what he's going to do with the humans while you're at it."

"All right, I will."

Saintcrow scowled when he opened the door and saw Vaughan on the porch. "You ready to go?"

"Not yet."

"So, what are you doing here?"

"We talked it over. We decided we need to know what's going on outside before we leave." He cleared his throat. "We want you to help us connect with others of our kind in the outside world, find out what we're up against when we leave here."

"Is that right?"

"Come on, you owe it to us."

"I don't owe you a damn thing."

"I know. We came here of our own accord and in spite of whatever was said earlier, we appreciate what you've done. You've taken good care of us."

"Uh-huh."

Vaughan grinned. "You don't buy that, huh?"

"Not for a minute," Saintcrow said.

"Would it help if I said please?"

Saintcrow shook his head in amusement. "I'll see what I can do."

"Oh, Lilith was wondering what you're going to do with the humans."

"Tell her to keep wondering."

Saintcrow stood at the door, staring out into the night long after Vaughan had taken his leave. So, the coven wanted to be brought up to date. No doubt they'd want cell phones and newspapers next. Letting them stay here had seemed like a good idea at the time. It had all started with Nolan. He had saved Browning from being staked by a couple of hunters and brought him here. Browning had asked to stay. He had found Lilith the same way, the ungrateful shrew. She'd been nothing but trouble the whole time she'd been here. Trent and Quinn had found the place by accident. He had run into Vaughan and the others on various trips outside and offered them his protection.

Well, he was tired of playing nursemaid. Hell, they were free to go, all of them. The sooner, the better, he thought, then paused. Without the coven, he had no need for the humans. He never fed on any of them, preferring to hunt outside. Still, Kadie would be lonely without someone to keep her company during the day. The men could go, but like it or not, the women would be staying.

Chapter 20

Kadie was surprised the next night, when, out of the blue, Saintcrow asked if she would like to go shopping with him.

"Sure," she said eagerly. "Where are we going?"

"To a local mall. I need to get something for the coven."

"I don't believe it!"

He shrugged. "It wasn't my idea, believe me. Are you ready?"

"Just let me get my jacket."

"Kadie?"

"What?"

"I'll want your promise that you won't do anything stupid."

"I promise," she said, and ran to get her coat.

It was a beautiful night for a drive. Kadie stared out the window, excited by the prospect of going shopping, even if it wasn't for her.

Saintcrow drove with the windows down, one arm resting on the back of her seat. It felt like they were flying down the road, making her hesitate to look at the speedometer.

She glanced at Saintcrow. "Can we turn on the radio?"

"Eager to hear the news of the day?"

"Can you blame me? I've been living in a vacuum for weeks."

With a shake of his head, he turned on the satellite radio and surfed the stations until he found a news program.

After five minutes, she'd heard enough. "It never changes, does it?"

"What's that?"

"The news." She skipped through the stations until she found one that played all oldies all the time. "It's always bad. Wars everywhere. Parents killing their children. Democrats and Republicans blaming each other for the horrible state of the economy, no one willing to take the blame for anything. It's so tiresome, and it never gets better. I don't know how you've stood it for nine hundred years."

"I rarely pay much attention to the news. The affairs of humanity don't have much effect on my kind. Sickness, wars, poverty, the price of gas . . . none of it matters. Our lives don't change. So long as people endure, we endure."

"Wow."

He grinned at her. "Wow, indeed."

"And as long as you endure, the people of Morgan Creek endure, for their lifetimes, anyway."

"So it goes."

She was still thinking about that when he pulled up in front of a covered mall. "Remember your promise," he warned when he opened her door.

Kadie took a deep breath as they entered the mall. She had always loved shopping, whether she was buying or just looking. There was something about wandering from store to store that appealed to her. One of her favorite comedians had remarked that some malls had birds, and how strange it must be for them, when going south for the winter meant flying to Sears.

She frowned when Saintcrow bought several iPhones. "What are those for?"

"The other vampires."

"Can I have my phone back?"

He looked at her a moment, then shrugged. "Why the hell not? There's just one thing—think carefully before you contact anyone. Because if anyone comes here looking for you, they'll never leave. You understand what I'm saying?"

"Perfectly."

"I hope so."

"Why iPhones?" she asked while waiting for the clerk to ring up his order.

"So they can stay in touch with each other on the outside."

"On the outside?" She stared at him. "I don't understand."

"I've agreed to let them go if that's what they want."

"That's wonderful!" Kadie exclaimed. "That means you won't need Marti and the others anymore. They can all go home!" Without noticing Saintcrow's silence, she thought how happy Marti would be to return to her husband and daughter. Kadie smiled. She couldn't wait to get back to Morgan Creek and tell Marti and the others the good news.

Saintcrow paid for the devices, then asked, "Where do you want to go now?"

"I could use some new clothes."

Saintcrow followed her as she wandered through Kohl's and Macy's. She had only to remark that she liked something—a pair of skinny jeans, a pink sweater, a lavender sweatshirt, a pair of white fuzzy slippers—and it was hers.

When they passed a Godiva candy store, she stopped. "Can I buy something for Marti and the others?"

"Why not? I'm Santa Claus, remember?"

Laughing, Kadie went inside and bought ten two-pound boxes of mixed chocolates for the human inhabitants of

Morgan Creek, and a box of dark chocolate truffles for herself. She couldn't wait to pass out the candy, thinking how excited everyone would be when she told them they would soon be free to leave town.

"Should I wrap these?" the saleswoman asked.

"All but the box of dark chocolates, please."

"Now what?" Saintcrow asked when they left the candy store.

"I think you should buy something."

"Me? I don't need anything."

"Yes, you do." She regarded him a moment. "I think you need a red sweater."

"Your reason being?"

"I think you'd look good in red. And it's my favorite color."

"Mine, too," he replied with a wicked grin.

Kadie grimaced. "Bloodred, no doubt."

Laughing, he drew her into his arms and kissed her, right there in front of the Godiva store, with people watching. And applauding.

Later, Saintcrow watched in amazement as she gorged herself on two slices of pepperoni pizza, three scoops of ice cream—chocolate, vanilla, and strawberry—and a churro.

"I'm stuffed," she moaned as they left the mall. "Why did you let me eat so much?"

He slipped his arm around her, his gaze sweeping the parking lot. "Like I could have stopped you." Lifting his head, he tested the air, though it was hard to detect anything other than the lingering scents of the veritable feast Kadie had devoured.

He paused when he caught a faint movement out of the corner of his eye.

"Something wrong?" Kadie asked.

"No." They were at the car now. And the shadows were getting closer.

Kadie moaned softly as he opened the rear door and tossed the packages inside. Wrapping her arms around her stomach, she said, "I think I'm going to be sick."

"Kadie, run!"

"What?"

"Run! Get the hell out of here!"

The urgency in his voice propelled her away from the car. Running as fast as she could, she sprinted toward the mall, then ducked behind a tree. There was no one following her.

Peering into the darkness, she watched four shadowy figures close in on Saintcrow. From this distance, it was hard to see what was happening. She heard the faint sound of scuffling, a hoarse cry of pain.

Should she go for help?

Hard on the heels of that thought came the realization that now was her chance to get away.

Instead, she crept back toward Saintcrow's car. The sounds of a struggle grew louder. Rounding the front of the car, she gasped. Four men wearing black clothing and hoods were trying to force Saintcrow to the ground. Even as she watched, he picked one of his attackers up and tossed him over the Corvette, sending him headfirst into a phone pole. With a sickening thud, the man slid to the ground and lay still.

The other three attackers launched themselves at Saintcrow again, their combined weight carrying him backward. They crashed to the ground with Saintcrow pinned beneath them. She heard muffled cries and groans, the smack of fists striking flesh. What were they doing to him?

Who were these guys?

They're vampire hunters.

One of them wielded a wooden stake. Without hesitation, Kadie sprinted across the lot toward the man on the ground.

Frantic, she searched him for some kind of weapon, felt a surge of relief when she found a gun in a shoulder holster. The pistol was heavier than she expected. Holding it in both hands, she slowly circled the car, dodging another of the men in black as he flew across the blacktop. He hit a concrete block with a sickening thud.

Kadie fired the gun into the air.

Startled, the two men hovering over Saintcrow looked up. She pointed the weapon at the biggest one. "Let him go!"

The man stared at her in amazement. "Lady, get the hell out of here!"

"I said let him go."

When the man shifted his weight, Saintcrow sprang to his feet. With a roar, he grabbed the two men by their throats, smashed their heads together, and tossed them aside. When he let them go, they sprawled facedown on the ground.

Kadie drew a shuddering breath when Saintcrow stepped into the moon's light. His skin was taut and pale. The whites of his eyes were tinged with red. Blood dripped from his fangs. He looked every inch the monster Rosemary declared him to be.

Seeing the horror on her face, he turned away, his hands clenched at his sides, his head lowered.

Kadie stared at his back, wondering why she was so shocked. She knew he was a vampire. She had felt his fangs at her throat. But never before had he looked so frightening. Never had she seen his eyes the color of blood. Except in her nightmares.

He turned slowly to face her, his body tense as if he expected her to turn and run screaming into the night.

Kadie took a deep breath, reminding herself she had nothing to fear from him. "Are they dead?" she asked, pleased when her voice hardly shook at all.

Some of the tension drained out of him. "Just unconscious."

"What about the other two?"

"They're dead." Prying the gun from her hand, he tucked it into the waistband of his jeans. "Come on, let's get out of here. That gunshot's sure to draw attention."

Burning rubber, he peeled out of the parking lot and didn't slow down until the mall was far behind them.

"What the hell were you thinking?" he asked. "I told you to run."

"You're bleeding." His shirt was torn in several places. A jagged piece of wood protruded from his stomach. A long gash spanned his chest from one side to the other. There was another cut along the side of his neck.

"Yeah."

"Doesn't that hurt?" she asked, pointing at the wood embedded in his flesh.

Biting back an oath, he withdrew the thing and tossed it away.

Kadie flinched. "Are you all right?"

"I will be. But the next time I tell you to run, you run. Those hunters would have killed you."

"Why? I'm not a vampire."

"They wouldn't have stopped to find that out. Guilt by association." He shook his head. "I shouldn't have brought you with me Why didn't you leave when you had the chance?"

"What?"

"You could have taken a taxi, gone to the airport. Left town. Why didn't you?"

"I would have, but all my camera equipment is still at your house."

He pulled the car off the road and turned sideways in his seat to face her.

Kadie met his gaze squarely, felt the brush of his mind

against her own. "What's the matter?" she asked. "Don't you believe me?"

"No."

"I promised I wouldn't do anything stupid."

"But you did," he said flatly. "You stayed when you should have run."

She thought about what he'd said as he pulled back onto the highway. Was it a warning? Had she made a mistake in staying?

She slid a glance at him. He was staring at the road ahead, his jaw rigid. What was he thinking? If only she could read *his* mind for a change.

By the time they returned to Morgan Creek, his wounds had healed, leaving no trace.

After seeing Kadie into the house, Saintcrow retreated to his lair to clean up. She didn't miss the fact that he took all the phones with him.

In her room, Kadie put her new clothes away, took a quick shower, changed into her nightgown, and went back downstairs.

You stayed when you should have run. Had he been trying to tell her something?

She curled up in a corner of the sofa, trying to dismiss his words from her mind, but it was impossible. They had sounded so ominous.

She couldn't stifle a little shiver of unease when he returned a short time later. He wore a pair of gray sweatpants and the red sweater she had picked out.

His favorite color. The color of blood.

"Are you all right?" he asked tersely.

She scrubbed her hands up and down her arms. "I'm a little cold," she lied.

He glanced at the fireplace and flames sprang to life in the hearth.

She stared up at him. He stood in front of the fireplace, looking incredibly tall and strong. Powerful. Supernatural.

She flinched when he took a step toward her. Forcing a smile, she said, "I was right. Red is your color."

He didn't miss the tremor in her voice. "What's wrong, Kadie?"

"Nothing," she said quickly. "What could be wrong?"

"What are you afraid of?" he asked, and then frowned. "You're afraid of me again. Why?" It was a stupid question. She had seen the monster beneath the civilized veneer he habitually wore.

"Because . . . I . . . what you said . . ."

"What I said?"

"You told me I stayed when I should have run. Why did you say that? What did you mean?"

"Only that you won't get another chance." He raked a hand through his hair, then sat beside her. "Vampires are notoriously selfish creatures."

"So?" She shook her head. What did that have to do with anything?

"I've never kept a woman with me," he said. "Most of us are solitary creatures by nature. I didn't want to share anything of myself with anyone else. And then you came along, and I found myself wanting your company."

"I still don't understand."

"When the other vampires go, you'll be staying here."

She had expected that. "You're not making any sense."

"You're staying," he said. "And because I want you here, the women will be staying, too."

"But why? You said you don't drink from them."

"I don't want you to be alone during the day. Here they are, and here they'll stay."

"I don't need them, Rylan. Let them leave. They have families. . . ."

"My mind's made up, Kadie. Let it go."

She clenched her teeth, horrified to think that Marti and the others would have to remain here because Saintcrow wanted her to have company. Suddenly, it was all too much. What kind of company would they be when they found out he was keeping them here because of her? They would probably never speak to her again, and she wouldn't blame them.

"I'm going to bed," she said abruptly. Avoiding his eyes, she rose from the sofa and hurried out of the room.

Saintcrow started after her. He flinched when he heard the slam of her door, the turn of the lock. As if a lock could keep him out.

Cursing under his breath, he left the house in search of prey. It was time to act like a vampire instead of a lovesick teenager.

Chapter 21

In the morning, Kadie found the bag with the boxes of Godiva chocolates on the table in the kitchen. She removed hers, then looked around for her phone, hoping Saintcrow had returned it, but it was nowhere in sight. Had he changed his mind about giving it back to her? She had hoped to call her mom and dad and assure them she was all right.

She lingered over a cup of coffee, wondering if she should tell Marti and the others that the vampires might be leaving. Thirty minutes later, she was still trying to decide. Grabbing the bag of chocolates, she drove to Marti's house for a little girl talk.

"Hi, come in," Marti said, smiling brightly. "I just made some cinnamon rolls. Would you like one?"

"I'd love it." Kadie followed her into the kitchen and sat at the table while Marti dished up cinnamon rolls still warm from the oven and poured two glasses of milk.

"So," she said, sitting at the table, "what brings you here so early?"

"I brought you a present." Kadie pulled one of the gaily wrapped boxes of candy from her tote bag and slid it toward Marti.

"A present? Why?"

"No reason." Kadie took a bite of the cinnamon roll. "These are great."

Marti quickly tore the paper off the box, her eyes widening with surprise. "Godiva chocolates!" she exclaimed. "My favorite. Where on earth did you get them?"

"I went shopping with Saintcrow last night. I bought some for everyone." She took another bite of her roll, then licked the sugar from her lips.

"Well, bless you," Marti said. She popped a truffle into her mouth, then closed her eyes, sighing with pleasure.

"You look like you're having great sex," Kadie remarked.

"Oh, chocolate is better than sex," Marti replied with a grin. "Except that sex doesn't go to your hips. So, where did you go? What was it like, to be outside?"

"We went to a mall. Rylan . . ."

Marti's brows shot up. "Rylan?"

"That's his name," Kadie said defensively.

"You're on a first name basis with him now?"

"Anyway, he bought me some new clothes. And he said I could have my phone back."

"He did! Kadie, that's great. Where is it? I can call Brad."

"He still has it. And even if I had it with me, it wouldn't be wise to call for help. Anyone who comes here would be trapped with us."

Shoulders sagging, Marti rested her elbows on the table, her chin propped in her hands. "Then what good is it?"

"It's a victory, of sorts. We can find out what's going on in the world."

"What difference does it make? We're no longer part of it."

"Saintcrow was attacked in the parking lot." She hadn't meant to share that, but the words slipped out.

"What? By who?"

"Vampire hunters. Four of the biggest men I've ever seen.

He killed two of them. Tossed them around like they were matchsticks."

"Why didn't you run away?"

"I don't know. I thought about it, but"—she shrugged— "I couldn't leave him."

Marti stared at her. "I don't believe what I'm hearing. You had a chance to get away from this place and you didn't take it?"

"Forget about that. I have something to tell you, but it's a secret. You can't tell anyone else, at least not yet."

Marti leaned forward, her dark eyes alight. "What is it?"

Kadie hesitated. Should she tell? Saintcrow hadn't told her not to. "The vampires might be leaving Morgan Creek."

"Leaving?" All the color drained from Marti's face.

"I thought you'd be happy."

"Happy?" Marti shook her head. "They'll kill us before they leave."

"Why would they do that?"

"So we can't tell anyone what happened here."

"No! No, they won't. You'll all be fine. Saintcrow will still take care of you."

"Why would he do that? If the vampires leave, there's no reason to keep us alive."

"Yes, there is, because I'll still be here."

"So?"

"So you'll all be staying, too." Kadie took a deep breath. "To keep me company."

Marti plucked another chocolate from the box and nibbled on it. "Well," she said, licking the chocolate from her lips. "I guess it's a good thing I like you."

Kadie spent the rest of the morning handing out boxes of candy. She was relieved when none of the women blamed her because Saintcrow refused to let them leave Morgan Creek.

She saved the men for last.

"Well, this is a first," Jeremy remarked when she handed him one of the boxes. "I've never had a lady buy me candy before."

Kadie went to Claude's house last. Grouchy as always, he was scowling when he opened the door. "What do you want?"

Kadie thrust the last box at him. "I brought you a present."

"Yeah? Why?"

Kadie shrugged. "Why not?"

He stared at the box for a moment, as if debating whether to give it back, then with a barely audible "thank you" he shut the door in her face.

Saintcrow laughed when she told him about Claude that night. "He always was a strange one."

"Jeremy said none of the vampires like him."

"That's not my problem."

"Were the vampires happy with the phones?"

"Yeah. They're all at the tavern, exchanging phone numbers and catching up on supernatural affairs."

"I don't remember ever hearing anything on the news about vampire hunters. Or about vampires, for that matter."

"The messages are relayed by encrypted e-mails."

"Oh. Have any hunters ever stumbled into Morgan Creek?"

"Just once."

She waited for him to elaborate. When he didn't, she surmised that the hunter hadn't lasted long. "Are there a lot of vampire hunters?"

He nodded. "And more every day. But it's all under the radar. Most of the population has no idea that we exist, or that there's a whole underground network hunting us."

"It doesn't make much sense to me for the vampires to leave here," she remarked. "Considering what's going on."

He shrugged. "Except for Lonigan and Quinn, they've all been here forty years or more. I guess they need a change of scenery." He didn't see any need to tell her that the real reason they wanted out was to hunt again. He couldn't blame them for that.

"I told Marti the vampires might be leaving, but that she and the others would have to stay."

"How'd she take it?"

"Pretty well, I guess, all things considered. Can I have my phone? I want to call my parents and let them know I'm all right."

She felt his mind brush hers, probing her thoughts, before he pulled her phone from his back pocket and handed it to her. "Be careful what you say," he warned, and left the room to give her some privacy.

Kadie quickly dialed her mom's number, blinking back her tears when she heard her mother's voice.

"Kadie! Where are you? We haven't heard from you in weeks. We've been so worried!"

"I'm fine, Mom. I got a little sidetracked." She forced a laugh. "You know how I am when I'm working, but I'm fine."

"Where are you?"

"Nowhere right now, sort of between ghost towns. I got lost."

"But you're all right?"

"I'm fine. I've . . . I've been getting some great shots. I'll send you some when I can. I'm sorry I waited so long to call, but I . . . I didn't have any cell service." It was hard to lie to her mom. She wasn't only her mother but her best friend. "How's Dad?"

"He's fine, honey. He's at work. There was a fire at the high school and he's tied up at the emergency room. He'll be sorry he missed your call."

Kadie took a deep breath, afraid to ask the next question. "How's Kathy?"

"Not well. The last infusion has worn off and there isn't any more available at the moment. Your father has been out every night hoping to find a new source."

"I guess she's asleep."

"Yes. You know how tired she gets."

Kadie nodded, choking back her tears. "I'll try to call tomorrow. And Mom? I love you."

"I love you, too, dear. Be careful."

"I will. Good night." Kadie closed the phone, then hugged it to her chest, trying not to cry. She needed to get home, needed to be with Kathy.

She blinked back her tears when Saintcrow returned.

"Everything okay at home?" he asked.

"Same as always. Thank you for letting me call."

"Tell me about your parents."

"My father's a surgeon. One of the best in the world. My mom's a housewife." She smiled wistfully. "One of the best in the world."

"You love them very much."

Kadie nodded. When she was a child, her parents had always come in at bedtime to hear her prayers and kiss her good night. They had shared bedtime stories and hot chocolate on cold winter evenings in front of the fire. Spent their summer vacations camping in the mountains. Her father had bought her her first camera when she was ten. She had quickly filled one scrapbook after another. Every few years, her father had bought her a new and better camera.

Saintcrow watched the play of emotions on her face as she thought about her childhood. He scarcely remembered his own parents. He had only been five or six when his father was killed in battle. His mother had remarried, only to pass away four years later, leaving Saintcrow with a stepfather he despised, and, eventually, a stepmother who tried to seduce him.

When he was sixteen, he'd run away from home and sought refuge in a neighboring castle where a knight took him on as a squire. He had spent the next four years in Sir Edward's service, dressing him in the morning, serving his meals, caring for his horse, cleaning the knight's armor, weapons, and shield. He had accompanied Sir Edward to tournaments and gone with him when he went to war. During this time, he had also learned to handle a sword and lance while wearing forty pounds of armor and riding a horse.

He had been just shy of his twenty-first year when Sir Edward deemed him worthy to become a knight. The day before the ceremony, Saintcrow donned a white tunic and red robes. He had spent the night in his room, meditating, praying for strength and courage, petitioning heaven for the purification of his immortal soul. Thanking heaven for Sir Edward's kindness and patience with a rebellious youth. He had loved that man, respected him as he had no other before or since.

In the morning, the chaplain blessed his sword, and then heard his confession.

Later, attired in his finest clothing, Saintcrow had knelt in front of Sir Edward, his head bowed, as his lord tapped him lightly with his sword on each shoulder and proclaimed him a knight of the realm. It had been the proudest moment of Saintcrow's life. It was one of the few memories he had clung to all these years.

"Rylan?"

"You'll see your parents again, Kadie," he said quietly.

"You mean it?"

The hope in her eyes went straight to his heart—a heart he had thought dead long ago. "I swear it," he said, his voice thick. "I swear it on my honor as a knight."

Later, Saintcrow stood beside Kadie's bed, wondering why she had never told him about her sister. She tried not to think about Kathy too often. Perhaps it was too painful. Or perhaps, with his ability to read her mind, she figured he already knew.

Watching her sleep, he longed to hold her in his arms, to make love to her until the sun came up, but, given all that had happened at the mall, he thought it best to wait a few days. He had never meant for her to see him like that, his skin drawn tight, his eyes blazing like the fires of hell, his fangs dripping blood. She had covered the horror she felt remarkably well, better than he had expected, but he knew it wasn't something she would soon forget.

Would she look at him now and see only a monster? If so, she wouldn't be the first. Or likely the last.

He lifted a lock of her hair, let it sift through his fingers. Since becoming a vampire, he had refused to let himself fall in love, had refused to let anyone—vampire or mortal—get close to him. But Kadie, clothed in youthful beauty and innocence, had captured his heart.

He had thought to keep her with him for a long, long time, but now, loving her, he knew he couldn't subject her to a life with him. He recalled, all too clearly, something Kadie had told him.

Only a monster keeps people enslaved, she'd said, her voice ringing with righteous indignation. And she was right. He was a monster.

A monster in love for the first time in his long, long existence. And so he would let her go.

But not yet.

Surely even a monster deserved a little happiness.

Chapter 22

Kadie woke feeling as if she hadn't had more than an hour or two of sleep. Her dreams had been filled with red-eyed demons and faceless monsters clad in black. Sometimes they had chased her. Sometimes they had attacked each other. Once she had dreamed she was buried alive in Leslie's grave. She had pounded on the lid of the coffin, screaming for help until her throat was raw, and all the while she could hear Saintcrow telling her she should have run while she had the chance. And always there had been blood, rivers of blood.

She banished her bad dreams with a hot shower and several cups of coffee. Sitting in the kitchen, staring out the window at a bright beautiful day, she found herself wondering what it would be like to never go out and about during the day. When the vampires slept, was it truly like death? Did they look like corpses, or merely like they were sleeping? What did Saintcrow look like? And why was she so obsessed with finding out? Was it because he didn't want her to? Still, if she was going to spend the rest of her life with him, then she wanted to know everything about him, including what he looked like when the sun was up and he was dead to the world. No pun intended, she thought with a grin.

Tonight, she would remind him he had promised there would be no secrets between them, then ask him to leave the door to his lair open.

After breakfast, she drove to Marti's to see if she'd like to go to lunch and a movie later that day. Marti suggested they ask Rosemary and the others and make a day of it.

"Why don't you go invite the others?" Kadie suggested. "I'll make some sandwiches and a cake and meet you all at the restaurant at noon."

"Great idea," Marti said. "After I invite everyone, I'll see what I can do about decorations, and we will have an unofficial celebration."

Kadie had just finished frosting a cake when the other women arrived. Marti had decorated the restaurant while Kadie fixed lunch. She had pushed two tables together and covered them with a bright yellow cloth. A vase held a bouquet of wildflowers. She had set the table with silverware instead of the plastic forks they sometimes used.

All the women were there, except Frankie.

"I invited her," Marti said, "but she wouldn't come."

"I wish we could convince her to spend time with us." Shirley shook her head. "She's so alone."

"I know," Kadie said. "I never see her unless it's in the tavern."

"I think she feels at home with the vampires because she can communicate with them. They can talk to her and read her answers in her mind."

"Maybe we should have invited the men," Kadie remarked.

"Well, I'm glad you didn't. We really can't indulge in girl talk when they're here. These sandwiches are delicious, Kadie."

"Thanks, Chelsea. It's just tuna with a little pickle and celery."

Rosemary smiled at Kadie. "This was a wonderful idea."

"We should party more often," Pauline said. "Maybe it would make the days go by faster."

"Sounds good to me," Marti agreed. "Sometimes I get so bored, I could scream."

"I'd like to drive a stake into the heart of every vampire here!" Rosemary said, her expression fierce. "I hate them all!"

"They're not that bad," Chelsea said. "I mean, they do take good care of us."

Rosemary scowled at her.

"Well, it's true. We each have a house of our own, and nice clothes, and food to eat, and . . ."

"We're slaves!" Hands fisted on her hips, Rosemary glared at Chelsea. "I don't care if they decked us out in furs and built us mansions and hired servants to wait on us, we'd still be slaves." She looked at Kadie. "I'm sorry. I didn't mean to spoil the mood."

"It's all right," Kadie said. "I understand how you feel. We'd all like to go home." But even as she spoke the words, she wondered if she really felt that way. If it meant never seeing Saintcrow again, would she leave Morgan Creek?

"So, how was lunch?" Saintcrow asked later that evening.

"It was fun, I guess. Rosemary is very bitter about . . . well, about everything. She's been here a long time. Why don't you let her go?"

"Would that please you?"

"Yes."

He considered it a moment. He knew Kadie was attracted to him, but he wanted more than that. He wanted her love. All of it. Perhaps letting the woman Rosemary go would be a step in that direction. "Very well. I will take her away tonight, when the others are asleep. But you are not to tell them she's been freed."

"What should I say?"

"Nothing. Let them think what they will."

"All right. Could I ask another favor?"

"You can ask." Although it wasn't necessary. He already knew what she wanted.

"I want to see you during the day."

"Why?"

"You see me when I'm asleep."

"It's hardly the same thing," he said dryly.

"Fair is fair. Besides, you promised there'd be no more secrets between us."

"This isn't a secret."

"Please, Rylan?"

The use of his first name, so sweet on her lips, was his undoing. "Very well. I will leave the door to my lair open to-morrow. But there's a price."

"Oh?" She knew what it would be, felt her whole body come alive in anticipation.

"Yes," he said. "Exactly that."

She forgot everything when he drew her into his arms, everything but the wonder and the magic of his touch, the in-toxication of his kisses, the sting of his fangs that should have been painful but filled her with sensual pleasure.

She wrapped her arms around his neck when he carried her to her bed, her hands clumsy in their haste as she un-dressed him. He was so beautiful, his body perfectly formed, his belly ridged with muscle, his limbs long and lean. He watched her, his eyes hot, as she removed her own clothing, then covered his body with hers.

They fit together well, she thought, her body somehow

molding to his. She ran her hands over him, loving the play of emotions on his face as her hands caressed him.

He gave her free rein until, with a growl of impatience, he tucked her beneath him.

She felt the sweet sting of his fangs at her throat as he possessed her with a fierceness he had never shown before.

"Mine." His voice whispered in her ear, echoed off the walls. "Mine!"

In the morning, she woke slowly, reluctant to leave the dream she'd been having. Even though she knew it was only her imagination, she could almost feel his hands stroking her skin, hear his voice whispering love words in her ear.

While showering, she could think of nothing but the exquisite feel of his skin against her own, the utter pleasure of their bodies becoming one, the fire in his eyes when he brought her to completion, the way he cried her name when he reached his own.

It wasn't until later that morning that she remembered he had agreed to let her see him while he slept. How could she have forgotten that? But then, with her mind and body still caught up in memories of the night before, maybe it was understandable.

Filled with excitement, she ran up the stairs to the turret room. The door leading down to the tunnel stood open. She smiled, grateful that she wouldn't be trapped down there until he woke. Turning on her flashlight, she hurried down the steps toward Saintcrow's lair at the end of the corridor.

She paused for a moment, suddenly unsure now that the moment was at hand. What if he looked like he was dead? He had been a vampire for more than nine hundred years. What if there was nothing but a skeleton in the coffin? Did she really want to see that?

Holding fast to her courage, she put her hand on the door. It was now or never.

A slight push, and the door opened into a large room. The walls were French blue, the carpet a shade darker. An antique mahogany wardrobe stood against the wall to the left. An old-fashioned four-poster bed with velvet hangings stood against the wall across from the door. There was nothing else in the room.

Was he in the bed? Weren't vampires supposed to sleep in coffins?

Taking a deep breath, she approached the bed and drew the velvet aside.

Saintcrow slept on his back, one arm at his side, the other across his waist. A sheet covered him from the waist down, his chest was bare. His skin looked paler than usual. As far as she could tell, he wasn't breathing. In repose, his face was still beautiful.

Did she dare touch him? Unable to resist, she laid her hand ever so lightly on his chest. His skin was cool, as were his lips when she traced them with her fingertips.

Was he naked beneath the sheet?

A little voice in the back of her mind urged her to peek, but she shook it off. It seemed a huge violation of his privacy.

She stayed a moment more, her curiosity urging her to peek into the wardrobe. After a brief battle with her conscience, she tiptoed out of the room. The door closed behind her.

Heart pounding, she ran up the stairs to the turret room, then made her way to the living room.

Sitting on the sofa, she tried to absorb what had just happened. It occurred to her that he must trust her a great deal to let her see him when he was helpless. What if she had brought the others with her? They could have killed him while he slept. She had no doubt that Claude Cooper would take Saintcrow's head without a second thought.

Suddenly restless, she went into the kitchen and opened the refrigerator. It was past time for lunch. And there was nothing to eat.

She grabbed the keys to the Corvette, making a mental grocery list as she unlocked the front door. She frowned when it wouldn't open. Was the lock jammed? She turned it this way and that. Nothing happened.

The back door wouldn't open, either. Neither would any of the windows.

So much for trust, she thought darkly. Did he really think she would betray him?

That she would tell the others where he slept? That she would invite them inside so they could destroy him?

He didn't trust her.

The idea hurt more than she would have thought possible.

She was waiting for him in the living room when the sun went down. One look at her face, at the way her arms were crossed over her chest, and he knew she was upset. He didn't have to read her mind to know why.

"It isn't a matter of trust, exactly," he said.

"Then what is it, exactly?"

"I haven't existed for over nine hundred years by being careless. None of the other humans in this town know where my lair is located. You wanted to see me at rest, and I let you. But to leave the door to my lair open during the day . . . ?" He shook his head. "I'm not that trusting."

"You trusted me. Why? I could have stabbed you while you slept, just like anyone else."

"I was willing to take my chances with you, but not with any of the others."

Somewhat mollified, she asked, "Can I go with you when you take Rosemary away?"

"If you like."

"Will you take her home?"

"If that's where she wants to go, although I'm sure she'll find it and everything else greatly changed after so many years."

Kadie nodded. Rosemary's husband had probably declared her dead after all this time. Her children would be grown now, probably married with kids of their own. Her husband could have remarried and had another family. How would Rosemary handle something like that? Kadie frowned. What would she do in a similar situation? How would she feel? How would she pick up her life on the outside after such an extended absence? The world had changed a lot in the twenty years Rosemary had been here.

"Maybe we should give her a choice," Kadie suggested. "Maybe, after all this time, she'd rather stay."

"And if she chooses to stay, then what?"

Kadie considered his question a moment. Of all the women in Morgan Creek, Marti had been there the shortest amount of time and had the youngest child. But of all the people in town, Marti was her favorite.

Shaking off her selfishness, Kadie said, "I think instead of Rosemary, you should let Marti go. She has a six-year-old daughter."

"You're sure?"

"Yes."

* * *

At midnight, Kadie and Saintcrow drove to Marti's house in Kadie's Durango. "Wait in the car," Saintcrow said. "I'll be right back."

He returned moments later, carrying a pajama-clad Marti in his arms. She was sound asleep, and remained asleep when he laid her on the backseat and shut the door.

"Remember," he said, sliding behind the wheel and putting the car in gear, "you can't tell anyone about this." His gaze met hers. "I'll know if you do."

Kadie nodded.

They reached the bridge a short time later. She felt a sudden apprehension as he drove across, but the Durango emerged onto the road without the slightest hesitation.

"How do you know where she lives?" Kadie asked.

"Driver's license."

"Oh. Aren't you afraid she'll tell people about you and the others?"

"No. I'll wipe the last five years from her mind. She won't remember anything."

Kadie stared at Saintcrow in amazement. She would never want to be a vampire. Their lifestyle was repugnant at best, but she couldn't help being in awe of his preternatural powers and abilities.

She gazed out the window, wondering about the other women and the lives they had left behind. They rarely spoke of their families. She supposed it was just too painful to think about people you loved when you were never going to see them again.

Kadie felt herself dozing off when Saintcrow pulled over to the curb. After shutting off the engine, he got out of the car and lifted Marti out of the backseat. Kadie stepped out onto the curb, then glanced up and down the street, wondering which house was Marti's.

"Do you want to tell her good-bye?" Saintcrow asked.

When Kadie nodded, Saintcrow spoke quietly to Marti, who woke instantly. She glanced at Saintcrow, her eyes wide with fear as he set her on her feet, until Kadie said, "Marti, it's all right. We're taking you home."

"What?" She glanced around, her eyes filled with confusion. "Why am I here?"

"Kadie convinced me to let you go," Saintcrow answered. "Come on." Holding Marti's arm, he started walking toward the corner.

Kadie followed the two of them as they turned the corner, then came to a stop in the middle of the block in front of a single-story, ranch-style house on a well-kept street. A pink bicycle lay on its side in the front yard. A rope swing hung from the branch of a tall oak tree.

Saintcrow released Marti's arm and stood back, giving the two women a little space.

"Marti, I'm going to miss you so much," Kadie said, blinking back her tears. "Thank you for making my days in Morgan Creek easier to bear."

Fighting tears of her own, Marti said, "How can I ever thank you?" She glanced at the house. "What if Brad doesn't want me anymore?"

"He hasn't remarried," Saintcrow said. "He still loves you. Now say your good-byes. It's getting late."

Kadie hugged Marti. "Be happy."

"Thank you so much. I don't know how you did this, but I'll never forget you."

Kadie wiped her eyes. "Yes, you will," she said, overcome by a wave of sadness as Saintcrow captured Marti's gaze with his. She felt a rush of preternatural power whisper over her skin.

A moment later, Marti was on the front porch and Kadie

and Saintcrow had darted out of sight around the side of the house.

Marti glanced around, looking confused, then rang the bell.

A few minutes later, the porch light came on and a man clad in a navy blue bathrobe stood in the open doorway. For a minute, he simply stared at Marti. Then, with a wordless cry, he threw his arms around her. "Marti! Thank God, you're back. Where have you been all this time?" He looked past her, his gaze sweeping up and down the sidewalk.

"I don't know," Marti said. "The last thing I remember is going for a walk . . ."

"It doesn't matter," Brad said, pulling her into the house. "All that matters is you're home. Teresa!" he called, his voice filled with happy tears. "Teresa, wake up! Mommy's home!"

Kadie wiped the tears from her eyes as she followed Saintcrow back to her car.

She was pensive on the ride home. Rosemary was wrong, she thought. All vampires weren't monsters. No monster would have done what Saintcrow had done tonight. She would never forget the look of surprise on Brad's face, the joy in his voice. She only wished she could have seen Marti reunited with her daughter.

"That was a wonderful thing you did," she said at last. "Thank you."

"It was a wonderful thing *you* did," he replied, sliding a glance in her direction. "I know Marti was your favorite. You spent a lot of time with her. I know you'll miss her more than you would any of the others."

Kadie didn't deny it. She would miss Marti dreadfully, but it had been the right thing to do. Once she had thought it through, Kadie had realized there was nothing for Rosemary to go back to, while Marti's life was still waiting for her.

Kadie smiled inwardly. She couldn't remember when she had felt so good. Was Saintcrow feeling good about it, too?

She studied his profile, thinking again how handsome he was. Maybe, if she played her cards rights, she would be able to convince him to let some of the other women go, as well.

Chapter 23

Kadie was roused out of bed early the next morning by someone pounding on the door. Slipping into her robe as she went, she hurried downstairs, wondering who it could be. No one ever came calling at Saintcrow's house. Belting her robe tightly, she opened the door.

"Jeremy, what are you doing here?" she exclaimed.

"The women sent me," he said, gasping for air.

"What's wrong?"

He held up his hand, then bent over, hands on his knees, while he caught his breath.

Kadie stared at him. It took only a moment to realize what had brought him here.

Straightening, he brushed a lock of hair out of his face. "Marti's missing," he said. "None of the women were up to the walk, so I volunteered to come and tell you."

"Missing?" she asked, feigning ignorance. "Are you sure?"

Jeremy nodded. "We've looked everywhere. No one's seen her since last night. You know what that means."

Kadie nodded. Everyone in town would assume that one of the vampires had killed her.

"I guess we'll never know which bloodsucker did it," Jeremy said bitterly.

"Does it really matter?" Kadie asked.

"No, I guess not." He glanced past her into the house. "Do you like it here?"

Kadie shrugged. "It's as good as anywhere else."

"What about Saintcrow? Is he treating you okay?"

"Yes. Better than I expected. When you go back to town, will you tell Rosemary and the others I'll be there as soon as I get dressed? Or you can wait, and I'll give you a lift."

"Thanks, that would be great. It's a long walk."

"I'd ask you in, but I'm not allowed to invite anyone inside. Sorry. I'll only be a minute." After closing and locking the door, Kadie hurried upstairs.

She dressed quickly in a pair of jeans and a sweater, tugged on socks and a pair of boots, ran a brush through her hair, and was out the front door fifteen minutes later.

Jeremy shook his head as he settled himself in the Corvette. "You sure hit the jackpot," he exclaimed, fastening his seat belt. "This car is sweet." He ran his hand over the dashboard. "And fast. Zero to sixty in less than four seconds."

"I wish I could let you drive it," Kadie said.

"Yeah, me too." He settled back in the seat, arms folded over his chest. "Like I said, you hit the jackpot. Living with the head vamp. Driving his car. None of the other bloodsuckers can feed off you. In this town, that's the brass ring."

"Is Lilith mean to you?"

"Mean? You have no idea. She's as mean as she is ugly." He tugged his shirt collar down, revealing several nasty-looking bites on the side of his neck. "She's an animal."

Kadie stared at the bite marks. Instead of neat holes, the marks were jagged and red.

"I've got bites in places I can't even show you. She doesn't bother to heal them and they're painful as hell. She doesn't like Cooper for some reason and now that Freeman's gone, I've become her favorite snack. She makes me do things, perverted, evil things . . ." He shook his head, his expression bitter. "I hope someone rips out her heart and she burns in hell."

"I'm so sorry," Kadie murmured. Casting about for a less gruesome subject, she asked, "What did you do before you came here?"

"I was engaged to be married, and studying to become an architect. I came out here for the weekend with a couple of buddies two summers ago. We got drunk and I guess we got separated. All I know is, when I came to, I was here. Alone."

"I'm sorry." The words were inadequate, but what else could she say? She wished she could tell him there was hope, that she might be able to persuade Saintcrow to let him go, but she had sworn not to reveal that Saintcrow had freed Marti and Carl, and if there was one thing she had learned, it was that it was impossible to keep secrets from Saintcrow.

"You can just let me off at my house," Jeremy said. "The ladies said they'd meet you in the library."

"Thanks. Why don't you come with me?"

He shook his head. "I need to get some rest while I can. Lilith will be wanting me as soon as the sun goes down."

Kadie nodded sympathetically, waved good-bye after dropping him off, then drove to the library. After shutting off the engine, she sat in the car a few moments, gathering her thoughts.

When she went in, Brittany waved at her from behind the desk. "Terrible thing about Marti," she said, her voice hushed.

Kadie nodded, then went into the conference room. Brittany followed her and quietly closed the door. All the town's women were there, including Frankie.

Rosemary's cheeks were tracked with tears. "She's dead, Kadie," she said, sobbing. "Marti's dead."

Kadie laid her hand on Rosemary's shoulder and gave it a squeeze. How could she do this? How could she let these women, who had known Marti far longer than she had, think their friend had been killed by a vampire? She suddenly hated Rylan Saintcrow for making her live a lie, and for causing these women unnecessary grief.

Listening as they shared memories of Marti, she was tempted to tell them the truth, that Marti was alive and well and home with her family. But then she looked at Rosemary, who had been here for twenty years, and at the others. Brittany had been here for almost as long. Would it be fair to admit that she had convinced Saintcrow to let Marti go? Would it give them hope for their own freedom? Would they expect her to do the same for them, and hate her when she couldn't?

She was glad when the gathering broke up.

Returning to the car, she sat behind the wheel for several moments before pulling away from the curb. As she drove toward Saintcrow's lair, her gaze was drawn to the mountains. It was a beautiful day. She had nothing to do. Why not go exploring?

On a long stretch of road, she put the pedal to the metal and found out why Saintcrow loved this car. Going zero to sixty in under four seconds felt like flying, but it was nothing compared to zooming down the road with the speedometer hovering near ninety. She had never driven that fast in her life and her good sense quickly took over. Saintcrow might survive an accident at that speed. She most certainly wouldn't.

She took a road that veered to the right and found herself in a part of the town she had never seen before. Vaughan had told her it had once been a cattle town, and here was the proof. After parking the car, she got out to stretch her legs. The place looked like an old western movie set, she thought, glancing around. There was a saloon, a telegraph office, a hotel. The buildings were in sad shape, roofs sagging, doors askew, the wood gray with age. The jail, made of red brick, had fared better, although the door was missing. Beyond the town, she spied what remained of a few corrals.

Picking her way across the rough ground, she peeked inside the dilapidated buildings, surprised to find furniture inside the hotel, or what was left of it. Animals had obviously taken refuge inside. The sofa pillows had been shredded, the insides used for nests. A faded picture of a naked woman hung over the bar in the saloon.

She tried to imagine what it must have been like to live there in the 1800s. No movies. No satellite radio. No electricity. No sports cars. Doing laundry by hand. Cooking on a woodstove.

"Definitely not for me," she decided.

Leaving the town behind, she walked toward the mountains. She hadn't been here before, but as long as she was, she might as well see if she couldn't find a way out.

She followed several trails. All were dead ends. She tried climbing a winding path that led toward the summit, but it grew increasingly narrow until it disappeared. Pausing to catch her breath, she stared upward. She had been foolish to think she could climb to the top before dusk. And even if she managed to reach the summit before sundown, what then? It would be dark soon and as badly as she wanted to leave this place, she wasn't foolish enough to wander around out here after dark. There could be wild animals. Snakes. And who knew what else?

With a sigh of resignation, she turned back, a sudden unease urging her to hurry. She began to run, unmindful of the brush that snagged her clothing and scratched her skin.

She glanced over her shoulder, her gaze darting right and left, her panic growing. Was that a vampire, or a shadow?

The cry of a night bird, or the wail of some earthbound spirit?

She sobbed with relief when she reached the safety of the car. She locked the doors, turned the key in the ignition, hit the lights.

And screamed.

Saintcrow loosed a pithy oath as he changed from a mass of swirling gray mist to his own form, opened the passenger door, and slid into the seat.

Kadie stared at him, her face pale, her eyes wide. "I thought you were a ghost."

"Sorry. I didn't mean to frighten you."

She pressed a hand to her heart. "Gee, I'm out here in the middle of nowhere, in the dark, alone," she remarked sarcastically. "Why would I be frightened?"

"What the hell are you doing out here, *alone,* anyway?"

"Just sightseeing."

"Not much to see," he mused, glancing around. "A few dilapidated old buildings and a couple of empty corrals."

"There aren't a lot of entertainment choices here. You can only watch so many movies, or read so many books, you know." She glanced out the side window, thinking that she had a lot more sympathy for animals forced to live out their lives in zoos. No matter how big or beautiful a cage might be, it was still a cage.

"Is that how you think of this place? As a cage?"

"You might not keep us behind bars," Kadie said bitterly, "but we're still just animals for you and the other vampires to prey on." She slid a glance at his face, recoiled at the fury smoldering in his eyes.

Folding his arms across his chest, he said, "Drive."

She kept her gaze on the road, afraid to look at him again. The words, *Don't bite the hand that feeds you,* kept running through her mind. Making Saintcrow angry was just stupid.

Her life, and the lives of the men and women in town, depended on his goodwill. Things in town could get a lot worse if he decided to stop providing them with food and drink. He didn't have to heat their homes, buy them new clothes, or supply them with new books and movies to help pass the time.

He didn't have to let them live.

All he had to do was withdraw his protection and they would be at the mercy of the other vampires.

She pulled into the driveway and turned off the ignition, then sat there, her eyes closed, her hands gripping the wheel, as she waited for him to say something.

Minutes passed.

When she opened her eyes, he was gone.

With a sigh, she went into the house and locked the door. Then, feeling uneasy, she turned on all the lights in the living room. A quick glance showed he was nowhere in sight. Where had he gone? Why had he been so angry?

"Just like a man," Kadie grumbled. "Can't handle the truth." Sitting on the sofa, she kicked off her shoes, then leaned back. Did he truly not understand how she and the others felt about being trapped in this place? Was she supposed to be grateful that he allowed her to live? Maybe he'd understand better if he'd ever been locked up.

A shimmer in the air, and he was beside her. "You think I don't know what it's like?" He stretched his legs out in front of him. "I've been locked up, Kadie, in a hole so deep and dark that no light penetrated. I was captured for a time during the Crusades. My only food was moldy bread and warm water, and I was glad to get it."

"I'm sorry, but a prison is still a prison."

He nodded. "Perhaps. But I would have given a year of my life for one day in a house like this, and another year for a hot bath and a decent meal. You think you and the others are being mistreated because I keep you here?" Standing, he removed his shirt, then turned his back to her.

Kadie gasped. From his shoulders to his waist, every inch of his skin was covered with a web of scars. Some were so faint as to be almost invisible. She had never noticed them before, but then, they always made love at night, often in the dark. The only one she'd been aware of was the long, ridged scar that ran from his shoulder to his waist.

He turned to look at her, his expression implacable. "I told you before. I need the women here. It isn't safe for us to hunt outside right now." He slid his arms into the sleeves of his shirt.

"You go outside."

He shrugged. "I'm older, stronger. Smarter."

"You care about the other vampires, don't you?"

He lifted one brow.

"If you didn't, you wouldn't worry about them."

He moved to the hearth, stood there, one arm braced on the mantel, staring at the coals. A fire sprang to life.

"You worry about them. I know you do. Why won't you admit it?"

Keeping his back to her, he said, very quietly, "I've spent nine hundred years trying not to care. On the outside, vampires are very territorial. We rarely share space. What we have here is unusual for our kind, and it only works because they don't have to hunt for prey. There's no competition, no worry about where to hide the bodies. As for humans . . . They live such a short time. If you stay with them, eventually you have to bury them." He shook his head. "Imagine how many women I could have watched wither and die if I'd allowed myself to fall in love."

Kadie stared at his back. People always said they wanted to live forever but suddenly it didn't seem like such a great idea.

She sat there for several moments, wanting to comfort him, but not knowing if her touch would be welcome.

Finally, she went to him. Hesitating a moment, she slid her arms around his waist and laid her cheek against his back. "I'm sorry, Rylan."

For a moment, his whole body went rigid. And then he turned and wrapped her in his embrace. He held her for a long time, one hand stroking up and down her back, his forehead pressed against hers.

"Kadie?"

It wasn't a question, not really.

But she knew what he wanted. What she wanted.

Taking him by the hand, she led him up to her room and closed the door, shutting out the rest of the world.

"You don't have to do this," Saintcrow said.

"I know." She squeezed his hand. "I want to." Moving closer, she clasped her hands behind his neck. "I think you need it."

"What makes you think that?"

"What makes you think you don't?"

"Are you reading my mind now?"

"I don't have to. You've spent centuries ignoring your emotions, pretending you don't care. Pretending that you can't risk loving anyone." She brushed her lips across his. "You can love me, Rylan. I'm young and healthy. I won't leave you for a long time. And when I start to grow old, you can let me go so you won't have to watch."

He gazed into her eyes, his mind probing hers, searching for the truth. With a shake of his head, he folded her into his arms and buried his face in the wealth of her hair. He was a vampire, a monster who preyed on others to sustain his own life.

What had he ever done to deserve her?

And how would he ever let her go?

Chapter 24

It was after midnight when Vaughan met with the other vampires in the tavern. A quick glance and he knew that Gil, Wes, and Lilith had fed earlier that night. He swore under his breath, wondering how often Saintcrow fed on the delectable Kadie Andrews. But for Saintcrow's high-handed tactics, the woman would still be his. He swallowed his anger. There were plenty of beautiful women on the outside and he intended to have his share. Blonde, brunette, redhead, bald. He didn't care. Variety was the spice of life and he had a lot of lost time to make up for.

"So," he said when he had the group's attention, "what are your thoughts?"

"I don't think it's as bad out there as Saintcrow wants us to believe," Quinn said. "According to the latest news, the hunters have withdrawn from most of the cities. There haven't been any reported hits in over a week."

"Maybe they're just lying low," Browning suggested.

Lambert snorted. "Why would they do that?"

"Who knows? But if we're ever gonna leave, this seems as good a time as any," Felix said. "I don't know about the rest of you, but I've had it."

Lilith nodded. "I agree with Felix. The time to go is now. The world has changed in the last forty years. I want to experience it."

"Admit it," Vaughan said. "You just want to kill something."

"And you don't?" she retorted.

Vaughan glanced around the room. "We're agreed then?"

"Agreed," Gil said. "Now, who's gonna break the news to Saintcrow?"

A knock on the front door brought Saintcrow to his feet. He glanced at Kadie. She was sleeping soundly.

After pulling on a pair of jeans, Saintcrow padded down the stairs. He lifted an inquisitive brow when he saw Vaughan standing on the front porch. "What the hell are you doing here?"

"The others are waiting at the tavern," Vaughan said. "They sent me to get you."

"Yeah? I can guess why."

"And you'd be right. We want out."

Saintcrow bit back an oath. He'd much rather be in bed holding Kadie in his arms than meeting with a bunch of unhappy vampires, but this night had been a long time coming. It was time to end it.

It took only moments for them to reach the tavern.

As Vaughan had said, the vampires of Morgan Creek were all inside. They looked up as he walked in, their expressions wary. He held the power of life and death in his hands, and they all knew it.

"All right," Saintcrow said. "I'll make this short and sweet. You want to go? Then get the hell out of here."

"You mean it?" Lambert asked.

"I said it, didn't I? Get whatever you're taking with you and meet me at the bridge in ten minutes."

"It's not like we aren't grateful for what you've done for us," Browning said. "It's just . . ."

"The clock's ticking," Saintcrow said. "Get a move on. I've got a woman waiting for me and my side of the bed is getting cold."

Lilith waited until the others were gone, then said, "I want to take Jeremy with me."

"No. He's mine."

"You never feed on any of them. What do you want him for?"

"To keep him away from you," Saintcrow retorted. "I'll see you at the bridge."

She glared at him, her eyes blazing with anger as she swept out the door.

Saintcrow stared after her. "Nothing stays the same," he mused. "Not even for vampires."

He met them at the bridge at the appointed time. Most of them carried luggage of one kind or another, but little else.

There was a ripple in the air as they crossed to the highway.

There were no good-byes. In moments, all the vampires were gone save for Vaughan.

"What are you waiting for?" Saintcrow asked.

"She should have been mine."

Saintcrow snorted. "Are you still upset about that?"

"I saw her first."

"And now she belongs to me." Saintcrow folded his arms across his chest. "Do you want to fight me for her?"

Vaughan shook his head. "You'd rip my heart out."

"Damn right. Now get the hell out of here before I change

my mind." Saintcrow stood there, gazing into the darkness, wondering what Kadie and the others would think when they discovered the vampires were gone. No doubt they would be relieved. He knew he was, just as he knew that Kadie was going to hound him to let all the humans go as well. Maybe she was right. Maybe it was time to turn them loose and leave this place.

Grunting softly, he returned home. Taking off his jeans, he crawled under the covers and drew Kadie into his arms. There were hours until dawn, hours to hold her close.

Smiling, Kadie lifted her arms over her head and stretched as she relived the night past. Rylan had made love to her so tenderly, it had brought tears to her eyes. Never before had she felt so loved, so cherished. Little had been said between them. No words of love had been declared. But there was a new depth to their relationship, one she dared not explore too closely. As much as she enjoyed his company and his lovemaking, she couldn't ignore the reality of what he was, or pretend they had a future together. There were some things that even love couldn't overcome. Not that she loved him, she reminded herself quickly, though falling for him would be all too easy. If only he was human. . . .

She blew out an impatient breath. No sense dwelling on what could never be. And with that thought in mind, she went into the bathroom to shower.

Closing her eyes, she imagined that it was Rylan's hands streaming over her body, his skin hot against her own, his mouth on hers, arousing her, carrying her away to places no mere mortal could ever take her.

Why did he have to be a vampire?

The thought was as effective as a splash of cold water.

Rinsing off, she grabbed a towel and stepped out of the

shower. Would it be so bad to be in love with a vampire? She studied her reflection in the mirror, her fingers lightly stroking the place where Rylan had bitten her the night before. Bitten her! So what if it felt wonderful? So what if his kisses and his loving only made her yearn for more? He wasn't human. Hadn't been human for hundreds of years. He had killed people. He fed on their blood.

On her blood. She had to remember that.

"England?" Kadie gaped at Saintcrow. "You want to take me to England?"

They were sitting on the sofa, in front of the fireplace. Kadie had just finished cleaning up the kitchen.

"Not if you don't want to go," he replied dryly.

"Of course, I want to go." England. Home of Big Ben, Trafalgar Square, Stonehenge, St. Paul's Cathedral, The Tower of London, Westminster Abbey, Windsor Castle— places she had heard about, read about, and longed to see.

She was a small-town girl. She had been born and raised in Morro Bay, a town with a population of less than eleven thousand. She had graduated high school, gone to college in San Luis Obispo, and worked part-time on the local newspaper. After selling a few stories, accompanied by her photographs, she had, much to her parents' dismay, bought the Durango and hit the road. To Kadie's surprise, her stories had gathered a following and the demand for her photographs had grown steadily. Of course, writing and photographing ghost towns and old mining sites didn't take her to too many big cities. Visiting England had long been a dream.

"I'd love to go," Kadie said. "But—can you leave here? What about the vampires? And Rosemary and the others? Who'll look after them?"

"The vampires are gone. They left last night."

Kadie stared at him, unable to believe what she was hearing. They were gone, just like that? "You don't mean to go off and just leave everyone else here, do you?" If Rosemary and the others couldn't leave town, they'd all starve to death in a few weeks, since Saintcrow was the one who arranged for supplies and brought them into town.

"Of course not," he said. "I'll make sure they get wherever they want to go."

"Are you going to tell them tonight?"

He shook his head. "I'm leaving that up to you. There are bound to be tears and questions I don't want to answer. You find out where they want to go, then make a list of who goes first, and I'll see that they get there."

"Why did you decide to do this?"

"Why the hell do you think?"

"I don't know."

"You had a hand in it, but so did Vaughan. He's been stirring the vampires up for some kind of revolt. I don't need that. They can take care of themselves. At least they think so, and I'm tired of babysitting the lot of them. And tired of this place. When everyone else is gone, we're leaving. I need to feed," he said abruptly, and vanished from her sight.

Kadie stared at the place where he had been standing. The vampires were gone. He was freeing Rosemary and Nancy and the others.

He was taking her to England.

It was a lot to think about. But the only thing on her mind now was Saintcrow.

He seemed different. Withdrawn. Almost angry. She wondered if he was hurt because the vampires had decided to leave. Even though he wouldn't admit it in a million years, she knew he worried about them. Which seemed odd to her. They were vampires. At the top of the food chain, so to speak. Other than vampire hunters and sunlight, what did they have to fear?

She waited an hour for Saintcrow to come back, and when he didn't, she drove to Rosemary's. The drapes were open, the house ablaze with lights; she saw several of the women milling about in the living room. Jeremy and Claude were sitting on the front porch stairs, swilling beer from bottles.

Kadie parked the car in the driveway. "Looks like a heck of a party," she remarked, making her way across the grass to the walkway.

"Darn right!" Jeremy said with a crooked smile. "The bloodsuckers are gone. The house on the hill is empty!"

Claude reached into the ice chest beside him and pulled out a bottle. "We're celebrating." It was obvious he'd had more than one beer. "Wanna drink?"

"No, thanks."

There was a party atmosphere inside the house, too. Kadie had never seen the women looking so happy, so relaxed.

"Kadie!" Rosemary hurried toward her and gave her a hug. "I'm so glad you're here! I guess you know the vampires are gone? We would have come to get you, but no one wanted to knock on Saintcrow's door in case he was still there. Is he?"

"Yes. I'm glad you're here. I need to talk to you. All of you."

The smile died on Rosemary's face. "I was right, wasn't I? He's going to kill us."

"No. No, nothing like that. He wants me to find out where you want to go."

"Go?" Rosemary took a step back and dropped onto a chair, one hand pressed to her heart. "He's going to let us go?"

"Who's going?" Donna asked, coming into the room.

"What?" Nancy hurried toward them, the wine in her glass sloshing over the rim onto her hand. "Kadie, are you leaving?"

"No." She shook her head. "We're all leaving."

In minutes, everyone was gathered around her, all talking at once.

Kadie raised her hand for silence. "Please, quiet down and I'll tell you what I know."

In minutes, they were all looking at her expectantly. Jeremy and Claude stood shoulder-to-shoulder in the doorway, propping each other up. Frankie, always a loner, stood by herself, a bottle of diet soda in her hand.

"Saintcrow is leaving Morgan Creek," Kadie said, glancing around the room. "He told me to get a list of where you all wanted to go, and he'd see that you get there."

This announcement was met with another burst of excited chatter.

"What if we don't want to go?" The question, though quietly spoken, brought all other conversation to a halt as everyone turned to look at Rosemary.

"You don't want to leave?" Kadie stared at Rosemary, unable to believe what she'd heard. Rosemary had been here the longest and hated it the most.

Rosemary glanced at the others. "Where am I going to go? The world I knew is gone. My children are grown and probably have children of their own."

"But, Rose, don't you want to see them?" Shirley asked.

"They won't know me. I won't know them." She shrugged. "This is my home now. With the vampires gone, it could be a nice place to live."

"But, how will you get along?" Kadie asked.

"I don't know."

"You'll be all alone," Chelsea said.

"No, she won't," Brittany said, moving to stand beside Rosemary. "I don't have anywhere to go, either."

"Nor do I," Donna said. "I don't have any children. My husband and I were divorced five years before I got trapped here."

Kadie shook her head, bewildered. She had been certain they would all be champing at the bit to leave Morgan Creek. "Well, those of you who intend to leave need to decide where you want to go. As for the rest of you, I'll let him know that you'd like to stay, but I don't know if he'll agree to that."

"He owes it to us," Rosemary said, her voice, as always, tinged with bitterness when she spoke about the vampires in general and Saintcrow in particular.

"Well, I'm leaving," Jeremy said decisively, "just as soon as I can."

"Me, too," Claude said. "You couldn't pay me enough to stay here one minute longer than I have to."

Frankie nodded vigorously.

"And if that bloodsucker's footing the bill, then it's Hawaii for me!" Jeremy exclaimed, pumping his arm in the air. "What do you say, Claude?"

"Why the hell not? I've got nowhere else to go, and no one waiting for me when I get there!"

Frankie tapped her chest, then pointed at Jeremy.

"Sure, Frankie," Jeremy said. "You can come along, too. What about the rest of you?"

Chelsea shook her head. "I'm going home. I want to see my folks." She bit down on her lower lip. "I hope my dad is still alive. He was having some health problems last time I saw him."

"I've only been here a few years," Nancy said, "so it's home for me, too, although I'm sure my fiancé has stopped waiting by now."

"It's home for me, too," Pauline said. "My house isn't far from here. My mother lives with me. I just hope she's been able to look after things while I've been gone."

"What about you, Shirley?" Kadie asked.

"I don't know. I had a good job as a teacher back home, good friends. But I've been gone so long . . . I just don't know how I'd explain my absence." Her eyes widened. "He'll erase our memories, won't he? We won't remember any of this."

"I don't know," Kadie said. It was the truth. She didn't know. But Saintcrow had erased the memory of this place and everything that had happened here from Marti's mind. Had he done the same to Carl? Would he do it to Rosemary and the others?

"What difference does it make?" Jeremy asked. "Why would you want to remember this place?"

"Because it's part of my life," Shirley said, a note of panic evident in her voice. "Maybe not a good part, but still, I don't want some vampire messing with my mind."

"It's not right," Pauline said. "Sure, I hate this place, but I've grown to love all of you. I don't want to forget that."

"He'll have to wipe this place from our minds." Claude cracked his knuckles. "He can't have us running around telling people about what those bloodsuckers did to us."

Nancy took Kadie's hands in hers. "You've got to talk to him, Kadie. Convince him that we won't tell anyone."

Kadie shook her head. "I'll try, but I don't think he'll listen to me. If there's one thing I've learned about Saintcrow, it's that he takes security very seriously."

"This is so unfair!" Shirley exclaimed. "He's stolen years of our lives, and now he wants to steal our memories, as well! What kind of monster is he?"

* * *

Saintcrow stood in the shadows outside Rosemary's house, Shirley's question echoing in his mind. *What kind of monster is he?*

A good question, to be sure, he mused as he pondered what his answer would be.

Just your typical monster, was the first response that came to mind, even though it wasn't true. He wasn't a typical monster. He was a master vampire, one of the oldest of his kind, practically indestructible, virtually immortal. He had lived hundreds of years before any of the people in the house had been born; he would live hundreds of years after they were dust.

Monster. The others in the house might think of him that way, but not Kadie. She was still a little afraid of him, still in awe of his preternatural powers, but she no longer saw him as a monster or, if she did, she hid it well.

Swearing under his breath, he walked up the stairs. He hadn't intended to interact with those inside, but after listening to their conversation, he'd changed his mind. The people gathered in the house had two choices. He doubted they would be thrilled with either one.

A stillness like death settled over the men and women in the living room when he stepped inside. Rosemary looked at him with ill-disguised loathing. Chelsea with fear. Nancy and Shirley with apprehension. The men with suspicion. Kadie with curiosity.

He decided to get right to the point. "I know Kadie has told you that I've decided to let you go. And that you're concerned about having your memories of this place erased." His gaze swept the room, resting briefly on each face. "I can understand your apprehension. However, it doesn't concern me. I don't really give a damn what any of you want, or what you think. I know humans spend a lot of time worrying about right and wrong and about what's fair. The only thing I worry about is survival. I haven't existed as long as I have by taking chances or putting my fate in the hands of others. So, it comes down to this. I can erase your memories of the time you spent in this place and let you go. Or I can end your life. The choice is yours. For those of you who want to stay here, that's fine. I won't erase your memories of each other, only your memories of what went on here. If that seems harsh . . .." He shrugged. "You can let me know your decision tomorrow night," he said, then vanished from their sight.

Kadie glanced around the living room. Most of the faces registered shock to one degree or another. She couldn't blame them, although the choice seemed relatively easy to her. *Always choose life.* That had been her grandmother's motto.

"Well," Jeremy said, "that's pretty cut and dried. His way or no way. I'm goin' to bed." He swayed unsteadily as he staggered toward the front door, then glanced over his shoulder. "Anybody wanna come with me?"

To Kadie's surprise, Chelsea followed Jeremy out of the house.

"How long has *that* been going on?" Shirley asked.

"Not long," Pauline said.

There were a few scattered remarks about Saintcrow, none of them favorable. Nancy and the others were subdued and thoughtful as they took their leave, until only Rosemary and Kadie remained.

"It isn't fair," Rosemary declared.

"I know."

"Are you going to stay with him?"

"I don't have any choice. He hasn't offered to let me go."

"Would you leave if you had the choice?"

"I honestly don't know." Kadie shook her head. "If he wasn't a vampire, I'd probably fall in love with him."

"Are you sure you're not already in love with him?"

"I'm sure," Kadie said adamantly.

And wondered if it was the truth.

Chapter 25

Saintcrow was standing in front of the fireplace in the living room when Kadie returned to his house.

She cast about for something to say, but nothing came to mind. She understood his reasoning, just as she understood why Rosemary and the others objected.

"Do you think I'm wrong?" he asked. "Do you think I'm a monster?"

Curling up in the chair beside the hearth, she tucked her legs beneath her. "No," she said quietly. "I don't think you're a monster."

"But you think it's wrong for me to take away their memories?"

"Yes, but I can understand why you think it's necessary."

"But you don't approve?"

"No. What difference does it make if they tell people about this place after you've gone? If there are vampire hunters, then there are already people who know you exist. Just because I didn't know before I came here . . ."

"My point exactly. Other than hunters, very few people believe in vampires. The ones who know about us are fewer still. I'd like to keep it that way."

Moving away from the hearth, Saintcrow knelt in front of

her. "I will not put my existence—or your life—in jeopardy for a handful of people who mean nothing to me. If enough people start to believe, more hunters will come. In the old days, long before you were born, the mere mention of the word *vampire* was enough to send men and women thronging the streets wielding torches and axes. Very few vampires were destroyed but a great many innocent men and women were killed."

It was an impassioned speech, one that resonated with truth and logic from Saintcrow's point of view, and reminded her, yet again, of the differences between them. Though he had once been human, he no longer thought of himself as such. Was it possible for them to have any kind of life together with a gulf like that between them? A gulf only she could cross, and then only if she was willing to give up her humanity to become what he was.

He lifted one brow, mute evidence that he had been reading her mind.

"Rylan, will you let me go with the others?"

He shook his head. "No."

"Will you ever let me go?"

"Perhaps. In time."

She bit down on her lower lip to keep from begging for her freedom. What was the point when she knew it wouldn't do any good?

"You can lie to yourself, Kadie, but you can't lie to me."

"What do you mean?"

"You don't really want to leave me. I know it. And you know it." He snorted softly. "Even Rosemary knows it."

"I hate you." She spoke the words, but there was no heat behind them. And no truth.

He drew her down onto his lap, then wrapped his arms around her. "If I can't have your love," he murmured, lightly stroking her cheek, "I'll take your hatred."

The trouble was she didn't hate him, even though she knew she should. Why didn't she? He had stolen her freedom. He was keeping her from her family. He was a vampire. Yet there was an indefinable connection between them. Even now, the wanting in his eyes warmed her to the depths of her soul. Yes, he was a vampire. Some might consider him a monster. But there was goodness in him. Kindness. Tenderness. He had spared Carl Freeman's life. He had let her buy chocolates for Marti and the others. Right or wrong, wisdom or folly, she wanted to be with him.

"It'll take a few days to send the others where they want to go," he said. "In the meantime, pack up whatever you want to take with you."

"Do you mind if I call my mom and dad tomorrow?"

"No."

Her quick smile was his reward.

Kadie woke late after a restless night. Her dreams were fragmented, filled with nightmare images of Saintcrow eliminating everyone in Morgan Creek. In one scene, she walked streets littered with desiccated corpses. In another, she was the only living creature left in town. Unable to escape, with no way to obtain food or drink, she saw herself wasting away. On the brink of death.

Her own horrified scream had roused her.

Sitting up, she clutched the covers to her chest, felt a slow smile chase away the last remnants of her nightmare when she saw the pale pink rose petals scattered across the bedspread. A vase, overflowing with roses, stood in the center of the dresser.

Picking up a handful of petals, she crushed them in her hand, then breathed in the delicate fragrance.

Vampire or not, he knew the way to her heart.

Later, after a shower and a cup of coffee, she called her parents to let them know she was doing well, she was going to England, and she wasn't sure for how long.

"England!" her mother exclaimed. "That's a long way from Morro Bay."

"I know, but . . ."

"Kadie, what's going on? Have you met someone?"

"I never could fool you, could I?"

"Who is he? What does he do? When will we meet him?"

"Slow down, Mom. His name is Rylan and . . ."

"He's the reason you got sidetracked, isn't he?" her mother said, a smile in her voice.

"Well . . ."

"I knew it! I've never known you to get lost."

That was true enough on the road, Kadie thought, but she was in unfamiliar territory where Saintcrow was concerned. "I'll tell you all about it some other time. How's Kathy?"

"She seems to be in remission at the moment."

"Great. Can you put her on the phone?"

"I'm sorry, she's not here. She's gone on an overnight camping trip with Susie and her family."

"That's wonderful!"

"She'll be so sorry she missed your call. Hang on. Dad wants to talk to you."

"All right. Love you, Mom."

"Kadie, darlin'!" Her dad's voice boomed over the line. "When are you coming home?"

"I'm not sure. I'm going to England with a friend."

"What kind of 'friend'?"

"A guy friend, Dad. How are you?"

"Hey, we're not changing the subject. When do I get to meet this 'guy'? What's his name? Where did you meet him? Do I need my shotgun?"

Kadie laughed. "I'll bring him home as soon as I can.

And no, you don't need your shotgun. Listen, I've got to go," she said before he could ask any more questions she couldn't answer. "I'll call you soon. Give Mom a hug for me."

"I know what you're doing," her father said. "But we'll talk about this again. Oh, wait, before I forget. Did you get a new phone? I've been trying to call you for weeks."

"Sorry, the battery went dead and I . . . I lost the charger. It took me a while to replace it. Talk to you soon."

After saying good-bye, Kadie sat there a moment. How could she even think of leaving the country when her sister was so ill? Even though Kathy was doing better now, there was no telling how long it would be before she had a relapse.

Kadie blew out a sigh. Whether she wanted to go or not, she really had no choice. Closing her eyes, she uttered a silent prayer that Kathy would hold on long enough for her father to determine the cause of her illness and find a cure.

She sat back on the sofa, her legs stretched out in front of her. So, her parents wanted to meet Rylan. She found herself grinning as she tried to imagine introducing Saintcrow to her family. *Hi, Kathy. Mom, Dad. This is Rylan Saintcrow. I'm his prisoner. Oh, by the way, he's a vampire.* Yeah, that would go over real well.

Too curious to wait until tonight to find out what Rosemary and the others had decided, she drove to Rosemary's house. When no one answered her knock, she drove to town. She found everyone but Chelsea and Jeremy in the restaurant.

All eyes turned toward her as she stepped inside.

Kadie hesitated. Was she imagining things, or was there a look of hostility in their eyes? "Would you rather I left?" she asked.

"Of course not," Nancy said. "We can't afford to make an enemy of you."

Kadie stared at the other woman. "What does that mean?"

"It's us against him," Donna said. "And you're with him."

"Guilty by association, is that it? None of this is my doing. If it wasn't for me . . ." Kadie pressed her lips together. She had promised not to tell anyone about Marti or Carl. Hurt beyond belief, she left the restaurant.

She laid rubber as she peeled out of the parking lot. With no destination in mind, she left the business district behind. She supposed she couldn't blame them for the way they felt. For the first time, it occurred to her that if and when Saintcrow let her go, he would probably erase all her memories of this place from her mind.

And she would hate him for it.

Kadie was loading her dinner dishes into the dishwasher when Saintcrow appeared in the kitchen.

"Shall we go get this over with?" he asked, coming up behind her.

"I'm not going."

"Why not?"

"I'm no longer one of them."

"You never were."

She whirled around to face him. "I went to see them this afternoon. I felt like . . . like they hated me."

"I know the feeling. Nevertheless, I think they'll be more at ease if you're there."

"No."

"This is not open for discussion. Are you ready?"

There was no point arguing. Wordlessly, she followed him out of the house and into the car. She refused to look at him. Instead, she concentrated on building a wall in her mind so he couldn't read her thoughts.

"Very good," he remarked. "With practice, you might be able to keep me out."

She glared at him, then turned and looked out the window once more. So, it was possible to keep him out of her head. Concentrating, she added height and depth to her mental barrier.

The human residents of Morgan Creek were all gathered at the restaurant again.

Kadie hung back as Saintcrow strode through the door. His gaze swept the room, his power a tangible thing. "I've come for your decisions," he said curtly.

It came as no surprise to Kadie that they all chose to have their memories erased.

Saintcrow nodded. "Next, I need to know where you wish to go. Rosemary?"

"I want to stay here, with Donna and Brittany."

Saintcrow shoved his hands in his pockets, bored with the whole thing. "Okay by me."

"Me and Jeremy and Frankie want to go to Hawaii," Claude said.

"Uh, about that," Jeremy said. "Chelsea wants to go home, and I'm going with her."

Claude shrugged. "Looks like it's just you and me, Frankie," he said, and she smiled.

"I'll have tickets for you tomorrow night," Saintcrow said.

"I'd also like to go home," Nancy decided.

Saintcrow nodded, then looked at Shirley. "What about you?"

"If Rosemary and the others don't mind, I think I'll stay here."

"The more, the merrier," Rosemary declared, and Donna and Brittany nodded in agreement.

"Pauline?"

"My house is only a few miles from here. I'm going home."

"All right, then," Saintcrow said. "Those bound for Hawaii will leave tomorrow night. Chelsea, you and Jeremy be ready to leave Wednesday night. Nancy, I'll take you home on Thursday." He glanced around the room. "Feel free to take anything you want with you. Claude, Frankie, I'll come for you tomorrow at sunset. Pauline, you can leave tomorrow night, as well. Kadie, let's go."

She followed him outside, feeling more alone than she ever had in her life.

When they returned to Saintcrow's lair, she went straight to her room and closed the door.

She should have known he would follow her.

"How long do you intend to give me the silent treatment?" He stood in the doorway, one shoulder braced against the jamb, his hands shoved into his pants pockets.

She shrugged.

"Do you think me a monster now?"

"I don't know what to think. My parents want to meet you." She pressed a hand to her mouth, wondering what had prompted her to say such a thing.

He stared at her, his eyes narrowed. "You told them about me?"

"Of course not! But I had to give them some reason for not coming home, and when my mother suspected there was a man involved . . . I told her we were going to England." She folded her arms across her chest. "I'm going to bed."

"So early?"

She nodded.

"If you want me, you know where to find me," he said, and left the room.

Kadie stared after him, confused by her anger. He was only doing what he had to do to protect himself. And even though he hadn't said so, she thought that erasing his memory from the minds of the others was probably for their protection, as well. Who knew what would happen if they told someone they had been living in a town with vampires?

Those who didn't believe in such creatures would likely think them delusional, and those who did believe might try to force them to tell what they knew.

She sat on the edge of the bed, one hand absently moving back and forth over the bedspread before picking up the pillow Saintcrow slept on and burying her face in its softness. His scent filled her nostrils and stirred a familiar longing deep within her.

If you want me, you know where to find me.

Kadie stared at the door.

Her mind told her to stay where she was.

Her heart urged her to run to him.

Before she could talk herself out of it, she hurried out the door.

Saintcrow looked up when Kadie entered the living room. To his credit, he didn't look smug.

"I was hoping you would come," he said quietly.

She stood in the doorway, uncertain of what to do now that she was there.

He made the decision for her by holding out his arms.

Sitting beside him was like coming home, she thought, sighing as his arms closed around her.

"You won't hurt them, will you?" she asked as his hand caressed her shoulder.

"No. It's quite painless. I'll simply remove their memories of Morgan Creek and replace them with other memories. Jeremy and Chelsea will think they were old school friends. Frankie and Claude will remember meeting at a restaurant. Rosemary and the women who decided to stay here will remember each other, but their memories of how they met will change."

"Will you wipe away all my memories of you, of this place, when you tire of me?"

His knuckles stroked her cheek. "I will never tire of you, Kadie."

"And you'll never let me go, either, will you?"

"Perhaps, in time, you'll stop asking."

Cupping her face in his hands, he rained featherlight kisses on her eyelids, her cheeks, the tip of her nose, the corners of her mouth. Kisses that, though ever so gentle, sent shock waves of pleasure coursing through her, igniting her nerve endings, energizing every cell, until she was breathlessly aware of his every touch as his hands caressed her.

She slid her hands under his shirt, desperate to touch him in return, to taste him, to feel his weight bearing her down as their bodies merged.

When he stood, carrying her with him, she wrapped her arms around his neck and rested her head on his shoulder.

Right or wrong, she was his for as long as he wanted her.

Chapter 26

The next few days passed in a flurry of activity. Kadie adjusted her hours to Saintcrow's, so that she slept most of the day. Rising in the late afternoon, she showered, dressed, did whatever housekeeping needed to be done, and ate dinner before Saintcrow arose.

Tuesday night, she accompanied Saintcrow, Claude, and Frankie to the airport. Saintcrow gave Frankie and Claude a thousand dollars each, and then, while telling them good-bye, he erased the memory of Morgan Creek and the vampires from their minds.

On Wednesday night, Saintcrow drove her, Chelsea, and Jeremy to Chelsea's home in Rexburg. He gave them the same amount of cash he had given to Frankie and Claude, and after Kadie hugged Chelsea, Saintcrow wiped all memory of vampires from their minds. The only thing Chelsea and Jeremy would remember was that they had met while in Wyoming.

Thursday night, Kadie was surprised to find Nancy's car gassed up and idling in front of Saintcrow's lair.

"Her parents live just a few miles from here," Saintcrow said.

Nancy was sitting on the front porch when they arrived. Her eyes widened in surprise when he pulled into the driveway.

"Do you want to drive?" Saintcrow asked after stowing Nancy's belongings in the trunk.

Nancy shook her head. "It's been years," she said, and climbed into the backseat.

When they arrived at her parents' house, Nancy hesitated on the sidewalk. "Maybe I'm doing the wrong thing."

"I'm sure your parents will be thrilled to see you," Kadie said, wondering at her reluctance.

"I hope so, although we didn't part on the best of terms. My father didn't want me to marry Troy and we had a terrible fight." She let out a sigh. "I guess that doesn't matter now. I'm sure Troy has found someone else."

"I hope everything works out for you," Kadie said, giving her friend a hug.

"Thank you, Kadie. You've been a good friend. If you'd never come to Morgan Creek . . ." Her voice trailed off as the porch light came on.

Glancing past Nancy, Kadie saw a man staring at them out of one of the front windows.

"Time to go," Saintcrow said. He pulled Nancy's suitcase from the trunk and dropped it on the sidewalk, then pressed a wad of bills into Nancy's hand.

Kadie felt the rush of his power as his mind brushed Nancy's. Saintcrow pulled Kadie into the shadows when the front door opened.

The man who had been watching them from the window stepped onto the front porch, peering into the darkness. "Nancy? Nancy, honey, is that you?"

With a joyful cry, Nancy ran up the steps and into her father's arms.

Kadie smiled, touched by the scene on the porch.

"You ready to go home?" Saintcrow asked.

"How are we going to get there?" Kadie had scarcely spoken the words when she felt an odd rush of wind in her face. The next thing she knew, she was standing in Saint-crow's living room, wrapped in his arms. "How did you do that?" she asked when she'd gathered her wits about her.

He shrugged. "Talent."

"Seriously, how did you do that?"

"I'm not sure. I just think about where I want to be, and I'm there. Comes in handy when you're trying to outrun a mob wielding pitchforks."

"Pitchforks?" Kadie asked, brows raised in amusement.

"Pitchforks. Swords. Torches. Wooden stakes. Holy water. You know, the good old days."

"I can't tell if you're serious or just putting me on."

"A little of both."

"Sounds like you've had an exciting life. Or death," she added with a grin.

"Yeah. Well, life and death got a whole lot more inter-esting when you showed up."

"You made quite a change in my life, too." With a sigh, she rested her cheek against his chest.

"I didn't mean to complicate your life, Kadie."

"I don't mind so much anymore."

"I'll make it up to you one day, I promise."

"Are we still leaving here tomorrow night?"

"Would you rather stay?"

"No. It'll seem strange, though, not being here, not seeing everyone." She looked up at him. "Will Rosemary and the others be all right, staying here by themselves?"

"I don't know. I can't predict the future. I'll leave them some cash, gas up their cars, provide them with cell phones. The rest is up to them. I could be wrong, but I don't think they'll stay long, now that the others are gone."

Cupping her chin in his palm, he smiled at her. "There's a big world out there, Kadie. I look forward to seeing it anew through your eyes."

In the morning, Kadie woke feeling excited at the prospect of going to England, and depressed at the thought of saying good-bye to those who had decided to stay in Morgan Creek. Since becoming a freelance photographer, she hadn't spent much time at home. Her high school friends were all married now, raising families, caught up in their own lives. The ladies in town were the closest friends she'd had since college.

After breakfast, she folded her clothing and placed it in her suitcase. When that was done, she left the house. She spent the next few hours photographing every house and business in Morgan Creek; when she'd finished, she drove out of town and took photos of the countryside and the mountains. Driving back, she paused to take photos of Saintcrow's lair from several angles, then drove back to town, stopping on the way to photograph Blair House.

Nearing the town, she wondered if Saintcrow expected her to leave her Durango here. She hated to leave it behind when she had paid it off only a few months ago.

It was a little after two when she pulled up in front of Brittany's house. Not looking forward to saying good-bye, she knocked on the door.

Only, it was Donna who answered. "Kadie, I'm so glad you're here."

"What's wrong?"

"Brittany . . . she's . . ." Tears spilled down Donna's cheeks and she dashed them away. "I think she's . . . dead."

"What? Where is she?"

"In her room. There's an empty bottle of sleeping pills on the table beside her bed. She's not breathing."

Kadie hurried into Brittany's room. She had never seen anyone who was dead before, but one look and she knew Brittany was gone. Whoever said dead people just looked like they were sleeping had never seen one. "Does anyone else know?"

Donna shook her head.

Blinking back her tears, Kadie drew the covers over Brittany.

"We need to tell the others," Donna said, sniffling.

Nodding, Kadie said, "We'll take my car."

After picking up Rosemary and Shirley, Kadie drove to Donna's house.

"What are we doing here?" Rosemary asked when Kadie pulled up in the driveway.

"We were all going to meet at Brittany's house in just a few minutes," Shirley added.

"There's been a change in plans," Kadie said as they trooped into the house.

Once inside, Donna glanced at Kadie. "You tell them."

"Tell us what?" Rosemary asked sharply. "What's wrong? Has Saintcrow changed his mind about leaving?"

"No." Kadie took a deep breath. "Brittany took her own life last night."

Shirley shook her head. "I don't believe it."

Rosemary's eyes widened, and then she began to cry. "I should have known," she said, sniffling.

"What do you mean?" Kadie asked.

"We had dinner together last night," Rosemary said, wiping her eyes. "She was acting strange, kind of nervous and uptight. And she was drinking. A lot. Something she never did. I asked her several times what was bothering her, but she wouldn't tell me." She shook her head. "I knew something was wrong when we said good night. She hugged me and . . . thanked me for being her friend, and . . ." Rosemary buried her face in her hands. "I never should have left her alone."

"You couldn't have known what she intended," Kadie said.

"But why?" Donna asked plaintively. "Why would she do such a thing now?"

It was the same question Kadie put to Saintcrow when he rose that night.

"I should have seen this coming." He shoved his hands into the pockets of his jeans.

"What do you mean?"

"They've been prisoners here a long time. They haven't had to think for themselves. Everything has been provided. The thought of being on her own, having to look after herself . . ." He shrugged. "It was probably more than she could handle."

"But she wasn't going to be alone," Kadie said. "She seemed happy to be staying here with Rosemary and the others."

"Well, apparently she wasn't. I'll bury her tonight."

"I want to be there. And I know the others will, too."

An hour later, Kadie stood beside Brittany's grave with Donna, Shirley, and Rosemary. Rosemary had dressed Brittany in her favorite lavender skirt and sweater, applied a bit of makeup, brushed her hair. Saintcrow had provided a gleaming white casket. Kadie was afraid to ask where it came from, but couldn't help wondering if he'd kept a spare somewhere in the house.

Kadie bowed her head and closed her eyes as Shirley began to recite the Lord's Prayer. Then, curious to see how Saintcrow reacted when someone prayed, Kadie opened her eyes, let out a cry of alarm when Rosemary pulled a wooden stake from inside her coat.

Shrieking, "This is all your fault!" Rosemary lunged toward Saintcrow, murder in her eyes.

Fangs bared, his eyes blazing red, he sidestepped deftly and plucked the stake from her hand.

Coming up short, Rosemary stared at him, all the color draining from her face.

Donna and Shirley had looked up in time to see Saintcrow snatch the stake from Rosemary's hand. Now, hugging each other, they stared at Rosemary as if seeing her for the first time.

With a hiss, Saintcrow reached for his attacker.

"No!" Without thinking of her own peril, Kadie darted between them. "Rylan, don't hurt her!" She laid her hand on his arm. "Please."

He glowered at her for several taut moments, then vanished from sight.

Kadie put her arms around Rosemary. "Are you all right?"

"I wish I'd killed him."

"I'm sorry you feel that way."

"How can you stay with him?" Rosemary pushed Kadie away. "I don't understand how you can endure being around him. Did you see his face? He's a monster, Kadie. Mark my words. You'll rue the day if you go with him."

Kadie glanced at Donna and Shirley. From their expressions, she could see that they felt the same.

"I'll drive you back to town," Kadie said stiffly. If it hadn't been such a long walk, and in the dark, she was certain they all would have refused. As it was, Rosemary climbed into the backseat with Shirley, leaving Donna to take the passenger seat.

No one spoke on the way back.

Kadie parked in front of Donna's house, but left the engine running. "The barrier will be down in the morning. Your cars will all have a tank full of gas. You'll find cell phones and some cash waiting for you, courtesy of the monster," she said, her voice tight. "Good-bye."

She kept her eyes straight ahead as the women got out of the car. As soon as the doors were closed, she sped away.

She didn't look back.

Kadie's steps were dragging when she climbed the stairs to Saintcrow's house. She had expected to find him waiting for her in the living room, but the house was dark and he was nowhere to be seen.

Switching on the light, she sank down on the sofa and closed her eyes. She hadn't had time to really get to know the women in town, or to develop deep, lasting friendships, the kind that took years, but she hadn't expected them to turn on her like that. And yet, how could she have expected them to do otherwise? They had been prisoners in Morgan Creek for years. Heaven knew they had ample reason to hate the vampires, and Saintcrow most of all, for treating them so callously.

Was Rosemary right? Was she crazy to stay with Saintcrow? To trust him?

"Having second thoughts?"

Kadie bolted upright at the sound of his voice. Standing, he towered over her, tall and dark, his power a tangible presence in the room. She stared up at him. He looked as he always did, but in her mind's eye she saw him as he had been earlier, his fangs bared, his eyes red as hellfire. Would he have killed Rosemary if she hadn't stopped him? Would he have killed them all?

"Not that I'd blame you." He sat at the other end of the sofa, careful not to touch her. "Kadie?"

"They hate me," she said, her voice thick with unshed tears. "I thought they were my friends, but they hate me."

"It's my fault, not yours. So, where does that leave us?"

"What do you mean?"

"There's a suite waiting for us at the best hotel in London. Do we go, or do we stay here?"

"I want to go home." She held up her hand, afraid to hear what he was going to say. "I want to see my parents. I miss them. I'll come back. I promise. I just need to see them for a little while." *And Kathy,* she thought. She needed to see her sister. "Don't you trust me?"

He snorted softly. "Should I?"

Strangely hurt, she said, "I thought you already did."

"Why have you never told me about your sister?"

"You know about Kathy?" she asked, then wondered why she was so surprised.

He nodded. "Why didn't you ever tell me about her?"

"I'm not sure. I thought about it, thinking it might convince you to let me go. But then . . ."

"You were afraid you'd hate me if I refused and she died while you were here."

She nodded.

"I wouldn't have let you go," he said. "But I would have taken you home."

"Will you take me now?"

"If you wish."

"Would you do one more thing for me?"

He waited, knowing what was coming.

"Let Rosemary and Donna and Shirley keep their memories."

"We've already talked about this."

"I know, but I can't believe that the three of them are any danger to you. I think you're wrong. I don't think they'll ever leave here. And what if some of the vampires come back? If you erase their memories, they won't know they're in danger until it's too late. Please, Rylan."

It was the sweet entreaty of his name on her lips that was his undoing. "All right, Kadie. You win." It was a risk, letting the women keep their memories. But not too big a risk, as long as they stayed in Morgan Creek. And he'd make sure of that before he left.

"Rylan?"

He took her hands in his. "Before I take you home, there's one thing you need to know."

"What's that?"

"Should you decide to make a run for it, I will always be able to find you. No matter where you go, I will be able to hunt you down."

"Hunt me down? I don't think I like the sound of that. It makes me feel like . . ."

"Prey?"

She nodded.

"I'm a vampire, Kadie. A predator. Humans are what I prey on."

"I know." She looked at their joined hands. His so large and strong. Hers small, powerless in the grip of his. "Why are you telling me this?"

"Because if you decide to take off during the day in hopes of escaping me, it won't work. You're mine," he said, an odd note of regret in his voice. "And you'll be mine for as long as it pleases me."

"Didn't we already have this conversation?"

"I just wanted to make sure you understand."

"Will you be mine as long as it pleases me?"

His smile was melancholy. "I'm sure you will tire of me long before I tire of you."

"That's no answer."

"I'll be yours for as long as you wish."

He drew her into his arms, his lips claiming hers. At that moment, she told herself that nothing else mattered, not even the little voice in the back of her head that whispered she was prey.

Chapter 27

"How shall I introduce you?" Kadie asked. She had packed a bag earlier that night, and then Saintcrow had used his preternatural power to transport them to Morro Bay.

Their first stop had been at a car rental agency where Saintcrow had picked out a low-slung sports model. Now, as she stood on the front porch of her parents' house, it suddenly occurred to her that she was about to present a vampire to a surgeon and a housewife who were active in their church and their community and who had lived in the same small town all their lives. If they knew vampires existed, they had never discussed it, at least not in front of Kadie or her sister.

"Perhaps you can just tell them I'm a friend."

"A friend I brought home from work?" she asked with a wry grin.

"Or you could say I followed you, like a stray puppy."

"Some puppy," Kadie remarked as she opened the door and stepped into the foyer. "Mom? Dad?" She dropped her suitcase on the floor. "I'm home."

Still standing on the porch, Saintcrow watched as a dark-haired woman with bright blue eyes ran forward to hug Kadie.

"I'm so glad to see you!" her mother cried. "We were beginning to worry about you."

"That's what mothers are for," Kadie said, hugging her mother in return. "Is Dad home?"

"No. He took Kathy to the hospital this afternoon. I just got home myself a few minutes ago."

"Is she all right?" Kadie asked anxiously.

"She's been feeling poorly the last few days, so Dad took her in for another treatment. If all goes well, she'll be home in a few days." Mrs. Andrews hugged her daughter again. "I'm so glad you're home. Kathy's been asking for you." Moving to shut the front door, she noticed the stranger on the front porch for the first time. "Kadie, you didn't tell me you brought company."

"This is my . . . my friend, Rylan Saintcrow. Rylan, this is my mother, Carolyn Andrews."

"I'm pleased to meet you, Mr. Saintcrow." Carolyn looked at Kadie. "Where are your manners?" Extending her hand, Mrs. Andrews said, "Come in, won't you?"

Summoning his best manners, he murmured, "Thank you, ma'am," as he shook her hand.

"Please, call me Carolyn," she said with a smile. Tucking Kadie's arm in hers, Mrs. Andrews led the way into the living room. She and Kadie sat together on the sofa.

Saintcrow trailed behind, his gaze moving quickly over the room. The furniture was old but expensive and well taken care of. A piano stood in one corner, the lid covered with photographs of varying sizes, all depicting Kadie and another, younger girl, in various stages of growth. The pictures on the mantel displayed photos he was certain Kadie had taken.

His gaze rested on Kadie's mother. She was a pretty woman in her late forties. She carried herself with the air of a woman who had never known want. Now and then, she ran her fingertips over the large filigreed silver cross that hung from a silver chain around her neck.

"So, tell me all about this last trip," Carolyn was saying. "Did you get any great shots?"

Their voices faded into the background as Saintcrow sat in the overstuffed chair across from the sofa, absorbing the smells of the house—soap, shampoo, shaving cream, toothpaste, the lingering odor of cooked food, disinfectant, the fragrance of the flowers on the table beside the sofa. The smell of an apple pie wafted from the kitchen. And overall, another scent he recognized all too well. The scent of vampire blood.

He was aware of the curious glances Kadie's mother occasionally sent in his direction, and after she and Kadie had played catch-up, she turned to him with a smile.

"So, Mr. Saintcrow, tell me about yourself. What do you do?"

"I don't have a job, as such. I'm rather fortunate in that I'm able to live off my investments," he said smoothly. "And please, call me Rylan."

"You must have a lot of spare time on your hands. What do you do to keep busy?"

"Mother, really!" Kadie exclaimed.

"It's all right, Kadie. I support several people who live in a small town that has no other source of income."

Carolyn's eyes widened in surprise. "That's very generous of you. It must be terribly satisfying, using your money to help others."

"Yes, indeed."

"Oh! Where are my manners?" Mrs. Andrews exclaimed. "Have you two had dinner?"

"We ate earlier, Mom."

"How about dessert? There's a fresh apple pie in the kitchen, still warm from the oven."

"Sounds great." Kadie looked at Saintcrow, a twinkle in her eye. "It's too bad you're on a diet. My mom makes the world's best apple pie."

"A diet?" Mrs. Andrews shook her head. "You look fit as a fiddle to me."

"Trying to cut down on carbs," Saintcrow replied.

"Yes, of course," Mrs. Andrews said with a sigh. "Everyone's so worried about cholesterol these days. Kadie, why don't you come help me in the kitchen?"

Saintcrow grinned inwardly, amused by Mrs. Andrews's not-so-subtle way of getting Kadie out of the room. He had no doubt that Kadie's mother was eager to get her daughter alone for a few minutes, anxious to find out more about their guest. It was obvious mother and daughter were very close.

Rising, he wandered around the room, pausing to look more closely at several of Kadie's photographs. She really was a talented photographer, he thought, admiring a black-and-white, wide-angle shot she had taken of some of the houses in Bodie. Moving on, he noticed several of her articles were framed on the wall behind the piano.

He was about to resume his seat when the front door opened and a tall, angular man with close-cropped black hair and brown eyes entered the house. The man came up short when he saw a stranger in his living room.

"Dr. Andrews?" Saintcrow said.

"Yes. And you'd be . . . ?"

"Rylan Saintcrow. I'm a friend of Kadie's."

Dr. Andrews studied him through narrowed eyes. "Where's Carolyn?"

"Right here," Mrs. Andrews said, hurrying out to greet her husband.

"Dad!" Kadie ran to her father and threw her arms around him.

"Hey, pumpkin!" Dr. Andrews said, hugging her close. "Welcome home."

Warmth crept through Kadie at the sound of her childhood nickname. "I see you've met Rylan," she said, smiling. "Rylan, this is my dad, Ralph Andrews."

The two men shook hands.

"Rylan came to my rescue when my car ran out of gas," Kadie explained. She tugged on her father's arm, leading him to the sofa. She sat down, and her parents sat on either side of her.

Saintcrow took the chair he had occupied earlier.

"So, Kadie, where have you been all this time?" Andrews was talking to his daughter, but his gaze never left Saintcrow's face.

"Rylan is the benefactor of a small town in Wyoming. I've been staying there. I got some great shots. I can't wait to print them."

"A benefactor?" Dr. Andrews remarked.

"Yes," Saintcrow said, his gaze meeting that of Kadie's father. "I have a bit of money. I find if you take care of people, they'll take care of you."

"I see. Will you be staying long?"

Saintcrow shrugged. "I'm not sure."

Mrs. Andrews laid her hand on her husband's arm. "No more questions, Ralph. We were about to have some pie. Would you like a slice?"

Dr. Andrews nodded.

Motioning for Kadie to stay where she was, Mrs. Andrews went into the kitchen. She returned moments later carrying a tray bearing three slices of pie and four cups of coffee.

Saintcrow accepted one of the cups without comment.

He grinned when Kadie looked at him, one brow lifted in amusement.

"How was your day, dear?" Mrs. Andrews asked. "Did the Perkins boy respond to the new treatment?"

"Yes, he's going home tomorrow."

"So soon? That's wonderful." Mrs. Andrews beamed with pride.

"My father's quite a famous doctor," Kadie said. "Patients with terminal illnesses come to him from all over the world."

"They call him the miracle worker," Mrs. Andrews said. "He's been written up in all the medical journals."

"Unfortunately, I haven't been able to cure my own daughter."

Saintcrow nodded sympathetically. He sat back, the cup untouched in his hand, listening to the Andrews family discuss their day. After getting Kathy settled in at the hospital, Dr. Andrews had spent the morning in surgery and the afternoon making rounds. Mrs. Andrews volunteered as a teacher's aide in a school for handicapped children three days a week. Interspersed in their conversation about the day's activities were questions for Kadie: Had she sold the photographs she had taken in Silverton? Not yet. How long was she going to stay? She wasn't sure. Where was she thinking of going next? England, with Rylan.

They spent the next half hour making polite conversation, and then Dr. Andrews said he felt like some fresh air and asked Saintcrow if he would join him out on the patio.

Saintcrow followed the man outside, waited patiently for him to say what was on his mind. He didn't have to wait long.

"Does my daughter know you're a vampire?"

"She knows. But she doesn't know you're a hunter, does she?"

If Andrews was surprised, he didn't show it.

"That's what I thought. I'm betting your wife doesn't know, either."

"She has her suspicions."

Saintcrow nodded. Most hunters chose not to marry, knowing that their wives and children could be used against them. He shook his head when Andrews reached casually inside his jacket. "I wouldn't, if I were you."

Andrews froze, then, very carefully lowered his arm to his side. "If you hurt Kadie, I'll hunt you down if it takes the rest of my life."

"I'm not going to hurt her. And just so you know, the only way you can destroy me is by taking my head. And I don't intend to let that happen."

Curiosity flared in Andrews's eyes. "I've never heard of a vampire who couldn't be destroyed by a stake in the heart."

Saintcrow shrugged. "I'm a very old vampire. Not much can hurt me anymore." He leaned back against one of the patio supports, his arms folded across his chest. "Are there a lot of vampires here in Morro Bay?"

"Not anymore."

Saintcrow raked a hand through his hair. He had a feeling Andrews would be a formidable enemy. He also had a feeling that he knew what kind of "miracle" the good doctor was using to cure his patients. "What do you do with the bodies after you take their blood?"

The color drained from Ralph Andrews's face.

"That's how you perform all those miracles, isn't it? By infusing your patients with a little vampire blood." He wondered why it didn't work on the doctor's daughter.

"It's only fair, isn't it?" Andrews retorted. "Human blood sustained their lives. It's only right that they return the favor."

Andrews was a smooth character, Saintcrow mused. He knew the doctor was afraid of him. He could hear the rapid beating of the man's heart, smell the fear on his skin. He let him sweat for a few more moments before saying, "Relax,

I'm not going to give your secrets away. And I'm not in the revenge business."

"What are your intentions toward my daughter?"

"I'm going to take her to England and show her a good time."

"And if I refuse to let her go?"

"I wouldn't try it if I were you. Besides, she's a big girl, capable of making her own decisions."

"And after England, then what?"

Saintcrow shrugged. "I haven't thought that far ahead. Shall we go back inside?"

Kadie's parents went upstairs to bed a short time later.

"What did you and my dad talk about for so long?" Kadie asked when she and Rylan were finally alone.

"Just guy talk." He stretched his arm across the back of the sofa. "He told me a little about his practice and asked me what my intentions were."

"He didn't! What did you say?"

"I told him we planned to go to England, and that I hadn't thought beyond that."

"Oh."

"You sound disappointed."

She shook her head. "No, I . . ." She *was* disappointed. Even though she kept reminding herself that he was a vampire and they had no real future together, she couldn't imagine her life without him in it.

"Kadie?"

"It's late," she said, blinking rapidly. "I'll go make sure there are clean sheets on the bed in the guest room."

When she started to rise, his hand on her arm stayed her. "I won't be sleeping here."

"Where will you go?"

"I'll find a place, don't worry."

"But what will I tell my folks? They'll expect you to stay with us."

"Tell them whatever you want. Tell them I came to town on business and I had an early meeting. Whatever. I'll see you tomorrow night."

She nodded, but looked none too happy.

"I'll miss you, too." He stroked her cheek with his fingertips.

One touch, and she wanted to pull him down on the sofa, to pour herself over him, to absorb his very essence. It had been days since he had made love to her. She wanted him. Needed him.

He smiled at her, a smugly masculine smile. "I want you, too, sweetheart."

"Then take me, now."

"Here? Under your father's roof?" He shook his head. "I don't think so." He could imagine her father's righteous indignation if he found the two of them together, could almost feel the sting of the blade as Andrews lopped off his head. But it didn't keep him from taking Kadie in his arms and kissing her. She was light to his darkness, a blanket of warmth to turn away the chill, a ray of hope that chased away his occasional bouts of despair.

Hugging him close, she ran her tongue along the side of his neck.

He hissed a word she didn't understand under his breath.

Pleased by that reaction, she climbed onto his lap and kissed him, long and hard, until, with a low growl, he planted his hands on either side of her head and took control of the kiss, his fingers tangling in her hair, his tongue plundering her mouth. He kissed her until they were both breathless, then, in a single sinuous move, he stood and placed her on her feet.

She stared up at him.

"Go to bed, Kadie," he said.

"But . . ."

"I need to feed and find a place to rest. I'll see you tomorrow night."

"You're going?" How could he leave her now, when she was on fire for him?

But she was talking to empty air.

Saintcrow strolled down the quiet streets of Kadie's neighborhood, his hands shoved in his pockets. Most of the houses were dark. Here and there, a dog barked at his passing. A cat hissed at him, then turned and ran away. A short time later, a police car slowed as it passed him, but then moved on.

He grinned inwardly, bemused by fate's sense of humor at bringing him into the home of an active vampire hunter. He wondered absently how many vampires Andrews had dispatched, and how he had discovered the healing properties of vampire blood. Had it been by accident, or had the good doctor done a little experimenting on the side? He wondered what kind of illness Kadie's sister had and why the blood of his kind failed to heal her, or at least put the symptoms into remission for an extended length of time.

Turning right, he came to a strip mall. Most of the businesses were dark, but a sign in the window of a small tavern announced it was open. Pushing through the door, he quickly scanned the occupants—a couple of young men playing pinball in the corner, a middle-aged couple sitting at the far end of the bar, a man and a woman at a nearby table who had eyes only for each other.

Moving to the bar, Saintcrow ordered a glass of red wine. He sipped it slowly, and waited. A short time later two young women—a blonde and a redhead—entered the bar, laughing.

Both were pretty, but he liked the way the redhead smelled. When she looked in his direction, he smiled. It was as easy as that.

Two minutes later, he bought her a drink to quench her thirst.

Three minutes after that, she was quenching his.

Chapter 28

Kadie woke to the heavenly smell of coffee brewing. With a sigh, she closed her eyes. It was good to be home, to sleep in her own bed. For years, she had considered getting a place of her own. She was certainly old enough. She could afford it. But she was home so seldom, it just didn't seem worth it. She thought fleetingly of Saintcrow's house . . . and bolted upright.

Where was he? Where had he spent the night?

With a sigh, she flopped back on the pillows. Why was she worrying about him? He was a big boy. He'd been taking care of himself for over nine hundred years.

The promise of fresh, hot coffee drew her to the kitchen.

"Good morning, sunshine," her mother said.

"Hi, Mom. Dad."

"Mornin', pumpkin. Good to have you home again," her father said. "How long are you staying this time?"

"I'm not sure." Kadie poured herself a cup of coffee, then sat at the table, thinking again how good it felt to be back home.

Minutes later, her mother placed a platter of French toast and bacon on the table.

"Should we wait for your friend?" her mother asked.

"No. Rylan's gone for the day. Business of some kind."

Her father nodded. "Right."

Kadie looked at him sharply, wondering at his skeptical tone. "He'll be back tonight, probably after dinner."

Her father grunted thoughtfully.

Kadie frowned. If she didn't know better, she would have thought her father suspected something.

Later, sitting out on the patio doing her nails, she wondered how Donna, Shirley, and Rosemary were getting along. Had they stayed in Morgan Creek, or had Brittany's death soured them on the idea? She wondered how Marti was doing, and if Chelsea had found it hard to settle back into life at home, and if Jeremy had stayed with Chelsea, and if Frankie and Claude were having a good time in Hawaii. And then she wondered about the vampires. Had they stayed together? Where were they now? Were they enjoying their freedom, or wishing they had stayed in Morgan Creek, where it was safe?

She looked up, smiling, when her mother pulled a chair up beside her and sat down.

"You seem lost in thought," Mrs. Andrews remarked. "Anything you want to share?"

"No, I was just thinking about some of the strange stories I heard while I was traveling," Kadie said, choosing her words carefully.

"What kinds of strange stories?"

"Oh, you know. Tales of ghosts and things that go bump in the night. I guess it's really not all that unusual, considering where my work takes me. But then I heard someone say vampires were real, and . . ."

"Vampires?" Mrs. Andrews laughed. "Kadie, really."

"And they said there were vampire hunters."

"You're serious, aren't you?"

Kadie nodded. "I remember reading something about vampires in the paper years ago, but I didn't pay much attention. I mean, who believes in vampires?"

"Well, there are always stories," Mrs. Andrews said, her brow furrowing. "But no one's ever proved they exist. Why, just day before yesterday there was a story on the news about a body being found drained of blood in the alley behind Kitner Road. But your father saw the body and told me the report had been exaggerated."

"Well, that's a relief."

"Yes, indeed. So, tell me about your young man."

Kadie grinned inwardly, thinking that her "young" man hadn't been young in centuries. "He's just a guy I met. We sort of hit it off and when he asked me to go to England with him, I said I would. I'm due for a vacation."

"He seems very nice, and I know you've been making your own decisions for years, but, Kadie, do you think it's wise to go off with a man you've known such a short time?"

"I'll be fine, Mom," Kadie said, reaching over to give her mom's hand a squeeze. "I've been with Rylan for several weeks." And she knew him in ways her mother would surely frown on.

After lunch, Kadie and her mother drove to the hospital to see Kathy. It broke Kadie's heart to see her little sister looking so thin and pale.

She pasted a smile on her face as she hurried to her sister's bedside and gave her a hug. "How's my angel?"

"Kadie! I'm so glad to see you."

"I missed you, too." Reaching into her bag, Kadie pulled out a beribboned package. "Here you go," she said. "A souvenir from Wyoming, as promised."

"You didn't forget!" Kathy quickly tore off the wrappings,

opened the box, and pulled out a porcelain doll dressed in the garb of a Cheyenne bride. "I love her!" she exclaimed. "Thank you!"

While Kathy admired her new doll, Kadie looked up and met her mother's tear-filled eyes and knew, in that moment, that Kathy's days were numbered.

It was near dark when Kadie and her mother headed home from the hospital. Kadie's father was sitting on the front porch, reading one of his medical journals, when Kadie and her mother arrived.

Dinner passed congenially. Sitting at the table, her father told them about his day at the hospital. They had just finished dessert when the doorbell rang.

"I suspect that will be your young man," Kadie's mother said. "You go entertain him. Dad can help me with the dishes."

"Thanks, Mom!" Kadie jumped up, her heart beating with anticipation as she ran to open the door.

"You're still here," Saintcrow remarked, sounding surprised.

"Did you think I'd run off? What would be the point if you can find me?"

He smiled as he drew her into his arms and kissed her. "Am I interrupting anything?" he asked, his breath warm against her ear.

"No. We just finished dinner." There was something different about him, Kadie thought, though she couldn't say what it was. Shrugging the thought aside, she took him by the hand and led the way into the living room. Sitting on the sofa, she patted the cushion beside her. "So," she asked, eyes twinkling, "did you sleep well?"

"Like the dead," he replied, slipping his arm around her shoulders.

"I missed you."

"I missed you, too." His gaze rested on her lips. "How much longer do you want to stay here?"

"At least a few more days," she said, thinking about her sister. "You're ready to leave, aren't you?"

"The sooner, the better." His fingertips stroked her arm. "I want you all to myself."

"After we go to England, will we come back here?"

"I don't think so."

Before Kadie could ask where else he wanted to go, her father came into the room.

Dr. Andrews settled down in his easy chair, his gaze resting speculatively on Saintcrow. "How was your day?" he asked.

Saintcrow shrugged. "Quiet."

Dr. Andrews grinned wryly. "I thought it might be. So, Kadie, your mom tells me you were asking about vampires."

Kadie slid a glance at Saintcrow, then said, "It was nothing. Just some idle gossip I overheard."

"I don't want you upsetting your mother with that kind of talk."

Kadie nodded. Was she imagining things, or was there some silent communication going on between her father and Saintcrow? There was definitely an air of tension in the room that hadn't been there before her father arrived. What did it mean?

"Kadie, I'd love a cup of coffee," Dr. Andrews said. "And ask your mother if there's any of that pie left."

When Kadie left the room, Dr. Andrews leaned forward. "A man was killed here night before last. Drained of blood and tossed in a trash bin."

"I wasn't here night before last," Saintcrow said.

"This is the third death in the last week."

"And?"

Andrews drummed his fingers on the arm of his chair. "I can't find the killer."

"What do you want me to do, find him for you?"

"That's exactly what I want."

Saintcrow snorted. "You're the hunter, not me."

"Dammit, I need your help." Andrews jumped out of his chair and began to pace the floor. "If he isn't stopped, he'll kill again."

"Probably."

Andrews glared at him. "And you don't give a damn, do you?"

Saintcrow blew out a sigh. That was the trouble. He did care. But hunting his own kind . . . That left a bad taste in his mouth. He looked up as Kadie and her mother entered the room. This wasn't his town, but a vampire who killed so often and didn't dispose of his kills was a danger to everyone. Sliding a glance at Andrews, he said, "I'll see what I can do."

It was with some surprise that Saintcrow found himself driving along a narrow road with Kadie's father later that night. They were about two miles out of town when Andrews slowed the car.

"This is where we found the first body," the doctor said, pointing to a culvert. "The man was a transient. We're still waiting for some ID."

Saintcrow sniffed the air. The vampire's scent was faint, but he'd know it if he smelled it again.

The second body had been found in an abandoned warehouse. "Jack Wheldon," Andrews said. "He was the general manager of the First National Bank."

The third body had been found in a Dumpster in an alley.

"The same vampire killed them all," Saintcrow said.

"How can you be sure?"

"His scent. It's the same at all three sites."

"Can you follow it back to his lair?"

"Why? Are you going to try to destroy him tonight?"

"Are you crazy? I'll do it tomorrow, when the sun's up."

"And take his blood?"

"Do you have a problem with that?" Andrews asked, his voice curt.

"Actually, I do, but I can live with it."

"Let's go then."

Saintcrow leaned back as Andrews drove back toward the city. They hadn't gone far when Saintcrow said, "Pull over."

Andrews parked on the side of the road, then peered out the window at the abandoned building situated on a patch of barren ground. "You think he's in there?"

Saintcrow nodded.

"Doesn't seem very secure to me," the doctor remarked, frowning.

Saintcrow shrugged one shoulder. "It's concrete and steel. I imagine he's figured out a way to lock it from the inside when he's at rest."

"No doubt," Andrews agreed.

"Well, I'm outta here," Saintcrow said, opening the car door. "The rest is up to you."

"Where are you going?"

"I found the vampire for you. Now I need to find a human for me," he said, and vanished into the darkness.

Later, after satisfying his thirst, he began to feel guilty about leading Andrews to the vampire's lair. He thought about it for a few minutes, then returned to the lair of the other vampire. A single breath told him the killer Andrews was hunting was still inside.

Saintcrow hesitated a moment, then rapped on the door. "Hey, come on out."

The door creaked open and Saintcrow found himself face-to-face with a tall, dark-haired young man. A fledgling.

"Who are you?" the vampire demanded, his tone surly. "What are you doing here?"

"Maybe saving your life."

"What's that supposed to mean?"

"You might want to clean up your act. Those dead bodies you've left lying around are attracting attention from the local hunters."

The fledgling snorted disdainfully. "Let 'em come."

Saintcrow frowned. "How old are you?"

"Twenty-three."

"I meant how long have you been a vampire?"

"Oh. I don't know. A couple of days. A week. Time has no meaning anymore."

"What's your name?"

"Micah Ravenwood."

"Where's your master?"

"I don't have a master. Who the hell are you, anyway?"

"Saintcrow."

Ravenwood's eyes widened. "Rylan Saintcrow?" He hissed a curse.

"You've heard of me?"

"Yeah. The creature who turned me, she mentioned you."

Saintcrow lifted one brow. "What was her name?"

"Lilith."

Now it was Saintcrow's turn to swear. "She's here?" The vampire community wasn't small, so the chances of meeting another vampire who knew Lilith seemed like more than coincidence

"No. I was doing a shoot in Cody, Wyoming."

"You're an actor?"

"I wanted to be. I'd just scored my first speaking role."

"And your last."

"Yeah."

"So, where'd you meet Lilith?"

"At a singles' bar in Cody."

"Go on."

"There's nothing more to tell." Ravenwood looked away, hands clenched at his sides.

"You're lying. She seduced you, didn't she?"

"Yeah, she took me into this big house and one thing led to another. At first, it was . . . nice, but then . . ."

"Go on."

"She humiliated me in ways I'd rather not repeat. Made me do things . . . When I woke up the next night, she was gone, and I was . . . hungry." Ravenwood's gaze slid away from Saintcrow's. "I think I went a little crazy."

Saintcrow swore under his breath. It wasn't uncommon for untutored fledglings to go on a killing spree. "So, Lilith turned you and left you there without telling you anything?"

"What's to tell? I'm a bloodsucker now. A monster. If I ever see her again, I'll kill her."

"Not if I see her first. Are you thinking about staying here in Morro Bay?"

"Yeah. I can't go back home. I've never been to California before, so I figured, what the hell. I might even take up night surfing."

"If you're planning to hang around, you'll need to find a new lair before sunrise."

"Why? What's wrong with the one I have?"

"One of the hunters I mentioned, he knows where you take your rest."

"How the hell does he know that?"

"Because I told him where to find you."

"What?" Hands clenched, Ravenwood took a menacing step forward, his eyes blazing red. "Why the hell did you do that?"

Knowing the other vampire would be able to feel it, Saintcrow gathered his power around him. "If you attack me, it'll be the last thing you ever do."

Ravenwood backed up a step. He might have been a new vampire, but he wasn't a fool.

"There's a little bar on the corner of Ninth Street," Saintcrow said. "Meet me out back tomorrow after midnight and I'll answer any questions you have about your new lifestyle."

"I'll be there."

"Remember what I said about a new lair. It'll be dawn soon."

With a curt nod, Ravenwood took off.

Saintcrow stood there a moment, considering what Ravenwood had said about Lilith. One way or another, she had to be stopped.

It hadn't taken her long to sire a new vampire. Had she made more? And if so, why? And what about the others? Had they stayed in Wyoming? Were they all out kicking up their heels, preying on unwary humans, making fledglings, and abandoning them without telling them what they needed to know to survive?

Shoving his hands in his pants pockets, Saintcrow headed back toward the Andrewses' house. Fledglings were notoriously unpredictable, he thought as he turned the corner onto Kadie's street. Had he made a mistake in warning the other vampire?

And then there was Kadie's father. Saintcrow shook his head. Of all the luck, falling in love with the daughter of a hunter. Once again, it occurred to him that fate was likely having a good laugh at his expense.

He was a block from Kadie's house when he heard muted footsteps easing up behind him. Damn! Either Andrews had lied to him or the man was ignorant of the fact that he wasn't the only hunter in town.

The hunter's heartbeat increased as his footsteps drew nearer. Saintcrow could smell his excitement. The blood rushing through the hunter's veins teased Saintcrow's hunger and only the fact that this was Kadie's town kept him from grabbing the man and taking him down. He rarely took a life these days, but turnabout was fair play.

Instead, he let the hunter creep up on him, then grabbed the guy by the throat and shoved him against a cinderblock wall. "You lookin' for me?"

The man glared at him but said nothing. He was of medium height with sloping shoulders and a barrel chest.

Most vampire hunters were born with an extra gene passed from father to son that gave them the ability to recognize vampires. It was, Saintcrow thought, nature's way of keeping a balance between good and evil.

Saintcrow relieved him of three wooden stakes, which he broke in half and tossed into the bushes alongside the wall before emptying a vial of holy water. When that was done, he captured the man's gaze with his.

Looking deep into his eyes, he said, "You won't hunt any more vampires. From now on, the thought of doing violence, the sight of any blood but your own, will make you violently ill. If anyone questions you, you won't remember me or this conversation. You understand?"

The hunter nodded.

"What's your name?"

"Brian Kirk."

"All right, Kirk," Saintcrow said, giving him a push. "Get the hell out of here."

With a nod, the hunter hurried back the way he'd come.

Saintcrow stared after the man, thinking he probably hadn't seen the last of the hunters in this town.

Chapter 29

Saintcrow arrived at Kadie's house just after dinner. After exchanging pleasantries with the doctor and his wife, Saintcrow asked Kadie if she'd like to go for a drive.

"I'd love to," she said. "Just let me grab a jacket."

When she left the room, Ralph Andrews said, "I trust you won't be out too long."

"I'll have her home before dawn," Saintcrow promised with a wry grin. "You can count on that."

"I'm ready," Kadie said as she came back into the room. "Dad, stop worrying about me. I'm a big girl now, remember?"

"I'm your father," he said. "It's my job to worry."

Kadie hugged her mother, gave her father a kiss on the cheek; then, holding Saintcrow's hand, they left the house.

"What is it with you and fast cars?" she said as he held open the door to the sleek, metallic blue Porsche.

He shrugged. "What can I say? Fast cars, fast women."

She stuck her tongue out at him when he slid behind the wheel. "Where are we going?"

"Just somewhere we can be alone."

"Any particular reason why we need to be alone?" Kadie asked, settling herself in the seat.

"I can think of one or two."

"I'm sure you can," she replied primly.

Saintcrow chuckled. "Don't go all schoolgirl innocent on me now."

"Can I ask you something?"

"Sure."

"All the stories about vampires say they can't be seen in a mirror, and that garlic repels them, and holy water burns them. Is that true?"

"It depends on the vampire. We're solid. We can be seen in a mirror. Garlic stinks but it doesn't repel us. Holy water won't burn me, although it burns new vampires. Fire . . . that's something else."

"What about silver crosses?"

He shook his head as he made a left turn and headed for the beach. "They no longer have any power to thwart me." Silver didn't affect him, save for weapons that were made out of it. Though they wouldn't kill him, wounds inflicted by solid silver took longer to heal and were infinitely more painful.

"Wooden stakes?"

He slid a glance in her direction. "I'm not sure I like the tone of this conversation."

"I'm just curious."

"A wooden stake through the heart will destroy most vampires."

"Most?"

"You'll be happy to know that I'm impervious." As he had told her father, the only way to destroy him now was to take his head. Even fire wouldn't destroy him, although it took decades of agony spent deep in the earth to recover.

"What about other vampires?"

"A stake to the heart will destroy most of them. We grow

stronger and harder to kill as we grow older. Anything else you want to know?"

Kadie shook her head, thoughts of vampires receding as she stared out at the ocean, beautiful and peaceful under the light of the moon.

They reached the marina a short time later. Saintcrow parked the car, then they walked down to the water.

"This is such a pretty place," Kadie remarked. "Have you ever been here?"

"Once, a long time ago." He glanced at the Morro Rock, which was the town's most famous feature. "Do you know how the rock got its name?"

"I seem to recall some explorer named it."

Saintcrow nodded. "Juan Rodriguez Cabrillo. He discovered it in 1542 while exploring the Pacific Ocean. It's said he named it El Morro because it reminded him of the head-wrap of a Moor."

"I've lived here all my life and never knew that."

"Well, that's how it usually is. People don't pay much attention to the attractions close to home."

"I love this place," Kadie said. Once surrounded by water, the northern channel had been filled in to create a harbor. The public wasn't allowed to climb the rock, not only because it was dangerous, but because it was a reserve for the peregrine falcon. "We used to camp here a lot when I was younger. The only spanking I ever got was when my best friend dared me to climb the rock."

Kicking off her sandals, she started to walk down the beach, which was deserted at this time of night. A short time later, she began to run.

Saintcrow watched her for several minutes, admiring her curvy bottom, the way the moon cast silver highlights in her hair, the sound of her heart as it began to beat fast. All his predatory instincts came to life as he watched her run away from him. Yanking off his boots and socks, he pursued her.

She let out a squeal when he grabbed her around the waist and carried her to the ground, twisting at the last minute so that she landed on top of him. She stared down at him, breathless, a hint of fear in her eyes.

He took a deep breath, inhaling the fragrance of her hair and skin, the tempting scent of her blood. Cupping the back of her head, he kissed her. The salty smells of sea and sand clung to her skin. He tasted it on her lips.

She moaned softly as he rolled over, tucking her beneath him. She wrapped her arms around him, drawing him closer. And all the while, she made little hungry sounds deep in her throat.

Holding her close, he whisked them up into the hills above the bay. Removing his long leather coat, he held her to his chest with one arm while he spread his coat on the ground, then lowered her onto it. With hands that moved faster than her eyes could follow, he removed her clothing and his own, and then he gathered her body to his, his hunger for her blood, his longing for her body, merging in a maelstrom of desire that would not be ignored.

She writhed beneath him, as eager as he, her hands roaming over him, now caressing him, now raking her nails across his back, down his chest.

With a low growl, he buried himself deep within her, felt her answering cry of pleasure as desire engulfed them.

Loosing a contented sigh, Kadie ran her fingertips through Rylan's hair. She never wanted to move, never wanted to let him go.

"I must be heavy," he remarked, raising himself up on his elbows.

She wrapped her arms more tightly around him. "I don't care."

Chuckling softly, he quickly rolled over, carrying her with him so she was now on top. "That's better."

She smiled at him, thinking she had never been this happy. She started to tell him she loved him, but she bit back the words, her joy slipping away like a wave returning to the sea. There had been no words of love spoken between them. Right or wrong, silly or not, she wanted him to say it first.

Saintcrow stroked Kadie's cheek, brushed a kiss across her lips. So, she wanted the words, did she? He kissed her again, longer and more deeply. He had never intended to fall in love with her. Relationships between humans and vampires rarely ended well. He didn't want to hurt Kadie. Better to keep the words locked inside. Once spoken, they could not be taken back.

The fact that her father was a hunter only complicated matters. There was no way Andrews was ever going to welcome a vampire into the family, nor did Saintcrow trust the man. Kadie's father might decide to try ridding the world of one more vampire regardless of his daughter's feelings.

And there were other hunters in town. He had smelled them on the drive to the beach.

"What are you thinking about?" Kadie asked. "You look so far away."

"Just thinking about you," he admitted quietly, "and how lucky I am to have you in my life."

Kadie stared at him, the words *I love you* begging to be said. But, again, she held them back.

Sitting up, he gathered her into his arms and held her close. *I love you, too*, he thought, stroking her hair. *More than you'll ever know*.

* * *

"I wish you didn't have to go." They were parked in front of her house. "Where do you spend the day, anyway?"

"Nearby." He kissed the tip of her nose. "It's late. You should go to bed."

She squeezed his hand. "Come with me."

He laughed at that. Finding him in Kadie's bed would give her father one more reason to take his head. "I'll see you tomorrow night."

"It's early yet," she said, pouting.

"I know, but I need to feed." It wasn't a lie, just not the whole truth. Before he fed, he needed to meet with Raven-wood.

"All right. Good night, Rylan."

"Sweet dreams, darlin'."

She lifted her face for his kiss, closed her eyes as his mouth covered hers.

Drawing back, Saintcrow reached across her to open the door. "You'd best get in the house," he said, "before I take you right here, right now."

"I wouldn't mind." A saucy grin curved her lips as she got out of the car. On the sidewalk, she blew him a kiss, then, reluctantly, went up the walkway and into the house.

Kadie shut the door. On her way to her room, she paused when she heard voices coming from the back of the house. Without turning on any lights, she tiptoed down the hallway to her father's den. Light shone beneath the closed door.

She was about to turn and tiptoe away when she heard the word *vampire*.

With all her senses suddenly alert, she placed her ear against the door.

"Are you sure it's Saintcrow?" A man's voice. One she didn't recognize.

"I'm sure," her father said.

Kadie smothered a gasp. Her father knew Rylan was a vampire? How was that even possible?

"Damn! That'll be quite a feather in our cap, taking him out." This from another man with a slight English accent.

"Don't start posing for pictures yet, Harry," her father said. "He won't be easy to kill."

"I don't care how tough you think he is," Harry said. "A stake to the heart works every time."

"Not on this one. He told me himself that the only way to destroy him is to take his head."

Kadie pressed a hand to her heart. What was going on? Why was her father discussing vampires with these two men? And how had he come to know so much about the subject?

Flashes of past memories sprang to her mind—memories of the large, oblong wooden box she had found while looking for hidden birthday presents in the basement the year she turned twelve. It had been filled with a variety of odd-looking sharp implements. When she'd asked her father about it, he had told her they were medical instruments used in surgery. How often had she seen him leave the house early in the mornings on his day off, carrying that box?

She shook her head, astonished by the turn of her thoughts. Her father was a hunter. It explained why her mother, who preferred gold jewelry, always wore a large silver cross on a silver chain. Kadie had asked her about it once. Her mother had replied that it had been a gift from Ralph and she had promised never to take it off. Did her mother know she was married to a vampire hunter? Or had she thought the cross merely a sentimental gift from the man she loved? Now that she thought about it, Kathy had been wearing one in the hospital when she'd visited her there.

"What about that other vampire?" the first man asked.

"The one who was supposed to have a lair in the old Hedley building."

"He's gone. I think Saintcrow warned him away."

"So, now there's two bloodsuckers in town that we know of," Harry muttered sourly. "And that's two too many."

"Let's worry about the other one for now," her father said. "As long as Kadie's here, we can be pretty sure that Saintcrow is nearby."

"A vampire dating your daughter," the first man said, a note of irony in his voice. "It would be funny if it wasn't so dangerous."

"I know what I'm doing, Gordon."

Kadie tensed at the sound of chairs being moved.

"Let's call it a night," her father said. "I'll meet the two of you at the usual place in the morning and we'll see if we can track down the other vampire."

Pivoting on her heel, Kadie hastened down the hallway and up the stairs to her room. Her father was a hunter. It was unbelievable. Inconceivable.

But all too true.

Safe in her room, Kadie closed the door, her mind racing. Thank goodness Saintcrow was planning to leave town soon. As far as she was concerned, the sooner the better. She told herself her father wouldn't attack him, but she knew the other two hunters would have no qualms about taking Rylan's head.

And neither, said a worrisome little voice in the back of her mind, would her father, whether she wanted to admit it or not.

Twenty minutes after midnight, Saintcrow found Raven-wood pacing the parking lot behind the bar.

"You're late," Ravenwood said.

"Sorry. I had a date."

"A date? With a mortal? How can you stand to be near them and not sink your fangs into them?"

"A lifetime of practicing self-control."

Ravenwood snorted.

"I didn't say it was easy. Lilith shouldn't have left you without telling you a few things."

"Yeah, like what?"

"For one thing, she should have told you that you don't have to kill when you feed, and that if you do take a life, you need to dispose of the body where it won't be found. If you want to keep your head longer than a few months, it's best not to leave a trail of bodies in your wake."

"I don't want to kill! I hate that. But once I start . . ." Ravenwood shook his head. "It's just so hard to stop once I start drinking. Who knew that people were so fragile? Or that their blood tasted so good?"

"I know how intoxicating the hunt can be. Believe me, I know. But you don't have to be a monster if you don't want to be. It'll get easier as you get older. Feed more than once a night. Try drinking a little from several people instead of taking from just one until you learn to control your hunger."

"Does that really work?"

"If you give it a chance. Did you find a new lair?"

"Yeah. Thanks for the heads-up."

"Just one more thing. If you go rogue in this town, I'll hunt you down myself."

Chapter 30

In the morning, it was difficult for Kadie to sit at the breakfast table with her father and pretend she hadn't overheard his conversation the night before. She had a million questions she was dying to ask him, like when had he become a vampire hunter, and if her mother knew, and how many vampires he had killed, and did he really intend to hunt Saintcrow.

Those questions and more chased themselves through her mind as she listened to her mother and father discuss their plans for the day, the weather, the latest headlines, Kathy's prognosis.

"In a word, not good," her father said. "It's taking her longer each time to absorb the infusion. And the effects aren't lasting as long as they should."

Kadie studied her father surreptitiously. How was it possible that he'd managed to hide the fact that he was a hunter from her and her mother all these years?

"Kadie, you're very quiet this morning," her father said. "Is everything all right?"

"Yes, of course. I'm just a little tired."

"I'm not surprised," her mother said. "You were out pretty late last night."

"Quite the night owl, your friend," her father remarked.

Kadie looked at him sharply. Was he fishing? Trying to find out if she knew Saintcrow was a vampire?

"Are you serious about Mr. Saintcrow?" her mother asked. "I was under the impression you'd just met."

"I'm in love with him."

Her father rose from the table so abruptly that his chair tumbled to the floor with a loud crash.

"For goodness' sake, Ralph, what's gotten into you?"

"Nothing." He righted the chair, then stood with one hand braced on the back. "Is he in love with you?"

"I don't know."

Her father glanced at his watch. "I'm late for a meeting." He drained his coffee cup, kissed her mother on the cheek, and strode out of the room.

Was he going after the other vampire, Kadie wondered, or going hunting for Rylan? Questions flooded her mind. How did her father find those he hunted? What did he do with the bodies? Were the hunters organized? Sanctioned by the government?

"Where is Mr. Saintcrow?" her mother asked.

"Attending to business," Kadie said. "He'll be back tonight." But not if she could help it. He wasn't safe here.

The day passed with agonizing slowness. Her mother took her to lunch and then they spent the rest of the afternoon at the hospital with Kathy. Carolyn read to Kathy for a while, and then the three of them played a few hands of Uno. Later, Kathy challenged Kadie to a game of checkers. It was impossible for Kadie to concentrate. She was concerned about her sister's illness, worried by the fact that Rylan was in danger and there was no way to warn him.

"You're not paying attention," Kathy said when she beat Kadie three games in a row. "Is something wrong?"

"No, of course not," Kadie said, smiling as she set up the checkerboard again. "This game is mine."

Kadie and her mother left the hospital an hour later. By then, Kadie's nerves were so taut, it was all she could do to keep from screaming.

At home, her mother went into the kitchen to start dinner.

Kadie stood at the window in the living room, staring out. Where was her father? Where was Rylan? Was the young vampire Saintcrow had told her about still alive, or had her father and his friends hunted him down and driven a stake into his heart?

She swallowed the bile that rose in her throat when she imagined a hunter destroying Rylan.

She let the curtain fall back into place when she saw her father coming up the walk. Outwardly, he looked the same as always, but he was forever changed in her eyes. He was a doctor, sworn to save lives. How could he, in good conscience, destroy life? And even as she pondered that question, she knew what his answer would be. He wasn't taking a life. Vampires were already dead.

She felt herself tense as he opened the door.

"Hey, pumpkin," he said cheerfully. "Were you waiting for me?"

She shook her head. Did he smell like blood, or was it just her imagination?

"Something wrong?" He shrugged out of his suit jacket and tossed it over the back of the sofa. "Is your mother home?"

"She's in the kitchen. Fixing dinner. Pork chops. And stuffing."

"Good. I'm starved." He regarded her a moment, his brow furrowed. "Kadie?"

"How was your day?"

"Same as always. Kathy told me she beat you at checkers.

Your visit really cheered her up." He glanced around the room. "Saintcrow not here yet?"

"No."

"Well, it's still early," her father remarked, and headed for the kitchen calling his wife's name.

Kadie stared after him. She had known him all her life, she thought, and yet she didn't really know him at all.

Kadie was a nervous wreck by the time Saintcrow arrived. As quickly as she could, she hustled him out of the house.

"What's going on?" he asked as he pulled away from the curb.

"We have to leave. My dad's a hunter, and so are two of his friends."

"I know."

"You do? How did he find out about you? And why aren't you more upset?"

"I doubt if he intends to try and take my head while I'm at your house. He'll never find me when I'm at rest, and if he did . . ." He shrugged.

Kadie stared at him. "You wouldn't hurt him?"

Saintcrow glanced in the rearview mirror. "No, but his friends are fair game."

"I don't believe this." She shook her head. "Does my mother know?"

"If she does, she hides it well."

"I think we should leave tomorrow night. My dad's friends want your head."

"So do a lot of other people, but I'm still using it."

"This isn't funny!"

"Kadie, stop worrying."

"But . . ."

"Enough." He glanced over his shoulder, then stepped on the gas. "I didn't get this old by being careless."

"Did you warn that fledgling you told me about that my dad was after him?"

"Ravenwood? Yeah. I felt responsible for him."

"Why?"

"Lilith turned him."

"Lilith!" Kadie's eyes grew wide. "She's here, in Wyoming? You don't think she'll go back to Morgan Creek, do you?"

The thought of the vampires returning to Morgan Creek made Kadie sick with fear for Rosemary and Shirley and Donna. Now that Saintcrow was gone, there was no one to protect her friends. The vampires could do whatever they liked, kill whomever they wished. For all she knew, her friends could already be dead.

"I don't know if she's gone back there or not," Saintcrow said, "but I need to find out." It had never occurred to him that any of the vampires would return. He didn't think the men would kill the women. As for Lilith, she had never preyed on the females before, but she was unpredictable at best. If anything happened to the humans, the guilt would be his.

"When are we leaving?" Kadie asked anxiously.

"We?"

"Were you going without me?"

"I thought you wanted your freedom."

"So did I. What's wrong?" Kadie asked, frowning, when he glanced in the rearview mirror again.

At the corner, he turned right, then pulled over to the curb in front of a small strip mall. It was closed at this time of the night.

"Why are we stopping?" Kadie asked.

"We're being followed. Stay here."

Before she could ask what was going on, Saintcrow disappeared into the darkness. She glanced out both side windows, gasped when she looked out the back and saw Saintcrow yank a man out of the driver's side of a black car. The man came out swinging, a stake clutched in one hand. He drove it into Saintcrow's shoulder. And Saintcrow hurled the man against one of the buildings.

A second man bolted out of the passenger side. Scrambling over the hood of the car, he plunged a long-bladed knife into Saintcrow's back and gave it a sharp twist.

Saintcrow shook his attacker off, grabbed him by the throat, and tossed him after the other man.

It was over in moments.

Before Kadie could get out of the car to see how badly Saintcrow was hurt, he had jerked the stake out of his shoulder, yanked the knife out of his back, and was again sitting behind the wheel.

Kadie stared at him. His shirt was soaked with blood.

"I'm all right," he said curtly.

She shook her head. Then, unable to resist, she glanced in the rearview window. The two men were still sprawled on the sidewalk. Unmoving.

Were they dead? She bit down on her lower lip, trapping the question in her throat.

Saintcrow pulled away from the curb. Keeping his eyes on the road, he said, "You're not going to faint on me, are you?"

She shook her head, one hand pressed to her heart.

Saintcrow drove for several miles before pulling to a stop alongside a park. Switching off the engine, he got out of the car, removed his shirt, and used it to wipe the blood from his shoulder and back. Wadding it up, he tossed it into a cement waste receptacle.

Kadie stared at him. In the faint glow of the headlights,

she could see that his face was set in implacable lines. Was he in pain? Being stabbed might not be fatal to him, but she couldn't help thinking it must be painful, vampire or not.

Saintcrow clenched his hands at his sides. He could feel Kadie watching him, sense her amazement as the wound in his shoulder began to heal.

After taking several deep breaths, he returned to the car. "Are you all right?" he asked.

"That's a good question, only I should be asking it." The nasty-looking gash in his shoulder was healing right before her eyes, the skin knitting together as if by magic. "Does it hurt?"

"I've had worse."

"There's blood on the seat."

He shrugged, as if it wasn't important.

"Do you think my father sent them after you?"

"I don't know. Maybe. It doesn't matter." Word of his presence had no doubt spread to nearby towns. Taking him out would be quite a coup for any hunter who managed to cut off his head.

"Are they . . . ?"

"One's dead. The other one's gonna have a nasty concussion."

"Were they . . . ?" She swallowed hard. "Were they friends of my dad's?"

"Probably. Come on, I'll take you home."

"But . . ."

"Don't argue with me. Not now." The wound in his shoulder was minor; the one in his back, made by a jagged silver blade, hurt like the very devil and would take longer to heal. Right now, he was in desperate need of blood to replace what was trickling down his back.

Kadie had a lot to think about on the ride home. Her

father was a hunter, and there were others in town like him, men who wanted to kill Rylan.

Rylan had killed a man. What would her father's reaction be when he found out?

Rylan was going back to Morgan Creek to find out if Lilith was there. And if she was, what did that mean for Rosemary and the others?

Kadie's head was throbbing by the time they reached her house.

Saintcrow pulled up to the curb, his nostrils flaring. Andrews had company.

"Rylan . . ."

"Stop worrying about me."

Kadie nodded, worried by how pale he looked, by the fact that the house lights were on so late, and by the unfamiliar cars in the driveway. She glanced at the house, quickly exited the car when she saw her father step out onto the porch. Was that a gun in his hand?

She looked back at Saintcrow. "Go!"

Kadie hurried up to the porch, determined to get some answers. One look at her father's face and she swept past him into the house, her heart pounding with fear for the man she loved.

Two men stood in front of the hearth, their bodies rigid, their faces expressionless, as if they had been carved from stone.

Kadie turned to look at her father, who'd followed her inside. "What's going on?"

"Saintcrow," her father said. "Where's he staying?"

"I don't know."

"He killed a man tonight," her father said. "A man who was a friend of mine."

"Your friend tried to kill Rylan. What was he supposed to do?"

"He's a vampire, Kadie."

She took a deep breath. "I know that."

"You know?" Disbelief swept every other emotion from her father's face. "You know? And you're dating him? Are you out of your mind? He's a monster. A killer. Dammit, he's not even alive!" He took a step forward. "You haven't . . ." He sucked in a deep breath. "Never mind, I don't want to know. Just tell me where to find him."

"I have no idea. And I wouldn't tell you if I did."

"Kadie." Her father moved toward her, one hand outstretched. "I understand you're infatuated with him, but whatever your feelings for this creature might be, they aren't real."

"Dad . . ."

"Let's leave it alone for now, Kadie. We'll talk in the morning."

Kadie nodded. She spared a brief glance for the two men in front of the fireplace, then went up the stairs to bed, only to lie there, wide awake, unable to sleep for the questions that plagued her.

Was Rylan safe?

Had his wounds healed?

And, most troubling of all, how many others were hunting him?

Thinking a glass of warm milk might help her sleep, she tiptoed down the stairs, only to pause when she heard voices on the front porch.

". . . tomorrow night."

"We'll be ready." Her father's voice.

"What about your wife and daughter?"

"Leave that to me."

Hearing muffled farewells, Kadie scurried back up the stairs, dived into bed, and pulled the covers up to her chin.

Tomorrow night? She clutched the bedspread in her fists. What was happening tomorrow night?

Chiding himself for not going back to the vacant house he was currently using as a lair, Saintcrow stood outside a rundown tavern on the outskirts of town, waiting for some unwary drunk to exit. Under other circumstances, he would have gone inside, but being shirtless, his pants stained with blood, he would surely have drawn attention, and that was one thing he didn't need right now.

So, he stood in the shadows and waited.

It was nearing one A.M. before a middle-aged couple staggered out the door. He mesmerized them both, ordered them into the car—the woman in front, the man in the back. He took the woman first. Her blood was thin and tasted strongly of alcohol, but he was in no condition to be choosy. He took as much as he dared, then got into the backseat. The man's blood tasted vile. He drank as much as he could stand, wiped the memory from their minds, and sent them on their way.

Feeling only marginally better, he drove back to Kadie's house. The two cars that had been parked in the driveway earlier were gone. The lights were out. Opening his senses, he knew Kadie's parents were asleep. Kadie was awake. And worried.

He sat there a moment, the engine purring softly while he debated the wisdom of stealing a few minutes with her under her father's roof.

He had just decided it was a really bad idea when the curtains at her window parted and he saw her staring down at him.

She gestured for him to wait for her. A few moments later, she ran down the porch steps and slid into the car.

"You've got to get out of town!" she said. "My father knows you killed his friend. He asked me all kinds of questions tonight. . . ."

Saintcrow pressed his fingers to her lips. "Hey, slow down."

She pulled his hand away from her mouth and pressed it to her breast. "This is serious!" She took a deep breath. "Don't you understand? No matter how this turns out, someone I love is going to get hurt."

Saintcrow nodded. She was right. He didn't want to kill her father or the others, but after nine hundred years, he had a strong sense of survival. If threatened, he would do whatever was necessary. But, worse than the thought of killing Kadie's father was the very real fear that she might be caught in the cross fire. And that was one risk he refused to take.

"Don't worry," he said. "Nothing's going to happen."

"There's a little dance club off the highway," Kadie said. "Wait for me there tomorrow night. I'll meet you after my dad goes out. And then we can go to England, as we planned." She hated the thought of leaving Kathy again so soon, but she would call her every day.

Saintcrow nodded. "Be careful."

"You, too."

She leaned forward for his kiss, her eyelids fluttering down as his hand curled around her nape. He kissed her deeply, his fingers tunneling up into her hair.

She was breathless when he drew away.

"You'd better go." He glanced at the house. "Your father's waking up."

"All right. Until tomorrow night."

He watched her run up the stairs. She turned and waved, and then closed the door.

With his preternatural senses, he tracked her movements through the house, waved when she peeked out the window.

"I love you, Kadie mine," he murmured.

He put the car in gear and pulled away from the curb. He didn't look back.

The next day seemed twice as long as usual. In the morning, her father asked her again if she knew where Saintcrow spent the day. She was grateful that she could honestly say she didn't.

She and her mother went to the hospital to visit Kathy shortly after lunch. Kadie smiled and hugged her sister, wondering how she was going to go off to England and leave Kathy behind. Her sister seemed to be growing weaker every day. There were faint shadows under her eyes, hollows in her cheeks.

"Do you have an appointment, Kadie?" her mother asked when they stepped out into the hall so a nurse could draw Kathy's blood. "You keep looking at your watch."

"No," Kadie replied quickly. "I was just checking the time. Kathy's favorite teen heartthrob is going to be on one of the talk shows this afternoon."

The day passed quietly. Kadie hugged her sister good-bye, wondering again how she could even think of leaving her.

Kadie forced herself to relax on the drive home. It wouldn't do to arouse her father's suspicion. She was in the kitchen helping her mother prepare dinner when he came home from work.

Conversation at the dinner table seemed strained to Kadie. Her parents exchanged several looks that she couldn't interpret.

"Another wonderful meal," her father said, pushing away from the table. "You outdid yourself, Caro. Kadie, could I see you for a few minutes?"

"Can't it wait until I help Mom clear the table?"

"It's all right," her mother said. "Go along, dear."

Filled with apprehension, Kadie followed her father into his study.

"Where is he?" her father asked. "He's usually here by now."

"I honestly don't know."

"But he's coming over later?"

Kadie shook her head. "I don't know."

"And you wouldn't tell me if you did," he said, and there was no mistaking the disappointment in his voice.

If things had been strained at the dinner table, they were more so when she followed her father into the living room. Her mother switched on the TV and Kadie tried to lose herself in what was on the screen, but it was impossible.

At nine o'clock, the two men Kadie had seen last night arrived, along with another man.

"Kadie, Carolyn, I'd like you to meet Rob, Gordon, and Harry. They're associates of mine. Rob and Gordon and I are going out for a while. We have a little business to attend to."

"Nothing serious, I hope," Carolyn said.

"Nothing to worry about. Just something I couldn't take care of this afternoon. Harry will be staying here. He's going to spend the night."

"Oh?" Carolyn Andrews frowned at her husband.

"It's not a problem, is it?" Ralph asked.

"No, of course not," Carolyn replied, as if having a strange man stay the night was an everyday occurrence.

At ten thirty, Kadie excused herself and went into the kitchen on the pretense of getting a glass of water. Plucking her mother's car keys from the hook beside the back door, she tucked them into the pocket of her jeans. Returning to the living room, she said, "I think I'm going to bed, Mom. It was nice to meet you, sir."

Harry nodded, but said nothing.

In her room, Kadie changed into a pair of black jeans and a dark shirt, then stood by the door, listening. A short time later, she heard her mother show their guest to the spare room and bid him good night.

Kadie waited half an hour before opening her window and shinnying down the tree outside her bedroom.

Grateful that her mother had left her car in the driveway, Kadie slid behind the wheel. She backed slowly out of the driveway, keeping the lights off until she reached the end of the block.

Since there was little traffic at that time of night, it took less than twenty minutes to reach the club.

Inside, she sat at the bar to wait for Saintcrow. Excitement fluttered in her stomach every time the door opened, followed by a sharp stab of disappointment when Saintcrow failed to arrive.

Midnight came and went and still there was no sign of him.

Kadie jumped up when her father and his two friends entered the bar. No doubt her mother had discovered her absence and told her father. All he'd had to do was search for her mother's car.

"Where is he?" her father asked, his voice harsh.

"I don't know." The tears that stung her eyes were real. "I don't know."

Her father insisted on staying until the bar closed. Taking Rob and Gordon aside, he spoke to them for a few minutes, and then he drove her home.

Kadie stared out the passenger window, her heart breaking, her cheeks wet with tears as she faced the truth. Now that she no longer wanted it, Saintcrow had given her the freedom she had pleaded for so many times in the past.

Chapter 31

Saintcrow arrived in Morgan Creek shortly after midnight. He had spent the last two weeks trying to convince himself he had done the right thing. Spending those few days with Kadie and her family, seeing how much they all loved her, how she loved them, had made him realize that leaving her was the right thing to do. Who was he to take her away from her home and family? He had nothing to offer her. With him, she would never have a normal life. Never have children. He envisioned her with a family of her own, a husband who could share her whole life, a man who wasn't hunted by other men, who didn't shun the sun, or exist on the blood of others.

Yes, leaving had been the right thing to do, and he had never been more miserable in his whole wretched life.

A quick stroll through the residential section told him that the women were safe in their homes. Before leaving town, Saintcrow had given each woman ownership of the house in which she resided, which meant that no vampire could enter their homes without an invitation. Hopefully, the women were wise enough to remember that. He noted that two of them were sleeping soundly; one was awake.

He walked around Blair House. It was empty at the

moment, but Lilith's scent was fresh. When had she come back? And where was she now?

His own home seemed colder and more lonely than ever without Kadie. How had he ever lived without her? What was the point in continuing his existence when she was no longer here?

He wandered up the stairs to her room. Standing in the doorway, he took a deep breath, filling his nostrils with her scent, remembering the taste of her lips, the warmth of her skin, the way she cried his name as she writhed beneath him. He had admired her spunk, the way she defended the other women. Marti and the others were free because of Kadie's concern for them. Carl Freeman owed his life to her.

Feeling foolish but unable to help himself, he took the pillow from her bed and carried it down to his lair.

Hugging it close, he tumbled into oblivion with her scent all around him.

"He's back."

"Who?" Donna asked, and then her eyes widened. "How do you know?"

"I saw him out in front of my house late last night."

Shirley and Donna stared at her.

"Are you sure it was him?" Shirley asked. They were sitting in the restaurant, having dinner together, something they did most nights. The town was quiet now, with only the three of them. But, thanks to the cell phones Saintcrow had given them, and the TVs they had ordered, they were no longer cut off from the rest of the world.

Donna shook her head. "Why would he come back?"

"What if some of the others came with him?" Rosemary shivered. "Remember when Lilith was here a few days ago? That creature is pure evil!"

Shirley nodded.

"Maybe we should leave," Donna suggested. "Staying seemed like a good idea before, but now . . ." She lifted a hand to her neck. "If he's back, maybe they're all coming back. I can't go through that again."

"I think you're right," Shirley said. "Where should we go?"

"I don't want to leave," Rosemary said. "I know you'll think I'm crazy, but this is my home now."

Donna looked at her friend as if she'd lost her mind.

"I understand how you feel," Shirley said. "It'll be hard getting used to living around a lot of people again, but there's safety in numbers. I think we should go."

"He never bothered us before," Donna said. "I'm willing to stay a few days and see what happens. But if Lilith and the others come back, then I'm leaving."

"Unless he prevents it again," Shirley said. Though she hated to admit it, she didn't really want to leave, either. She glanced at her friends. "Let's think about it and decide tomorrow."

"If we have a tomorrow," Rosemary said darkly.

Chapter 32

Kadie braked her rental car at the bridge. Though she had been away from Morgan Creek for only a short time, it was like returning to another world. Once she had hoped to leave this accursed place and never see it again, but she'd had to come back. She was certain Saintcrow was here.

Taking a deep breath, Kadie drove across the bridge; then, curious, she put the car in reverse. She breathed a sigh of relief when the car crossed to the other side, and then she frowned.

Maybe he wasn't here.

Maybe he had gone to England without her.

As long as she was here, she decided to check on Rosemary and Shirley and Donna and see how they were getting along. And if Lilith was here? She thrust the troubling thought from her mind as she crossed the bridge a second time.

It hadn't been easy, leaving her sister. Kathy looked more frail every day even though she insisted she felt fine. Kadie knew her mother was worrying herself sick. As for her father . . . Kadie shook her head. In the last few weeks, he had rarely been home and when he was, he was surly and withdrawn.

Kadie was about to turn up Oak Avenue toward the residential section when she noticed a car parked in front of the restaurant. Pulling in behind it, she smiled when she saw Shirley and Donna sitting at one of the tables near the window.

Shirley noticed her at the same time.

Kadie waved and then she was inside and they were all hugging each other and talking at once.

". . . glad to see you."

". . . never thought we'd see you again, Kadie."

"Why on earth did you come back here?" Rosemary asked when the first wave of excitement passed.

Kadie sat down. The other women resumed their seats.

"Are you hungry?" Shirley asked. "We had an early dinner. There's some ham and mashed potatoes left."

"No, thanks, I ate on the road. As for why I came back . . ." Kadie lifted her shoulders and let them fall. "I was hoping Saintcrow was here."

The women exchanged glances.

"He's here," Rosemary said curtly.

"We've been thinking that maybe since he's come back, we should leave," Shirley remarked.

"He's here?" Kadie asked. "You're sure?"

Donna nodded. "Rosemary saw him outside her house late last night."

Kadie blew out a sigh of relief. This morning, she had waited until her father left the house and her mother went to her yoga class, then booked a flight to Cody. She had rented a car at the airport and driven here, so tense she had stopped only to grab a bite to eat.

"I can't believe you're still with him." Rosemary's voice carried a familiar bitterness.

"Why did he come back without you?" Donna asked.

Kadie shook her head. "It's a long story."

Shirley leaned back in her chair. "Well, let's hear it."

"When we left here, he took me home. Imagine my surprise when I discovered that my father is a vampire hunter."

"What?" Donna's eyes widened in surprise.

"You're kidding," Shirley said, and burst out laughing.

"It's not funny, and I'm not kidding. Anyway, two of my dad's acquaintances, who are also hunters, attacked Saintcrow. He killed one of them, which naturally didn't sit well with my dad. Rylan and I made plans to go away together, but he left without me." She paused, swallowing hard. "He didn't even tell me good-bye."

"You're better off without him," Shirley said, "even if you don't think so."

"You're in love with him," Rosemary said, disbelief evident in her voice.

Kadie nodded. "I know you all think he's a monster, but he isn't, not with me. He's kind and thoughtful and"—she bit down on her lower lip—"I don't want to live without him."

"Is he in love with you?" Shirley asked.

"I don't know. He's never said so, but then, I never told him how I feel, either. If he doesn't love me, I'll have to live with it. But, one way or another, I have to know." She glanced out the window. One of the mansion's turrets was barely visible in the distance. "I *have* to know."

The conversation turned to other things, and Kadie learned that tourists had wandered into town on several occasions, hoping to find something to eat. She was even more surprised to learn that her friends had actually made a few dollars serving food and that on a couple of occasions they had rented vacant houses to travelers looking for a place to spend the night.

"We're thinking of painting the inside of the restaurant white or beige, and making new curtains and tablecloths," Shirley said with a grin. "I was thinking a red-and-white check would look nice."

Kadie nodded, remembering the red-and-white check-ered tablecloths at the Italian restaurant where she and Saintcrow had gone to dinner.

"Of course, Donna likes yellow, and Rosemary wants blue. Who knows, if we can decide on the décor, we might just make this place a success."

"I was thinking we could turn the old hotel into a bed and breakfast," Donna said. "I went in there the other day. It's full of dust and cobwebs, but a little paint would go a long way to making it presentable. With a little work, we could make a nice living here."

Ever the pessimist, Rosemary said, "Of course, all these plans will come to naught if the vampires decide to come back."

The sun was setting when Kadie took her leave, promis-ing Rosemary and the other two women that she would see them again tomorrow.

Eager as she was to see Saintcrow, Kadie drove slowly up the narrow road that led to the big gray stone mansion. She had no idea what she would do if he didn't want her there. If he didn't, she would just have to live with it. But one way or another, she wanted to know why he had left without a word.

She parked the car, then sat there, drumming her finger-tips on the steering wheel as she realized she had no way to get into the house if he was still at rest. One thing was for certain: if any of the other vampires were here, Kadie didn't want to be caught out in the open after dark, alone.

Grabbing her handbag, she got out of the car and hurried up to the front door. She was about to knock when it opened.

Saintcrow stood there clad in a pair of faded jeans and nothing else.

"Kadie, when I caught your scent, I thought I was dreaming, but of course, that's impossible, since vampires don't dream. What are you doing here?"

"Since you don't seem very happy to see me, I guess I'm making a big mistake."

"Not happy?" He shook his head. "*Happy* doesn't begin to describe it." Taking her by the hand, he pulled her gently into the house and closed the door. "How did you find me?"

"I just knew you'd be here." She gazed up into his eyes. "Aren't you going to kiss me?"

"Of course." Drawing her into his arms, he kissed her as if it had been years since he'd last held her instead of only weeks.

When he broke the kiss, he led her to the sofa and drew her down beside him. "I never thought you'd come back here of your own free will."

"I never thought you'd leave me without so much as a good-bye."

"All things considered, I thought it was for the best."

"Oh? Best for who?"

"For you, of course. You once told me I had no right to keep you or the others here against their will. After spending time with you and your family, I realized that you were right. I thoughtlessly ruined lives, broke up families, deprived children of their parents. And if my conscience ever bothered me, I excused myself because I'm a vampire, a hunter, and humans are my prey." He held up his hand when she started to speak. "Then I watched you with your family. I've been a vampire for so long, I'd forgotten what it was like to be a part of one. You love them. They love you. I can't give you a normal life. I can't give you children. And your father will never accept me."

"I don't care about all that." She took a deep breath. "All that matters is that I love you. And if you love me . . ."

"*If?* Kadie, you must know how I feel."

"You never said it."

"Neither have you. I love you, Kadie. All I want is for you to be happy."

"You make me happy."

"Do your parents know where you are?"

"No! I left them a note saying I was going back to work and that I'd call them in a few weeks."

"So, where do we go from here?"

"I guess that's up to you. If you want me to stay, I will. If you don't . . ." She clenched her hands in her lap, her eyes searching his as she waited for his answer.

"Kadie." He pulled her gently into his arms. "Stay as long as you wish."

Her eyelids fluttered down as he lowered his head to claim her lips with his. His kiss, velvety soft and feather-light, put all her doubts to flight.

They talked far into the night, making plans, dreaming dreams. He made love to her tenderly, vowing he would always love her, never leave her again.

She fell asleep in his arms.

It was after three A.M. when Saintcrow left the house, drawn outside by Lilith's scent. She had been anxious to leave this place, so why did she keep returning?

A thought took him to Blair House. He found her on the

sofa in the front parlor, her head bent over the neck of a burly young man with coffee-colored skin and long black hair. If she was surprised to see Saintcrow, she hid it well.

He stood in the doorway while she finished feeding. When she was done, she delicately wiped her mouth on the young man's shirt.

"What are you doing here, Lilith? Besides satisfying your rapacious thirst?"

She shrugged.

"I met a fledgling of yours. Ravenwood?"

"How is he?" She eased the man out of her arms and he fell limply to the floor.

"Lucky to be alive." As was the man she had just preyed upon, Saintcrow thought. "Next time you turn someone, you might stick around long enough to show him the ropes, you know, tell him what to expect, how to survive."

"He made me angry."

"How long are you planning to stay here?"

She shrugged again. "Does it matter?"

"Not if you behave yourself."

She rose in a long, sinuous movement that reminded him of a snake uncoiling.

Saintcrow lifted one brow when she swayed toward him. "Did you ever think about what it would be like if we got together?"

He snorted. "I'd as soon bed a pit viper."

Her eyes blazed red. "I can't believe that puny mortal is more to your liking," she retorted, her voice thick with scorn. "But then, I never understood why you protected the humans that came here. They're nothing. Less than nothing."

"I don't want any more deaths in my town." He jerked his chin toward the man on the floor. "And that includes him."

She glared at Saintcrow, mute.

"I mean it, Lilith. The mortals have a saying. It's my way or the highway. Don't forget it."

Kadie woke in bed, alone, late the next morning, with no memory of how she had gotten there. She knew a moment of disappointment because Saintcrow had left before dawn, then shrugged it off. It was, she thought, something she would have to get used to if she intended to spend the rest of her life with a vampire.

The ringing of her phone brought her back to the present. Glancing at the display, she hesitated to answer it, but there was no point in worrying her mother any more than she had to.

Forcing a note of cheerfulness into her voice, she said, "Hi, Mom."

"Kadie. Where are you?"

"Dad. Is Mom okay?"

"She's fine."

"Why are you using her phone?"

"Because I knew you wouldn't answer if you thought it was me. Where are you?"

"Daddy, please just leave us alone."

"So, you're with him."

"I love him, and nothing you say will change that. Please accept it. He's not a monster. He doesn't kill people when he . . . when he drinks from them. He's treated me with nothing but kindness."

"He's got you under his spell, Kadie. Can't you see that? You've got to listen to me and come home, if not for your sake, then for your mother's. She's worried about you."

"You told her about Rylan?"

"Of course not."

Kadie drummed her fingertips on the edge of the night

table. "You didn't have to tell her, did you? She already knew."

"Kadie, I'm asking you one last time to come home. I can't be responsible for what happens if you don't."

With that ominous declaration, her father ended the call.

Feeling sick to her stomach, Kadie dressed and drove into town. She was surprised to see a black van parked up on the hill in front of Blair House. Had Lilith returned without Saintcrow knowing?

That seemed doubtful.

Another car she didn't recognize was parked in front of the restaurant. A good sign, she thought, remembering Donna's hopes of finding a way to make a living in Morgan Creek. It was a pretty place, what with the mountains and the trees. But, as Rosemary said, the future hinged on whether the vampires returned. She wondered if Saintcrow could cast some kind of spell that would keep the vampires out, the way he had once kept the humans in.

Kadie parked the car and went into the restaurant.

Rosemary smiled at her from behind the counter.

Three men stood at the cash register, waiting for Donna to ring up their bill. They all wore long, dark coats and shuttered expressions.

Shirley was in the kitchen.

Kadie took a seat at the counter.

"What'll you have?" Rosemary asked. "Shirley made an apple pie last night."

"Sounds good," Kadie said.

"Coffee?"

"Please."

Kadie glanced at the three men. They didn't look like tourists. She felt a shiver run down her spine when one of them looked up and caught her staring. She quickly looked away.

"What's wrong, Kadie?" Rosemary asked. "You look like you've seen a ghost."

"Nothing. I . . . I . . ." She bit down on her lower lip. She was just being paranoid, she thought. But she couldn't shake the feeling that the three men were hunters, and that they had come to Morgan Creek to destroy Saintcrow.

In the back of her mind, she heard her father saying he wouldn't be responsible for what happened if she didn't come home. Had he sent those men here? If so, how had he found her? And even as she asked the question, she knew the answer. He had traced her cell phone to this location.

Was her father here, too? Maybe up at Blair House, looking for vampires to kill?

"Rosemary," she said quietly, "are there any other vampires in town?"

"Not right now. Lilith's been here a couple of times, but she hasn't come near any of us. Why?"

"I think those men who just left are hunters."

Chapter 33

In the darkness of his lair, Saintcrow stirred, then came fully awake as the scent of freshly spilled blood stung his nostrils.

Vampire blood.

Lilith's blood.

There were strangers in town. Strangers who smelled of blood and death.

Hunters.

Saintcrow opened his preternatural senses, honing in on his blood link to Kadie. It was midafternoon and she was in the restaurant with the other women.

A thought took him to Blair House. The scent of freshly spilled blood was strong inside. He found Lilith in her bedroom. A thick wooden stake made of hawthorn had been driven into her heart while she was at rest. The skin of her face was gray and shriveled, her white nightgown dyed red with her blood.

Saintcrow ran his fingertips over the stake. The hunters were Old School, he mused. In times past, people had believed stakes had to be made from ash or hawthorn or black thorn in order to be effective when, in truth, one kind of wood served as well as another.

Taking hold of the stake, he eased it from her chest and tossed it aside, then wrapped her body in one of the blankets. He would come back later tonight and bury her.

There was no sign of the young man she had preyed on. Either the hunters had taken him away, or he had left on his own early this morning, after the sun had sent Lilith to her rest.

The young man's fate was immaterial. Saintcrow's only concern was for Kadie. After ascertaining that she wasn't in any danger, he was about to return to his lair when his senses warned him that the hunters were now prowling through his house. Saintcrow cursed himself for his carelessness. After the vampires and most of the humans had left town he had lowered the wards on the front door to make it easier for Kadie to come and go. Reinstating the wards had slipped his mind, or maybe he had been unconsciously hoping some hunter would find him and put him out of his misery when he returned without her.

He had two choices, he thought. He could go home and kill the hunters. Or he could stay here. One thing was certain—he had to decide soon. He could feel the dark sleep stealing over him again, dragging him down toward oblivion.

Swearing vociferously, he slid under Lilith's bed. There was no hurry to go after the hunters. Now that he had their scent, finding them would be easy.

With that thought in mind, he closed his eyes and surrendered to the darkness once more.

It was near dusk when Kadie left the restaurant. She had spent the afternoon with Shirley and the other two women. Donna had brought out a deck of cards and they had spent the day playing canasta and nibbling on potato chips and

M&Ms. They had enjoyed an early dinner together and then Kadie had taken her leave, eager to see Saintcrow and tell him about the strangers she'd seen.

After parking the car, she hurried up the stairs, only to come to an abrupt halt when she saw that the front door had been forced open and was now hanging by one hinge.

Nudging it open a little farther, she leaned inside. "Rylan?"

An eerie silence greeted her.

She called his name a little louder and when there was still no answer, she crossed the threshold, cautiously glancing to the left and the right.

Someone had been here, but who?

The answer came swiftly to mind. The hunters, of course. Where were they now? Were they still inside? Had they found Saintcrow's lair?

The thought spurred her forward. Grabbing the poker from the fireplace, she ran up the stairs to the turret room. The tapestry lay in a heap on the floor.

She stood there, the poker clenched in her hand, debating whether to open the door leading to Saintcrow's lair, when she heard faint cries coming from the other side. The hunters! Had they forced open the door to Saintcrow's lair and destroyed him? Whether they had gotten past the second door and made it into Saintcrow's lair or not, they were now trapped inside the tunnel.

She started to open the door, then hesitated. If they had killed Saintcrow, the hunters could stay there and rot for all she cared. But what if they hadn't? What if Saintcrow was still safe? He would surely kill them if he found them.

She bit down on the inside corner of her lip. Did she want to be responsible for that?

She was about to open the door when she felt a hand on her shoulder. With a shriek, she whirled around, the poker raised to strike, only to come face-to-face with Saintcrow, his eyes blazing with fury.

Taking the poker from her hand, he said, "Don't even think about opening that door."

Kadie pressed a hand to her heart. "What are you doing out here?"

"The men in the tunnel have had a busy day. They destroyed Lilith while she slept, and then they came here, looking for me. Only I wasn't at home."

"Where were you?"

"I spent the day at Blair House. I went over there to find out what had happened to Lilith, and I finished my rest there."

Kadie glanced at the door. "What are you going to do with them?"

"I'm not sure."

"Would they have been able to break down the door to your lair?"

"Perhaps."

"You're not going to . . . ?" She stared up at him. Sometimes she forgot he was a vampire, a creature with supernatural abilities she could scarcely comprehend, but it was blatantly evident now. Three men had come to destroy him. What right did she have to plead for their lives? And yet, how could she not? "You won't . . . ?"

"Kill them?" A muscle clenched in his jaw. "Are you asking me to spare them?"

She nodded.

His gaze held hers for several moments, and then the red faded from his eyes and he was Rylan again.

"Get away from the door, Kadie."

She quickly backed away, her foot catching in the fallen tapestry so that she stumbled.

He caught her arm, steadying her. "Careful."

With a nod, she scooped up the tapestry, then scooted into the hallway, still within sight of the door. Whatever happened next, she was going to be there to see it.

When Saintcrow was certain Kadie was safely out of the way, he opened the door.

The three men inside blinked at him, the color draining from their faces when they realized they were staring into the face of the man they had come to destroy. The hunter at the top of the stairs loosed a cry undoubtedly meant to boost his courage as he charged forward, a stout wooden stake clutched in his right hand.

Saintcrow grabbed the man by the collar of his coat and tossed him against the wall. The hunter crumpled to the floor, a thin trickle of blood leaking from his forehead.

The other two came through the door together, only to meet the same fate as the first man, although one of them managed to drive a stake into Saintcrow's left shoulder before his head hit the wall.

Grimacing, Saintcrow jerked the wood from his shoulder and threw it down the stairs.

Kadie glanced at the three fallen hunters. "What now?"

"I'm going to wipe this place and everything that happened here from their minds. And then I'm going to make the mere idea of hunting vampires so repellent to them that the very thought of it will make them violently ill."

"You can do that?"

He nodded. "Why don't you go downstairs and wait for me? I'll join you as soon as I can."

"But . . ."

"Get out of here, Kadie."

With a huff of exasperation, she tossed the tapestry at him, then flounced down the staircase.

Saintcrow grinned as he listened to her angry footsteps.

After rehanging the tapestry, he knelt beside the first hunter. The sooner he sent these idiots on their way, the sooner he could spend time with his woman.

Kadie was playing solitaire at the kitchen table when Saintcrow strolled into the room. He looked extremely satisfied with himself.

"Are they gone?" she asked coolly.

"Yeah. They won't be staking any more vampires."

Kadie nodded. "That's good." She placed a red nine on a black ten, then dropped the rest of the cards on the table as she put a disquieting thought into words. "I think my father figured out where I was and sent those men here."

"It doesn't matter."

"You're not upset?"

"No, why should I be?"

"They killed Lilith. If I hadn't come back here, they wouldn't have found you. You could have been killed, too."

He lifted one brow.

"Well, excuse me for worrying!"

Laughing, Saintcrow dragged her chair away from the table, then drew her into his arms. "Kadie, my love, stop worrying about me. I can take care of myself, and you, too. As for Lilith . . ." He shrugged. The world was better off without her.

He was about to suggest they take a walk when his nostrils flared. A moment later, there was a knock at the front door.

Kadie looked up at Saintcrow. "Are you expecting someone?"

"No, but I guess I shouldn't be surprised he's here."

"Who's here?"

"Lilith's fledgling. Micah Ravenwood."

Saintcrow gave Kadie's hand a squeeze, then went to greet his guest.

Kadie trailed at Saintcrow's heels. She hung back a little when he opened the door. He didn't invite the other vampire into the house.

Lilith's fledgling stood almost as tall as Saintcrow. He was a good-looking man with dark brown hair, brown eyes, and dusky skin. Kadie guessed he was probably in his mid-twenties.

"What the devil are you doing here?" Saintcrow demanded.

"I'm not sure. I felt something strange when I woke tonight." Ravenwood shook his head. "I don't know what it was, or how to describe it . . ."

"Lilith was destroyed this afternoon," Saintcrow said. "What you felt on waking was the breaking of the blood bond between you."

"What does that mean, exactly?"

"It means your sire is dead and you're on your own. Ideally, she should have stayed with you the first few months until you were comfortable with your new lifestyle."

"So, what do I do now?"

Saintcrow shrugged. "Anything you want. Just don't do it here."

"Where is she? I mean, did you bury her or do old vampires just go up in smoke?"

"I buried her. The town cemetery is just a few miles down the road."

"Would you mind if I"—he cleared his throat—"if I stopped by there on my way out of town?"

"Suit yourself."

"Well, so long, then."

"The women in town are off-limits," Saintcrow said. "Remember that."

With a wave of his hand, Ravenwood ambled down the stairs and drove off in a black Chevy truck.

With a shake of his head, Saintcrow shut the door. He couldn't imagine why Ravenwood wanted to visit Lilith's grave, unless it was to make sure she was dead.

Kadie had returned to the living room. Saintcrow found her curled up in a corner of the sofa. She held a throw pillow to her breast. She looked up when he entered the room.

"You told Ravenwood he knew Lilith was dead because of the blood bond they shared," Kadie said, her brow furrowed in thought. "How does that work?"

"I'm not sure how it works, only that it does."

"So, when a vampire turns someone, it forms a bond?"

He nodded. "It's similar to the bond between us."

"What do you mean?"

"I've tasted your blood, Kadie. I'll always be able to find you."

"Does it work both ways?"

"Uh-huh. It's how you knew I was here."

He could see the wheels turning in her mind as she considered that.

"So, it wasn't just a lucky guess, or intuition."

"No."

"And it works, no matter how far apart we are?"

"Pretty much." He sat beside her, his arm curling around her shoulders. "So, here we are, alone at last."

She smiled up at him. "So we are."

His fingertips skated up and down her arm, an innocent caress, in and of itself, and yet her body responded to his touch like a flower opening to the sun.

"Our hotel suite is still waiting for us in England," he said, "if you'd still like to go."

"Oh, I would." The sooner, the better, she thought, all

things considered. And then she frowned. "Are there hunters all over the world?"

"Yeah, pretty much, although the good ole USA seems to have more than its share."

"Why is that?"

"Until recently, there weren't a lot of vampires here. Most of the vampires tended to live in Romania and the surrounding countries. Many of my kind hate change. Moving means locating a new lair, learning a new language. But in the last hundred years, as it grew more and more dangerous in Transylvania and Bulgaria, vampires started leaving in droves. A good many of them came here."

"How long have you been here?"

"I came to California just days after Marshall struck it rich at Sutter's Mill."

"Really? Wow. What was it like?"

"Those were wild times. In the beginning, you could pick nuggets up off the ground. I made a good part of my fortune then. I scoured the streams and riverbeds at night while the miners were asleep. I still have the first gold nugget I found."

"That's amazing." It explained a lot, she mused. Like how he could drive such an expensive car, and how he could afford to maintain a whole town and feed everyone in it.

"It was a great time to be a vampire. During the seven years of the strike, over three hundred thousand people flocked to California. As news of the strike spread, people came from all over the world—Hawaii, Australia, Latin America, Europe, China. There was quite a mix," he said, grinning with the memory. "Probably the best hunting ground I've ever known."

"Thanks for sharing that."

"Sorry." She didn't know the half of it, he thought. All those nationalities in one place, each with its own unique scent and taste. A real smorgasbord. No one in the States had really believed in vampires back then. Oh, there had been stories and myths carried from the Old Country, but few people truly believed.

Unfortunately for his kind, that had changed over the years. He feared it was only a matter of time before some idiot snapped a picture of one of his kind draining some unfortunate mortal and posted it on YouTube. The crap would surely hit the fan. Before digital cameras, it had been impossible to photograph vampires, but thanks to new technology, that was no longer the case. If the day ever came when the government got involved and started posting bounties on their heads, there'd be no place to hide.

Feeling the weight of Kadie's gaze, he shook off his morbid thoughts. "How soon can you be ready to leave?" It had been a long time since he'd been back to England and he had a sudden longing to see the Hodder Valley in Lancashire, to show Kadie the view from Hadrian's Wall in Northumberland, to stroll the streets of Liverpool and London, to visit the castle in Durham, a fortress so impregnable that the city was one of the few places that had never been captured by the Scots.

"Give me a day to pack and I'll be ready to go. Are the plane tickets still good?"

"What tickets?"

"We're going by boat?"

Saintcrow laughed softly. "Boats and planes are too slow, Kadie, my love."

She stared at him a moment, and then grinned. "Ah. Air Saintcrow."

He grinned back at her, then kissed the tip of her nose. "Kadie, what did I ever do without you?"

"I don't know." She slipped her hand under his shirt, her

fingers running lightly over his stomach. "But I don't intend to ever let you be without me again."

Saintcrow's gaze met hers and she knew he was thinking the same thing she was. . . . It was a promise made by a mortal to a vampire.

A promise she could never keep.

Chapter 34

Micah stood in the shadows alongside the driveway leading to Saintcrow's house, his hands clenching and un-clenching as he watched three men get into a late-model sedan and drive away. They were hunters. They had destroyed his sire. He'd had no feelings for Lilith, hated her for what she had done to him, and yet he had an overpowering need to avenge her death.

With preternatural speed, he raced ahead.

When the hunters reached the bridge, he was waiting for them. The driver braked hard when he saw Micah blocking his path.

The man in the passenger seat got out of the car. "What the heck are you doing, you idiot? Get off the bridge."

Micah frowned. This was a hunter? An indrawn breath carried the faint scent of Lilith's blood, but he detected no malice in the man, no sense of danger. What the hell?

The man in the backseat leaned his head out the window. "What's going on, Rob?"

"I don't know," Rob replied.

Now the driver rolled down his window. "Hey, buddy, do you need a lift?"

Micah shook his head. Muttering, "No, thanks," he

moved out of the way. He would have sworn the men in the car were hunters. Could he have been wrong? They smelled like hunters, but they didn't act like hunters.

Still puzzling over their odd behavior, he strolled back to town.

Everything was locked up tight.

With nothing to do, he turned his thoughts to finding a secure spot to spend the day. The first place that came to mind was the cemetery. It should have struck him as morbid. Not long ago, it would have. But what the hell, he was dead, after all. And his sire was there. He had visited her grave earlier. There had been no marker. Saintcrow had buried her deep, smoothed the earth, replaced the grass. There was nothing to show where Lilith was buried. Saintcrow had told him the blood bond was broken, so he had no explanation for how he'd known where to find her, but find her he had.

This whole lifestyle was bizarre, he mused glumly. Just when his life and career had been on the upswing, Lilith had wiped it all away. She had stolen his life, his hopes, his dreams, and left him with nothing but an insatiable thirst.

He was glad they'd destroyed her.

Walking through the residential area, he noted that all the houses were dark. Only three were inhabited. He paused in front of the first one where he detected a heartbeat. It belonged to an older woman, as did the second house.

The occupant of the third house wasn't as old as the other two. She wasn't asleep. And she wasn't in the house, but in the backyard, crying softly.

Curious, he walked around to the rear of the house. He found the woman lying in a heap at the bottom of a set of stairs that led into the kitchen. There was blood matted in her hair. One ankle was swollen.

She let out a shriek when she saw him.

"Hey, calm down. I'm not going to hurt you."

She stared at him, her eyes wide with panic, her heart beating wildly as she tried to scrabble away from him.

He knelt beside her. "Take it easy."

"Go away!"

"You need help, lady. That's a nasty bump on your head. What happened?"

"I . . . I slipped on the steps. I think I might have passed out." She cringed when he reached for her. "What are you going to do?"

"I'm going to take you inside and bandage your head and your ankle."

"No! You can't come inside!"

Micah snorted. "Lady, if I was going to kill you, I could just do it here."

She blinked at him, as if that had never occurred to her.

He settled her in his arms. "So, are you going to invite me in or not?"

Chapter 35

Kadie spent part of the morning packing. Saintcrow had told her he would buy her a new wardrobe in England, so packing hadn't taken long—her makeup, toothbrush, hairbrush and comb, her favorite underwear, her cell phone. The last thing she packed was the enormously expensive bottle of Clive Christian No. 1. No way was she leaving that behind.

With the day stretching before her, she decided to go into town for lunch and to tell Rosemary and the others good-bye.

She had thought to find them in the restaurant, but it was closed up tight. Frowning, Kadie went to Shirley's house.

Rosemary answered the door. "Kadie, hi."

"Hi. What's going on?"

"Shirley had an accident last night."

"What happened? Is she all right?"

"She's fine. Come on in. She's resting."

Kadie followed Rosemary into Shirley's bedroom. Passing through the living room, Kadie noticed there was a new TV and DVD player on a stand across from the sofa. She wondered absently if the other women had also bought flat screens.

Stepping into Shirley's bedroom, Kadie saw that Donna was already there.

After exchanging hellos, Kadie took the empty chair beside Shirley's bed. "What happened?"

Shirley shook her head. "It was so silly. I'd been watering the plants by the back porch. The stairs got wet and I slipped and hit my head and twisted my ankle."

"Do you need a doctor?"

"No."

"You should have called one of us to come and stay with you," Kadie said. "You should have been watched through the night in case you had a concussion."

Shirley lowered her gaze. "Well, actually, I did have someone stay the night with me."

"Oh?" Kadie glanced at Rosemary and then at Donna.

"It wasn't me," Donna said.

Rosemary shook her head. "Or me."

"Then who was it?" Kadie asked.

"A vampire," Rosemary muttered, her voice dripping with venom.

"He was very nice," Shirley said defensively. "He carried me into the house. After he treated the cut in my head and wrapped my ankle with an ace bandage, he fixed me a cup of tea, then tucked me in."

"Micah," Kadie guessed.

"Yes." Shirley smiled faintly. "Do you know him?"

"Not really. He came here looking for Lilith."

"Lilith? Why?"

"She turned him," Kadie said. "You know those hunters who were here? They killed her, and somehow Micah knew she was dead."

"He was very sweet," Shirley remarked. "If Saintcrow is anything like him, I can understand why you stay with him."

"Sweet!" Rosemary exclaimed. "I think that bump on the head scrambled your brains!"

"They aren't all monsters," Kadie said.

"I'll never believe that." Rosemary shook her head. "She's lucky to be alive. And now that she's invited him inside, she'll never be safe."

"I'm not afraid of him," Shirley said. "If I was younger . . ."

Donna stared at her. "You don't mean that."

Shirley lifted her chin defiantly "Yes, I do."

"He's bewitched you." Grabbing her handbag from the dresser, Rosemary left the room.

"I think she's right. You aren't thinking clearly." Donna patted Shirley's hand. "I'll see you later."

When they were alone, Shirley looked at Kadie. "You don't think I'm crazy, do you?"

"Of course not."

"Do you think he's still here?"

"I don't know. You want to see him again, don't you?"

Shirley nodded. "It was nice, having a man to talk to, even though I'm probably old enough to be his mother."

"Can I get you anything?"

"A drink from the fountain of youth would be nice."

"I'll see what I can do."

Later, back at Saintcrow's house, Kadie thought about what Shirley had said about a fountain of youth. In a few years, Kadie might be wishing for a sip out of Ponce de León's magic fountain herself. Right now, she and Saintcrow looked like the perfect couple. But that wouldn't last forever. She was growing older every day.

She was standing in front of the mirror, fretting over things that could not be changed, when Saintcrow came up behind her.

Slipping his arms around her waist, he nuzzled her neck. "How's my girl?"

"How do I look?"

"Beautiful, as always."

"Never mind. Is Micah still in town?"

"Yeah." He was quiet a moment, and then he frowned. "What the devil is he doing at Shirley's house?"

"She fell last night and he went to her rescue."

Saintcrow's gaze met hers in the mirror.

Kadie shrugged. "He spent the night with her."

Saintcrow raised his eyebrows.

"Not like that!" Kadie exclaimed. "He stayed to look after her because she hit her head."

"And now she fancies him." It wasn't a question.

"It seems that way." Kadie frowned. "Did Micah do some kind of vampire mojo to make her like him?"

Saintcrow lifted one brow. "Vampire mojo?"

"That's what Vaughan called it. So, did he?"

"How the hell should I know?"

"I thought you knew everything."

He lifted his head, his eyes narrowing. "Your father's here."

"What? Where?" She glanced over her shoulder, as if she expected to see him standing behind her.

"He's coming up the driveway."

"You don't think I called him, do you?"

"I know you didn't."

Kadie tugged on his hand. "Let's go. Now. Before he gets here."

"It's too late. He's at the door. Why don't you let him in?"

"No! You can't kill him. He's my father!"

"Did I say anything about killing him?"

"What's he doing here?"

"He's come after you. Your sister's in the hospital again, but this time it's worse."

"I don't believe that. He would have called me."

"Kadie, go let him in."

Her hands were shaking when she opened the door. "Dad, what are you doing here?"

"I'm here to take you home."

Saintcrow folded his arms over his chest. "What makes you think I'll let Kadie go?"

"Kathy's dying."

A cry of denial rose in Kadie's throat. She had known this day was coming, but the shock of hearing it put into words, the finality of it, was even worse than she had expected.

"At most, she has only a few days left. Her last wish is to see Kadie."

Saintcrow shook his head.

"You think I'm lying?" Andrews asked.

"I'm not in the habit of trusting vampire slayers, or helping them."

"Yeah, I heard what you did to Rob, and Clarke and Gordon. Three of the best hunters in the world, and you ruined them."

Saintcrow shrugged. "Would you rather I'd killed them?"

"Come with us and you'll see I'm telling the truth," Ralph said. "I have a plane waiting. It leaves in forty minutes."

"Rylan, please." Kadie stared at him, her eyes glazed with unshed tears. "My sister's dying! I've got to go."

"I know. Tell me what hospital she's in. I'll meet you there."

Ralph stared at him, his eyes narrowed, and then he nodded. "Very well." He pulled a card from his coat pocket and handed it to Saintcrow. "Room 305. Let's go, Kadie."

Kadie stared at Saintcrow. She didn't want to leave him. To her surprise, she realized she didn't trust her father, that, deep down, she found herself questioning his motives. Was her sister really at death's door, or was this simply her father's way of getting her away from Saintcrow? The thought left her feeling horribly guilty. Surely her father wouldn't lie to her about something as serious as Kathy's welfare. "Rylan?"

"It's all right, Kadie," he said quietly. "Go with him. I'll meet you there."

Kadie kissed him on the cheek, then followed her father out of the house and into the car. She glanced out the back window as her father put the Buick in gear, unable to shake off the nagging suspicion that she was making a terrible mistake.

Saintcrow stood in the living room, silent and still, as he considered his next move. He had let his mind brush Ralph's. Either the man was telling the truth, or he was a master at hiding what he was really thinking.

It would take Kadie and her father less than two hours to fly from Morgan Creek to Morro Bay, another half an hour or so to leave the airport and drive to the hospital. He had seen the worry in Kadie's eyes, and it hadn't been for her sister. It had been for him. The thought warmed him as few things had. His sweet, fragile female was worried about him, afraid her father was up to no good, that the story about Kathy being in the hospital had been a ruse to get her away from Saintcrow.

Well, they'd know if she was right soon enough.

Going to his lair, he changed into a pair of black jeans and a black shirt, pulled on a black leather jacket, and went in search of Ravenwood.

He found the vampire in Shirley's house. The woman was on the sofa, wrapped in a blanket, her left leg propped on a pillow on the coffee table. Ravenwood sat beside her. They were watching a movie on a small flat-screen TV. Saintcrow shook his head, thinking that technology had come to Morgan Creek in his brief absence.

Vampire and human both looked up when he entered the house. The woman's eyes widened in fear. The vampire's eyes narrowed as he gained his feet, his hands clenching at his sides.

"Relax," Saintcrow said. "I just stopped by to tell you I'm leaving. I'm not sure when I'll be back." Reaching into his pocket, he withdrew the key to the Corvette and tossed it at Ravenwood. "Don't wrap it around a phone pole."

Micah stared at the key. "What's going on?"

"I'm not sure. If I'm not back in a few days, the car is yours. Look after the women." With a nod in Shirley's direction, Saintcrow left the house.

Shirley looked at Micah. "What was that all about?"

He shook his head. "Beats the hell out of me." Micah tossed the key to the Corvette in the air, and caught it in his hand. "How'd you like to go for a drive?"

Shirley stared at him. "Are you serious?"

"Sure. It's a beautiful night. What do you say?"

"How do I know you won't . . . you know?"

"You don't think I'd do anything to make Saintcrow mad at me, do you?"

"I hope not."

"Come on," he said, and smiled at her.

His smile was her undoing. The dimples in his cheeks gave him an innocent, boyish look that was somehow irresistible.

Moments later, she was sitting beside him in Saintcrow's Corvette, holding on for dear life as he sped down the highway. At any other time, she would have been scared to death, but with Micah, she wasn't afraid.

For the first time since she had wandered into Morgan Creek, she felt young and carefree. Laughter bubbled up inside her and she let it out, not caring that Micah looked at her as if she was slightly insane.

"Anyplace in particular you'd like to go?"

"Why are you doing this?" she asked.

"Doing what?"

"Spending time with me? I'm old enough to be your mother."

"Really? You don't look that old. Besides, it's just a date. We aren't getting married."

Shirley laughed again, liking him even more. "I'd like to go somewhere for an ice cream sundae . . . Oh, never mind. I forgot you can't eat anything."

"Well, maybe you'll let me have a taste of you later, and I can taste it that way."

"You're kidding! You can taste what I eat?"

Now it was his turn to laugh. "No, but that would be great, wouldn't it?"

"I guess so."

For a time, they rode in silence. Shirley kept glancing at him, unable to believe this gorgeous vampire wanted to spend time with her. In spite of Micah's words to the contrary, she was forty-five and she looked it even though she still felt like a teenager. She recalled a conversation the women had had one night. It seemed, no matter what their age, from forty to sixty, they all felt young on the inside. They'd all laughed when Donna said she sometimes looked in the mirror and found herself wondering who that old lady was staring back at her. Shirley knew the feeling.

A short time later, Micah pulled up in front of a Baskin-Robbins where Shirley ordered a hot fudge sundae with extra whipped cream and extra fudge.

"It doesn't bother you, watching me eat?" she asked when they were seated at one of the tables.

"A little. I haven't been a vampire very long. I can still remember what food tasted like."

"What do you miss the most?"

"Peanut butter and jelly sandwiches," he said, grinning. "And beer."

"Did you have a family, before?"

"Well, sure. Mom, dad, sisters, brothers."

"Do they know what you are?"

"No. I haven't seen them since I was turned. As far as they know, I'm working in Cody."

How awful, she thought, to have been turned against your will. "Are you going to tell them?"

"I don't know. Probably not. My dad's not in the best of health. Something like this could kill him."

"Did you have a sweetheart?"

"Several," he admitted.

She wasn't surprised. With his dimples, sexy smile, and beautiful dark brown eyes, he had probably charmed every girl he met.

"What about you?" he asked. "Were you married?"

"No."

"Why didn't you leave with the others?"

"Oh, I don't know. I didn't really have anything to go back to." She took several bites of ice cream. "Have you . . . Never mind."

"You can ask me anything," Micah said.

"No, it was nothing."

"You wanted to know if I've killed anyone," he said quietly.

"It's none of my business."

"I have," he said, not meeting her eyes. "I didn't mean to. I didn't want to, but . . ." He shook his head. "I couldn't stop." He'd never forget how it had felt, draining the life out of that old derelict. He'd probably saved the man from a slow, lingering death on the streets, but that didn't ease his guilt.

"I don't know a lot about vampires," Shirley said, "but I know it takes time to control the hunger." She took a last bite of her sundae. "Are you ready to go?"

"Yeah." He was subdued on the ride back to Morgan Creek.

Shirley found herself watching him surreptitiously as he drove, admiring his profile, the confident way he handled the Corvette.

She was sorry when he pulled up in front of her house thirty minutes later. She hadn't expected him to walk her to her door. Or to take her in his arms on the porch.

Flustered, she murmured, "Thank you, Micah. It was fun."

"Maybe we can do it again."

"Maybe."

She stared up at him. He was going to kiss her. The thought filled her with excitement and trepidation. It had been years since anyone kissed her.

He lowered his head toward hers, then paused. "You okay with this?"

Shirley nodded, unable to speak, as his arm slid around her waist. When his mouth covered hers, she felt like she was sixteen again.

Chapter 36

Opening all his preternatural senses, Saintcrow circled the hospital. Overlying all the other odors was the scent of blood, some from the living, some from the dead. The sharp stink of antiseptic and urine overshadowed the smell of death and fear. Kadie was not there, though he caught her father's scent. Where was Kadie?

Dissolving into mist, he entered the hospital. The first hunter was in the lobby, hiding behind a newspaper. The second was near the elevators, ostensibly waiting for the next car.

Saintcrow drifted up to the third floor. A pair of hunters stood at the far end of the corridor, trying to look inconspicuous and failing miserably.

He paused at the entrance to Room 305. It was a private room. Through the open door, he saw Kadie's father standing beside the bed. A short, rotund man in a white coat and black shoes stood on the other side, his head bent over a chart.

A girl lay on the bed covered by a thin blanket. Her face was pale, her cheeks gaunt. Her heartbeat was slow and uneven.

After moving into the room, Saintcrow willed the door

closed, then assumed his own form. "What's going on? Where's Kadie?"

The hunter dressed like a doctor whirled around, one hand slipping into the pocket of his lab coat.

Ralph Andrews lifted his arm, the gun in his hand aimed at Saintcrow's heart. "She's not here."

"I can see that. Where is she?"

"Safe from you."

"So, this was all a ruse to get me here?"

"No. My daughter is dying," Andrews said. "I may lose her, but I won't lose Kadie to a monster."

Saintcrow shook his head. "Andrews, you're a damn fool. Put that gun away. I can break both your necks before you can pull the trigger."

Scowling, Andrews shoved the pistol into the waistband of his trousers.

Saintcrow was about to turn away when he felt a sharp stabbing pain in the middle of his back. He started to turn, only to collapse as the world went black.

He woke slowly, his senses sluggish. Where the hell was he? Unable to move, he glanced from left to right. He was in a dark room, lying on a gurney, his arms and legs strapped down. A heaviness unlike anything he had ever experienced burned inside of him, searing his veins. Fire itself had not caused him such agony.

What the hell had happened?

A door opened somewhere behind him. The sound of footsteps, and Ralph Andrews appeared beside him, a needle in one hand, a tray in the other. Removing several vials from the tray, he placed them on the end of the gurney.

Andrews jabbed the needle into Saintcrow's arm, filling

one container and then another with blood so dark it was almost black.

"Is that for your daughter?"

Andrews nodded. "It occurred to me that the reason the effects from the blood of the other vampires lasted such a short time was because they were all relatively young. I decided I needed someone far older. Someone like you. Blood as old as yours should heal Kathy completely."

"What the hell did you use to knock me out?"

Andrews shrugged. "I'm not sure. I told a Nobel prize–winning research scientist everything I know about vampires and asked if it was possible to find something to render them powerless. I wasn't even sure it would bring you down, but Kathy's time is running out, and it was a risk I was willing to take."

Andrews drew a deep breath, let it out in a long slow sigh. "If it works, I'll drain the rest of your blood. I have several young patients at death's door. I'll need to do it quickly. Although vampire blood heals remarkably well, it's viable outside the body for only a day or two."

Outside the body. Saintcrow swore under his breath. He didn't have to ask what the future held for him after that. He could read it in the man's mind. Once Andrews had bled him dry, the doctor would make a quick visit to an old friend who worked at the town cemetery. Saintcrow swallowed a rising bubble of panic. Completely drained of blood, even a vampire as old as he wouldn't survive being cremated.

"I'm sorry," Andrews said. "But you see how it is? I'm a father and a hunter . . ." He shrugged, as if that made everything all right. Placing the vials on the tray, he left the room, closing and locking the door behind him.

Saintcrow closed his eyes against the pain burning through him. Damn! What had Andrews used to immobilize him? And how the hell was he going to get out of here when he couldn't move?

Kadie! She was his only hope. Forcing himself to relax, he opened the blood bond that linked them together. The pain, more excruciating than anything he had ever known, made it hard to think, hard to concentrate.

Kadie. I need you. Kadie! Dammit, hear me!

Rylan? He heard the worry in her mind. *Where are you?*

That was the sixty-four-thousand-dollar question, wasn't it? He tried to respond, but darkness beckoned and he fell into it, hoping for a respite from the agony burning through him.

Rylan? Rylan! Why didn't he answer?

Kadie paced the floor, her thoughts flying in a dozen directions at once. But one thing she was sure of, her father was behind this.

She pounded her fists on the door, screamed for someone to release her, but to no avail. Screamed until she was hoarse and then she began to pace the basement floor. This couldn't be happening. How could she have lived with her father her whole life and never known him for what he was? When they'd returned to Morro Bay, he had told her, in a voice as calm as a summer day, that he had been born to be a hunter. It was in his blood. He had grinned when he said that, as if it was some kind of joke. He was, he said, locking her up for a few days for her own good.

If she'd had any lingering doubts about her feelings for Rylan, they had all been laid to rest when Kadie realized her father intended to destroy him. She had to get out of here, had to get help. But from who? And how?

Pausing, Kadie smacked herself on the forehead. Her father had taken her purse, but neglected to take her cell phone. Fishing it out of her pocket, she checked the time, then quickly punched in Shirley's number, grateful she'd asked for it before leaving Morgan Creek.

Shirley answered on the second ring. "Hi, Kadie. I'm so . . ."

"Shirley, listen to me. Is Micah there?"

"Yes, why?"

"I don't have time to explain. Can I talk to him, please?"

"Sure."

"Hey, Kadie."

"Micah, Saintcrow's in danger. I need you here. Now."

"What's going on?"

"I'll explain when you get here. I'm locked in the basement of my house." She gave him the address. "I don't know if my father's home, but don't let him see you."

"Don't worry."

"Hurry!"

"I'm already on my way."

Kadie resumed pacing the floor. Micah was a young vampire. Was he able to move from place to place as quickly as Rylan? What if it took hours for him to get here? Hours that they didn't have?

She was contemplating calling Shirley again when Micah materialized in front of her. "So, what's up?"

Kadie's hand flew to her throat. "Micah! You scared me out of a year's growth."

"Sorry. I'd think you'd be used to it, living with Saintcrow and all."

She waved his apology aside. "Can you get me out of here?"

"Sure." He wrapped his arm around her waist. "Hang on."

A heartbeat later they were standing in the backyard.

"Where is he?" Micah asked.

"I don't know! All I know is he's in danger."

"I'm assuming he drank from you?"

"Yes."

"Then you should be able to find him."

Kadie nodded. Somehow, she'd known Saintcrow had returned to Morgan Creek, but she had no idea how she'd come by that knowledge. "So, how do I go about locating him?"

"Concentrate on the bond between you."

"How do I do that?"

"It's like an invisible connection. Once you find it, you can follow it."

Kadie closed her eyes. She pictured Saintcrow in her mind, searching for the invisible link that bound them together. It took her several minutes but gradually she became aware that she was being drawn out of the backyard.

Opening her eyes, she hurried out onto the street, Micah at her side.

"Do you know where he is?" the vampire asked.

"Not exactly."

"Too bad. We could get there a lot faster if you knew where we were going."

Kadie?

Rylan! I'm coming. Where are you?

The hospital. In the basement, I think.

Are you all right?

He didn't answer. Before she could ask again, she felt a horrible burning sensation shooting through her veins.

"Hey!" Ravenwood grabbed her when she started to fall. "What the hell?"

Kadie groaned. "He's in pain. Terrible pain. And my father . . . he's bleeding him." She wrapped her arms around Micah's neck. "The hospital. Hurry."

"Just tell me how to get there." Swinging her into his arms, Micah followed her directions to the hospital. He stopped in the parking lot. "Now what?"

"Well, we can't go in the front door. We'll have to go in through the service entrance."

He nodded. "I'll follow you."

They moved stealthily through the shadows of the parking lot, then slipped in one of the doors at the back.

"Can you still feel him?" Micah asked as they stepped into one of the service elevators.

"Yes." There were several storage rooms in the basement. She paused briefly in front of each one, until she came to the last door on the right. "He's in there," she whispered, and prayed they weren't too late.

Chapter 37

Taking a deep breath, Kadie turned the door handle. And nothing happened. "It's locked."

Reaching past her, Micah grasped the knob, gave it a twist and a push, and the door flew open.

Kadie switched on the light, gasped when she saw Saintcrow strapped to a table. His eyes were closed. His body twitched convulsively.

"Rylan." His name whispered past her lips as she hurried toward him. "Rylan, can you hear me?" She stared at him, appalled by how pale and weak he looked. She was only vaguely aware of Micah closing the door behind them.

Saintcrow's eyes opened. "Kadie?"

"He needs blood," Micah said, removing the straps from Saintcrow's hands and feet. "Human blood. Preferably fresh."

Kadie didn't waste time asking how he knew that. Slipping one arm under Saintcrow's head, she held her wrist to his lips. "Drink, Rylan." Seeing the refusal in his eyes, she shook her head. "Just do it."

Saintcrow glanced sideways at Micah. "Don't let me take too much."

Micah nodded.

Saintcrow looked up at Kadie; then grasped her forearm in his hands.

Kadie gasped as his fangs pierced her flesh, closed her eyes as he drank from her. He had tasted her in the past, in moments of passion, but never like this. For the first time, she felt like prey.

She glanced over her shoulder when the door opened. "Dad!"

Andrews glanced from his daughter to Micah to Saint-crow. "What the hell!"

What happened next happened very fast yet Saintcrow experienced it all in horrifying slow motion.

Andrews pulled a gun from his coat pocket. His first shot was for Micah, who reeled backward when the bullet grazed the side of his head.

Summoning what little strength Kadie's blood had given him, Saintcrow sat up, rage pulsing through every fiber of his being.

Andrews took a step backward, his finger curling around the trigger.

With a cry, Kadie threw herself between Saintcrow and her father as Andrews fired the gun twice in rapid succession.

A wordless shriek of denial rose in Andrews's throat as bright red stains blossomed across Kadie's chest and belly. She stared at him, her eyes wide with disbelief. A moment later, her legs gave way.

Saintcrow caught her before she hit the floor. She lay limp in his arms, her eyes closed, her face as pale as death.

"What have I done? Kadie . . ." Andrews stared at Saint-crow, his face almost as ashen as his daughter's. "Is she . . . ?"

"Not yet." Kadie's heartbeat was barely discernable. Her life's blood was warm where it dripped onto his arm. He was tempted to take her away from here, but she needed a doctor. And she needed one right now.

"Bring her upstairs," Andrews said, his voice thick with unshed tears.

Saintcrow glanced at Ravenwood.

"Go on." Micah pressed a hand to his head. "I'm fine. If you need me, I'll be in Morgan Creek."

With a nod, Saintcrow settled Kadie in his arms and followed Andrews upstairs. Moments later, Kadie was being wheeled into surgery. Andrews left to get his wife.

Alone in the hallway, Saintcrow dissolved into mist and floated into Kadie's room. He hovered near the ceiling while the nurses prepped her for surgery. He had seen blood and death in every form imaginable, caused a good deal of it himself, but watching the surgical team work on the woman he loved was the hardest thing he had ever done. The bullets, silver hollow points specially made for vampires and fired at close range, had done an incredible amount of internal damage.

Saintcrow didn't have to read the surgeon's mind to know that her chances of survival were slim at best. He could see it in the man's eyes.

When the operation was over, they moved Kadie into intensive care. As soon as she was settled, her parents hurried into the room. Carolyn Andrews grasped her daughter's hand and held it tight, as if she could will her daughter to get better.

Ralph Andrews stood by his daughter's bed, unmoving. The last two hours had aged him. His skin looked sallow, his eyes filled with quiet desperation and guilt.

Father and mother stood on opposite sides of the bed, not speaking, not looking at each other. Kadie lay unmoving, her face chalk white. The only sound in the room was her mother's muffled sobs and the hiss and wheeze of the machines that monitored Kadie's every breath.

Time lost all meaning.

326 *Amanda Ashley*

A nurse came in periodically to check Kadie's vital signs, rubber soles shushing over the tile floor.

Carolyn's tears gradually subsided. When she spoke to her husband, her whispered words sounded as loud as pistol shots in the stillness of the room. "This is all your fault."

The softly spoken words struck Ralph with the force of a blow. He reeled backward several steps, one hand raised as if to ward off her accusation, and then his face crumpled, his shoulders shaking as sobs wracked his body.

When Kadie's vital signs grew weaker, Saintcrow materialized in the room.

"You!" Carolyn exclaimed. "What are you doing here?"

"Taking what's mine."

"No! You can't! Ralph, stop him!"

"Carolyn, shut up." Ralph Andrews drew a deep breath. "He's the only one who can save her."

Ignoring Kadie's parents, Saintcrow went to her side. After biting into his wrist, he parted Kadie's lips.

Carolyn gasped and looked away as several drops of dark red blood trickled into her daughter's mouth.

Kadie grimaced, her eyelids fluttering open as she swallowed. She gazed up at him, her eyes filled with confusion and pain. "Rylan? What happened?"

He took her hand in his. "Listen to me. You're in the hospital. You don't have long. . . ."

A sob rose in Carolyn's throat. "No!"

Saintcrow ignored her. "You only have two choices. I can turn you, or . . ."

He didn't have to put the second choice into words, which was a good thing, because he couldn't bring himself to say it, couldn't imagine continuing his existence without her.

Ralph moved to the other side of the bed, his eyes hard. "What the hell are you saying, vampire? Just give her some of your blood and she'll be fine."

"She's too far gone."

"I've saved dozens of people using vampire blood," Ralph insisted, a note of desperation in his voice. "Kathy's already doing better."

"I doubt if any of the others were shot at close range with bullets meant for my kind. Dammit!" he snarled. "We're out of time."

"No." Andrews shook his head as his daughter flat-lined. "No!"

Scooping Kadie into his arms, Saintcrow willed the two of them out of the hospital.

A thought took him home, to his lair in Morgan Creek.

He just hoped he wasn't too late.

Chapter 38

Saintcrow stood beside the bed in his lair. There had been other times in his long life when what he wanted wasn't right, but never before had he faced a decision like the one he had to make now.

Kadie was only a few moments away from death. Her body was shutting down. They had never discussed the possibility of her becoming a vampire. She had never expressed any interest in the Dark Gift. He knew that, deep down, she found his lifestyle repulsive.

Sitting on the edge of the mattress, he stroked her cheek. It was cold, so cold. Her breathing stopped.

Should he let her slip away into eternity?

Would she hate him if he didn't let her go?

How was he to know what to do?

Desperate to buy a little time, he bit into his wrist and forced a few drops of his blood down her throat, hoping it would revive her long enough for him to ask her what he should do.

"Kadie? Kadie! Dammit, wake up!" He shook her lightly, then a little harder. "Kadie! You will do as I say and open your eyes!"

He hadn't expected it to work, but a moment later she was staring up at him.

"Rylan?"

"Kadie, listen to me. You're dying. What do you want me to do?"

"Do?"

"I can save you."

"Be . . . like you?"

"Yes, but you need to decide right now."

"I . . . don't want . . . to be . . . vampire."

He nodded, knowing, in that moment, that his life had no meaning without her. When her life was over, he would bury her in the cemetery, and then he would burrow into the ground and sleep beside her.

"Don't . . . want . . . to leave you."

Taking her hand in his, he said, "I love you, Kadie. I should have told you that sooner, and often."

"Love . . . you." Her eyelids fluttered down. For a moment, he thought she was gone, but then her hand squeezed his. "Want to . . . stay . . . with you."

"Are you sure? You know what that means?"

"Do it." Her hand fell away from his, her heartbeat slowed again.

"Dammit! Kadie, hang on!"

She had to live long enough for him to drink from her, long enough for her to drink from him.

Tears stung his eyes as he pulled her into his arms. She was weak, so weak. With a sob and a prayer he had no right to utter, he drank from her, drank until her heart stuttered, and then, cradling her to his chest, he bit into his wrist and held it to her lips, one hand lightly stroking her throat, urging her to swallow. Had he taken too much? Waited too long?

"Drink, Kadie," he pleaded desperately. "Drink."

Nothing.

"Kadie, dammit, don't leave me!"

One swallow, two, three. She clutched his arm, drinking greedily.

Saintcrow blew out a sigh of relief as a hint of color gradually returned to her cheeks. Her heartbeat grew stronger.

"That's my girl." He closed his eyes, content to let her drink her fill.

Later, when she was sleeping soundly, he left his lair.

Feeling restless, he walked down the driveway and kept going, his mind filled with thoughts of Kadie. She would sleep through the night and the next day and when she woke tomorrow night, she would be a vampire. Would she regret her decision? Or would she embrace her new lifestyle? Only time would tell.

He paused when he caught Ravenwood's scent. A moment later, the other vampire came into view.

"How is she?" Micah asked.

"Sleeping."

"You turned her, didn't you?"

Saintcrow nodded. "It was her choice. She was dying."

Micah shook his head. "I hope it works out, man."

"Thanks. And thanks for helping Kadie find me."

"How'd you know about that?"

"I read it in her mind."

"So, how'd Andrews bring you down? I thought you were impervious to just about everything."

"Yeah, me, too. Apparently some scientist came up with a Mickey Finn for vampires."

"What the hell's a Mickey Finn?"

"You are young, aren't you? It's an old slang term for a drink laced with drugs to knock you out."

"What are you going to do about Kadie's old man?"

"I haven't decided." Saintcrow drew a deep breath, then frowned. "You've been with Shirley."

Ravenwood nodded. "Yeah. We've been . . . dating."

"Dating? She's a little old for you, isn't she?"

"Maybe, but . . ." Micah shrugged. "I like her, you know?"

"Have you fed on her?"

"Hell, no!" Micah said. "Not that I haven't wanted to." He glanced toward Saintcrow's lair. "Guess I'll have to find a new place to hole up during the day."

"Sorry."

"Don't worry about it. I hope Kadie'll be all right."

"Yeah." Saintcrow raked a hand through his hair. "Me, too."

Later, walking back to his lair, he couldn't help wondering how what he had done tonight would affect his relationship with Kadie. Being selfish and territorial, vampires rarely paired off. That so many of them had lived together in Morgan Creek had been something unique. There were numerous stories of vampires who had destroyed their fledglings, stories of fledglings who had turned on their sires, and of fledglings who had so despised what had been done to them, that they had destroyed themselves.

It was out of his hands now, Saintcrow mused as he made his way down to his lair and closed the door. There was no way of knowing how Kadie would react to her new life.

For good or ill, tomorrow night would tell the tale.

Kadie woke feeling as if she were waking from a nightmare. Or maybe, she thought, looking around, she was still dreaming. The room was pitch black, yet she could see everything in vivid detail—each individual stitch in the blanket that covered her, the finest grain in the wood of the wardrobe, the hairline crack in the ceiling.

A moth fluttered in one corner. Not only could she see the tiny creature clearly, she could hear the whisper of its delicate white wings.

A deep breath carried Saintcrow's scent, and she realized that she was in his bed.

Sitting up, she wrapped her arms around her middle, a groan rising in her throat as a pain unlike anything she had ever known knotted in the pit of her stomach.

"Kadie."

She turned toward the sound of his voice. He stood on the far side of the room, watching her intently. He looked the same as always, and yet different. It was as if she was seeing him clearly for the first time.

"How do you feel?"

"Weird. This is the strangest dream I've ever had."

He smiled faintly. "I'll bet."

"My stomach hurts. I've never felt pain in a dream before."

He nodded. "I can make it go away, if you want."

"Please."

He was beside her while she was still speaking. A distant part of her mind told her she had to be dreaming. Otherwise, the sight of him biting into his wrist would have made her a little queasy. The scent of the blood oozing to the surface wouldn't have smelled so inviting.

When he held his arm out toward her, it seemed like the most natural thing in the world to lower her head and drink.

Surprisingly, it eased the pain in her stomach and she fell back on the mattress, and back into oblivion.

When she woke again, Saintcrow was lying on his side next to her.

"How are you feeling, Kadie?"

"Why do you keep asking me that?"

"Do you know where you are?"

"In your lair."

"Do you know why?"

"Because I'm dreaming." She smiled at him. "I've never had a dream quite like this one."

"Listen to me," he said. "You're not dreaming."

"Of course I am."

"What's the last thing you remember?"

"What do you mean?"

"Your old man came to tell you that your sister was dying and wanted to see you. Do you remember that?"

She frowned. Hadn't that been part of her nightmare?

"Kadie?"

"I remember that. But we didn't go to the hospital."

"Where did you go?"

"He took me home. And locked me in the basement . . . and then I heard your voice in my head. I called Micah for help." Her frown deepened. "He took me to the hospital to find you. You were strapped to a table. . . . My dad pulled a gun and . . . and he shot me." She threw back the covers, her hands moving over her breast and belly. There were no wounds. But of course there weren't. It had been a dream. "And then I woke up here."

"What else do you remember?"

"I was dying. You begged me not to leave you. . . ."

He nodded. "What else?"

"I said I wanted to stay with you. . . ." She grimaced. "You gave me your blood."

He nodded again, every nerve on edge as he waited for her to make the connection.

Sitting up, she ran her hands up and down her arms, patted her face with her fingertips. "Vampire."

The whispered word hung in the air between them.

"I'm a vampire." She stared at him, her hands clenching and unclenching at her sides. "I can't be a vampire. It's not possible. Rylan, tell me I'm dreaming, please."

"Would it be so bad if it was true?"

"I don't want to give up steak and cheesecake, or lying on the beach in the sun, or playing golf with my dad. . . ." Her eyes grew wide. "My father will hate me now!"

"Kadie, calm down."

"How can I? I'm not blaming you. I asked for this, but . . . I've changed my mind."

"There's no going back." He cupped her face in his hands. "Look at me. There were only two choices, Kadie. This, or death."

"I can't be a vampire! I don't want to spend the day locked inside a dark room. I don't want to drink blood." But she had, hadn't she? Or had that been part of the dream?

Drawing her into his arms, Saintcrow said, "We all think that way, at first. Your body has already accepted the change. It will take your mind a little longer to adjust. As for the blood . . ." He made a shallow slice in his palm and held it out to her.

Kadie stared at the crimson liquid in his cupped hand. With her enhanced vision, it looked deeper, brighter, redder than anything she had ever seen. No wonder it was Saintcrow's favorite color. An indrawn breath carried the scent to her nostrils, warm, sweet, sweeter than anything she had ever known. She licked her lips, felt a moment of shock as one of her teeth—one of her fangs—pricked her tongue. It didn't matter. She couldn't stop staring at the blood pooled in his hand.

"Do you want it?" Saintcrow asked.

She glared at him. "No."

"Liar."

"I hate you."

"I know. Do you want it?"

"You know I do."

"Then take it."

She leaned forward, torn between her body's craving and her mind's revulsion.

Her body won.

She lapped it up like a kitten at a bowl of cream.

When she finished, she turned her back toward him, unable to meet his gaze.

"Kadie?"

She wiped her hand across her mouth, then shook her head. "Go away."

"You're embarrassed."

She nodded.

"There's no need to be."

"Did you ever feel like this? As if you'd lost yourself?"

"Yeah. It's common for our kind to feel that way at first."

"Our kind," she repeated, her voice ever so soft. And then she lifted her head, her nostrils flaring. "What is that?"

"What's what?"

"That sound? Like . . . like distant drums."

"They're heartbeats, Kadie. The heartbeats of the people in town. Compelling, aren't they?"

She nodded. Compelling was putting it mildly. The sound sparked her hunger.

"Kadie, look at me. Tell me what you're thinking." He could have read her mind, but he wanted her to put it into words.

She shook her head, still not meeting his gaze.

"Okay, I'll tell you. You want to go into town, sink your fangs into the first mortal you meet, and drink that person dry. Am I right?"

"Yes!" She turned on him, her eyes filled with torment. "Help me, Rylan. I don't want to be a monster."

"Shh." He slipped his arm around her shoulders and

drew her close. "You're not a monster, sweetheart. You never will be. I won't let that happen." He kissed her cheeks, the tip of her nose, licked a bit of blood from the corner of her mouth. "Get dressed, my lovely fledgling. We're going hunting."

"I feel like a ninja," Kadie remarked, staring at herself in a store window. She was clad in black from head to foot.

"You're a creature of the night now," Saintcrow said with a wicked grin. "You need to look the part."

"Very funny."

"Lighten up, Kadie. Hunting is supposed to be fun."

"Right."

"You didn't enjoy it?"

She had, but she didn't want to admit it. It didn't seem right. Saintcrow had called a young man to him, mesmerized him, and offered him to Kadie. She had expected to feel revulsion at what she was doing—after all, she was biting another human being—and hesitation at doing what should have been disgusting. Instead, she had drawn him close and bitten him where Saintcrow instructed. The taste, which should have repulsed her, was warm and sweet and satisfying in a way she had never expected. She had thought to feel guilty, but that hadn't happened, either. Somehow, her whole view of the world had changed.

"You didn't hurt him, Kadie. People give more when they're donating blood than you took. Just think of it this way—you needed blood and he was a donor. All we did was cut out the middle man."

She stared at him, then burst out laughing.

Saintcrow laughed with her, then took her in his arms and kissed her. She was going to be all right.

* * *

"What about my parents?" Kadie asked much later that night. After hunting, they had returned to Saintcrow's lair. Now, they were lying in his bed, wrapped in each other's arms.

"What about them?"

"I should let them know I'm all right."

"Are you sure about that?"

"Yes. No. I don't know." She bit down on her lower lip, her expression troubled. "My dad will hate me now, won't he?"

Saintcrow blew out a breath. He didn't know Ralph Andrews well enough to answer Kadie's question. Was the man fanatic enough to destroy his own daughter? Or did he love her enough to accept her as she was now? Saintcrow was pretty certain that no matter how Andrews felt about his daughter's transformation, the fact that Saintcrow had turned her would only make the man hate him more.

"Rylan?"

"I don't know, sweetheart."

"I'm not human anymore, am I?"

"That depends on you. You can be a monster if you choose, or you can be Kadie who's on a restricted liquid diet."

She poked him in the ribs with her elbow. "Very funny. This is no time for jokes."

"This is the perfect time for jokes. It's good for relieving tension." He smiled at her, his eyes hot. "Of course, I can think of another way that's even better."

"I'll just bet you can," she murmured dryly. But she didn't object when he rose over her.

One thing about being a vampire. She could make love all night long and never get tired.

Chapter 39

Shirley stared at herself in the mirror. She was over forty, and yet she looked younger and happier than she ever had in her whole life. And it was all because of Micah. Sometimes she felt like a dirty old woman lusting after such a young man, but he was all she could think of. So far, she hadn't said anything about her feelings for Micah to Rosemary and Donna. She knew they would both think she was insane for wanting to spend time with a vampire, and maybe she was. But he had become the most important thing in her life.

She was pretty sure Rosemary and Donna suspected something was going on. This afternoon, she had caught the two of them staring at her speculatively time and again.

Well, let them think whatever they would, she thought as she brushed her hair, then changed into a white skirt and a frilly pink silk blouse. She was hoping Micah would come by. And maybe, if she was lucky, he would steal more than kisses tonight.

When the doorbell rang, she ran down the stairs, as excited as a teenager going out on her first date.

Micah whistled softly when she opened the door. "Wow, you look beautiful!"

"Thank you."

"I hope you don't mind my stopping by. I mean, you look like you're going out."

"No, I was just . . ." She hesitated, felt her cheeks grow hot as she blurted, "I was hoping you'd come by."

He smiled at her. "I was hoping you'd say that."

She smiled back, the warmth in his eyes making her toes curl in anticipation.

"Do you want to go out?" he asked. "It's a nice night for a walk."

"Sure." When he offered his hand, she took it, excitement curling in the pit of her stomach as his fingers closed over hers.

They walked in silence for a time, then Micah said, "Why do you stay here? This place is like a ghost town."

"I don't know. I've been here so long, it seems like home."

"You don't have any family anywhere?"

"Not really. A few cousins in Maine. How big is your family?"

"I've got five younger sisters and four older brothers. I'm right in the middle."

"You must be Mormon or Catholic."

Micah laughed. "Staunch Catholics."

"Have you seen them since you became a vampire?" she asked, and thought how strange it was to be talking about vampires as if it was no different from discussing the weather.

"No. I called my mom shortly after it happened. Told her I wouldn't be home for a while. She thinks I'm on location, working on a movie." He shook his head. "Lilith put an end to my career before it ever got started."

"I'm sorry."

He shrugged. "No sense crying over what can't be changed."

Shirley nodded. She couldn't argue with that.

She looked down at her hand in his. The movies had lost

a good thing, she thought, admiring his profile. He was incredibly handsome. If only she wasn't so old.

A moment later, he stopped walking. She glanced around, noting they had left the residential area behind and had reached the park. There were no lights here. "Something wrong?" she asked, suddenly nervous at being alone in the dark with a vampire, even one she found undeniably attractive.

"No."

"What is it?"

He made a soft sound of amusement. "I want you, too."

"What?" She looked up at him, startled by his words because they so clearly echoed her own thoughts.

"I can read your mind, Shirl. I know you've got the hots for me, and that it embarrasses you."

She turned away from him, her cheeks flaming.

He moved closer, his hands folding over her shoulders, pulling her body back against his. She felt his lips, cool against the side of her neck, the gentle brush of his fangs on her skin.

"You've been driving me crazy," he whispered. "I can't stop thinking about you. Wanting you."

She didn't know what to think, what to say, and then he was turning her around to face him, lowering his head to claim her lips with his, and there was no more time for thought, no need for words.

She trembled with anticipation when he swung her into his arms and carried her deeper into the park. Lowering her onto a patch of soft grass, he stretched out beside her. "Don't be afraid, pretty girl. I won't hurt you."

She gazed into his eyes, eyes with a faint red gleam, and wondered why she believed him.

* * *

Later, curled up against his side, she smiled. She hadn't felt this happy or this content in more years than she cared to remember. He had made love to her ever so gently, as if he was afraid she might shatter in his arms.

"Are you all right?" he asked.

"Never better." She turned her head to look at him. "How old are you?"

"Twenty-three."

She groaned softly. She was nearly twice his age. But that wasn't the worst of it. She would continue to grow older, and he would forever be twenty-three. It just wasn't fair.

But right now, with his hands gently caressing her, it didn't seem to matter.

Chapter 40

"You're serious?" Saintcrow asked. "You want to go for a walk? Now?"

Kadie nodded. "I'm nervous about the whole 'sleep like death' thing. I need to go outside and . . . I don't know. I just feel like I need to get out of here."

"All right. Get dressed and we'll go."

Fifteen minutes later, they were running side by side through the town.

"This is incredible!" Kadie exclaimed as they raced up one dark street and down another. The houses were a blur as they sped past. She felt invincible, as if nothing could stop her or even slow her down. And she wasn't even breathing hard!

Saintcrow kept pace with her, grinning the whole time. She was, he thought, going to make a wonderful vampire.

He came to an abrupt halt when they reached the park.

Kadie stopped beside him. "What's wrong?"

"I smell blood."

Lifting her head, Kadie took a deep breath. And it was there, a faint coppery scent that made her mouth water.

"Ravenwood's in the park," Saintcrow said. "With Shirley. Come on."

Kadie hurried after him. "You don't think he'd . . . ?" They were there before she finished her question. And, indeed, Shirley and Ravenwood were together, but Shirley wasn't in any danger, at least not the fatal kind.

Micah threw his jacket over Shirley, shielding her nakedness, then stood, his eyes blazing with anger. "What the hell are you doing here?"

"Checking up on my people," Saintcrow replied mildly. He glanced at Shirley, huddled beneath Micah's jacket. She refused to look at him or Kadie. Dropping down on one knee, Saintcrow took hold of her chin and turned her head to the side. The blood on her neck looked black in the moonlight. "He bit you."

Shirley stared at Saintcrow, mute.

"Are you all right with that?" he asked.

Shirley nodded. Then, finding her voice, she said, "He asked me if it was okay, and I said yes."

"He didn't take you against your will?"

"No."

With a nod, Saintcrow stood. "Sorry for the interruption."

Ravenwood snorted. "Why don't you take your fledgling home and mind your own business?"

Eyes wide with disbelief, Shirley stared at Kadie.

"This is still my town," Saintcrow reminded him. "Whatever you do here is my business."

Kadie was quiet on the walk back home. Shirley hadn't said anything, but Kadie had seen the horror reflected in her friend's eyes. Which seemed odd, in a way, since Shirley seemed to be pretty enamored of a vampire herself.

"Hey, you okay?" Saintcrow asked.

"Why wouldn't I be?"

"I saw the way Shirley looked at you, as if you'd suddenly grown horns and a tail."

"Or fangs," Kadie muttered bitterly. "It's okay for her to roll around in the grass with a vampire, let him bite her, but my becoming a vampire is horrible?"

"Don't let it bother you, sweetheart."

"I can't help it. She was my friend. At least I thought she was."

"You're being a little hard on her, don't you think?"

"Am I?"

"What if the situation were reversed? Would you be happy for her?"

"No, I guess not," she admitted, then shook her head. "But I never thought I'd see any of the women in Morgan Creek willingly spend time with a vampire."

"Never say never." And so saying, he swung her into his arms and willed them back to the sofa in his house.

It was going to be dawn soon, and he wanted to spend what was left of the night making love to his woman, if she had no objection.

Kadie snuggled against him, her head resting on his shoulder.

"Are you feeling any better about being a vampire?" Saintcrow asked. It probably wasn't the best question to ask, all things considered.

Kadie thought about it a moment, then said, "I think so. It's not as bad as I thought it would be." In fact, it wasn't nearly as bad as she'd thought it would be. She didn't remember ever feeling so strong. True, she had lost the daylight, but lately she had spent most of her days waiting for darkness so she could be with Rylan. "Will you teach me how to zap myself from one place to another?"

"It's not really something you have to be taught." He ran

his hand up and down her thigh. "You just have to concentrate on where you'd like to be, and you're there."

"What if I want someone to go with me?"

"You just need to be touching them."

"Like when you brought us to Morro Bay?"

"Exactly."

"So, I don't need any magic words? I don't have to practice. All I have to do is want to be somewhere . . . ?"

Saintcrow laughed out loud as he suddenly found himself in his bed beside her.

"And I'm there," she finished, grinning broadly.

"See? Nothing to it. Here's another good trick," he said, and in a move that would have been too quick for any but vampire eyes to follow, he had relieved her of all her clothing.

Kadie made a face at him; then, proving what a good student she was, she undressed him; looking smug, she flipped him onto his back and straddled his hips.

"I should have turned you months ago," Saintcrow remarked. "You're a natural."

"A natural?" she asked skeptically. "Is there any such thing as a 'natural' vampire?"

"Some take to it better than others. You never know how anyone will react, once it's done. Even people who've asked to be turned sometimes can't handle it. I've known a few who destroyed themselves soon after they were brought across."

"Ravenwood seems okay with it."

"Yeah. He'll be a master vampire one of these days."

"What does that mean, exactly?"

"It's usually a vampire who's survived longer than most. Someone who's staked out a territory and managed to defend it against all comers."

"Someone like you." She ran her finger along the silvery

scar that ran from his shoulder to his navel, marveling that he had survived such a wound.

He nodded.

"Have you made very many vampires?"

"Just one, a long time ago. It didn't turn out well."

"What do you mean?"

"Like I said, some people can't handle it. Gregor couldn't. The lust for blood drove him crazy. And I mean insane. He wiped out a whole village."

"That's terrible!"

"Yeah."

"What happened to him, I'm afraid to ask."

"Just what you're thinking. I hunted him down and destroyed him."

Kadie stared at him for several moments, debating whether she wanted to know how one vampire destroyed another. After thinking about it, she decided she'd rather not hear the details. Instead, she asked another question. "Are all vampires created equal?"

"No. It depends a good deal on who sired you. Ravenwood was turned by Lilith, which puts him in the upper ten percent. Most of the vampires who resided here weren't very powerful, which is why they came here in the first place. You, on the other hand, were turned by the oldest vampire in the country, which makes you very powerful indeed."

He sucked in a breath as her hand moved lower. "And thus endeth the lesson on Vampires 101."

Wrapping his arms around her, he rolled over, and after settling her beneath him, he demonstrated the remarkable staying power of a nine-hundred-year-old master vampire.

Chapter 41

After spending the night in Micah's arms, it was difficult for Shirley to sit in the restaurant with Rosemary and Donna the next morning, and even more difficult to concentrate on what they were saying. All she could think about was the handsome young vampire who had made love to her into the wee small hours of the morning, and how anxious she was to see him again. It had been years since she had made love. Truth be told, she had never really been crazy about it. Until last night.

"Shirley, what do you think? Shirley?" Rosemary tapped her on the forehead. "Hey, are you in there?"

"What? Oh, sorry, I was . . . um . . ."

"Not here. That's for sure. Donna thinks we should drive into Cody for the day, have lunch, do some shopping. Do you want to go?"

"Oh. Sure, why not?"

"Are you all right?" Rosemary asked. "You seem a little . . . distracted."

"I'm fine." She smiled faintly. "Really fine."

"She has that look," Donna said.

"What look?" Shirley asked.

Donna folded her arms over her chest. "The same one Kadie wore after she'd been with Saintcrow for a while."

"Don't be ridiculous!"

Rosemary nodded. "I think you're right."

"It's that young vampire, isn't it?" Donna leaned forward. "Come on, 'fess up."

Shirley slumped in her seat. "All right. I've seen him a couple of times."

"First Kadie, and now you." Rosemary sighed. "I just don't see the attraction."

"Speaking of Kadie, she hasn't been around lately," Donna said. "I hope she's all right."

"Oh, she's all right," Shirley muttered. "But she won't be coming in here for lunch anymore."

Rosemary and Donna both looked at her sharply.

"He turned her," Shirley said.

Rosemary looked stricken. "Are you sure about that?"

"I'm sure. I saw her last night."

"I was afraid that would happen. It was just a matter of time." Donna looked at Shirley. "If you're not careful, it'll happen to you, too."

Eager to change the subject, Shirley pointed at two men approaching the restaurant, "Customers." One was in his early thirties, the other in his fifties. Both were well dressed.

"I'll cook," Rosemary said, rising.

"I'll play waitress," Shirley offered.

"I guess that leaves me with the dishes," Donna remarked, following Rosemary into the kitchen.

Shirley went to greet their guests. "Good afternoon, gentlemen. Would you prefer a table or a booth?"

"Either one is fine," the older man said.

"Right this way." Shirley led them to a booth by the window and offered them each a handwritten menu. "Coffee?"

Both men nodded.

Shirley hurried into the kitchen. "Do those two look like trouble," she asked, filling two cups with coffee, "or is it just my imagination?"

"They remind me of the hunters that were here not long ago," Rosemary whispered.

"You don't think they're here for Kadie, do you?" Donna asked.

"I don't know, but I don't think so. How could they have found out about her so quickly? They're probably here for Saintcrow."

"But if they find him, they'll find her!" Donna exclaimed. "We've got to warn them."

"Yes," Shirley agreed. "But how?" Vampires slept during the day. Everyone knew that. Her breath caught in her throat as a new thought occurred. She had no idea where Micah spent the day now that Saintcrow had returned. She couldn't warn him even if she wanted to.

"You'd better go take their order," Rosemary suggested.

"Right." Returning to the table, Shirley forced a smile as she set the cups in front of the men. "What can I get for you gentlemen?"

"A little information," the older man said.

"Sir?"

"I'm looking for my daughter. Kadie Andrews. She lived here a while back. Have you seen her lately?"

"Last I heard, she went home," Shirley said. "And her boyfriend with her."

"You're sure?"

Shirley nodded. "Do you need more time to decide?"

"No. Is there anyone else in town besides the three of you?"

"No one else lives here," Shirley said.

"I'm sure of that," Andrews said dryly. "I'll have a roast beef sandwich and fries."

"I'll have the same," the younger man said.

"Coming right up," Shirley said, and hurried into the kitchen.

"What did they say?" Donna asked.

"They're looking for Kadie. The older man is her father."

"Her father? Really?" Rosemary spread mayonnaise on four slices of bread. "Well, she should be safe then."

Shirley pulled a package of roast beef out of the refrigerator. "I'm not so sure about that."

"But he's her father," Donna said. "You don't think . . . ?"

"You didn't see his eyes," Shirley said. "That man scares me." And suddenly she wasn't worried only for Kadie's life, but for Saintcrow's and Micah's, as well. If those men were hunters, there was nothing to stop them from breaking into the lairs of the vampires. Nothing at all.

Saintcrow stirred, his vampire senses warning him that someone was prowling through the house upstairs. He swore when he realized there were two hunters on the premises and one of them was Kadie's father. Damn. He should have known Andrews would show up in Morgan Creek sooner or later. Andrews had been here before. It was inevitable that he would show up again.

Rising, Saintcrow smoothed the covers over Kadie, then moved toward the door. With his preternatural hearing, it was easy to follow the movements of the two men as they explored the house, making lewd comments about the Undead as they opened doors, poking inside closets and cupboards.

Saintcrow shook his head. Did they really expect to find him stretched out in the linen closet, or holed up in one of the kitchen cupboards?

"What makes you think she's here?" Andrews's companion asked.

"I don't know where else to look." Andrews slammed a door. "He took her out of the hospital and I haven't heard from her since. For all I know, she's . . . Dammit, Harry, keep looking."

"I don't think we should even be here," Harry remarked. "You know what happened to Gordon and Rob and Clarke when they came nosing around this place. Hell, they don't even know who they are anymore."

"Let's check the upstairs," Andrews suggested. "Maybe we'll find your *cojones* there."

Harry snorted. "Are you even listening to me?"

"No. You're not saying anything I want to hear."

Saintcrow swore softly as the two men tromped up the stairs toward the turret rooms. And then they were in the one that led to his lair. No one had ever gotten past the door that led to his inner sanctuary. There was no reason to think Andrews would succeed where others had failed.

He heard their feet shuffling as they circled the room.

"Hey," Andrews said, a note of excitement in his voice. "There's a door here!"

As Saintcrow listened to the two men move cautiously down the stairs and along the narrow corridor, he pulled on a pair of jeans. Defending himself in the nude was something he had done only once before, and vowed would never happen again.

Moments later, he heard them at the door, rapping, pounding, hammering, swearing, but the door, made of reinforced steel and warded with preternatural power, held fast.

He listened with growing amusement as the hunters returned to the door at the top of the stairs and discovered that the way in did not allow for a way out. He heard the rising panic in their voices, the rapid beating of frightened human hearts as the hunters realized they would be the hunted when the sun went down.

Assured that there was no imminent danger to himself or Kadie, he went back to bed.

Kadie woke enfolded in Saintcrow's arms. For a moment, she was content to lie there and contemplate the events of the last few days. Amazing, how quickly her life had turned upside down. She had discovered that her father was a vampire hunter and that her mother knew all about it and had faithfully kept his secret. Kadie still had trouble accepting that fact. Hardest of all to wrap her mind around was the change in her own life. It didn't seem possible that her world had changed so drastically in such a short time. She was a vampire. There was no way to deny it. She had fangs. She had consumed human blood. But it didn't seem real.

When a familiar scent reached her, she bolted upright. Her father was here! When she swung her legs over the edge of the bed, Saintcrow laid a restraining hand on her arm.

"Where are you going?" he asked.

"My father's here."

"I know. He's been trapped in the tunnel since early this afternoon."

"Is he all right?"

"For now."

Her gaze searched his. "What does that mean?"

"It means he's here with another hunter."

"Does he know about me?"

"No." He sat up, head cocked to one side. "Shirley and Ravenwood are here."

"In the house?"

"Knocking on the front door. Let's go see what they want."

"What about my father?"

"He's not going anywhere."

Saintcrow took her by the hand. A moment later, they materialized at the front door.

"Good evening," Saintcrow drawled. "What brings you here?"

"We came by to make sure you two were all right," Ravenwood replied. "Shirley thought there might be a couple of hunters in town."

"Yeah, they're trapped in my lair."

Shirley looked at Kadie. "So, you know one of them is your father?"

Kadie nodded, then looked at Saintcrow.

When he shrugged, Kadie invited Micah and Shirley inside.

Shirley hesitated before following Micah across the threshold, but curiosity prompted her to enter the house. In all the years she had lived in Morgan Creek, this was the first time she had been inside a vampire's lair.

Saintcrow and Kadie sat side by side on the sofa.

Shirley sank onto the love seat next to Ravenwood, her gaze darting around the room. She wasn't up-to-date on the latest home fashions, but there was no mistaking that the furniture in the room was top of the line. She couldn't help wondering if the armor in the corner was genuine or just a remarkably good reproduction.

"What are you going to do with the hunters?" Ravenwood asked.

"There are only two choices," Saintcrow replied. "Kill them or wipe their memories." He glanced at Kadie. "I suppose the latter."

Ravenwood frowned thoughtfully. "I've done that a few times, of course, but I couldn't help wondering how long-lasting it is. When you erase a memory, does it ever come back?"

"Not if you do it right."

"What, exactly, are you going to erase?" Kadie asked.

Saintcrow rubbed a hand over his jaw. "Their memories of this place, for one thing. And all memory of being hunters, as well as their knowledge that we're vampires."

"How can that work?" Kadie asked. "My father probably knows a lot of hunters."

"Doesn't matter," Saintcrow said. "Thinking about vampires will cause both of them severe headaches." There was no guarantee that Andrews or any of the others would never regain their memories of what they were. Hunting was in their blood. But it was either erase their memories or kill them. And with Kadie's father, that wasn't an option.

"What about hypnosis?" Ravenwood asked. "Could a good hypnotist restore their memories?"

"Let's not go looking for trouble," Saintcrow advised. "We've got more than enough to go around."

"You don't think Kadie's father would hurt her, do you?" Shirley asked.

"No, but he'd do his damnedest to destroy the rest of us." Saintcrow looked at Kadie. "Are you going to be all right with this?"

"I don't know what else you can do. What about my mother?"

Saintcrow clucked softly. He had forgotten about Carolyn Andrews. "I'll have to do something about her, too." He grinned as he wrapped his arm around Kadie. "Your family is a lot of trouble, you know that?"

"I know, but we're a package deal," Kadie said with an impish grin, and then, seeing Shirley's expression, she frowned. "Are you okay?"

Shirley nodded. "I can't stop thinking about how surreal this all is."

"Surreal?" Kadie repeated, and then she nodded as understanding dawned. Shirley was surrounded by vampires and it was making her uncomfortable. "Do Rosemary and Donna know about me?"

"Yes."

Micah laid his hand on Shirley's arm. "You doing okay? You look a little pale."

Unable to keep the hurt from her voice, Kadie said, "I think she wants to leave."

"Kadie, I . . ."

"It's all right, Shirley."

Kadie blinked back unwanted tears when Ravenwood and Shirley left the house.

"How can she be so upset about me being a vampire when she's obviously in love with one?"

"I don't know. Maybe it's easier for her to accept Micah because he was already a vampire when she met him." He wrapped his arm around her shoulders. "I wouldn't worry about it. She'll come around, in time."

"I hope so." In her job, wandering from ghost town to ghost town, holed up in hotel rooms to write her articles, she hadn't had time to make many friends. She had grown close to the women in Morgan Creek. It hurt to think they would look at her differently now, that they might be afraid of her.

Saintcrow gave her shoulders a squeeze, "I'm sorry, Kadie. I never thought about how being a vampire would affect you." He shook his head. "Only how losing you would affect me. Selfish, as always."

"You saved my life."

"I didn't want to go on without you. Selfish, like I said."

"I wouldn't have wanted to live without you, either." Cupping his face in her hands, she kissed him. "Now, let's go see my dad."

Chapter 42

It took quite a bit of convincing on Saintcrow's part, but he finally managed to persuade Kadie to remain in the living room while he went to take care of their visitors. After promising that he wouldn't do any permanent damage to either man, Saintcrow made his way down to his lair.

He stood outside the door for a moment, listening to their conversation as they tried to decide what they would do when he confronted them. When they ran out of ideas, he lit the candles in the wall sconce, then opened the door.

Harry and Ralph sat side by side on the top step. They blinked at the light when he opened the door.

When they lunged at him, Saintcrow held up his hand. They fell back when they hit the invisible barrier.

Saintcrow crossed his arms. "Harry, I'll deal with you first. Come here."

Unable to refuse, the man crossed the threshold into the turret room, then stopped, prevented from moving any farther.

"What are you going to do to him?" Andrews demanded.

"Whatever I want," Saintcrow replied, and slammed the door.

He spoke to Harry's mind, erasing everything that

had to do with vampires and hunters. After implanting a posthypnotic suggestion, he told Harry to wait in the car for Andrews, then sent him on his way.

Andrews's face was livid when Saintcrow opened the door. "Where's Harry? What have you done to him?"

"He's fine."

"I don't believe you."

"I don't give a damn what you believe. You've interfered in my life for the last time."

The threat didn't faze Andrews. "Where's my daughter?" he asked belligerently. "What have you done to her?"

"I saved her life."

Andrews's face went from belligerent to furious. "You turned her into a bloodsucking monster, didn't you? Damn you! I'll kill you for that."

"No, you won't. When I'm through with you, the very word *vampire* will give you the mother of all headaches. You won't remember anything about being a hunter, nor will you recognize a vampire when you see one."

Doubt shadowed Andrews's eyes for the first time. "What do you mean?"

"Just what you think I mean," Saintcrow replied coldly.

"No!" Andrews staggered back, his arms raised to shield his face, as if that would save him. "Dammit, you can't do this!"

Saintcrow bared his fangs and let his eyes go red. "I can kill you, if you'd rather. Makes no difference to me."

Andrews's face paled. His arms fell limply to his sides as all the fight drained out of him. "Go on then, kill me. I'd prefer it."

"I'd be glad to oblige," Saintcrow said, and meant it. "But Kadie would never forgive me."

* * *

Kadie paced the living room floor. Try as she might, she couldn't hear what was going on in the tunnel. Harry had come down from the turret room twenty minutes ago. He had smiled at her, asked how she was, then told her he was going to wait for her father in the car. When he left the house, he was whistling softly.

Ten minutes passed and there was no sign of her father. Kadie tried to read his thoughts. When she couldn't, she realized Saintcrow was preventing it. What was taking so long? Was her father all right?

She hurried to the staircase, then paused when her father and Saintcrow appeared on the landing.

"Kadie!" Her father's expression seemed jovial as he hurried down the stairs to embrace her. "I hate to cut my visit short, but I've been gone too long already."

Kadie looked at Saintcrow over her father's shoulder.

He nodded. *Just play along.*

"Sure, Dad, I understand," Kadie said, hoping she was saying the right thing. "Tell Mom hi for me, and I'll see her soon."

"I will." He gave her a hug, then strode toward the door. "Good to see you again, Saintcrow," he called over his shoulder. "Take care of my girl."

Kadie waited until the door closed after her father, then looked askance at Rylan. "What did you do to him?"

"Just what I said I would. I wiped any memories of vampires or hunters from his mind."

"What about my mom?"

"It's all taken care of. The last thing they both remember is that you called to say you were spending some time in Morgan Creek with me and that they both approved."

"What about the other hunters that my dad knows?"

"Two are dead. I've dealt with Harry and three others.

There's only one left, and he's off hunting vampires in Florida. I'll deal with him when the time comes."

Kadie worried her lower lip between her teeth, then said, "When you saw my mom, did she say anything about Kathy?"

"No, but after I erased her memories, I went to the hospital to see your sister."

"How is she?"

"Greatly improved since you saw her last."

Kadie cocked her head to the side. "Did you have anything to do with that?"

"As a matter of fact, I did. When no one was looking, I hypnotized her, then I gave her a healthy dose of my blood. It should last her a good long time. When I left, the doctors were gathered around her bed, marveling at her miraculous recovery."

"But won't that make her a vampire now?"

"No. I didn't take any of her blood, only gave her some of mine."

"Oh, Rylan!" Kadie threw her arms around his neck. "I love you!"

"I know. So, I was thinking. We never made it to England. What would you think about going there on our honeymoon?"

"Honeymoon! Does that mean . . . ?" She drew a deep breath. "Are you asking me to marry you?"

"Sure sounds that way."

"But you said vampires rarely get married because they don't like to share territory. . . ."

"That's true."

"And because they exist for such a long time. . . ."

He placed his forefinger over her lips, stilling her words. "All true, Kadie, my love. But I can't imagine my life without you in it, no matter how long that might be. A hundred years or a thousand, I want to share them all with you. So, what do you say? Do you think you can put up with me that long?"

"You really are Santa Claus," she said. "You've given me everything I've ever wanted."

Kadie smiled as he drew her closer, his mouth covering hers in a long searing kiss that curled her toes and tripled her heart rate.

"Now that you're a vampire," Saintcrow murmured, "you'll be able to keep your promise."

"What promise is that?" she asked, though she knew perfectly well what he was talking about.

"Don't you remember?" he asked, feigning disappointment. "You promised to stay with me forever."

Warmth speared through Kadie as he swept her into his arms and carried her swiftly to their lair. "How could I forget?"

Lying side by side in their bed, Kadie smiled as she reached for him. And as his arms tightened around her and he claimed her lips with his, she wondered if even forever would be long enough.

Thrilling Suspense from
Beverly Barton